THE DEVIL SERIES BOOK TWO

THE EPIC SAGA CONTINUES

THE DEVIL BEHIND US

S.C. Wilson

The Devil Behind Us

Cover image copyright © www.fotosearch.com
Cover design © Serendipity Formats

ISBN 978-1-7323601-3-6

CHAPTER ONE

1864

Driving rain fell in sheets atop Mount Perish, the assault more insistent as the storm strengthened. Hail pelted the timber-framed structure Jesse McGinnis called home. Low-hanging branches thumped against the roof and a forked bolt of lightning cracked the sky. The flames from the evening cook fire danced, stirred by the drafts sneaking in through cracks in the chimney—swaying like ethereal dancers. The fire came alive.

Toby, oblivious to the sounds of nature playing out around him, slept soundly in the loft, his incessant snoring audible amidst the chaos. Below him, Jesse and Abby cuddled together in a warm tangle of arms and legs.

Jesse whispered, "Abs, we need to talk."

"Now?" Abby asked, her voice still husky from their love-making. She moaned, burrowing closer, head in the curve of Jesse's neck. The nook fit perfectly.

"You're going to have to decide what you really want."

Sighing, Abby disentangled herself from Jesse and rolled

onto her back. Moments before she'd had the most erotic experience of her life. This was not the time for serious talk.

Another loud clap of thunder shook the small cabin. The horses shifted restlessly, bumping against the adjacent wall, their own contribution to the noise. Toby's snoring remained uninterrupted.

Abby turned to face Jesse, her comfortable position belying her irritation. "I want to be with you," she said. "And, if that means living on top of a mountain, then so be it."

"You say that now, but you really have to think about what that would mean. You would be walking away from your life —your singing. What kind of life would you have here without that?"

"Thinking," Abby said, voice edgy. "That's all I've been doing."

A bolt of lightning lit up the small space, illuminating Abby's annoyed glare. She took a calming breath before continuing. "I know if I stay here with you, I'll have to give some things up. I won't miss them as much as you think: traveling around, singing in saloons, staying up all hours of the night. Those things don't mean as much to me as you do. I don't want that life anymore."

Abby was scared to death of walking away from the life she knew, only to live isolated on top of a mountain. The thought of walking away from Jesse was even more terrifying. She couldn't do that. In her heart, she knew she belonged with Jesse, no matter where life took them.

Jesse closed her eyes, her tension melting away. Abby's words were music to her ears, their melody soothing a dread that had been building in her thoughts. She couldn't imagine going back to a life without her. Jesse would be a fish out of water: scared, confused, and unable to breathe. She opened her eyes and continued. "I just don't want you to have any regrets, that's all."

"The only regret I'd have, Jes, is if I walked away from the only true love I've ever known."

Sharp when she started her declaration, Abby's words found their edge blunted. All that remained was the pure, unadulterated affirmation of her devotion.

Jesse swallowed hard against the large knot wedged in her throat. She pulled Abby close, wrapping her tightly in her arms. "I can't wait to start our—"

A loud shout from the loft interrupted her.

"It's ra-ra-raining in here," Toby yelled after being awakened by droplets of water landing on his cheek.

"I'll take care of it," Jesse shouted back as she jumped out of bed. Wasting no time, she tossed Abby her clothing and then scrambled to get dressed herself. She grabbed pots and pans and handed one of them to Abby, who was already halfway up the ladder to the loft.

"Here, catch it in this," Abby said, passing it up to him.

After making sure each leaking section of roof had a container beneath it, Jesse tossed another log on the fire. She and Abby returned to bed, opting to remain in their clothes. They held each other but did not sleep. They waited to speak until the steady rumble of Toby's snores once again cut through the patter of rain.

Abby whispered, "Are you going to tell him about us?"

"Um, I haven't even thought about that. Maybe we should just keep it between us—for now."

"You know he'll figure it out. Just because he stutters doesn't mean he's stupid." Abby smiled.

Jesse's brow furrowed. "I never thought he was stupid."

Abby leaned over and kissed her on the cheek. "I only said that because that's what he told me when we were coming up the mountain. Actually, he's very smart. I don't think he's as simple as he lets on. I think he's just had a hard time dealing with his stutter. He knows what he wants to say, he just has a hard time getting the words out sometimes."

Jesse's expression softened. "At least he's here and no one will make fun of him anymore."

"So, should we tell him?"

Jesse shook her head. "I'm not sure how to explain it. I'm not sure he'll understand. Hell, I'm not even sure I understand it myself."

"Let's just wait and see how things go. I'll do my best to behave myself around you, even though that may be awful hard to do." Abby winked. "Do you think you'll be up for traveling down soon? I know I won't be able to bring a lot back with me, but if I'm going to stay here with you, I'll need to go get some of my things. Oh, and I borrowed Edith's rifle. I wouldn't feel right if I didn't return it."

Jesse reached for Abby's hand. "I don't see any reason why we can't. Moon should be full in a couple weeks." She somehow kept the quiver from her voice, but it didn't matter.

Abby watched the discomfort pass quickly over Jesse's features like a shadow. She might have dismissed it as a trick of the flickering firelight had she not grown so close to her. "Is the pain bad?" she asked. "Maybe we shouldn't have—"

Jesse cut her off before she could say it out loud. "It's fine, really. Even if what we just did would have killed me, it would have been worth it," she said, grateful for the dim lighting masking the color she felt rising from her neck to her cheeks.

Abby stared into Jesse's green eyes, their effect powerful and immediate. Lifting Jesse's shirt, her fingertips caressed the toned muscles beneath. She whispered even lower, "I never knew I could feel that way." Her wandering hand paused when it found the fresh scar on Jesse's flank. "I still can't believe you got shot," she said, tone shifting with the abrupt change in mood. "You should've let me stay with you."

"I'm glad you didn't. You could've been shot, too. I wouldn't be able to live with myself if I caused you to get hurt."

"I still can't believe you found those men. I'm glad you took care of 'em. The world is a much better place."

"I shouldn't have done it," Jesse said, "but I couldn't stop myself. Makes me feel like I'm no better than them."

"Oh, Jes, there is a huge difference between you and them. Remember what I told you in the meadow—that day we went hunting—about Silas?"

"Yes, of course I remember."

"Well, does that make me like them, too?"

"No," Jesse said, "and don't think I can't see what you're doing."

"Good. Then you should know you did the right thing. Never doubt that. I call it justice."

Toby's loud snoring echoed over a distant roll of thunder.

"Sounds like the storm is moving out." Jesse pointed to the loft. "I still can't believe he's here." She shook her head, the joy of their reunion overshadowed by darker thoughts. "After all these years, I can still see him lying there—covered in blood, not moving. I thought for sure he was dead."

"I'm so happy you found each other." Abby spoke quickly, eager to pull Jesse back into the light. "You two have a lot of catching up to do. Oh, and you could've warned me about the Indians, though. When I saw them out front…well, I thought I was a goner."

"I was just as surprised as you were. I had no idea they lived up here," she said. "I've never seen or heard anyone other than Frieda."

"Didn't you ever go to the other side of the mountain?"

"Never. I've always stayed close to the cabin. Frieda always said if I went too far and got hurt, I'd be too far away to get help. She was right." She pointed to the scar on her arm. "I got bit by a rattler when I was twelve and if I'd been any farther away, well, let's just say things might have turned out different. So, I never had the desire to venture too far until Frieda told me how to cross the Devil's Fork."

"Thank God they keep an eye on the crossing and found you. They're wonderful people," Abby said. "And Aponi is just lovely. She's coming back here soon. Wants to check and see how we're doing."

"I can't wait to get to know them better."

Jesse and Abby lay awake for hours, talking well into the early morning. The sound of rain drumming on the roof mixed with the intermittent pings of drops landing in pots throughout the cabin.

Jesse had never felt more naïve as she listened to Abby speak, explaining everything she knew about Indians.

"Did you know Indians are actually hunted? Hated by some. An Indian scalp will fetch twenty-five cents. They pay five dollars for the entire head."

Jesse was sickened by this revelation. She listened, speechless and intent. Gooseflesh raised along her arms despite the warmth she shared with Abby.

"Most Indians have left their homes, but not because it's what they want. They have been forced to relocate and live on places called reservations. If they don't leave willingly, the government steps in and attacks their villages. Groups of men follow the soldiers. After an attack, they go in and seize any children left behind. There was a man who came in the saloon one day. He told me about these men being able to sell an Indian boy for around sixty dollars. A girl can go for as much as two hundred."

The more Jesse heard, the more it disgusted her. Having lived isolated for so long, she knew she really didn't have a clue about how things worked off the mountain. She'd been starting to believe it wasn't as scary as she'd thought all those years, but now she wasn't so sure. She had seen evil firsthand, had lost most of her family to bad men, but was still staggered by the scale of the horrors Abby described. She couldn't understand why all those people—so many men, women, and children—were being treated so horribly. After all, it was their land first, so what gave white men the right to take it from them? Then, to be brutalized based solely on the color of their skin was something she couldn't wrap her mind around. The way they were treated made her blood boil. She knew, should the time ever come, she would fight to her death to defend the Ponaks if necessary.

Abby woke in the morning with Jesse's arm wrapped around her. *Last night really did happen. It wasn't a dream.* She opened her eyelids slowly, letting the rows of shelves against the wall drift into focus. Safe in Jesse's embrace, the turmoil of the last several days behind them, she was finally free to contemplate what she had been ignoring for weeks.

Why couldn't Jes have come back a week sooner?

Abby reached down and placed a hand on her stomach. A woman knows her own body. She hadn't given much thought as to why she had missed her last monthly. Her cycle had been irregular at times, and she had skipped one on an occasion over the years. Now, she was terrified because she had missed two in a row for the first time in her life.

I'm so stupid. How could I have been so careless?

Abby thought Jesse was out of her life for good. Moving on made sense. She and Sam had only been intimate one time. It never crossed her mind this could happen. If she had known how things would turn out with Jesse, she never would have put herself in that position.

"Abs, you awake?" Jesse whispered, pulling Abby from her thoughts.

Abby sniffled. "Yeah."

"While Toby is sleeping, do you want to go with me and take a bath?"

Abby rolled over to face her. She tucked a stray strand of Jesse's hair behind her ear.

"Are you all right?" Jesse asked. "You look like you've been crying."

She considered telling her, but fear strangled her voice. "I'm just so happy. That's all."

"Me too. C'mon let's go."

Sunlight broke through the low-hanging clouds as the two made their way upstream, hand in hand. The smell of the freshly washed earth intoxicated them.

Jesse cupped Abby's face in her hands, and they kissed each other long and slow.

Jesse wondered if she would always feel a fluttering in her stomach. She hoped so. Hands trembling from nervousness, she untied the drawstring on Abby's nightgown, slowly slid it from her shoulders, and let it fall to the ground.

Abby, still uncomfortable being nude out in the open, quickly moved to cover her body.

Jesse reached out and placed a restraining hand on hers. "Don't hide yourself."

The soft touch and affirmation put Abby at ease.

"You're so b-beautiful," she stammered as soon as Abby lowered her arms.

The rigid set of Abby's shoulders relaxed and she tilted her head, allowing Jesse to kiss her neck and the soft curve of her jaw line. The gentle tickle of hot, wet lips elicited a shudder that ran through her entire body. She pulled away and moved to the edge of the stream. The morning air was cool against her exposed skin, and for once she didn't mind stepping into the slightly warmer water. Without a backwards glance, she waded out until she was waist deep and slipped beneath the surface, leaving just her head and shoulders visible. Only then did she turn to face the shoreline. She wore a seductive smile as she beckoned to Jesse with her finger.

Jesse hesitated barely long enough to remove her clothing before hurrying in. When their bodies came together at last, even the crisp mountain air could do nothing to cool their passion for one another, which had once again been unleashed.

CHAPTER TWO

J esse and Abby returned to the cabin on legs still tingling
from the early morning encounter. They exchanged a
knowing look, bemused and surprised, when they found
Toby outside and clearing away remnants of last night's storm.

"I wo-wondered where you two r-ran off to," Toby said
from behind the sticks piled high in his arms.

Jesse shoved her hands in her pockets and squirmed. "Uh,
we um…just went to wash up," she said, looking down at her
boots. She desperately wanted to change the subject before any
follow-up questions. "You hungry? I am."

"Starving," he said, dropping the load of sticks next to a
fire pit. The rain had saturated them, muffling their clatter as
they fell into a semblance of a pile. He paid no mind to the
damp streaks they left like shadows across his clothing.

"Let's clean this up later," Jesse said, gesturing at the
branches and other detritus strewn all about them, compliments of the storm. "How's fish sound?"

"Wonderful," Abby said. "Why don't you two go? You
have a lot of catching up to do."

"Don't you want to come?" Jesse asked.

"I don't think fishing is for me. Besides, you know how I feel about getting bait." Abby wrinkled her nose. She could almost feel the slimy worms wriggling against her fingertips.

"All right." Jesse chucked. "We'll be back soon."

After fetching her fishing pole, Jesse and Toby headed toward the stream.

Abby watched and waited until they reached a small bend, disappearing among the trees before climbing the porch steps. She closed the door and paced inside the cabin. As cozy as the small space was, it was her thoughts that kept her prisoner. The walls of her mind closed in, proving more formidable than the logs around her. Those, at least, had a door she could escape through.

She lifted her dress and ran her hand over her stomach. She knew she was being paranoid, but she couldn't help it. Time was plotting against her. Soon, she would no longer be able to hide her condition. The thought stirred her insides and made her feel sick. She lowered her dress, took a seat in the chair next to the fireplace, and cried into her hands.

Meanwhile, Jesse led the way, pole in hand, with Toby a few paces behind. He moved quietly for a large man. She kept glancing back over her shoulder to make sure he was still behind her.

"What?" Toby asked.

"Just making sure you're still with me. You're so quiet. It's kind of strange. You were always the one that led the way. You remember?"

He nodded. "I remember."

The siblings continued in silence, each lost in memories of their childhood days together. It seemed like a different lifetime. They'd been different people before having their youth so viciously stripped away.

They came to what Jesse considered to be the finest fishing hole on the mountain. Usually clear, today they found the water murky with brownish foam clinging to the rocks that broke the surface. Dragonflies swarmed the wildflowers growing in bunches along the banks, perfuming the air with their fragrance. The smell always reminded Jesse of fishing with her brother. She looked back, still in awe they were together again.

They stopped underneath a large oak. An old turtle, sunning himself on a log, swam away when he saw the pair emerge beneath the low-hanging branches. After collecting a few worms, Jesse watched Toby toss out his line.

"We're going to have to make you your own pole," she said, picking up a twig off the ground next her. "Do you remember our fishing hole back home? I loved that place."

He turned his head and met her gaze. "I remember. I re-remember a lot of th-things."

She pictured the boy she used to tease relentlessly. "Toby, I'm sorry for picking on you when we were little. I was such a brat."

He smiled. "Hey, th-th-that's what little sisters do."

"Still, I'm sorry. I've missed you so much. You being here is like living a dream. I still can't believe you're here."

"I've missed you too. It's just…" He scratched his head. "Well, wh-why do you look like that?"

"You mean why did I cut off my hair or why don't I wear dresses?"

"Both. You d-don't look like the s-s-sister I remember." Toby tapped his temple with his finger.

"A lot has changed since we were kids. I've had to do this. It was to keep me safe, but I don't have to pretend anymore."

Toby nodded, digesting the words. A more serious look came over his face. "Me either."

"What does that mean?" Jesse asked with a wide-eyed look.

"I've p-p-pretended too. When I woke up, after th-this," he pointed to the jagged scar on his forehead, "I couldn't talk like I used to. My words don't come out r-right. People just thought I was st-st-stupid and I just went along with it."

"Oh, Toby. I'm so sorry I wasn't there for you—"

"Not your fault. You didn't know."

"Maybe it's time we both stop pretending then," Jesse said, tossing the twig off to the side. "It'll be nice not having to hide who we really are anymore."

Toby smiled as if a weight had been lifted. He leaned closer and asked, tone shifting, "Do you think Ab—" A fish tugged on his line, demanding his attention. He stepped into the water and reached down. "Hey, it's a nice one," he said, holding the impressive trout up by the gills. Its dotted scales sparkled, catching sunlight from different angles as it flopped in his hand, continuing to resist. "Haven't caught one like th-this in years." After hooking a fresh worm and tossing out his line, he continued. "Do you th-think Abby likes me?"

"Of course she does. Why?" Her eyebrows narrowed. "Did she do something to make you think otherwise?"

Toby shook his head. "No. It's just…I like her. She probably th-thinks I'm stupid because when I'm around her she makes my stutter worse. She makes me nervous, but I like the feeling." He nudged Jesse's shoulder with his own.

Jesse, suddenly dizzy, reached out a steadying hand,

bringing it down hard on a large boulder. "You mean…you *like* her…like her? Like you want to court her?"

"Yes. You two are close and I wo-wondered if you know how she f-feels about me. I wanted to ask you before I say anything to her."

The revelation, although she knew it shouldn't, stunned her. Why wouldn't Toby be attracted to Abby? She simply hadn't imagined her brother having those types of feelings before. In her mind, he was still the silly boy she grew up with. "Uh…have you courted anyone before?"

"Kind of—once. A g-g-girl back in Granite Falls. But when her father found out, he said if he ever caught me speaking to her, he would sh-shoot me." Toby jerked the fishing pole, setting the hook. Never missing a beat, he pulled in another keeper as he continued. "Said his daughter wasn't going to be with some st-stupid stable boy."

Jesse watched him retrieve the fish with a sinking heart, instantly overwhelmed with guilt. She would lay down her life for her brother and wanted nothing more than for him to be happy. So lost in thought, she was oblivious to Toby speaking in the background.

He reached over and shook her by the shoulder. "Well?"

"Um, I want you to find someone…I really do. I just don't think Abby is the one."

"Why not?"

Jesse cleared her throat, buying time while she scrambled to find the right words. "Uh…because, she is already spoken for."

"She is? Oh, I didn't kn-know."

"Sit down," Jesse said, patting the rock next to her.

Toby pulled his line out of the water, set down the pole,

and took a seat next to her. He'd grown so much taller than the last time they'd sat beside a fishing hole, but the feeling was the same.

Jesse scratched the back of her neck. "I'm not sure how to tell you this, so, like Mother always told us, I'm just going to say it. Abby is…" She paused, losing the words again. She let out a long sigh. "Well, I love her and she loves me."

"I know you two are close. That's wh-why I wanted to ask you first. I didn't know she was spoken for. Is he in Ely?" Toby asked, rubbing the stubble on his chin.

Jesse smiled inwardly at the gesture. It was exactly what their older brother Daniel did when he was deep in thought. She remembered Toby imitating him, back when he only had pimples on his chin. Now a grown man, Toby had more hair on his face than Daniel was ever able to grow. An eternal teenager in Jesse's thoughts and heart, her oldest brother never had the chance to see what manhood would bring him.

She shook off the memory and let out another long sigh. "It means we love each other…like Mother and Father loved each other."

A series of confused expressions painted his face as he processed the information. His eyebrows arched when he finally understood. "You mean—"

Jesse cut him off before he could say it out loud. "Yes." Her ears burned. "I don't understand it either, but we can't help the way we feel about each other."

Toby sat in silence as he continued to turn it over in his head. "You two can't be together—like that!"

"Why?"

His brow furrowed. "Because, it's not right. What would Mother and Father th-think?"

"I hope they'd be happy for me, like I want you to be. That girl you liked in Granite Falls, what's her name?"

"Amy. Why?"

"The way you were attracted to Amy is the way I'm attracted to Abby. We can't control who we're attracted to. We're just drawn to certain people." Jesse's voice broke. "I tried not to be, but I can't help the way I feel."

An awkward silence hung in the air, broken only by a gentle weeping and the buzz of a nearby bee.

"Don't cry," Toby said. He nudged her shoulder again.

Jesse's body stiffened. She hurried to wipe away the tears pooling in the corners of her eyes. "I just don't want you to think less of me—or Abby." She placed her hand on his arm. "No one will ever have to know about us. It's our secret. I just couldn't keep it from you. I've—we've lost so much. We only get one life, and it could be snuffed out in the blink of an eye. I've found my happiness with Abby and what we do, well, it doesn't harm anyone. Can't you be happy for me?"

Toby sat in silence, forehead wrinkling as he thought about what she said. "I want you to be happy, but don't you want to get ma-married and have a family?"

Jesse smiled. "I already have a family. You, Abby, and me." She could see the tension slowly slip from her brother's face.

He leaned over and said, "Well, to be honest, I never could see you settling down with a man." He finished with a light-hearted jab to her ribs.

"So, you aren't mad or disappointed in me?"

"No. It's just…I'm not sure I understand it, but I want you to be happy," he said. "I r-really do."

"I know it's a lot to take in. I don't really understand it myself, but I do love her. I can't help it."

A smile spread across his face. "You never were the girly kind. It's like I had a little b-brother more than a little sister." He tugged on her short locks. "Looks like I still do."

She punched him in the arm, and they both laughed even though things still felt strained between them.

"Do you ever think about them?" Toby asked.

He didn't need to explain. She knew exactly who he was referring to.

"Every day."

"No ma-matter how hard I try, I can't remember that day. Will you tell me wh-what happened?"

Jesse bent her legs and rested her arms on her knees. "I went fishing that morning by myself. Father and Daniel were out hunting. You drove Mother and Jamie into town. You remember any of that?"

He shook his head. "No."

She paused, considering how best to tell him the rest of the story without going into too many of the gory details. "Well, you all got back from town first. You were in the barn tending to the horse when I got back. That's when we heard the screams. You hid me in the stall with Dakota, grabbed your rifle, and took off. I don't think I've ever been more scared in my life as I was watching you run out that barn door."

"Why'd they scream?"

"Four men were there. And not the good kind."

"Did Father know 'em?"

"No. I don't think so." She blew a calming breath as she stalled to find her next words. "I think they were there to rob us. Somehow you managed to get away but they caught you. From where I was hiding I couldn't see what they did to you, but the best I can figure is they hit you in the head with a rifle."

Toby rubbed the jagged scar on his forehead. "Must've been a helluva wa-wallop. Where were Father and Daniel?"

"They hadn't come back yet. I wanted to run out of the barn and do something, but I was too scared. I couldn't move."

Toby placed his hand over hers. "Being scared is probably the th-thing that saved you."

"I suppose," she said, although the thought always left a raw spot in the pit of her stomach, burning as if she had downed a bottle of whiskey. "Anyway," she continued, "after you were hurt I saw two of the men get on their horses and ride away. I was hoping, praying that the other two would do the same—but they didn't. They were inside when Father and Daniel got back. I wanted to warn them. I tried to yell but when I opened my mouth, nothing came out. They had no warning. They were ambushed as soon as they opened the door."

His chin trembled. "So, they shot Mother and Jamie too?"

"Yes," she said without hesitation. "Two more shots came right away." She had no intention of telling her brother what had really happened to their mother and sister. She may be smaller, but she was strong enough to shoulder that burden alone. "They didn't suffer."

"I know it can't be easy for you to talk about, but thanks for telling me."

Already the day was shaping up to be beautiful, the warmth of the sun chasing any hint of chill from the air. The birds had found their voices and all around them the trees vibrated with lighthearted trills. The few white clouds scudding across the sky cast shadows on the surface of the water.

They were nothing compared to the ones in Toby's mind as he contemplated everything he had heard.

"I lied to you when I said I didn't know the man who shot me," Jesse said, interrupting his thoughts. She had thought it better to lie to him rather than admit to being a murderer. If she were going to be honest with him, then she would tell him everything, even if it meant he thought less of her. "Those two men that stole our family from us...well, our paths crossed again when I went to Granite Falls. That's why Abby went to the waterfall that night. She led them there for me. I took care of them, but one of them managed to get off a shot first."

Several minutes went by and Toby still hadn't said anything.

Finally, Jesse couldn't take it any longer. "Well say something," she said, scared to hear the next words coming from her brother's mouth.

"You're horse shittin' me?"

Jesse's forehead wrinkled. It was not what she had been expecting him to say. "No, I'm not. I really did shoot them. I watched them die right in front of me."

The thought of his little sister having the tenacity to kill two men in cold blood was something he couldn't fathom. "You really did—swear it."

"Yes," she said. "I swear it."

"Pinky swear it."

She held out her little finger. "Pinky swear it," she said. She hadn't thought of their childhood vow in years. It brought a smile to her face despite their solemn conversation.

He hooked his little finger around hers and nodded in understanding. "And when Abby and I went back to the woods that night—"

"She was looking for me, but I wasn't there. I tried to ride back to Granite Falls but passed out somewhere along the way."

"So, Abby knows what really happened?" he asked.

"Yes. And now you do too. Do you think I'm a bad person?"

"Hell no. I'd of sh-shot 'em myself if I had the chance."

"You know, I never asked you. Why *did* you follow Abby out into the woods that night? You didn't even know her."

He laughed. "You're one to talk. Suppose you'd just met her and she asked you to go somewhere. Are you telling me you wo-wouldn't go?"

Jesse chuckled. "You make a good point. Speaking of Abby, we should probably start heading back and check on her."

Jesse, Abby, and Toby fell into the simple rhythm of life over the next two weeks. The trio worked together, getting as much done as possible before the upcoming trip to Ely.

Toby didn't understand his sister's attraction to another woman, but the more he witnessed them together, the more natural their relationship seemed. How could he have any reservations when it was obvious they cared deeply for one another? It wasn't what he was used to, but the abundance of love he saw between them was all the evidence he needed to know this was good and right. Besides, he knew it was nothing short of a miracle to have his sister back in his life and he would accept her with open arms—no matter what. Having suffered enough heartache, he was grateful his sister finally found her happiness.

Although Jesse moved slowly through her chores, her wounds continued to heal. She had her big brother back and Abby by her side. Life couldn't have been more perfect.

For Abby, anxiety and stress filled those two weeks. Worry about the life growing inside of her plagued nearly every thought. She had already started suffering from morning sickness. Her morning ritual usually began with a struggle to make it outside before vomiting. At night, she tossed and turned from nightmares in which Jesse found out about her situation. Terrified Jesse would notice the obvious swelling in her stomach, she used the sickness as an excuse not to be intimate.

Two days before setting out for Ely, Abby rested inside, too sick to help with morning chores. Toby chopped wood outside. Jesse was coming back from the lean-to for another load when he buried the axe in the chopping stump and pointed to the edge of the woods.

Jesse looked toward the tree line, relieved to see Aponi approaching. She hoped Aponi knew a different remedy to help Abby. The one she knew how to concoct did nothing to ease this unshakable ailment.

Food and fun filled the evening, culminating in Toby's spirited demonstration of the native dance. Jesse did her best to learn the steps while Abby and Aponi watched from the warmth of a blazing fire.

After exhausting himself, Toby went inside and made a blanket bed in front of the fireplace so that Aponi could sleep in the loft.

Jesse stood. "I think I'm going to have to call it a day, too."

Abby reached up and took hold of her hand, giving it a squeeze. "I won't be long," she said.

"All right. It's chilly out here, do you want me to bring you a blanket?"

Abby smiled up at her. "I'm fine. You go on in, I'll be in soon."

The moment the cabin door closed, Abby took hold of Aponi's arm. The expression on her face worried her friend even before the words came out in a panicked rush. "I need to talk to you."

"What is it? Are you all right?"

"No. No, I'm not. I can't believe this is happening—now. It's bad and I don't know what to do." Tears rolled down her cheeks, glistening in the firelight.

"You don't have to stay here. We can take you off mountain," Aponi said, wrapping her arm around Abby.

Abby pulled away to face her. "That's not it. I'm with child. I wasn't sure at first, but I'm certain now."

A small gasp escaped Aponi. "How far are you?"

"Almost three months."

Aponi shook her head. "Jesse no welcome child?"

"She doesn't know. I don't know how to tell her. She knows I had been seeing someone before she came back. I never told her we had been together…like that. Just when I thought I finally had my life together. Now, everything is ruined."

"Tell her. She may welcome child. Child gift from Great Spirit."

"She doesn't want children. We're going back to Ely in a couple days. I know someone who can help me get rid of it."

Abby placed her hand on her stomach. "She'll never have to know."

"Oh, Abby, I think you should tell her. Maybe she welcome child."

"The last time we talked about children, she said they were too big of a responsibility. A burden. I don't know how she'll take the news that Sam and I were—"

"Jesse loves you. You need to tell her."

"I know she does, but this could ruin everything. I just don't know what to do."

Aponi comforted Abby late into the night, trying to persuade her to confess the truth.

The next morning, Jesse found Aponi seated on one of the stump chairs outside. She took a seat beside her. "Could you do me a favor? Abby and I are leaving tomorrow. I'll need the horses to bring back a lot of supplies. Can you stay here with Toby until we get back?"

Aponi nodded. "Yes. I will stay."

"He'd probably be fine staying by himself, but I'd feel better about leaving if someone were here with him. Just in case. We'll be back as soon as we can." She leaned in closer to her. "Did Abby say anything to you last night about what's been bothering her? Does she not like it here?"

Aponi stiffened. "She likes being here. Living on top of a mountain takes some getting used to. You should talk to her."

"I've tried. She says everything's fine, but I don't believe her. Something's bothering her."

Aponi glanced toward the door, making sure they were alone. She leaned over and whispered, "She's—"

The door flung open and Abby came rushing out. She barely made it off the porch before being overcome by another bout of morning sickness.

Jesse gently rubbed her back. "You poor thing. I wish it were me."

Not if you knew the truth, Abby thought.

"I will make you some tea," Aponi said.

"I feel fine now. It passed."

Aponi shrugged her shoulders. "Well, I make you some anyway."

Jesse led Abby back inside. It took several tries but she managed to convince her to get back into bed. She took a seat on the edge and placed her hand on Abby's forehead. "Are you sure you're going to be up for making the trip tomorrow? Maybe Toby and I should—"

"I'll be fine," Abby said with a snap in her voice. "I have to go."

"I'm just worried about you."

Abby held Jesse's hand. "I'll be fine. Promise. Don't worry."

"I've been thinking. I want to tell Edith about me. Who I really am."

"Are you sure?"

"Yes. I think she'll understand. I want to be me again. I don't want to hide who I am anymore."

"I don't know how she'll take it. Some people might not be that understanding."

"I think she'll be shocked at first, but I think she'll come around and understand why I did it."

"I hope so."

"If I don't leave the mountain next year, that'll give my hair time to grow out. Then, in two years, who would even recognize me?" Avoiding resistance, Jesse switched the topic. "Aponi is going to stay here with Toby. That way we can get more supplies loaded on the horses. We'll need to stock up on what we need to get us through until we go back."

"Sounds like you have it all worked out," Abby said, tone pregnant with irritation, her moodiness a side effect of her condition. "You feel comfortable leaving Toby here?"

Jesse smiled. "He'll be just fine. You know he...never mind."

"What?" Abby asked.

Jesse's smiled widened.

Intrigued, Abby asked again, "What? Finish your sentence."

Jesse's mouth opened and then closed. She had considered telling Abby of her brother's feelings for her, but decided not to say anything. There was no reason to make things awkward between them. "Pretty women just make him nervous, that's all." Her smile vanished. "Are you sure you're all right? You haven't seemed yourself lately. Are you having doubts about living up here? Do you want to stay in Ely?"

"No. That's not it. I'm happy here with you. Actually, I've never been happier."

"Well...what's bothering you then?" Jesse reached down and took hold of her hand.

Abby stared wordlessly for a moment. "Do you ever think about what you're giving up, being with me?"

"I don't feel like I'm giving up anything. I have you and

Toby. I'm happy living here and can't think of anything else I could ever want or need."

"Children, Jes, do you ever think about having children?"

"I've never considered it. Is that what's wrong? Is that what you want?" Jesse asked, brows raised.

"Uh…no," Abby said, hesitantly. "I was just wondering how you felt about it. That's all. We've never really talked about you wanting children of your own."

"Abs, my life is complete the way it is. I don't want children. I guess I wasn't born with those instincts. Please don't think I'll ever have regrets about that."

"All right. I just wanted to make sure," Abby said, her tone somber.

Jesse went on to reassure her. "Don't worry about that. Ever. Things are perfect just the way they are." She leaned down and kissed Abby's forehead, only slightly convinced she had found the source of Abby's irritability.

CHAPTER THREE

J esse rolled over, hand instinctively reaching out. Still half asleep, the cold, empty space in the bed surprised her, but did not immediately alarm her. Only as her waking brain recognized her surroundings did she realize what was missing. Abby.

She bolted upright. There was no sign of anyone besides Toby, who still slept soundly on a blanket in front of the fireplace. She pulled pants over her long underwear in a state of panic, barely getting them up before rushing outside.

Relief washed over her. A familiar silhouette sat outside on the porch.

Abby, lost in an attempt to bring order to the chaos in her mind, hadn't heard the door open. She jumped when she felt Jesse's hand on her shoulder.

"Sorry, I didn't mean to scare you," Jesse said. "Did you get sick again?"

She placed her hand over Jesse's. "No. Just couldn't sleep."

"Are you sure you're up to making this trip?" Jesse took a seat on the carved stump beside her.

She nodded. "I'm ready to get it over with."

"Do you want some coffee?"

"No, thanks. I already had two cups of Aponi's special tea. It really helps, but," she leaned over and whispered, "it's not very good."

Jesse couldn't help but smile, her tongue going dry at the memory of acrid native remedies. "Believe me, I know. I'm just glad it helps. She showed me how to make it. I tasted the plant she uses and it really is bitter. I had to spit it out."

"I wanted to, but decided to give it a try. I haven't felt this good in days."

"Good. Now maybe you'll be able to keep some food down. You hungry? I can heat up something. It will be our last hot meal for a few days."

"We probably should." Abby tilted her head toward the door. "Are they still sleeping?"

"Toby is, but I'm not sure about Aponi. She's still in the loft."

"I don't want to wake 'em. I'll wait 'til they get up and then I'll whip us up something."

Jesse stood. "I'm going to start getting ready."

"Are you going to cut your hair?" Abby asked.

"Yes."

Abby got up, too. "I'll do it."

"I don't have scissors. Have you ever cut hair with a knife?" she asked, placing her hand on the sheath hanging on her hip.

"No, but I'll do my best." She raised an eyebrow. "If I mess it up, I'll just shave you bald."

"You're kidding…right?"

"Of course. Hand it here."

Jesse cocked her head, unsure, but drew the blade and

handed it to her. "Just a trim. And don't cut your finger. The blade is sharp enough to shave a frog's hair."

Toby walked outside, yawning and rubbing his bleary eyes with the palms of his hands. "I could use one of th-those myself," he said, running his fingers through his hair.

"You may want to wait and see how she does first," Jesse said, chuckling as she looked up at him.

"Ha, ha. Very funny." Abby tilted Jesse's head back down. "Now hold still so I don't cut off your ear."

Jesse flinched slightly as Abby separated a wide lock of hair from the side of her head and severed it with a quick slice. "Toby," she continued, chin resting on her chest, "you want us to bring you anything back?"

"I c-could use some clothes."

"I already thought of that. Anything else?"

"Naw, don't think so."

Abby stepped back to admire her handiwork. While it was technically a trim—Jesse's hair was considerably shorter—the only thing good about the uneven rat's nest was the smiling face beneath it. Loose tufts and cowlicks stuck out from various parts of her head.

"Well. How's it look?" Jesse asked.

Toby chuckled.

"Shush," said Abby, getting back to work with the knife. "I'm not done yet."

Having figured out the basics of cutting hair with a knife, Abby spent a few minutes getting Jesse into presentable condition. This time when she stepped back, her heart fluttered. The short-haired beauty in front of her looked much like the Jesse she first met and fell in love with.

Finished with Jesse's hair, Abby grinned at Toby and patted the old stump chair with her palm. It was his turn.

"I'm going to heat us up some food and start getting ready," Jesse said.

"This shouldn't take long. We'll be in shortly."

As she cut, she noticed the scar running along the right side of Toby's forehead. The violent wound demanded her attention. Trying not to look only seemed to make her more aware. Disturbing as it was from a distance, up close it was even more unsettling. The red and withered flesh was hideous in itself, but it was also a symbol of the evil their family had experienced. Although what she had gone through with Silas had been terrifying, she knew it was nothing compared to what Jesse and Toby had been through.

As ugly as it all was, it gave her a glimmer of hope. If they could overcome their tragic pasts, then somehow she would get through her current situation.

Jesse packed a few items in their saddlebags. Necessities only; they'd need plenty of room for the return trip. She did a quick tally of the money tin, but didn't find nearly enough to get everything they needed.

She put the money in her pocket and reached for another of Frieda's tins. The weight surprised her, as it always did, when she pulled it from the shelf. Inside, the gold Frieda had saved sparkled. Jesse selected the smallest chunk and replaced the lid. She reached to set it back on the shelf, but hesitated.

They needed to stock up for two years on the mountain. It might be smart to take two nuggets. She chose another piece, placed them both in her pocket, and returned the tin to the shelf. She hated to use the gold but hoped Frieda would understand. It wouldn't be wasted on luxuries, only necessities.

After the four shared a morning meal and finalized some last-minute details, Toby and Jesse went to the paddock and saddled the horses. Aponi used the opportunity to plead with Abby one final time to tell Jesse the truth.

"You need to tell her, Abby," she said. "Jesse may welcome child. She loves you."

"I know I should tell her, I just…" Abby paused. She really didn't know what to say or do.

Toby and Jesse came back with the horses, saving Abby from trying to finish the thought out loud. Aponi pleaded with her eyes. Abby looked away.

They hugged their goodbyes before Jesse and Abby mounted their horses. Toby and Aponi watched them fade into the woods, their final wave disappearing behind the green curtain of forest.

Low-hanging clouds covered the mountaintop, and a light wind, thick with the scent of pine, whistled along the slopes, rustling the trees. The horses descended, Buck leading the way along the familiar path, their pace steady. They moved in silence broken only by the snap of twigs beneath hooves.

Abby hadn't been herself in days. Jesse could see the difference, but each time she asked, Abby reassured her everything was fine. Jesse decided not to pry. Abby would open up to her when she was ready.

During the entire trip down, Abby prayed silently: she prayed for guidance, she prayed she was doing the right thing, and most of all, she prayed Jesse would never learn what she was about to do. It wrenched her heart in every direction. She felt so twisted inside that at any given moment she didn't know which way was up or which path led the right way.

Never had Abby given much thought to having children. She hadn't even thought it possible after her abusive husband's best efforts had failed. Now, being with child was the only thing she could think about.

On the third evening before they crossed the river, they bedded down, waiting on the moonlight to help guide them. Jesse tried to take advantage of the privacy. Abby hadn't let her touch her since they'd bathed in the stream two weeks ago. It wasn't from a lack of trying.

Spooning her from behind, Jesse brushed Abby's hair aside, exposing her neck. She kissed the soft skin. "I've missed you. This," she murmured, desperate to focus her attention on other areas. She felt Abby quiver against her body.

Abby, body covered with goose flesh, wanted nothing more than to make love with her. Raging hormones flooded her. She felt dizzy from her desire. Trying to resist her advances was physically and emotionally painful. She pulled Jesse's wandering hand tightly around her chest. "Jes, I'm so sorry. Please don't be mad."

Jesse leaned up on an elbow and looked at her. "I'm not mad. I just can't figure you out sometimes. Are you having doubts about us?"

Abby rolled over and placed her hand on Jesse's cheek. "Not one. Being with you is the only thing I'm sure of."

"Then what is it? I've missed being with you. I finally get you all to myself and you don't want me touching you—"

Abby cut her off. "That's not it. I love when you touch me. I just have a lot on my mind. This is all a big adjustment for me. That's all. Trust me, once I take care of a few loose ends, I'll be back to myself. Can you be patient with me, please?"

"I'm sorry. I didn't mean to—"

"You have nothing to apologize for. It's not you, it's me." She rolled back over and snuggled into Jesse's warm embrace. *Soon it will be over*, she thought, releasing a long, calming breath.

"Get some rest, Abs."

"You too, Jes."

Of course, neither one could relax. Although their bodies lay close, their troubled minds wandered in opposite directions. The chirping of crickets went unnoticed by both.

Jesse saw all the possible reasons why Abby could be so detached from her. Terrible scenarios flashed through her head, but the worst lingered like an unwanted guest. *What if Abby doesn't love me anymore?*

Abby wanted nothing more than to break down and cry. She considered telling Jesse the truth, but fear once again choked the words from her. She placed a hand on her stomach, an almost-protective habit she had developed.

Then it happened, or so Abby believed. Maybe it was caused by fatigue, or a mind overworked with too many worries. Either way, Abby could have sworn she felt something inside of her move, the tiniest shift. A confusing mixture of panic and elation filled her.

God help me, she silently agonized. *You can't have both. It's either Jes or this baby.*

Abby prayed she was making the right choice.

≈

They rode into town with darkness descending over them like the awkward silence that had loomed throughout the trip.

Abby leaned in her saddle and placed her hand on Jesse's leg. "Good luck telling Edith. Are you sure you don't want me to go with you?"

Jesse took her hand and gave it a kiss. "Yes. I think it's best if I tell her alone."

"All right. You have a good night and I'll see you in the morning," Abby said before turning toward The Foxtail.

Jesse got Buck settled into a stall for the night and headed inside. She found Edith in the kitchen, setting the table for supper. She lingered in the doorway until Edith noticed her, the shock knocking cutlery from her hand.

"Oh my God! I have been worried sick about you. Where have you been? Did Abby find you? Is she all right?" The questions spewed from her mouth.

"We're all fine, Edith. Really. Here's your rifle. Thanks for loaning it to Abby."

"Where is she?"

"At The Foxtail—"

"Abby said you might have been hurt. Said you got into a nasty fight."

"I had a run in with someone from my past," Jesse said, beginning the story she and Abby had come up with for this moment. "Words and blows were exchanged. When it was over, I knew my face was messed up. I didn't want anyone to see me looking like that. I went home. I shouldn't have made everyone worry. I'm sorry."

"I'm just glad everyone's all right."

"Edith...why don't you have a seat?" Jesse said as she pulled out a chair. "I have something to tell you."

Abby dismounted, tied Titan to the hitching post in back of The Foxtail, and entered through the rear door.

"Abby, no one has seen you in weeks!" Jules said. "Where have you been?" She pulled her close, her face painted with a mix of worry and relief.

Abby stepped back, breaking the embrace. "I'm all right. I had something urgent to tend to. I'll explain later. I just need to go get something from my room."

"Boone assumed you weren't coming back. Abby, he found someone to replace you. He gave her your room."

Abby felt dizzy. She placed a hand on the wall for support. "Where are all my things?"

"Boone told the new girl she could have 'em, but, Mabel told him she would keep your things for you. He didn't care what she said. Thankfully, Sam was here. He stepped in and convinced him to let Mabel keep your stuff. Everything is in her room."

"Is she here?"

"No, Boone sent most of the girls to the Rowdy Rabbit. There's a group of men from the railroad up there scouting the area. He's trying to get them to lay tracks through Granite Falls and wanted to show 'em a good time while they're in town."

"He's never one to pass up an opportunity to make money, is he? Look, I really need to go. I'll be back soon and we can catch up."

Abby hurried up the stairs and flung open the door to her old room. Someone had taken over. She saw none of her things. She closed the door and went down the hall to Mabel's room. She spotted most of her belongings stacked in one corner, and her periwinkle dress hung neatly on a hanger close by. She dug through the pile, flinging clothing on the floor until she found her music box.

Abby could feel her heart thumping as she opened the box and removed the false bottom. She let out a sigh of relief. Her life savings were still there—$327.00. She rolled it up and placed it in her coat pocket. After replacing the bottom, she returned it to the pile of possessions.

She and Titan left town, riding out into a nearby area she had never ventured to before. She had heard talk of a woman out here and stories about how she had taken care of women in a delicate condition. The thought of what she was about to do sickened her more than she ever imagined.

Maybe I should just tell Jes I want to stay in Ely. Then I could have this baby. What kind of life is that for a child? I don't even have a job.

Lightning forked across the sky, cracking the night in two. Abby felt the first drops of rain on her face. The thought flashed through her mind as fast as the next bolt streaked above her—maybe it was God trying to warn her. Maybe what she was about to do was an abomination.

For once, the dark and eerie woods caused her no fear or concern. Her mind was elsewhere, her hot tears mixing with the rain coming down in buckets. At times her horse barely kept his footing as he slipped on the muddy track. With words of encouragement, she urged him on as another streak of lightning lit the sky.

Weathered wood and rusted tin sheets made up the run-down shack at the end of the heavily wooded lane. Her heart sank instantly. Then she thought she felt it again—that tiny movement inside her.

It's just your nerves getting to you, she thought, willing herself to believe it. She brought Titan to a stop and put a settling hand on her stomach. She waited.

See, nothing. It's just your imagination. She continued onward, wanting to get it over with as soon as possible.

Dismounting, Abby took in a deep breath and paused. A gust of wind rustled the leaves and set the string of bones dangling from the sagging porch into an angry clatter. Abby shook a rickety post, testing its fortitude before securing Titan to it. She stepped up rotting steps to the weather-beaten door of the dilapidated shack, her face an infringement on a spider's web as she approached. She rapped on the door, her free hand swiping at the silky strand that clung to her cheek.

The latch clicked. Abby braced herself for whatever loomed behind the warped pine. The door squeaked open a crack, revealing the barrel of a shotgun. Candles cast little light inside. Abby could make out the shape of a stout figure. Nothing more. A shadow where a face should be.

"What do you want?" The voice was thick, husky.

Abby wasn't expecting it. If she hadn't known better, she would have thought she was talking to a man.

Another streak of lightning lit the sky, pulling a face from the gloom. Dark eyes glared from sunken sockets, which could have been a hundred years old, if not more. The map of deep lines covering the face spoke of a life that had not been kind. Long hair, white as new-fallen snow, shivered, disturbed by a sudden rush of wind. The old hands holding the weapon were steady, though, as they leveled the gun at Abby.

"I…uh…I heard about you. Heard you could help a

woman who was in trouble," Abby said, her voice rising as she competed with a rumble of thunder.

The woman studied Abby's body, squinting her eyes so hard Abby wondered if she'd closed them. "Get in here then," she said, opening the door wider. "How fer along is ya? Two?"

Abby stepped inside. "Almost three months," she said, wiping rain from her eyes. She blinked when the image persisted, and swallowed hard when she realized there was nothing wrong with her vision. The woman still looked the same, though something about the darkness within the hut seemed to accentuate her harsh features. It was as if death itself grinned at Abby when she smiled.

Abby shivered. Her clothes were soaked through and no fire burned in the stone hearth to warm her. Ash and chunks of charred wood, the remains of numerous fires, had grown into a cold, messy pile within. The shanty had a damp, earthy smell and it seemed no warmer than it had been outside.

The woman propped the gun on the wall next to the door. "No problem fer me, but I ain't gonna lie. You gonna feel it. I git twenty dollars. You got money?"

Abby turned away. The simple task of separating twenty dollars was complicated by nervous fingertips. She returned the roll of money to her coat pocket before facing the old woman. "Yes, here," she said, handing over the money.

"You git in there." The woman aimed a crooked finger at a door in similarly gnarled condition. "Git on the table. I'll fetch what I need. Take this." She handed Abby the candle.

Abby walked into the room and closed the door behind her. The wood felt cool against her back when she leaned on it but did nothing to ease her fear and panic. She breathed hard but slowly, making every effort to calm herself.

She could not contain a small shriek when a cat suddenly darted across the floor in front of her, hissing on its way.

She held out the candle, revealing the room in a flickering orange light. A large wooden table was in the center—stained brown on one end.

CHAPTER FOUR

"Hmm." Toby reached for one of the two cards left in Aponi's hand. The woman across the table betrayed no emotion, which he took as the sign he was looking for. He let go of the card and opted for the other one instead. He glanced at it, at his own hand and back, a slow smile stealing across his face. "You're the old m-maid!" he said, laughing, laying out a pair of deuces.

"That makes three in a row." Aponi tossed her lone card on the table and slid the pile toward him. "Shuffle the deck."

The familiar clatter of the door latch halted the flittering of cards between Toby's hands. Game forgotten, he rose quickly, knocking the chair over in his haste. The door had already opened by the time his hand was on his rifle.

Ahanu stood in the doorway.

"Come," Aponi said, motioning.

Toby picked up the overturned chair and did his best to hide his unease. Heart hammering against his ribs, he forced himself to take a calming breath. He didn't have many memories of that awful day in Granite Falls. Whatever evil was left of that day had wormed its way into the shadows of his mind, unseen and forgotten. It took swipes at Toby nevertheless. Since then, he'd become prone to panic.

When he was much younger it had been even harder to deal with. Without another soul to trust and confide in, he had huddled alone in the barn with the horses, knees pulled to his chest, feeling as if his heart would explode. He never knew what would cause the attacks or when they would happen.

Over the years, he'd learned to tame the worst of it. He released another calming breath and watched as one of the biggest men he had ever seen ducked his head and stepped into the cabin.

"Came to check on you. You no come back to tribe," Ahanu said.

"I'm fine. Just staying here until Jesse and Abby get back from place called Ely. Sit down."

Toby sat and slid one of the chairs with his boot. "I'll deal you in."

Ahanu took the offered chair, but shook his head. "Don't know white man game."

Toby and Aponi shared a knowing look. "We'll teach you," he said, picking up the cards.

Jesse took a seat at the kitchen table and motioned for Edith to join her.

"What is it?" Edith asked.

Jesse placed her hands on the table. She had no idea how Edith would take the news she was about to deliver. She felt unsteady. The familiarity of the wooden table, the place she had spent so much time over the last few years, had a soothing effect. Bracing herself against that solidity, she pushed on before she could change her mind. "I have something I need to tell you."

"I have some news of my own, but you go first." Edith patted Jesse's hand.

Jesse took a deep, steadying breath. She hoped she was doing the right thing by telling her the truth. *Just say it.* She cleared her throat. "I hope you don't think I'm—"

"Well, there's the disappearing man." Felix approached the table, a grin on his face. "Everyone all right?" he asked.

"We're fine," Jesse said as Felix took the seat across from her.

Edith stood and walked to the counter. "Jesse, we were just about to sit down and have supper. You're welcome to join us." She picked up a plate. "What did you want to tell me?"

"Thanks, Edith. I'm starved." Jesse shrugged. "It was nothing."

"I gotta take mine on the go," Felix said. "I gotta pick up a load of feed down in Big Oak. Charles can't make the run with me. If Tom wasn't needin' that grain tomorrow, I'd put it off. It's raining cats and dogs out there."

"I'll go with you." Jesse said.

"I could sure use the help. Job pays a dollar." Edith came over and placed a firm hand on his shoulder. "I meant two dollars," he said.

Edith patted him on the back and smiled.

Jesse nodded. Telling Edith the truth would have to wait. "So, what's your news?" she asked.

"Felix can tell you all about it on the way to Big Oak. You boys just hurry up and get some food in ya before you leave."

"We'll probably get back late tomorrow because of this rain. Will you open the store for me?"

"Sure thing," Edith said. "Don't rush. You two just be careful."

Her warning did not go unheeded. By the time they got the wagon rolling out of Ely, the wheels slid through mud thick like porridge.

"Damn rain. Might take us all night to get down there," Felix said, snapping the reins. Rain poured from the brims of their hats.

Abby rode through the dark street, tired and cold, but restless. She had to see Jesse tonight. She may not have the nerve later.

With Titan secured out front of Edith's place, she hurried inside. She went to the room Jesse always stayed in and let herself in. She crept toward the bed, arms stretched, and bumped into the footboard. Her hands found soft linens but no warm body within.

They must've decided not to go, Edith thought, hearing a noise across the hall. She climbed out of bed and pulled on her housecoat.

"Jesse?" Edith rapped her knuckles gently on the door. "You boys back already?"

Boys? Jes must not have told her yet. Abby opened the door. "He's not here. Where is he?"

"Abigail Flanagan." Edith pulled her close in a hug. "It's so good to see you. He went with Felix to pick up a load of feed down in Big Oak." She felt Abby's body tremble, felt the coldness seeping out of her. "You're soaking wet. Let me fetch you a towel and get you a change of clothes."

"Thanks, and I can just slip on one of Jesse's shirts. He won't mind."

Edith brought Abby a towel. "I'll put on the coffee and meet you in the kitchen. We have a lot of catching up to do," she said, pulling the door shut on her way out.

Abby was delighted to see the blazing glow coming from the fireplace in the kitchen. Although she was dry, and could feel the heat radiating through the oversized shirt, a shiver ran through her body. She was grateful when, at last, Edith handed her a warm mug.

"Are you all right, dear? You look upset."

"I just have a lot on my mind," Abby said, looking down into the cup. The liquid was as black as the despair eating away at her. "I'll be fine. How are you? Everything all right?"

"Well." Edith paused and put her palms flat on the table. "I do have some news. I'm getting married."

"Married? To who?"

"Felix. We just thought it was time. Oh, hell. I'll be honest. No need to keep it from you." Elated and unable to keep the news bottled up, Edith leaned over and whispered, "I'm going to have his baby."

Abby held Edith's hands. "Congratulations. I'm so happy for you two."

"Who would've thought? Isaac and I never conceived. Thought it was never in the cards for me. No one was more surprised than I was, that's for sure. Felix is a good man. He's going to make a great husband and father."

Abby's lip quivered. She bit it even as she felt her brow

furrow, the flood of tears unstoppable. She squinted against it, anyway, before stifling a sob with the palm of her hand.

"What is it? What's wrong?" Edith asked, pulling her chair closer. "It'll be all right. Nothing can be that bad."

"I...I'm with c-child, too," she said, her voice breaking as the words came tumbling out.

"Congratulations. That's wonderful news. A child is a true blessing. Jesse must be thrilled. Why are you so upset?"

"It's just not the right time. I went to the old house out by the Gleason farm. You know who I mean...don't you?"

"Agnes? You went to see her? But why? Why would you want to get rid of your baby—and why would Jesse let you go through that alone?" she said, brow creased in confusion.

"Jesse doesn't know. He doesn't want to have children. I've heard him say it. I'm just going to tell him when he gets back that it's over between us." Abby wiped her tears on Jesse's shirt-sleeve and continued. "He can go live his life and I will stay here and raise this baby on my own."

"Abby. You need...you have to tell him. It's the right thing to do. He may surprise you when he finds out."

Abby didn't want Edith to know the truth. "Edith, I've made up my mind. I'm letting him go." Resolute, she contin-ued. "I want him to be free and not tied down with a wife and child. His life would never be the same."

"I guess you know what's best. I just hope you're making the right decision."

"I am. I know I am." Abby scooted her chair back from the table. "I'm going to wait for him in his room. I want to tell him as soon as he gets back. I'm so sorry to be so emotional, especially after you told me your wonderful news. I really am happy for the two of you."

Edith paced the empty kitchen, the questions swirling in her mind. *Should I tell Jesse? He needs to know so he can step up and be the man Abby needs. Be a father. But, you know you shouldn't meddle in other's affairs.*

As tired as she was, Edith didn't go back to bed. Instead, she spent the remainder of the night pacing, feet unable to stop. She weighed the pros and cons, praying for some clarity about what she should do.

Wet clothes stuck to their skin and water seeped into their boots, but Jesse and Felix were grateful for even a small break from the torrent.

"We should make better time, at least, now that we're out of that," Felix said, snapping the reins. The horses slipped in the sludge.

"Oh, what was Edith going to tell me?" Jesse asked.

Felix grinned. "We're gettin' hitched."

"I'm so happy for you." Jesse slapped him on the back.

"There was no rush to get down here to pick up feed. I used it as an excuse. I ordered a ring for her and got the wire today that it was ready."

"Don't you sell rings at the Post?"

"I do, but they're just simple bands. I wanted something real special for her, so I had one engraved down in Big Oak."

Jesse nodded. "So, when's the big day?"

"Two days. Scratch that. It's after midnight, so tomorrow. It's kind of a rushed wedding, if you know what I mean."

"Not really."

"She's carrying my child. Best to get married before she

starts to show. Being unwed with a child can ruin a woman's reputation, ya know?"

Jesse nodded. "So, that's why you're marrying her? To save her honor?"

"Heck no! I love that woman. I've been asking her for years to marry me and she always said no. I guess this baby helped me finally convince her to settle down. Hey, you and Abby can stay for the weddin' can't ya?"

"I'm not sure. I need to get home."

"Well, I know Edith would love it if you two could make it. The whole town will be there."

"Maybe we can. I'd like to."

The mud sucked against the horses' hooves, each step of their struggle to pull the load splitting the night air with a wet gurgle.

Jesse shifted uncomfortably, her clothes chafing. "Have you ever sold gold before?" she asked.

"No. Never looked for it. The odds aren't in my favor. Why?"

"I found a couple nuggets and I need to get some things. What do I do? Just take it to a store and do some trading?"

"Absolutely not! Storeowners will haggle with you. You take that to a bank. They weigh it and you get paid per ounce. No negotiating."

"Is there a bank in Big Oak?"

"Yeah, sure."

"While you get the ring, do you mind if I run to the bank?"

"I'll do ya one better. I'll go with you, just in case you need my help."

"I'd appreciate that."

A slate gray sky met the pair as they rolled into town.

"We got some time to kill before the stores open. How about getting something hot to eat?" Felix asked.

"Sounds good," Jesse said with a cold shiver.

Over a hot plate of biscuits and gravy, Jesse asked what seemed to Felix a hundred questions about the wedding. Never having attended one before, she was curious about the upcoming ceremony. Felix explained it in detail.

After their meal, they drank coffee and read. Felix skimmed over the newspaper, while Jesse leafed through a magazine someone had left behind on the table. The front cover captured her attention. Studying an image beneath the headline she read, *Union Ships Destroy Confederate Fleet.* The illustration, depicting the battle at Mobile Bay, fascinated her.

She had never seen anything like those ships before. They were immense. In fact, she realized with a start, they were many times bigger than the building she sat in at that moment. Whole towns floated in the ocean, doing battle with giant guns. It was the stuff of fantasy.

She finished reading the article and let her eyes drift to the small image of a locomotive on the next page. Again, it was astonishing and new to her. The article stated trains were said to be so much faster than horses, yet smooth in their movement. Even though they were known to be terrifyingly loud, the idea of riding on one piqued her curiosity.

In that moment, it became clear how much she was missing out on, living atop the mountain. For the first time ever, she was having doubts about whether or not she wanted to continue the reclusive lifestyle.

She turned the page and gasped as the image on paper came to life—soldiers, their dead bodies splayed across a field like they were sleeping. Abby had told her about the war. Hearing about it and actually seeing proof of it were different things entirely. Seeing the brutality with her own eyes made it more real. The death on the page made her think of her own family, of their lifeless bodies, of the horror men inflict upon each other. *This world is going mad. Maybe it is best to stay on the mountain.*

Felix checked his pocket watch. "Stores are opening. We should get going," he said, giving Jesse a thankful reprieve from her thoughts.

As he steered the wagon toward the bank, he offered to make the transaction for her. Not knowing the first thing about cashing in gold, she happily agreed.

Jesse stood and watched as the teller weighed out the nuggets, studying the entire process. The man counted out the cash and Felix rolled it up and placed it in his pocket. When they stepped outside, Felix pulled Jesse into the alley beside the bank. "Don't let people see this," he said, handing her the roll of bills. "Money can make people crazy. You hide it."

Jesse stuffed it in her pocket. "Thanks for doing that for me."

"Welcome. Now, let's go get that ring."

More people and horses crowded the street as the town woke up. Unused to being around so many people, Jesse was somewhat disoriented. All the conversations around her, accents both unique and familiar, blended together into a wordless murmur. The sounds reminded her of the flowing water by the cabin.

Distracted by the townspeople, Jesse didn't notice their destination until she read the letters painted across the front window: Emporium. Beneath a red and white-striped awning in front of the store sat a long table, piled high with produce. She inhaled deeply. The fresh scents of ripened berries, peaches, and apples were so intoxicating she didn't want to follow Felix into the store, but he wasn't waiting around.

She was overcome by the size of the place. It was bigger than anything she'd ever seen—like those ships, perhaps. Everything one could imagine, all housed in this one building. A myriad of jams, jellies, and jars of honey lined the shelves. Baskets were piled high with potatoes, cucumbers, carrots, and vegetables she didn't recognize. Cured meats hung from the ceiling next to hanging scales.

Jesse tried to take it all in as she trailed Felix, who made a beeline toward the counter. The long, glass case held beautiful jewelry of every kind: rings, pocket watches, broaches, and necklaces. She focused her attention on the rows of rings, each one a work of art. She was mesmerized by the light as it glittered over the facets.

"Hey, Mr. Nicholas," the man behind the counter said. "I've got your ring in the back."

"Can I see that?" Jesse asked, catching the clerk's attention before he could walk away. She pointed to a cameo necklace.

The clerk slid open the back panel and reached inside.

Jesse held it in her hand. She liked the weight of it; it felt substantial, precious. "I'll take it," she said, handing it back to the salesman.

"Sure thing. Will that be all?"

"No. I have some other things I need," Jesse said.

"Is that for Abby?" Felix asked.

"Yes. Her birthday is coming up soon."

"Well done!" he said, clapping her on the back. "Hey, why

don't you get what you need while I finish up here. We need to get back soon."

She walked the aisles, amazed by the variety and amount of merchandise. The first thing that caught her attention was an area containing tack. Her eyes were drawn to a leather pannier box set. They were like saddlebags but much larger, almost the size of crates.

A salesman approached her. "Best there is."

"How do they work?"

"No special ropes, or fancy knots needed. They buckle to the cinch. Keeps them in place. You can haul a lot of equipment in these."

She looked at the price tag. "I'll take them."

"I'll take 'em up front for ya," he said.

Jesse continued to walk the store, selecting clothing for Toby and Abby—nothing fancy, just practical attire, along with thick, wool socks. She paused at numerous bins, which held every variety of seed possible. *How wonderful it would be to have a garden.* She picked up a scoop and filled small envelopes with an assortment of seeds. Her mouth watered at the phantom taste of what these little starts would become.

Felix found her wandering among the wool blankets. "Look at this. Do you think she'll like it?" he asked, opening the small velvet box. He pulled out the ring and handed it to her.

"Look." He pointed to the fine lettering along the inside of the gold band. *My beloved,* etched in a delicate script, stood out clearly.

"Felix, she'll love it."

"I hope so. You almost ready?"

She nodded.

Edith held a coat over her head, a shield against the persistent rain. She kept pace with the wagon as it rolled to a stop behind the trading post.

"I need to speak with you," she said, calling up to Jesse with concern written on her face. "It's urgent."

"Is it Abby?" Jesse asked, jumping down quickly. "Is she all right?"

"You just come inside with me."

A helplessness washed over Jesse as she followed on legs she could barely feel.

Edith sat by the wooden barrel. "Have a seat. What I'm about to tell you…well, just have a seat," she said.

Jesse sat down. "What's going on?"

She took hold of Jesse's hand and smiled. "Congratulations. You're going to be a father."

"What are you talking about? I can't be," she said, shaking her head.

"Oh, yes you can and you are. Abby told me."

"Told you what?" She leaned back and rubbed the scar on her forehead.

"That she is carrying your child."

Jesse felt dizzy. The light took on a different quality and the room spun. *What is going on?*

"Are you all right?"

"No. Not really." It was too much information to process. She put a hand to her brow, but the spinning continued.

How? When? It didn't seem possible. It wasn't possible.

When the thought came, it hit her with such force it nearly knocked her over.

Sam!

"She was going to get rid of it last night. She said you don't want to have children with her."

Jesse stood up so quickly stars twirled in front of her eyes. "I need to talk to her."

Before she could walk away, Edith grabbed her by the arm. "She's at my place. She spent the night in your room."

"Thanks for telling me."

"Just be gentle with her. She's in a fragile state of mind."

"I will," she said before hurrying out the door.

CHAPTER FIVE

E dith hung the feather duster on a peg in the back storeroom of the trading post. In between customers, she had swept the floors, dusted and straightened the many items along each row of shelving, and counted the money in the till several times. She refolded, arranged, and then rearranged the clothing.

Tidiness was not her only goal. The effort also gave Jesse and Abby some privacy back at her place. How much time they needed, she couldn't be sure. She simply continued working until she thought for sure she would go mad if she had to look at one more can or box.

Surely, the young couple had had plenty of time to work things out, she thought. She went to the back of the post to the small living quarters she had once shared with Isaac. She had let Felix get some much-needed rest after he had been up the night before.

She paused in the doorway, placing her hand on the memorable gouge in the frame's wood. It carried her back to when she and Isaac had completed the living quarters.

"There's plenty of clearance," she had said, peeking around the bureau she and Isaac were manhandling into the virgin structure.

"Are you sure?" he'd asked.

"Of course I'm sure. I wouldn't say it if I wasn't. Just lift your end a little higher."

Unfortunately, she never had been accurate at judging distance. She had been horrified by the deep gash, but Isaac never said a word about it. He'd never been a man who showed his temper or raised his voice at her. Her greatest regret was never being able to give him a child. It seemed a lifetime ago and yet, oddly, it seemed as if it happened only yesterday. She felt old. Where had all the time gone?

Oh, my word. I'm going to be forty-five when this child is born, she thought, placing a hand on the slight protrusion of her stomach, noticeable only to her. It felt surreal. She was overjoyed to be with child. Finally. After all these years. She shook off the musings and walked to the bed. "Felix. Wake up," she said, shaking him by the shoulder.

He rolled over and rubbed his eyes. "I'm up. I'm up."

"Don't go back to sleep. I'm going home."

"All right," he grumbled, tossing back the blanket.

Edith trod lightly down the hall when she arrived back home. Not wanting to interrupt the young couple, she put an ear to Jesse's door, hearing nothing but silence. Relieved they seemed to have worked things out, she tapped softly. "Hey," she said, "would you two like something to eat?"

The door flew open. "He's not back yet," Abby said. "Do you think they're all right?"

Edith stammered, searching for the words. "Uh...they... um, got back hours ago."

"They did?" Abby's forehead wrinkled.

"Yes. Jesse said he was coming here to talk to you."

Edith took Abby by the arm. *I told him and he ran*, she thought. *What have I done?* She led Abby to the bed, both to calm the panicking woman and to relieve her own roiling stomach. Neither one could handle much more agitation.

"Abby, I think you better sit down. I think we both should," Edith said, pulling Abby down beside her. "Please don't hate me." Edith took hold of her hand. "I had to tell him. I'm so sor—"

Abby jerked her hand away as if it had been burned. She jumped up with a fire in her eyes Edith had never seen before. "You told him I was—"

"Yes. I'm sorry," Edith said, cutting her off. "I'm so sorry."

"I told you I didn't want Jesse to know about this baby," Abby said, walking to the door.

"Where are you going?" Edith asked.

"To see if Buck's in the barn."

Abby's shoulders sank when she saw the empty stall. "He's gone." Her body shook as she sobbed. She felt Edith place a consoling hand on her back. "You had no right to say anything," she said, shrugging off her hand. "It wasn't your place."

Edith wilted. "Please! Please forgive me. I thought he was different."

"Well, now you know," Abby fired back. "I told you he didn't want children." She bent over, hands on her knees, trying to breathe through the quick and violent nausea.

Edith warily put an arm around her. "Let's get you back inside."

Abby allowed herself to be aided back to the bedroom. She

wept as she took a seat on the edge of the bed, her palms no help in stanching the flow. It dawned on her she had no right to be upset with Edith. In all actuality, she had done her a favor. Now, she wouldn't have to see the hurt she caused Jesse when she broke off their relationship. "I know I shouldn't be mad at you," she said in between sobs. "I did this to myself. I'm the one that ruined everything."

Edith rubbed her back. "Listen here. It takes two to make a baby. I can't believe Jesse is acting this way."

Fearing unjust repercussions against Jesse, she said, "Please, don't be upset with him—"

Edith interrupted. "Don't be upset with him," she said, scoffing, her lips pressed into a thin line. "Let me say this. Any man who runs out on a woman after he got her in trouble is no man at all." She could feel Abby's body trembling beside her. In an effort to calm her, she shifted the conversation off of Jesse. Edith's tone softened, "Look, I know this isn't how you probably pictured things, but everything will be all right."

Abby's chin quivered, her pain evident in the tears streaking her face. "No, it won't," she mumbled, her words choked almost incoherent by the sobs. "I'm going to have a baby and I don't even have a job."

Edith's body went still. "You don't sing at The Foxtail anymore?"

"No. Boone hired someone to replace me."

Edith moved closer and draped an arm around her. "I'd hire you to work for me, but I'm not going to rent rooms anymore." It pained her to say it, but she and Felix had decided to turn the hotel back into a home. "Listen," she said, "the Ely Grande Hotel will be opening soon. Maybe they will hire you to entertain the guests. If not, you could always see if they need a housekeeper. It would at least be a paying job."

"I don't even have a place to stay."

"Nonsense. You can stay here with us until you get on your feet. Somehow, we'll make this work. Why don't you lie down and get some rest. All this stress isn't good for you or your baby."

Abby curled into a ball and let Edith cover her with a blanket. "I'll be back to check on you later," she said, closing the door quietly behind her.

The next few hours were a living hell for Abby. The idea of breaking it off with Jesse was one thing—it actually happening was another. The pain of losing her was already more that she could stand. It felt like her heart was literally breaking. On top of that, she knew the only way to fix the turmoil she had created between Edith and Jesse was to come clean and tell Edith the truth that Sam Bowman was the father of her child.

At the other end of the house, Edith had resumed her pacing in the kitchen. Never had she felt so ashamed of herself. *If only I had kept my big mouth shut.* No matter how many times she repeated it, the fact remained she hadn't and the results had been disastrous. Unable to stand the guilt any longer, she headed to the barn, hoping the job of mucking out the stalls would take her mind off of the mess she'd created. Perhaps the unpleasant task would serve as penance.

The sound of an approaching horse shook Edith from her thoughts. She turned, grateful to see Buck's familiar muzzle coming around the side of the building. "Oh my heavens!" she said, dropping the pitchfork and running from the barn. "I'm so glad to see you! Where were you?"

"I had something I had to do. Is Abby still inside?" Jesse asked.

Edith reached up and placed a trembling hand on her leg. "Yes. So, you're not going to abandon her?"

"Abandon her?" Confusion painted her face. "What are you talking about?"

"I thought you were coming to talk to her earlier. When we didn't see Buck, we assumed you got cold feet and ran off."

Jesse slid to the ground and handed the reins over to Edith. "I rode him pretty hard. Will you tend to him so I can go talk to her?"

"Yes, of course," Edith said, waving her off.

Jesse hurried inside with her saddlebag draped over one shoulder. "Abs, you awake?" she asked, inching open the bedroom door.

Abby bolted upright. "Jes! You came back!"

"Of course I did," she said, pushing the door wide open. Once inside the room, she dropped her bag on the floor and slid the bolt lock in place. She put her hat on the post of the footboard and sat down beside her.

Abby locked her arms around Jesse in an embrace so tight the tremble of her body shook Jesse's.

"Hey, hey, hey, ssshhh," Jesse said. She pulled away, taking Abby's face in her hands. "Everything is going to be all right." She wiped away the tears with her thumbs. "I have just one question for you. Are you going to raise your child with Sam?"

Abby sniffled. "No. I don't want a life with him. I want one with you. But I've ruined everything. I'm so sorry."

"You didn't ruin anything and I was hoping you would say that," she said, a smile creeping across her face.

"Jes, I didn't know you were going to come back into my

life. If I had known there was a chance for us, I never would have been with him. I was trying to get on with—"

"Abs, you don't owe me an explanation. It's all right."

"But I'm going to have another man's child. How's that all right?"

"I'll be honest with you. I was really hurt and angry when I first found out. But I had no right to be. I was the one who kept pushing you away. You did nothing wrong." Jesse looked into her eyes. "All I know is that I love you and I want to be with you. No matter what."

"I love you too."

"I promise to be there for you and this child, if you'll allow me. And look, Edith already thinks I'm the father, so why say anything?"

Abby turned her head away. "But—"

"Look at me. Frieda taught me a lot of things, but the most important thing was you don't have to be a blood relative to be family."

"But you don't want children."

"I never considered it a possibility. I never wanted that life for myself. To marry a man and have children." She shook her head. "That's not the life for me." She took hold of Abby's hands. "I'm sorry I scared you. I didn't mean for you to think I ran off on you. I had to ride down to Big Oak."

"Didn't you just get back from there this morning?"

"I did. But I had to go back for something." She reached into her pocket and pulled out a small velvet box. "I wanted to have this just in case," she said, pulling it open. "I'd like to do right by you and this baby."

Abby's eyes widened at the sight of the shimmering gold band. "What are you saying?"

"I'm saying—asking if you'd consider being Mrs. Jesse McGinnis?"

Abby gasped. Her heart wanted nothing more than to say yes. Her conscience, however, couldn't allow it. "No, Jes," she said, chin trembling. "I can't."

"Why not?" Jesse asked, reaching out to stroke her hair.

"Because," she said, placing a hand on her stomach, "I can't put this burden on you."

Jesse fired back. "Burden! This child is not a burden. It's a blessing, and I want to help you raise it. I've never wanted anything more."

Abby's eyes widened. "Are you sure?"

"I've never been more sure of anything in my life. So, what do you say?" Jesse took her hand and slid the ring on her finger. "I hope I got the size right. It fit my little finger so I figured it might be your size."

A little large for her petite finger, the ring slid on with ease. Abby held out her hand, staring at the interlocking hands formed in metal. "Oh, Jes! Yes!"

Jesse rubbed her finger along the band. "The guy in Big Oak told me it's called a Fede ring, imported from Europe. Anytime you're scared or need me, just look at this ring and rest assured I will always be there to hold your hand no matter what life might throw at us."

Abby cupped Jesse's face in her hands and left a lingering kiss on her lips. An intruding thought made her pull away. "But I thought you didn't want to keep living like this. You didn't want to live this lie anymore."

"If I have to live the rest of my life as Jesse McGinnis so that I can be with you, then so be it." She shrugged.

Abby looked down at the ring. "I can't believe this is happening."

"Believe it. It's just the beginning for us." She scratched the back of her neck. "I have to admit, I'm nervous. I don't know anything about babies. Never been around one before."

"I'm new at this too, but I'm sure it will come naturally to you. To us."

She placed her hand on Abby's stomach. "I can't wait to meet her."

"And how do you know it's a girl?" Abby asked with a raised brow.

"I don't. Just a hunch. Hey, do you still have that blue dress?"

"It's in Mabel's room."

"Did you give it to her?"

"No. She's keeping my things for me. Boone hired someone to replace me. He gave my room to her."

"That's great news," Jesse said, nudging Abby's shoulder with her own.

"Great news?"

"Yeah, Boone did you a favor. You didn't want that life anymore anyway. Now you don't have to feel guilty about quittin' on him."

"I didn't think of it that way."

"Anyway, you're going to have to go get that dress. I just met with Frank Whitaker. Do you know who he is?"

"Yes, he's the justice of the peace around here."

"Well, you and I have an appointment with him tomorrow afternoon. He's already drawing up the paperwork so we can make this official." Jesse stood and reached for her saddlebag.

"I need to get out of these," she said, glancing down at her clothes.

Jesse unbuttoned her shirt and tossed it aside.

"Let me help you with that," Abby said, reaching to help remove the breast binding. "It's wet."

"Yeah, we got soaked last night," she said, holding out her arms, letting Abby unravel the strips of fabric. She savored the gentle tickle of her touch, but said nothing. She kicked off her boots and removed her pants while Abby watched. When she bent down to remove her damp socks, the muscle along the side of her abdomen flexed.

Abby didn't mean to stare. She just couldn't help herself. She was drawn to Jesse's exquisite form and couldn't resist the temptation any longer.

"You have an incredible body," she said, inching closer.

Jesse stood rooted in place, emerald eyes taking in the woman approaching her.

"I've missed being with you, touching you," Abby said, resting her head on Jesse's chest, arms wrapped loosely around her. She trailed her hands up Jesse's back, playing toned muscles like piano keys.

Jesse held her tight. "I've missed you, too."

Abby stood on the tips of her toes and put her mouth next to Jesse's ear. "I want to be with you," she whispered, nibbling a path along the side of her neck.

Stifling a yawn, Jesse said, "I'm sorry—"

"Oh, you poor thing," Abby said, realizing the obvious. "You've been up all night. Why don't you get some sleep?"

Jesse yawned again and looked down at her pruned toes. "I bought some things this morning, and I have to go get them off of Felix's wagon."

"It can wait." She handed Jesse a pair of long underwear. "You get some rest."

Her urge to argue about it was outweighed by fatigue. "Don't let me sleep too long."

"You just get some sleep," Abby said, picking up her damp clothing. "I'll be back later."

Jesse stretched out on the bed. "You don't want to lie down with me?"

"I need to go apologize to Edith. I'll take your stuff and let the sun dry 'em out."

"Um hmm." Jesse groaned, asleep before Abby reached the door.

Abby watched her sleeping form. "Sleep well, Jes," she whispered as she closed the bedroom door behind her on the way out.

A few hours later, Jesse woke to the sound of humming. She stayed silent, watching Abby at the bureau, writing on a piece of paper. On the floor were several sheets that had been wadded up and tossed aside.

Jesse looked at the mess. *Better get used to that if we're going to have a life together.* Something about Abby made her seem even more beautiful than usual. She bit her bottom lip as she puzzled over what was different. Then she remembered. *She's with child!*

Jesse focused on the knotty pine ceiling, a smile twitching at the corners of her mouth. *A baby. I wonder if it's a boy or a girl.* Then, it was as if she had been punched in the stomach. *A baby!* Her smile vanished. She lay there, mind racing. *The cabin is so small the way it is with Toby, Abby, and me. Now a baby. Will it be healthy? What if Abby has problems like her mother did?* The thought alone made her jerk.

"Oh, you're—" Abby stopped when she noticed Jesse's strained expression. "Are you all right? You're not having second thoughts are you?"

Jesse's eyes widened. "No. But I've been thinking. Do you want to have this baby on top of a mountain? What if something goes wrong?"

"Jes, I'll be fine. Women have babies all the time. Besides, we do have help. I'm sure our friends on the mountain have helped plenty of women birth babies over the years."

"What about the cabin? It's so small."

"The smaller the better. It will keep us close," she said, smiling. "Stop worrying about everything. We're going to be just fine. Relax, we have plenty of time to figure it all out."

"I just don't want anything to happen to you or the baby." Her thoughts scrambled, like a squirrel looking for a lost nut. "What are you writing?"

"Can't tell you, but you'll find out tom—"

"We should go."

"Where?"

"To get you something to eat. You're eating for two you know."

Abby smiled and made her way over to the bed. She sat and leaned down to kiss the scar on Jesse's forehead. "I have a feeling you're going to be really good at this parenting thing."

CHAPTER SIX

The hardwood floor in the back of the trading post dug into Jesse's hipbone. Knowing an unwed couple sharing a bed would be frowned upon, she gave Abby her room at Edith's. It wasn't ideal, but she was grateful to Felix for offering her the lodgings.

Unable to get comfortable, Jesse tossed back the blanket and got dressed. She found Felix up front, tallying money from the cash drawer. "Are you nervous?" she asked.

"Hey, morning. Not too bad—yet." Felix grinned, hiding any lingering anxiety behind his teeth. "How 'bout you?"

Jesse ran moist palms on her pants. "Terrified, really."

"Just remember to breathe and you'll do just fine," he said, leaning against the counter.

Jesse wondered if it could be as simple as he made it look and sound. She studied his attire. The striking suit, finished off with a black bow tie, made her feel insecure about her own appearance. She glanced down at her clothing, what she now felt were little more than rags. *I can't show up dressed like this.*

"I know you're not opening the store today, but could I get a couple of things?"

He waved her on. "Go ahead and get what you need."

She headed to the back of the store to change into a light blue shirt and black leather vest. She felt a little better. At the very least, she wouldn't stick out like a nun in a saloon.

A small group of women had gathered in Edith's bedroom, their mood apparent from the chatter bubbling out into the hallway.

"You're beautiful," Abby said. "One look at you and Felix will be so tongue tied he won't be able to speak." She pinned a flower in Edith's hair, stepped back, and checked the placement. It was passable, but it took another slight adjustment to achieve perfection.

Edith beamed. "Thank you for all your help. All of you. What time is it?" she asked for what seemed like the hundredth time.

"A little after eleven," one of them said. "Don't worry. We'll get you to the church on time."

A knock at the door was followed by the deep voice of a man. "Hey Sis! You in there?"

"Teddy!" Edith exclaimed, rushing to open the door.

The two hugged in the doorway for a long moment before she finally let go. "Let me see you," she said. "It's been so long. Where are Carol and the kids?"

He'd barely started his reply when two boys came tearing down the hallway, their cries drowning out his words. "Aunt Edith!" they hollered, practically bowling her over.

She hugged them before peeling them off. "Let me see you," she said, taking a step back. "Wow, you two are as big as men. How'd that happen?"

"Boys. Mind her dress."

Edith extended her arms. "Oh, Carol. So good to see you."

"Good to see you too," Carol said, returning the hug. "It's been way too long."

"It sure has." Edith looked around the room, feeling joy at the sight of each and every person. She could have savored the feeling forever. She might have, too, if she hadn't noticed the time or lack thereof. She could feel the big moment rushing up on her.

"I was beginning to think you weren't going to make it," Edith said.

"Stage was running behind," Teddy said. "But better late than never."

Edith turned and faced the women in the room. "Everyone, I want you to meet my brother, Theodore, and his wife, Carol. And these two handsome lads are my nephews, Tanner and Harrison." She introduced the women in the room, pointing as she said each name. "These are my dear friends: Fern, Hazel, Margaret, and Abby."

Teddy doffed his hat. "Nice to meet you ladies."

"You can put your things in the room across the hall," Edith said, pointing to the suitcases at his feet. "I'm almost ready."

When her relatives went across the hall, Abby said, "Edith, I'm going over to the church to check on things."

"All right. We'll be there shortly."

Jesse's reflection stared back at her in the mirror. She buttoned the vest and straightened her shirt collar. The stiff garment seemed to be doing its best to choke her. She wet her hands in the washbasin and combed her fingers through her hair, irritated that the unruly strands wouldn't stay down.

Why did she cut it so short? She cursed inwardly at Abby. Noticing Felix's ointment on the bureau top, she decided to try it—just a smidge. She parted and smoothed out her hair, forgoing her hat in an effort not to mess it up.

She went back to the front of the store and paid Felix for the clothing. "Hey, I'm going over to the—"

The bell above the door jingled and a man called out, "How's the happy groom!"

Felix put his hand on Jesse's shoulder. "Hank, this is Jesse. Jesse McGinnis. Jesse, this is my good friend, Hank Johansen."

Hank and Jesse greeted each other with a simple nod.

"So, you all ready for the big day?" Hank asked Felix.

"I think so."

"Good. Good. The wife made so many pies last night the house looked like a damn bakery. But boy, did they smell good. I tried to sneak a taste, but she wasn't havin' it..."

Their conversation faded into background noise as Jesse silently cataloged all she needed to get done. The mental list seemed to dwarf the time she had to finish everything. Felix and Edith's wedding ceremony was to take place at noon, with a gathering to follow right after. Then, she and Abby were meeting the justice of the peace at two o'clock. Plus, she still had to pack up, load the horses, and get to the river crossing by nightfall.

"I'm heading over to the church," she said, placing her hat on the counter, eager to get started on her day.

THE DEVIL BEHIND US

Felix reached behind the counter for a decanter of Scotch whiskey. "How about having a drink before we go?"

Jesse considered it, but declined. Today was too important. She wanted to have all her wits about her. "Thanks, but I'll pass. You fellas go ahead."

"All right. We'll be over shortly," Felix said, pouring whiskey into one of the shot glasses.

Jesse couldn't help but notice how different Ely seemed. It was almost eerie. Nothing moved as she made her way down the street: no people walking about, businesses closed for the day, grim silence instead of the typical hustle and bustle.

As she approached the end of the street, a line of wagons greeted her like a wooden snake basking in the sun. At the same time she noticed a slight hum, which grew as she neared the church. By the time she walked around to the back of the building, the din had grown into a full-blown clamor. She would have sworn the entire town was there.

Flower bouquets topped white linen tablecloths. Women arranged food dishes on long tables and men stood around, chatting in small groups. Several gentlemen hovered around a hog roasting on a spit. A few young ladies huddled together beneath a tall oak.

Jesse, still barely comfortable with town living, was overwhelmed by the throng of people. She noticed one of the women beneath the tree point her out to the group. Whatever the young lady had said made the others chuckle and blush. Jesse's whole body tensed when the one who pointed her out walked toward her.

"Hi, I'm Claudine," she said, laying a hand over her heart.

"Jesse."

Claudine stepped closer, erasing the distance between them. "So, are you a friend of the bride or the groom?"

"Uh…both, actually. How 'bout you?"

"Edith and my mother are friends. I see you're here alone. Would you like to—"

"Jesse," Abby called out, cutting Claudine off mid-sentence.

Jesse turned around. The sight of Abby in the periwinkle blue dress made her heart flutter.

"He's with me," Abby said, hooking her arm through Jesse's. Her gaze took in Claudine, sweeping over her from head to feet and back up again.

Jesse, unsure of what to say or do, stuffed her free hand in a pocket and squirmed. She didn't want to be rude, but had less of an idea about what to say or do than she had seconds earlier.

A few awkward moments passed before Claudine finally spoke. "Oh, I see," she said, turning to leave. "I should go. My friends are waiting."

Not wanting to be impolite, Jesse called out to her, "Enjoy the wedding."

"Looks like I can't leave you alone for a second," Abby said. Seeing another woman flirt with Jesse only increased her attraction for her.

"Abs, y-y-you look lo-lovely," Jesse said, stammering, awestruck by her beauty. "Ha. You have me sounding like Toby now."

Abby took in Jesse's appearance. She was glad to have her arm for support because suddenly her legs felt in danger of collapsing. "You don't look so bad yourself," she said, her look one of yearning as she ran her hands down the soft suede of Jesse's vest. "I missed you last night."

"I missed you, too. How'd ya sleep?"

"Not too good. I think I've gotten used to having you beside me. Hard to sleep when you're not there."

"I know what you mean."

"We should go in and get our seats," Abby said. "It'll be filling up soon."

The couple made their way inside and took their seats on a wooden pew, four rows back from the altar. Jesse watched as people filed in, tipping her head in acknowledgement at the few she recognized.

There was the man who sold Buck to her. Seated not far from him was the waitress from The Tin Plate who had served her that first time. *That seems like a lifetime ago.* So many things had changed since her first visit to Ely. She was remembering how scared and lonely she had been back then when a firm hand settled on her shoulder.

Frank Whitaker leaned down and said, "I've got the paperwork waiting for you at the office." Jesse nodded up at him. He let his hand fall and took a seat in the pew in front of them.

Abby placed her hand on Jesse's fidgeting leg. "You aren't nervous, are you?"

"I am," she admitted, moisture prickling her palms.

Inside, the church was lively as the pews filled. Abby leaned over and whispered, "Felix is here."

Jesse watched as he made his way down the aisle to the front of the church where he took his place next to the preacher.

"You think he's nervous?" Abby asked.

"How could he not—"

The sound of the church bell ringing caused Jesse, along with everyone else in the congregation, to stand and turn their attention toward the back of the church. When the bell finally stopped, its final peal spreading through the town in stark contrast to the deserted streets, Edith came in from the vestibule holding to the arm of her brother.

Abby tugged on Jesse's arm, forcing her to lean down. "That's Edith's brother, Teddy," she whispered.

Jesse nodded, never taking her eyes from Edith as she made her way down the aisle. Edith winked at them as she passed by.

Once at the front, Teddy gave Edith's hand to Felix. With her hand in his, Felix guided his bride-to-be up two small steps. Finally, they stood facing each other.

The preacher looked out over the congregation and asked for everyone to be seated. Jesse's leg bounced. She rested a palm on her thigh, trying to hold it in place.

Abby placed her hand on top of Jesse's. They were both nervous at the same thought. Soon, they would be the ones taking their vows.

This was the first wedding Jesse had ever attended. She sat intently, listening as the preacher performed the ceremony. Some of the specific language was lost on her, but not the overall meaning. This was an event celebrating the deep love between her friends. Jesse's stomach flopped at the idea of experiencing the same thing from up front where the lucky pair stood.

When it was over, and Felix had kissed his bride, the church erupted in cheers. The newlywed couple, hand-in-hand, made their way to the back of the church. The pews emptied and people spilled out onto the lawn, taking seats at the tables, waiting for Edith and Felix to join them.

Abby led Jesse to a table with two empty chairs where a family was already seated. "Jesse, this is Joe Mulligan and his family. They own The Tin Plate. Joe, this is my fiancé, Jesse McGinnis."

Jesse reached across the table to shake Joe's hand.

Before Joe took his seat, he said, "This is my wife, Mary, and our kids: Tommy, Harriet, Henry, Susan, Jackson, Vivian, William, and baby Lulu." He pointed out each one as he said their names.

"Nice to meet all of you," Jesse said. She did a quick mental calculation. *Holy hell. Eight kids.* The idea of raising one suddenly didn't seem so daunting.

"So, have you two picked a date yet?" Mary asked.

"Actually, we're meeting with Mr. Whitaker this afternoon," Abby said.

"Well, congratulations to the both of you," Joe said, raising his glass of lemonade. "We wish you—" He stopped when he heard the announcement.

"It is my honor to introduce to you Mr. and Mrs. Felix Nicholas!" the preacher called from his perch on the back steps of the church. Everyone stood and clapped as the couple made their way down. The preacher continued, "Now, let's enjoy this wonderful bounty our women have prepared."

Jesse watched everyone make a beeline for the food. She had never seen so much at one time. Everyone in town must have brought their prize dish.

Abby asked, "Mary, how old is she?"

"Goin' on three weeks now," she said, cradling the baby in her arms as she stood from her chair.

"Why don't you let me hold her for you while you get your plate?" Abby asked.

"That's so kind of you. Thank you." She carried her baby over and gently placed her in Abby's arms.

"Jesse, isn't she beautiful?" Abby asked. She couldn't take eyes off the sleeping infant cuddled in her arms.

"She is. She's so tiny. Look at those little fingers."

"You want to hold her?" Abby asked.

Jesse shook her head and put her hands up in a defensive gesture. She may as well have asked her to hold a rabid badger.

Joe returned to the table with a heaping plate of food. "Go on. You won't break her," he said with a chuckle. "Besides, the way you two keep looking at each other…well, something tells me it won't be long before you have a brood of your own."

Jesse looked at Abby, a knowing smile playing at the corners of her mouth.

After sharing a meal with the Mulligans, Jesse asked, "Joe, do you have the time?"

He tugged on a chain and pulled his watch from a pocket in his vest. "Day's flying by," he said, looking down at the watch face. "It's already quarter to two." He snapped the watch closed and stuck it back in his pocket before one of the smaller children could pull it from his hand.

Jesse had stood and was preparing to pull out Abby's chair for her when Felix and Edith approached their table. "You two ready?" Felix asked.

"Yes, we were just about to leave," Jesse said.

"Well, I just saw Frank leaving. Come on. We're going with you." He turned toward the crowd and raised his voice above the clamor. "Folks, we'll be right back. Please enjoy yourselves."

Frank Whitaker was already working at his desk when the two couples entered his office. He greeted them and glanced up at the wall clock as he scooted back in his chair. After fetching a book off the top of one of his filing cabinets, he pushed open the swinging gate separating the waiting area from his office space. "You two stand right there and face each other," he said, pointing to a specific spot on the floor. Once Abby and Jesse were in place, he continued. "All right. Are you folks ready?"

Abby and Jesse nodded.

He opened to a marked page in the book and began to recite the words. "We are brought together today to join this man, Jesse McGinnis, and this woman, Abigail Flanagan, in matrimony. This is a solemn vow they pledge to each other. Do you, Jesse McGinnis, take Abigail Flanagan as your lawfully wedded wife, to have and to hold from this day forward, for better or worse, for richer for poorer. Will you love, honor, and cherish her in sickness and in health as long as you both shall live?" He looked up at Jesse.

"I do. I will," Jesse said, releasing her pent-up breath.

"And do you, Abigail Flanagan, take Jesse McGinnis as your lawfully wedded husband, to have and to hold from this day forward, for better for worse, for richer for poorer, in sickness and in health, to love, honor, and obey him—"

Jesse held up her hand. "Stop. This isn't right."

Abby felt faint. *Jes can't go through with it.* She felt her strength wane, and the room began to spin. Edith reached out a steadying hand.

"Abs, are you all right?" Jesse asked. "Do you need to sit?"

"Oh, Jes. You should've said something sooner if you were having second thoughts."

Jesse's brow furrowed. "What are you talking about? I'm not having second thoughts."

"Then why did you stop him?"

Jesse reached out and took hold of Abby's hands. "Oh, Abs. I'm not stopping because I don't want us to get married. I'm stopping because I don't want you to agree to obey me. We're equal partners in this." She turned to Frank. "Can you just ask her the same thing you asked me, please?"

Frank scratched the back of his head. Never had anyone made such a request from him. "I can. I guess," he said, shrugging. "Shall I proceed?"

"Yes. Please," Jesse said.

"Do you, Abigail Flanagan, take Jesse McGinnis as your lawfully wedded husband, to have and to hold from this day forward? For better or worse, for richer, for poorer? Will you love, honor, and cherish him in sickness and in health as long as you both shall live?" He looked up from his book.

"I do and I will," she said, body trembling.

"Jesse do you have the ring?" he asked.

She pulled it from her vest pocket.

"You may place it on her finger."

Her hands shook as she slipped the shiny-gold band on Abby's finger.

"If no one has any objections." He paused, glancing from Edith to Felix before continuing. "All right, then. By the powers vested in me by the state of California, I now pronounce you husband and wife. You may kiss your *equal* bride." He finished with a crisp nod, and slapped the book closed.

Jesse leaned forward and brushed Abby's lips with a kiss. Not used to this kind of display in front of others, she could feel a hot flush spread across her face.

"All right, I just need some signatures," Frank said, indicating the correct line for each of them. After signing their names, Felix and Edith added theirs as witnesses.

Abby, Edith, and Felix stepped outside and waited beneath the awning while Jesse settled the bill for Frank's services.

"It's been taken care of," Edith said in a low voice. "They should have it there by the time we get back."

"Thank you," Abby said. "I hope he likes it."

Felix leaned closer. "I have a feeling he's gonna love it."

CHAPTER SEVEN

A s soon as Jesse stepped out of the office, she felt like she could breathe again. The tightness she had been feeling in her chest during the ceremony was gone. It wasn't the fresh breeze, or the warmth of the afternoon sun making her feel as if a weight had been lifted. She had hated being the center of attention.

"Thank you," Jesse said, extending a hand to Felix. "It meant the world to Abby and me having you both here."

"We wouldn't have missed it," Felix said, his grip firm. "Now come with us over to the store. We have a little something for the two of you."

Inside the trading post, Edith stepped behind the counter and pulled something from underneath. "Here," she said, bringing up a wicker basket. "A little gift from us."

Abby opened the lid, delighted to find a hamper full of yarn, knitting needles, scissors, string, and an assortment of stickpins.

"Thought you could use this," Edith said. "You do know how to sew, don't you?"

"Yes. My mother taught me when I was little." Abby smiled, memories of the past flittering through her mind like passing butterflies. "It's been a long time, but it should come back to me."

"Good. I figured this will come in handy."

Abby hugged Edith and Felix, throwing her arms around them and pulling them in tight.

"Thank you," Jesse said, picking her hat off the counter. "Thank you both for everything. We're sure going to miss you."

Still in Abby's embrace, Edith furrowed her brow. "You aren't leaving now are you?"

"Yes. We still have to pack up," Jesse said, setting the hat on her head. "We have a long trip ahead of us."

Abby let her arms fall to her sides and stepped back. She gave Edith a troubled look.

Thinking on her feet, Edith blurted, "You just have to come back to the church and have a slice of Mrs. Johansen's pie."

"I appreciate the offer but we really do need—"

Abby placed her hand on Jesse's arm. "Come on, Jes. It won't take that long."

A tiny smile parted Jesse's lips. "All right," she said, unable to deny her.

When they returned to the festivities behind the church, Jesse noticed a familiar piano sitting out in the churchyard. "Hey Abs," she said, leaning in, "isn't that the piano from The Foxtail?"

"Yes. I went there last night to drop off a letter for Mabel since I won't get to see her. While I was there, I made arrangements to use it. Edith and Felix had some men go get it while we were at Mr. Whitaker's."

Before she had a chance to ask why, Felix made an announcement. "Everyone, can I have your attention?" he asked. When the chatter continued, his words lost in the crowd, he raised his voice. "Everyone." He called loudly through his cupped hands.

A hush fell over the guests when they realized someone was speaking. He waited until everyone had turned in his direction before he continued. "I want to thank you all for being part of our special day. Edith and I are blessed to have each of you here. We consider all of you part of our family." He skimmed the familiar faces in the crowd. "Today is not only a special day for us, but for our friends, Jesse and Abby, who also just got married."

Jesse felt her face burn when everyone turned and looked at them.

Abby seemed to be taking it all in stride. She had, after all, been comfortable as the center of attention for years as a performer. Abby shrugged and squeezed Jesse's hand.

It was comforting, though Jesse was still eager for everyone to stop looking in their direction.

Felix continued. "Mrs. Abigail McGinnis would like it if you all would indulge her while she gives her husband his wedding gift."

Abby leaned over and whispered in Jesse's ear. "I wrote this for you. I hope you like it."

Jesse couldn't believe it. *That's what she's been working on!*

A round of applause accompanied Abby as she made her way over to the piano. She took a seat, staring down at the ivory keys as if seeing them for the first time. She positioned her hands, making sure her finger placement was correct, and closed her eyes.

She had performed in front of hundreds of people over the years, but never had she felt as nervous as she did in that moment. Of course, this was a different audience. Here, everybody was a friend at worst and family at best. She wasn't here to earn their tips. Despite the size of the gathering, Abby was really only playing for an audience of one.

It was so quiet she swore she could hear the footsteps of a cricket. Any mistake that might get lost in the din and clatter of a saloon would ring loud and clear here. She drew a deep breath and released it slowly as her fingers moved across the keys.

When I was just a young girl
To fairy tales I'd cling
Hoping dreaming praying
True love my wish would bring

I'd sit beside my window
Whisper to the dark
Willing someone out there
To heed my faint remark

I looked to the heavens
Prayed to God above
Asked Him for a chance to find
My one true love
But as it often happens
The light of day shone through

Like the fading starlight
Some wishes don't come true

The years began to pass
I feared I'd walk alone
The dreaming of a young girl
Finally I'd outgrown

I'd all but given up on love
Chanced one last look to see
The shining light that pierced the night
And led your soul to me

I looked upon the mountain
Braved the river wide
Walked away from all I knew
To travel by your side

Now when I look to heaven
I finally see it's true
If you only find the right star
Wishes can come true

When Abby had finished, she tuned out the applause and focused her attention on Jesse, who was difficult to read even in normal circumstances. She searched for a sign, any kind of reaction that could tell her what Jesse was feeling.

Jesse, face hidden beneath the brim of her hat, added her applause to the mix. The fact Abby was willing to express their love in such a public way made her weak. She pulled the brim lower still, trying to hide her eyes. Holding back her tears prickled. Never had she been touched so deeply or had anyone expose themselves in such a way. Her emotions rushed over her in a torrent.

Abby was vaguely aware of the people around her as she walked toward Jesse. Nerves on edge, she twisted her wedding ring. "Well…did you like it?"

Jesse lifted the brim of her hat and met her gaze for gaze. Her eyes glistened with tears. "It was absolutely beautiful," she said, her voice quivering. She brought her mouth close to Abby's ear. "What are people going to think of your new husband?" Her throat tightened. "Grown men aren't supposed to cry."

"I just wanted you to know how much you mean to me," Abby said, tearful at the sight of Jesse's red-rimmed eyes. "I love you more than you could ever know, Jes." She ran her hand down Jesse's arm. "Now and forever. Say, how about getting out of here so we can start our life together?"

"Let's go," Jesse said, taking her by the hand.

They practically had to fight their way to Edith and Felix's table. Hands reached out for shakes, pats, and hugs. Smiling faces couldn't stop congratulating the pair or complimenting the beautiful song. The joy was palpable, if a bit smothering to Jesse.

When they finally made it through the gauntlet, Jesse said, "We're going to head out now."

Jesse and Felix shook hands across the table and said their goodbyes.

When they had finished, Edith pulled Jesse and Abby off to one side. "I wish you didn't have to leave so soon. I'm going to miss you two." Taking hold of Abby's hands, she whispered, "And I can't wait to meet your little one. You know, the next time we see each other we'll both have babies on our hips."

Abby nodded in agreement. She whispered, "I reckon so. And I can't wait to see your baby."

Smiling, Edith released her hands and stepped back. "You two take care of yourselves, and don't be strangers."

"We will," Jesse said. "Thank you for everything."

With several miles to cover before sundown, Jesse and Abby set out traveling as fast as their supply-laden horses would allow. They rode together on Buck, Titan tethered behind with a length of rope. Jesse held the reins loosely with one hand, her other wrapped firmly around Abby's waist as they moseyed along the secluded path in the woods that led the way home.

Jesse asked, "Do you think we're the only two women to be together?"

"No. I'm sure there're others."

Jesse cleared her throat. "Can I ask you something? And you promise not to get mad?"

Abby placed her hand on top of Jesse's. "Sure. I promise."

"Do you like being with men?" Jesse bit down on her lip, but failed to chew down the warmth spreading up into her face.

Abby squirmed in the saddle.

"I'm trying to understand. If you're attracted to men, then how are you attracted to me?"

Abby stared down at the saddle horn, trying to figure out the best way to explain her feelings. She wasn't sure there was an explanation. "I think if I had met you as a woman...well...

I can't imagine we would've ended up together. Don't take this the wrong way, but I'm not attracted to women."

"But that's exactly what I am," she said, leaning back to put some distance between them.

Abby put her hand on Jesse's leg. "I know. But you're different."

"But, when I don't have clothes on, how are you attracted to what you see?"

She rubbed Jesse's leg. "It's hard to explain."

"Try. I need to know."

Abby drew in a breath and released a heavy sigh. "I think getting to know you before I found out the truth made me see you in a different way. When I look at you I see more than just flesh. I see so much more…" She paused, searching for words. "Jes, I see you for exactly who you are. A person who is smart, strong, loving, and kind. I see the person I fell in love with. The person I love unconditionally. The person I want to spend the rest of my life with. I just see you."

"Hmm." Jesse contemplated Abby's words. Then she asked, "But what if I decided not to look like this anymore and had gone back to looking like a woman? Would you still be with me?"

Abby silently pondered the scenario for a moment. She glanced down at the hand holding the reins, and the one which had a firm grip around her middle. They were rough and calloused from years of hard work. She realized she didn't think of them as being either masculine or feminine. They were simply Jesse's. And they were perfect. She interlaced her fingers with Jesse's before continuing. "I have never loved anyone more than I love you. I can say this with certainty. I will be with you no matter how you choose to look. I'm in love with you, not the clothing you wear." She chuckled under her breath. "I guess I was wrong before. I am attracted to a woman after all."

A few minutes later, Jesse got the nerve to ask something that had been weighing on her mind for some time. "You know I've never been with a man, so the only thing I know is what I saw when I was a kid. It wasn't like that for you was it?" She craned her neck in an attempt to see Abby's face.

Not only was Jesse's openness to talk about such things new to Abby, so was her understanding when it came to her relationship with Sam. She knew how most men would have reacted when they found out she had been intimate with someone else. They would have considered her damaged goods. This was just one more thing setting Jesse apart. In her heart she knew Jesse wasn't asking to be judgmental, she was merely concerned for her well-being. Even so, some of it was hard for her to discuss.

Abby placed her hand on her stomach. "You mean when I was with Sam?"

"Yes. When you shared your bed with him. He didn't hurt you, did he?"

An unnatural quietness lingered and Abby felt herself blush before she spoke. "Do you really want to talk about that?" she said, fidgeting with her ring.

"Yes, or I wouldn't have brought it up," she said, tone sincere.

Abby wanted to hide underneath the saddle. There was no way to escape the embarrassing question. "No, Jes. He didn't hurt me."

"Did you enjoy it—I'm only asking because I want to

know if you like having…you know…with men, then how can you like being with me?"

Abby didn't need to search for words this time. She turned in the saddle to face her. "No one has ever made me feel the way you make me feel. With men, it's basically about their needs. Their pleasure. You're the only one who has ever put my pleasure first. Does that make sense?"

"I suppose," Jesse said, still somewhat confused. "But I don't have what they have. You know what I mean?"

Discussing male genitalia, especially in the broad daylight, made Abby uncomfortable. The leather squeaked underneath her when she shifted again. She released a long breath and cleared her throat. Her tone was low, almost a whisper when she spoke.

"I've only been with two men in my life, but I can tell you this. The way you touch me—the things you do to me—out pleasures anything I have ever experienced with either of them. Being with you is like the best of both worlds. You're outwardly strong, yet your touch is tender. The things you do to me…well." She shook her head. "I didn't even know my body could feel like that."

Silence doused them, thick like molasses. Abby hoped Jesse didn't press for more information about the night she gave her body to Sam. It wasn't something she was comfortable talking about, especially with her.

Jesse softly brushed the hair away from Abby's neck. Slowly, she whispered kisses along the heated skin.

Abby's body shivered with each touch of Jesse's lips. She leaned her head to one side, granting Jesse unrestricted access. "Um, don't you start something you can't finish," she advised, body covered with goose flesh.

Jesse nipped tenderly on Abby's earlobe as she reached forward and slowly used her fingers to draw Abby's dress and petticoat higher, exposing the bare skin beneath. "Oh, I can finish," she murmured, sliding her hand up the inside of Abby's thigh.

CHAPTER EIGHT

Sunlight broke through the haze atop Mount Perish, the morning rays making quick work of drying the dew-drenched grass. Small waves lapped along the shoreline beside where Jesse and Abby still slept. Instead of returning to the cabin, they had stolen one last night alone, choosing a bed beneath the stars.

Jesse woke slowly, her right arm draped around Abby's waist, a small smile curving the edges of her mouth. The cedar-scented smoke that hung over the camp tickled her nose even before she saw the smoldering embers. As much as she hated to take her hands off of Abby, the fire would die without her help. She slid out from under the wool blanket and knelt to add another log, holding her hands over the heat for warmth as she watched the wood catch.

"Mornin', Jes," Abby said, her breath visible in the chilly air.

Jesse blew a warm breath into her cupped hands. "Good morning." She rubbed them together, trying to trap the heat. "Do you want me to put on the coffee?"

Abby hesitated. "Um, since we are so close to the cabin, how about we wait and have it with Toby and Aponi?"

"All right. Let me put this out and we can be on our way," she said, kicking dirt to douse the newly kindled flames.

The mirrored surface of the lake reflected their campsite, and Abby found herself staring at it wistfully. For a moment, she saw them as they were just hours before, beneath the silvery light of the moon, arms and legs entwined below the surface. She closed her eyes, letting the memory wash over her, a rosy flush crawling up her neck.

"Mmm, last night was wonderful," she murmured, still unwilling to open her eyes and break the spell. She could still feel Jesse's touch on her body—all over her body. "You were incredible."

The smile Abby's words brought quickly faded. Jesse walked over and sat down beside her. She placed her hand lightly on Abby's stomach. "Do you think it's safe for her?" she asked. "Maybe we shouldn't...you know."

Abby opened her eyes, rolled over, and met Jesse's gaze. "Don't worry, it's fine," she said, placing her hand on top of Jesse's. "So, you're sticking with a girl?"

"Yep. That's what my gut says, anyway."

"Will you be disappointed if I give you a son?"

Jesse looked dazed the moment Abby's words registered with her.

"You do realize I didn't agree to marry you just for this baby to have your name or protect my honor," Abby said. "This child will be as much yours as it is mine. We are equal partners in this, right?"

Abby's words touched her deeply. She felt the sentiment as physical warmth which started in her heart and radiated through her entire body. The glow encapsulated all three of them: Jesse, Abby, and the baby. Their baby. She had offered to help Abby raise her child, but she hadn't realized until that moment Abby considered the unborn child to be hers as well. Her heart was full.

"Yes. Partners." Jesse pushed down the lump in her throat. "And honestly, I don't care what you have. As long as you and the baby are fine, that's all that matters." Jesse rubbed the scar on her forehead.

"What is it?" Abby asked, understanding the subliminal gesture meant Jesse was deep in thought.

"I'm not sure how this is going to work. Won't this child be confused about having two mothers?"

"Oh, Jes, why would you even think that? If anyone would understand, I thought for sure you would." She let out a long sigh. "I know Frieda didn't give birth to you, but wouldn't you say she was a mother to you just as much as Sarah?"

A smile crept across her face, unbidden, at the mention of her old mentor. "She was."

"See? I don't think our child could ever have too much love. I think it will be blessed to have two loving parents. Look, we have plenty of time, so let's just figure it out as we go?" Abby put a warm hand on the back of Jesse's neck. She pulled her down and met her lips with her own before whispering, "I think it will be a boy. Either way, one of us is going to be right."

"It's good to see home again," Abby said when the cabin came into view. Its rough-hewn logs, old and weathered, had never looked so welcoming.

Jesse loosely wrapped Buck's reins around the paddock fence and made a beeline straight for the door. Abby was a little shocked. Jesse was one to stick to a routine. She usually tended to the horses before doing anything else.

Her excitement was contagious, though. Abby followed close behind, her heart thumping, peeking anxiously around Jesse's shoulder as the cabin door swung open. Inside, she saw Toby and Aponi seated at the table, a deck of cards splayed out in front of them. With them was a man she had never seen before.

After a morning spent tending to the horses and catching up on everything that had taken place since everyone had last been together, the topic of conversation soon changed course. Aponi and Ahanu invited each of them to come see their village on the other side of the mountain. As much as Jesse wanted to go, she had to decline when she found out they would have to make the journey on foot. There was no way she could leave the horses unsupervised, knowing they would be at risk of attack by predators. Fortunately, Ahanu graciously offered to stay behind to care for them.

With their plans solidified, Abby took Jesse by the hand and led her outside to a spot halfway between the cabin and the stream. "This is the perfect place," she said, over the babbling sound of water. "We need to plant this." She opened her hand, revealing an acorn on her palm. "It's an old marriage tradition. It's said that when a couple plants a tree in their yard, it symbolizes putting down roots. This acorn, over time, will grow and strengthen, just like our relationship."

"I love that." Jesse knelt, pulled her knife from its sheath, and used it to gouge out a piece of sod.

Abby dropped the acorn into the hole and together they covered it with dirt.

As Jesse finished patting down the soil, Abby placed her hand on top of hers. Over the small heap, their lips met.

Jesse, Abby, Toby, and Aponi set out early for their trip to the other side of the mountain. Jesse paid careful attention to each detail along the way, as she had on her first trip to Ely. She wasn't sure why but it was better to know the way than not.

It took them just over six hours to reach the native village on the western side of the mountain.

Kaga approached. "Welcome," he said warmly. "Burning Bush, you come."

Jesse glanced at Abby.

"Go on," Abby said, waving her on. "We'll be fine."

Kaga led her to a hidden area deep in one of the hollows of the mountain. Just inside the entrance she stopped, scanning the cavernous space. Pictographs covered the vast stone walls. Although she had no idea what the markings meant, she had a pretty good idea they somehow documented the lives of these people. A fire burned in the center of the space, a group of men seated around it.

"Come. Sit." A white-haired man motioned to her.

Jesse sat in the open space they'd made, legs crossed in front of her.

"You go off mountain. You speak with white men?" one of the elders asked.

Jesse nodded. "I did."

"Any talk 'em come on mountain?"

A chill overtook Jesse's body, almost as if she'd been dunked in cold water. She understood at once their concerns. She too was worried, frightened even, about the possibility of men crossing the river and invading the mountain. "No. No men are coming."

"We know 'em come someday. White men always come."

Jesse nodded in agreement. As much as she hated it, as much as she knew in her heart it was wrong, it seemed inevitable. She knew all too well one day white men would indeed find a way to cross the Devil's Fork.

"We need to know when 'em come. We no let 'em take our land. We fight," said another tribe elder.

Jesse knew what white men were capable of and she knew these kind people had the right to defend what was theirs. This rational perspective did nothing to temper the horror at the thought.

It will be war. The dead bodies from the magazine in Big Oak flashed through her mind. She felt sick.

"If I get word of anyone planning to cross the river, I will warn you," Jesse said, trying to keep her voice from quavering. "I'll stand beside you no matter the cost. We'll stand together and protect our mountain."

The men nodded to one another. The elder man who had invited her to the group held up a long wooden pipe. The decorative beads and feathers swayed slightly in his aged fingers as he lit it.

The shaking hands, the pipe, and especially the fragrant aroma escaping from it, all reminded Jesse so much of Frieda that for a moment she was back at the cabin, sitting on the old stump chair. She had forgotten how much she missed that smell.

The man seated next to her bumped her arm with his own, rousing her from the memory. He offered her the pipe. She graciously accepted it and took a long drag. A coughing fit overcame her as she passed it to the man on her right. The men chuckled, though their humor was not cruel.

Through watering eyes she watched as the pipe circled around to her once more. Smarter this time, she took a hit, but not quite as deep as the previous one. She coughed less this time as she eyed the pipe traveling in her direction again.

She managed not to cough on her third try. She blew smoke, passed the pipe, and let the room spin. Perhaps the coughing fits had been her body's defense against what now made her feel like a child's top. She pressed her palms to the cold stone floor, trying to slow the whirling sensation.

When it slowed, she found herself staring at the drawings on the walls. One depiction in particular caught her attention. It documented tribal history she knew. It was her history.

A young girl, hair painted red with hematite, was being hunted by a bear. The scene showed a native stick-man with his arrow trained on the beast. In the next images, the stick-man stood over the dead bear, and then he carried the young girl to a cabin where she was placed in the open arms of a woman. The bright ocher markings rippled and blurred into a river of blood as the imagery took motion. Her body felt numb.

"Eo ahst dik o tonk Burning Bush tuminik Great Spirit," one of the men said, his voice deep and muffled. The group laughed out loud.

Jesse understood his words—smoking the pipe could make one see the Great Spirit.

I don't think this is what Frieda used to smoke. The thought wasn't funny, but she couldn't stop herself from laughing.

The men around her stood. Jesse, trying to be straight-faced, followed suit. She focused her attention on the tribe elder directly across the fire from her as she swayed, a haze of smoke rising between them.

The elder took out his bone knife and used it to slice his palm. He handed it to Jesse over the flames, mimicking for her to do the same. She paused, the sharp blade resting against her palm as she gathered her nerve. Sucking in a breath, she drew the blade across her hand. Swallowing the pain, she stared as her blood pooled and then spilled onto the cave floor. Strangely, there was no pain.

The elder extended his hand over the fire and she met it with her own. They held their grip tight as all those gathered placed their hands on top of hers and the elder's. The sizzle of blood falling into the flames echoed in the quiet of the great space.

As their vitality mixed and burned together, the old man reached into the pouch hanging off his hip. He drew out a pinch of powder and tossed it into the blaze. Colored flames leaped up, lighting almost every nook and cranny in the entire cavern.

The man released her hand. Ceremony completed, the man next to Jesse took her hand and wrapped it tightly. "Burning Bush one of us," the man said, securing the wound with a small strip of hide. "We feast now."

Jesse squinted as she followed the men back out into the bright sunlight. Cut off from the sun, she'd forgotten it was daytime. Or was that another effect of the pipe? She still felt strange. She plopped down on the grass beside Abby and almost fell over.

"What happened to you?" Abby half-shouted, taking hold of her bandaged hand. She cradled it gently.

"I'm fine. It was part of my…I guess you could say initiation," she said, eyes glossed over. She leaned over and whispered in Abby's ear, "I wish we were back at the lake."

Jesse felt like she had no self control. She wasn't normally so blunt, but it was as if whatever was on her mind came spilling out of her mouth.

Abby smiled and whispered back, "Maybe we can sneak off later and—"

"Are you hungry?" Jesse asked. "I'm starving."

Whatever she had smoked was making it hard for her to stay focused.

Abby looked at her more closely. Only a hint of green remained visible in the narrow slits of her eyes. "Have you been drinking?"

"Nope. Smokin'," she said with a chuckle. She fell back to the ground with a grunt. Though she made no move to get up, Abby could tell from her grin she was doing just fine.

Abby knew right then Jesse was inebriated from whatever she had smoked. "Let me get you something to eat."

Before she could stand, Jesse called up to her. "You're a good woman, Abigail Flanagan!"

That evening they joined the others in celebrating Jesse's induction. They danced, feasted, and commemorated the newest member of the Ponak Tribe well into the early morning hours.

CHAPTER NINE

Fortunately for Jesse, Frieda had taught her the proper way to treat and dress a wound. With the aid of a salve she made from pine tree sap, the laceration on her hand was healing nicely. Even so, it was still a hindrance. She took added precautions in everything she did in an effort to keep the cut from reopening. The last thing she needed was an infection. If she lost her hand, she'd be nearly helpless. Helpless on the mountain was as good as dead. Simply feeding the horses took time and patience. Extra time was a luxury she didn't have.

Even before the weather turned bitter cold, Jesse brooded over the upcoming winter. She had to. Too many lives were depending on her. From the first hint of dawn, until everything around her was swallowed in shadow, she pushed herself. She was tireless in her efforts, racing against the calendar. It was a race she didn't intend to lose. As the daylight hours grew shorter, her anxiety grew stronger. She agonized there wouldn't be enough time for her to finish everything that needed to be done.

Abby's concern grew as well when, night after night, Jesse

entered the cabin with boots dragging across the floor on legs too tired to lift them. She could see the toll the winter preparations were taking on her even with Toby's help. Regardless of how hard she and Toby worked, the list never seemed to dwindle. There was always more game to hunt, traps to check, meat to smoke, berries to collect, and hay to bundle.

No matter how many times Abby pleaded to help, Jesse refused, thinking her condition too fragile for such strenuous activities. Much to Abby's chagrin, Jesse preferred to keep her safely tucked away in the cabin, working on a project she considered perfect for someone in her state. Not only would it make Abby feel like she was contributing, it would also give her some semblance of privacy when the baby came.

Abby, with a stockpile of Jesse's old tanned animal hides at her feet, opened the sewing kit Edith had put together. She selected one of the sturdiest needles and the heaviest string in the basket. While she liked the idea of a curtain to hang beneath the loft, and the privacy it would afford, she did not like being treated like a damsel in distress.

Abby pulled two of the hides onto her lap and began stitching them together, rehearsing what she was going to say when Jesse returned that evening. When they had taken their vows, nowhere did it say one of them had the right to shut the other away in the cabin, like some captive seamstress. She explicitly remembered Jesse stopping the ceremony to have the word obey removed from the vows.

When Jesse came through the door that evening, Abby took one look at her and forgot every rejoinder she had planned. Even the smile Jesse offered her looked tired. Her heart softened. She knew Jesse was only doing what she thought was best for her and their unborn child. Crossing the room, Abby wrapped her arms around her, vowing silently to be less argumentative.

Did I put away enough wood? Do I need to smoke more meat? Will there be enough hay for the horses? Jesse knew those questions would taunt her in the days to come. She was in a trance of exhaustion by the time she came through the door each night with barely enough energy to sit at the table and eat the meals Abby prepared. Afterwards, she cleaned up and went straight to bed, falling asleep as soon as her head touched the pillow.

A couple of weeks later, Abby set the baby blanket she was sewing in her lap and rubbed her tired eyes. It had been yet another evening alone by the fire, and in the low light of the cabin, she felt more lonely than usual. Yawning, she got up and closed the curtain that Jesse had hung earlier in the day.

She undressed as quietly as she could in an effort not to wake Jesse. As she was about to slip on her nightgown, she was startled by a ragged whisper.

"You're so beautiful," Jesse murmured, her voice raspy from sleep.

"Oh," Abby said, quickly moving to cover her ample body. "I thought you were asleep."

Jesse sat on the edge of the bed and reached out to take hold of Abby. "Don't hide yourself. You've never looked more beautiful than you do right now." She pulled Abby's hands closer, kissing each one in turn.

Abby looked down at her distended belly. "I'm so fat."

"You're not fat. You're carrying a baby." Jesse leaned in

close to Abby's stomach. "Tell your mother she's beautiful?" She placed her ear against Abby's swollen abdomen as if listening for a response. "She agreed with me," she said, kissing Abby's belly. "Good night little one." She stifled a yawn. "We'll see you soon."

"If I'm so beautiful then why don't you touch me anymore? Are you not attracted to me?"

Despite her exhaustion, Jesse wanted nothing more than to be with Abby. Sometimes it took every ounce of willpower she had to stop herself from initiating something between them. Fearing harm to the baby, she would keep feigning fatigue whenever an opportunity presented itself.

"Nothing could be further from the truth," she said, faking a yawn. "It's just been a long day and I'm tired." Her statement was followed by a genuine yawn this time. "Let's get some sleep." She crawled back under the covers.

By the time Abby had slipped her nightgown on over her head, Jesse was sound asleep. She crawled into bed beside her. Their bodies were so close Abby could feel the heat coming off of her. *How can two people be so close and yet so far apart,* she wondered?

Even before the start of winter, the frigid temperature was too bitter to venture outside for any length of time. Jesse had years of experience to draw on when it came to cabin fever, and this time she planned accordingly. She had set aside a pile of hand-hewn wood in one corner of the cabin. It was the perfect time to build the cradle she had already started constructing in her mind.

A couple of weeks into the project, Jesse and Toby sat working, their attention focused on assembling the framework. Abby sat in the rocker, knitting on a baby outfit. Pops and crackles from the fire went unnoticed, dwarfed by the ever-present winds howling through the pines.

Abby was engrossed in her work, humming to herself, when her rocker came to an abrupt halt. Her eyes widened. "Jes, come here!"

"What is it?" Jesse asked, hurrying to her side. "What's wrong?"

Abby took hold of her hand and placed her palm flat against her stomach. "Do you feel that?"

Jesse wasn't sure what she was supposed to feel. "No. I don't feel anything."

"Wait." Abby stayed completely still, keeping Jesse's hand pressed firmly in place.

A few moments later, Jesse felt something shift against her hand. "Was that—"

"Yes."

Jesse wrinkled her nose. "Does it hurt when she moves like that?"

"No. It feels more like a flutter."

Jesse shifted her hand, and waited. She smiled when she felt the gentle sensation once more. "She sure is active this morning."

Abby chuckled. "He sure is."

Long winter days turned into even longer winter nights. When Jesse wasn't busy working on the cradle, she worked on the plain wooden box she had given Abby for her birthday. Initially, she'd planned to give her the cameo necklace. Her plan had changed when she'd had to exchange it in order to be able to afford her wedding ring. The box would never be as beautiful as the necklace but at least now, with so much time on her hands, she could give it the attention it deserved. As she sat for hours carving intricate flowers into its top, she glanced at Abby from time to time. Pity pulled at her insides.

Abby's stomach had grown considerably larger in a short span of time. Jesse knew she drove the others crazy with her constant pacing but she couldn't stop herself. While she was overjoyed at the idea of the baby coming, at the same time, she had never been more terrified in her life. Especially knowing Abby's own mother had died giving birth to her sister. She didn't know what she would do if something were to happen to either Abby or the baby.

Abby was miserable. Her own body had betrayed her. Everything hurt from her engorged breasts, to her lower back, all the way down to her swollen feet. She no longer had ankles. Her fingers were so swollen she couldn't even wear her wedding ring. Something as simple as bending had become impossible. At night, if she was lucky enough to find a comfortable position in the bed, it wouldn't take long before she had to move due to bouts of indigestion.

Jesse and Toby figured out when to come close and when they should give tear-prone Abby her much needed space.

Jesse did anything she could think of to make Abby more comfortable. She rubbed her swollen, achy feet, massaged her lower back, and did her best to assure her everything she was going through was only temporary. Even though they had moved the outhouse closer to the cabin for Abby's convenience before the weather had turned, it became clear by Abby's waddle the short jaunt was too much for her. Jesse offered to bring her the old pan Frieda had used. The fury in Abby's eyes was colder than the ice coating the windowpane. Some things she was willing to sacrifice for her unborn child, but her dignity while using a chamber pot was not one of them. It was bad enough Jesse had to help her bathe. So, in an effort to help Abby maintain her last remaining thread of normalcy, Jesse and Toby were diligent in keeping the path to the outhouse clear of snow. It was the least they could do for her.

On January 31st, Jesse dragged the cradle over to the bed where Abby lay. She already knew the answer, but asked the question anyway. "Pain is pretty bad today. Isn't it?"

Abby's sleep had been sporadic. No matter what she tried, she couldn't find a comfortable position. She'd tossed and turned all night long. Jesse had wanted to shove a pillow over her own head in order to drown out Abby's groaning. She knew better than to do it, though, or risk finding herself sleeping in an uncomfortable position.

"I don't recall ever feeling so miserable in my life," Abby said. "I'm never going to go through this again. That you can be sure of." She released a long slow breath, moaning as she arched her back in an effort to alleviate the pain.

"I'm sorry you feel so bad. I wish there was something I could do."

"Did you get it finished?" she asked, attempting to take her mind off the pain.

"Almost. It still wobbles a little when it rocks though." Jesse gave it a push to demonstrate. "I think it just needs a little more taken off the—"

Abby sat up with a grunt. A protective hand, guided by

instinct, went to her stomach when a strong contraction shuddered through her. She thought she had felt them intermittently throughout the night, but hadn't been sure. This time there was no doubt in her mind. "I think the baby might be coming today," she said, her voice smothered with worry.

Jesse sprang to her feet, her hands laced through her hair. "But you aren't due for at least another month."

"I don't think he cares," she said through clenched teeth.

CHAPTER TEN

Strong gusts of wind had been relentlessly buffeting the cabin. Toby could hear the creaking and moaning of the log timbers in between Abby's intermittent groans. As he knelt to place a log on the fire, another violent squall swept across the porch, rattling the door on its hinges. He glanced over his shoulder at Jesse sitting vigil beside Abby. Neither one of them seemed to notice anything outside the realm of their bedroom. He paced around the table in the center of the room and stopped when Abby cried out again as another contraction ripped through her body. *I wish I could do something to help her*, he thought, pulling the curtain closed to give her some privacy.

"Will you hand me that blanket?" Abby asked Jesse through gritted teeth. She shifted her body, trying to find a comfortable position. It was as if her own muscles conspired against her. Nothing felt natural. Jesse started to cover her with the blanket, but Abby grabbed her arm. "No. Put it under me." She lifted her bottom slightly, allowing Jesse to slip it beneath her.

A few minutes later, Abby's eyes widened and she grabbed her stomach. "I think I'm going to be sick." She quickly put her hand over her mouth.

Jesse fetched an old pan and held back Abby's hair each time the sickness overwhelmed her, keeping a cool rag pressed on the back of her neck.

Abby's breath came out in one long rush. She pushed a balled fist into the small of her back, her face twisted in pain.

Jesse stood up. "Here, why don't you roll on your side and I'll rub your back." She helped Abby turn and then set to work kneading the muscles, sore from months of straining. The tension had formed knots like stones beneath her skin.

A few minutes in that position were all Abby could tolerate before her body demanded something different. She rolled onto her back, clutching a piece of the blanket in her fist.

"It should all be over with soon," Jesse said.

Abby pushed out what she intended to be a calming breath. "Not necessarily. A friend of mine was in labor for nineteen hours. I'm not sure I can do this. I've never been in so much pain before." The words spilled out in an anxious gush almost as violent as the purge that had roiled her minutes earlier.

Jesse blotted her forehead with the cool rag. "Yes, you can. We'll get through this together." She bent over and kissed Abby's cheek, blotched from the heat of her efforts. "I can't wait to meet her—" She stopped when Abby's eyes went wide. "What is it? What's wrong?"

Abby clutched her arm. "I think my water just broke."

Jesse heard the door open and close, but the sound barely registered as background noise. Her attention was focused solely on Abby. She pulled back the cover and saw a damp shadow spread on the blanket beneath Abby. "Let's get you out of these wet things," she said, helping her lean forward. Jesse gingerly pulled off the nightgown, careful of Abby's swollen belly and tender breasts, and then covered her up with a blanket.

Abby grimaced at the sight of the nightgown. She had been wearing it for the last three months, the only clothing she could fit into. The garment was her own work, sewn out of material from Frieda's old dresses. She never wanted to see it again. "I can't wait to burn that thing," she said, clenching her teeth through another contraction.

"Abs, I'm so sorry." Jesse took hold of her hand. "I wish there was something I could do to take away your pain."

Abby blew through pursed lips. "You just stay here with me and like you said, we'll get through this."

Time crawled over the next several hours, it's passing marked only by the increasing tempo of Abby's contractions. Waves of pain, which had been coming at intervals of twenty minutes near midday, now came within minutes of each other. Her pain was visibly, audibly more intense now. The contractions came consistently, urging her along, until finally, her body's insistence was too compelling to resist any longer.

Abby said, "I need to push." She leaned forward, grabbed hold of her bent knees, and bore down. Her pulse slammed in her ears, getting louder with each quick beat of her heart. After a few seconds, she released her grip and lay back. "Will you look? Hopefully, you'll see a head."

Jesse cautiously peered underneath the blanket, unsure of what to expect. She tilted her head in surprise. The part of Abby she had become quite familiar with now looked engorged and red. She pushed the thought from her mind. "No. I don't see anything." Jesse asked, "Do you think something is wrong?"

"I don't think so. I just think he's going to be stubborn about this."

"She." Jesse clarified with a wink. She wrung out a cloth and dabbed the beads of sweat from Abby's forehead. "Do you know you've never looked more beautiful than you do right now?" She tucked a stray strand of Abby's hair behind her ear.

"Oh, I'm sure I look—"Abby cried out as another sharp contraction rippled through her. She moaned. "It hurts so— " Pain racked the words from her mouth.

Jesse held Abby's bent knee. "Do you want to try pushing again?"

Abby leaned forward and bore down. She pushed for as long as she could, eyes squeezed, face reddening, and then leaned back, winded. "Do you see the head?"

Jesse looked again. She shook her head. "No."

Abby tossed and twisted in the bed as the worst contraction yet hit her, fighting hard for control of her body. She arched her back, head pressing almost through the pillow. Her lips quivered as a moan escaped. "I think something might be wrong," she cried out, each word more breathless, worry painted on her face. "You should be able to see the head by now."

Jesse had spent months agonizing over something exactly like this. She was scared to death Abby would have trouble giving birth. She felt as if she were trapped in a nightmare. It took everything inside her to tamp down her fear, but she knew she had to. Abby and the baby depended on her. The thought steeled her. "Let's try again. Slow, deep breaths," she said gently, coaxing Abby to lean up and push. "She's got to be getting close."

Abby leaned forward, pushing with every ounce of strength her small frame could muster. The seconds until she was spent felt like hours. She collapsed back on the bed. "How 'bout now? Can you see it?" The words were barely a miserable groan. Her tears would not stop.

"No. I don't see anything. What can I do?"

Abby licked her dried lips. "Can you get me some water?"

Jesse slipped through the curtain, realizing for the first time Toby wasn't inside. Then, she noticed his coat, the one Abby and she had made for him out of deer hides, gloves, and hat were gone as well. She opened the front door, shielding her face against the small, sharp bits of grit kicked up by the strong wind. It was then she recalled hearing the cabin door open several hours prior. She came to the only possible conclusion. *Oh, shit. He must've gone to get help.*

The tribe lived hours away when the weather was favorable. Even though it hadn't snowed in days, the air was bitter cold. Deadly cold.

He's going to freeze to death out there. Jesse heard Abby calling out for her. It took all her strength to push the door closed against the relenting force of the wind. Cup of water forgotten, she hurried to Abby's bedside.

Abby could tell by Jesse's face something was amiss. "What's wrong?"

Jesse deflected the question. Abby had enough to deal with. "Nothing," she said. "I'm just worried about you. Do you want to try pushing again?"

Abby leaned forward and grabbed her knees. She dug her

heels into the mattress as she bore down with her next contraction, pushing with all her might.

"Keep pushing. You're doing fine," Jesse said, her consolation lost beneath yet another excruciating spasm.

Abby's strength gave out. She released her grip and fell exhausted back onto the bed. "It burns. It burns so bad. Do you see the baby?"

Jesse looked. "I don't see—" She stopped speaking and looked again, wanting to be sure. "I don't see a head. I don't see anything."

Abby gasped and the color drained from her face. "I think the baby is stuck."

Jesse's gaze darted up at her. Her eyes went wide, as did her mouth. "What does that mean? Is that bad? What can I do?" she asked, pitch rising.

Abby squirmed in discomfort. "I don't know what to do," she said, clutching her stomach.

"You seem to have those shooting pains more often now. She has to be getting close," Jesse said. "Try pushing again."

Each time Abby pushed, Jesse searched for signs the baby was emerging from its hiding spot. And each time she saw nothing, another wave of fear rippled through her.

Minutes ticked by with little progress. She pushed when she felt the need, only to exert herself, the pain worse. With each contraction, Abby pushed harder, making her feel as if her body was being torn apart. Guttural sounds ripped her throat as each attempt left her more physically and mentally drained.

Jesse, normally calm, felt fear take hold. What started as a spark in the pit of her stomach grew into a blaze, threatening to engulf her. All of her inadequacy was finally exposed. A snowball out of control, she paced restlessly, hands lost in a tangle of hair, as she stared down the avalanche of complications she knew was heading their way. She stopped pacing and stood facing the wall beside the bed. She remembered the pain of her dislocated finger and recalled biting on the stick. She reached for a snowshoe and lifted it from its peg. Without a thought, she took her knife and cut a piece of rawhide binding.

"Bite on this the next time. It will help," she said.

After enduring one of the worst contractions so far, Abby fell back, panting, eyes closed. Pain was the only thing she knew. *How did women endure this? Survive this?*

Some didn't, Abby knew. Behind closed lids, her mind drifted, took her away, to a different time, a different home. She had promised herself she wouldn't go back there—wouldn't think about the day her mother died. Yet, there she was, back in that tiny house, hands pressed over her ears, listening as her mother fought to bring her sister into the world. A tear rolled down her cheek as she reached to take hold of Jesse's hand, her grip no stronger than a breeze. "Jesse," she whispered.

"Yes?"

"I want you to do something for me," she said, voice crackling and weak.

Jesse kissed the back of her hand. "Anything."

"I might not make it through this. If I don't, I want you to take the baby. Cut it out of me if you have to. Don't let it—"

"Dammit! Don't you do this! Don't you quit. Come on, let's try pushing again."

"I can't push anymore. I can't." Her chin trembled. "I'm so tired."

"Yes, you can," Jesse said, pulling her forward by the arms. She put Abby's hands on her knees, pressing down on them with her own palms to add their strength. "Now push! Push as hard as you can."

Abby tried, but like all the attempts before, nothing happened save for a momentary increase in the pain and pressure. She crumbled back onto the bed. "Promise me you—"

"I can't! I won't make that promise, so don't ask me to."

"Come here," Abby said, voice fading, barely a whisper.

Jesse lay down beside her, thumb caressing Abby's cheek.

"You must. I'm begging you. Don't let our child die," Abby said, trailing her fingers through Jesse's hair.

"Please, Abs. Don't ask me to do that. Neither of you are going to die." Jesse pleaded, trying to swallow the lump growing in her throat. "We'll get through this. You can't give up. You can't."

Abby held Jesse's face in her hands. "I'm begging you. If I don't make it, you have to get our baby out. Please. Promise me. Our baby's life depends on you."

Jesse turned away, unable to face her.

Abby placed her hand on Jesse's cheek, turning her head back, forcing her to meet her gaze. "Do you promise?"

Jesse stayed silent. She felt her resolve crumbling and swallowed the lump that went down like shards of glass. Looking into Abby's eyes, she relented. "I'll do what needs to be done. I promise. But right now I need you to be strong. I need you to try again." She put her hands on Abby's shoulder and helped her lean up. "Now push. Come on. You can do this."

Just then, the door opened, letting in a gust of wind that buffeted the heavy curtain. Jesse and Abby were both stunned when Aponi appeared from behind it, rushing to remove her coat as she hurried to the bedside.

Abby had never been more relieved in her life. As much as she loved Jesse, as much as she needed her, she knew Aponi was the one who would have the knowledge and experience to help right now.

"It's stuck. She's been pushing and pushing, but nothing," Jesse said. "I don't know what to do."

"Let me see." Aponi pulled back the blanket. "Um hum," she muttered as she placed her hands on Abby's abdomen and felt around. She knew what had to be done. "Abby, I need you to get out of this bed. Jesse, go get a chair." She aided a frail Abby to her feet. "Baby hard to come when you lay on your back. Must squat," she said, bending her knees enough to comfortably mimic the position. Then she instructed Jesse to sit in the chair at the foot of the bed.

"What can I do?" Jesse asked, straddling the chair.

"You just sit there and keep it from falling over. Abby, you hold on," Aponi said, placing Abby's hands on the back of the chair for support. She put a blanket on the floor underneath Abby. "Now, squat down and push," she said, her tone demanding.

On legs so weak and shaky Abby feared she would collapse, she held tight to the chair and squatted. Her body shook, her body hurt. Determined, she bore down until she felt something shift inside her.

"Again," Aponi said, reaching up. "It's coming. Push again."

Jesse kept her hands over Abby's as she continued to push. "Come on. You can do this," she said.

Abby's strength waned. She wanted to collapse, let her

aching body fall across the bed. But Jesse and Aponi were insistent and wouldn't allow her to give up.

After several more attempts, Jesse leaned down for a look. At last, something was different. Jesse saw a head. "Abs, you're doing it. She's almost out," she said, excitement radiating through her voice. "Push!"

The words had barely left Jesse's mouth when the baby shot out so quickly she couldn't tell if it was a boy or a girl. All she could make out was that it was fleshy and wet. Aponi had it in her arms, cleaning away the mucous with a rag. Jesse strained for a better look. She was sure it was a girl.

Abby's strength finally gave out. Her limbs turned to water and she sagged. She draped her arms around Jesse, resting her head on a shoulder like dead weight. Jesse kissed the top of her head.

The sudden silence rang in their ears.

"Is it all right?" Abby asked, lifting her head, trying to see for herself. "I don't hear—"

A shrill cry split through the still.

"He's fine," Aponi said, smile spreading across her face.

Relieved, Abby looked at Jesse. "He," she said, grinning. "We have a son—" Pain silenced her. She grabbed her stomach. "Something's not right."

Aponi put the baby on the bed and reached up between Abby's legs. "I feel it."

"Feel what?" Abby asked.

Aponi leaned around her and looked up. "A head! Now push!"

A head. Jesse repeated the words. It took her several seconds to comprehend what that meant. Then, she felt a tingle shoot through her body. Blackness filled her vision. She crashed to the floor, striking her head on Frieda's old trunk at the end of the bed.

"Jesse. Jesse. Jesse." The muffled words slowly crept in her ears, like penetrating through a pillow. "Jesse! Jesse wake up."

The words loud and clear now, Jesse blinked and blinked again, studying the apparition standing over her. Slowly, Aponi came into focus. She winced from the pain and put up a hand, felt the cool touch of a rag on her forehead.

"You're bleeding," Aponi said. "Keep pressing."

Jesse cleared her throat. "The baby? Is it all right?"

"You mean babies," Aponi said with a wide grin. "Yes, they and Mother are fine. Come. See." She helped Jesse to her feet.

Jesse saw Abby covered with a blanket in bed. Two tiny heads poked out, one cradled in each of her arms.

"We were both right. Look, we have a son and a daughter," she said, voice raspy, blue eyes sparkling with pride.

Jesse unconsciously lowered the rag and sat down beside her.

Abby took Jesse's hand and guided the wet cloth back to her forehead. "Keep pressure on it. You're still bleeding."

Still in shock, Jesse sat in silence.

"Well, say something," Abby said.

Jesse opened her mouth to speak, but it was as if the part of her brain that processed speech had shut down. The apparent danger behind them, she finally felt the effects of these frantic, sleepless hours. She stammered. "You had tw-twins?"

"Uh, huh." Abby nodded.

With one hand holding the rag over her wound, Jesse warily used the other to pull back the blanket enough for a better look. Curled up on Abby's naked body were the tiniest, most beautiful beings she had ever seen. She ran her cupped hand lightly over the top of the baby's head nearest to her. "It's so soft. It feels like peach fuzz." She stuck out a finger and the baby boy grabbed hold. "They look like you," Jesse said, eyes meeting Abby's.

Glancing down at one of the babies, Abby said, "Jesse, this is Jim."

"Jim?" She lightly placed her thumb over the tiny fingers wrapped around her own.

"Yes, after your father." She tilted her head towards the baby girl. "If you don't mind, I'd like to call her Gwen, after my grandmother, Gwyneth."

Jesse was overcome with emotion, tears pooling in her eyes. "I love those names."

Baby Gwen puckered her face and cried. Jesse's own tears finally spilled over and fell, slipping quietly down her face.

"Would you hold him while I see if I can get her to nurse?" Abby asked.

Jesse didn't move, unsure of what to do. Aponi picked up the baby and carefully placed him in Jesse's bent arm. She rocked him as she kept the pressure on her bleeding wound. She focused on the eyes staring back at her. "He's perfect," she whispered, looking over at Abby.

Jesse had never seen a mother nurse a baby before. Gwen latching on was one of the sweetest things she had ever witnessed. Hands full, she had no way to wipe away the tears streaming down her face. She swiped her wet cheeks against her shoulders, smearing the salty flow more than drying it. "Has Toby seen them?" she asked.

Aponi shook her head. "He's not here."

Jesse looked up. "He didn't come back with you?"

"No. He's with the tribe. Running Cloud is taking care of him."

"Taking care of him. What happened?" Jesse asked, worry shaking her voice.

Aponi placed a consoling hand on her shoulder. "He's got the blackness in his feet."

Jesse's heart sank. She knew exactly what Aponi was talking about—frostbite.

CHAPTER ELEVEN

J esse woke to soft grunting and squeaking emanating from the cradle next to the bed. Abby was finally resting peacefully, and she didn't want to wake her. She rolled quietly out of bed and tiptoed to the cradle. Jim was fast asleep, yet his lips pursed as if searching for his mother.

"Good morning, Gwen," she said, feeling the smile stretch across her face. The infant's icy-blue eyes stared at her intently as she reached for the tiny bundle. "What do you say we let them sleep?" she whispered, picking her up. "I've seen squirrels bigger than you."

Jesse sat in the rocker beside the fireplace, Gwen cradled in her arms. "You're so beautiful," she said, " just like your mother." She caressed Gwen's cheek as they rocked, and then pulled her hand back. She feared her calloused skin would somehow hurt the baby. She felt as soft and fragile a thing as Jesse had ever handled.

She remembered what Joe Mulligan had told her at the wedding—about babies not being breakable. She wasn't sure about that. She'd err on the side of caution. Either way, Gwen seemed to enjoy the interaction.

Jesse held the baby in her lap, supporting Gwen's little head in her palm. A tiny arm poked out of the blanket Abby had knitted, and the smallest hand she had ever seen clutched hold of her finger. Gwen's grip had more strength behind it than she anticipated. She again noticed the intense blue eyes.

"You're going to be a handful just like your mother, aren't you?" she whispered, nuzzling Gwen and taking in her baby scent.

Jesse couldn't help but think of Toby as she rocked Gwen softly. "I can't wait for you to meet your uncle. He saved your life. Actually, he saved mine too," she said softly. "If something would've happened to your mother…well, I couldn't imagine a life without her. See, I'm quite fond of her."

"I'm quite fond of you too," Abby said, startling her. She put a hand on Jesse's shoulder and kissed the top of her head. "I should see if she's hungry."

Jesse carefully transferred the baby to Abby's open arms as if worried she'd shatter. "I'll put on the coffee."

Aponi climbed down from the loft just as Jesse was adding another log to the fire. She took a seat in one of the rocking chairs.

"Be honest with me," Jesse said, prying the wood into place with the poker. "How bad is he?"

"I'm not sure. We rushed him inside as soon as he got there. He could barely walk. I only saw the blackness briefly when they took off his boots. He was more worried about Abby. He said she was in trouble and told me to get here fast."

Jesse stood. "Do you think they can save his feet?"

"Running Cloud is good with medicine. But can't bring things back to life. Dead is dead."

Jesse's heart sank. She knew blackness meant dead flesh. Frostbite was one of the most dangerous predators on the mountain. Its invisible claws loomed a greater, more imminent threat than any bear or wildcat.

Jesse jabbed with the poker. "I need to see him," she said. Her words came out tinged with fire like the sparks she sent spiraling.

"I'm worried for him, too. Toby means much to me."

Jesse, concerned about her brother's well being, missed the subtle hint from Aponi. "You know, there was a time when I thought I had lost him forever. I can't lose him again."

Aponi stood and put a warm hand on her shoulder. "I know your past. Now that Abby's out of danger, I will return to tribe and check on him."

Jesse shook her head and grabbed Aponi's hand. "No. Will you stay here with her instead? You're more of a help to her than I am. I don't know anything about babies, and if something should happen…" Jesse paused, eyes glistening as a series of possibilities flashed through her head, each one too terrible to consider. She pushed them away. "Well," she said, gulping back her fear, "I'd feel a whole lot better if you were here."

Aponi smiled and nodded. "I will stay."

Jesse patted Aponi's hand, still resting on her shoulder. "Thank you."

Aponi's willingness to help did little to put her mind at ease, knowing the situation had become dire for her brother. She left the immediate heat of the fire and took a seat on the edge of the bed, listening as Abby sang to a nursing Gwen.

The day is finally done
Time to sleep my little one

The man in the moon sits way up high
Softly singing lullabies

He sprinkles stardust on your head
Sending sweet dreams to your bed

No harm shall come upon you
With Mama by your side

So dance among the stars my child
With angels as your guide

You'll wake with sunshine kisses
Bluebirds and their songs

For now sleep softly child
Safe in Mama's arms

Of all the times she'd heard Abby sing, this was by far her best performance. Gooseflesh prickled her skin as Abby's voice filled the small cabin. The love coming through in her voice was so pure and radiant it shook Jesse to her core.

"That was beautiful." Jesse cupped Gwen's head, rubbing the soft peach fuzz with her thumb. "She really is something special, isn't she?"

Abby nodded and smiled. "She's perfect," she said. "Why don't you lay down with us? You've got to be exhausted."

Jesse absolutely did want to lay down and stretch her body

out beside Abby and Gwen, but the thought gave her a sharp tinge of guilt. She knew Abby wasn't going to be happy with the news she would be leaving. She figured she might as well be blunt about it.

"I can't. I'm going to—" A shrill cry cut Jesse short. She got up and went to the cradle. "Now, what's all the ruckus about?" she asked, leaning over Jim. She winced, then buried her nose in the crook of her elbow.

"Oh, is he needing a change?" Abby asked.

Jesse lowered her arm. "How can something so tiny put off such a smell?"

Abby chuckled. "Let me finish with her and I'll clean him up."

"Abs, I got this." Jesse gently picked up the infant, more confident this time.

"Do you know how?"

Jesse's brow furrowed. She wasn't clueless. "Yes. I watched you two do it yesterday. It didn't look that difficult."

She removed the dirty diaper, trying her best not to retch in front of Abby. She rung out a rag and cleaned up the mess, still marveling that such a sweet little thing could create such an ungodly stink.

Once he was clean, she replaced the diaper and left him on the bed next to Abby before going to wash the soiled cloths.

As she hung the clean diaper and rag in front of the fire-place to dry, Abby asked, "Can you come burp her so I can feed him?"

Jesse held Gwen against her chest and paced the cabin, softly patting her on the back. Once she heard the tiny belch, she went to speak with Abby. She held Gwen in her arms as a protective shield.

"Please don't be mad," Jesse said, "but I have to leave. I'm going to check on Toby."

Abby scowled. "Right now?"

"Yes. Aponi is going to stay here with you. She'll be more help to you than I will."

"Jesse, don't think I don't care about him, because I do. I just don't think you should leave right now." Abby tilted her head toward the door and pleaded with her eyes. "It's freezing out there."

"There's a break in the weather, so now's my chance. I can't just sit here. I have to go. He's my brother. Please understand."

"Can you even find their village?"

"Abs, I remember the way. Don't fret about that. I have to go. He risked his life for us."

"I know he did, but what if something happens to you? What good would that do?"

Jesse took a seat beside her. She did not have an answer that would satisfy anyone, even herself. She cradled Gwen in her arm, using her hand to support her head. Her other she placed on Abby's leg. "I'll be just fine," she said. "Nothing's going to happen to me. I'll be back as soon as I can."

Abby didn't say a word. She didn't need to. Her look said it all.

Jesse kissed Gwen and gently placed her in the cradle. She dressed in layers: long underwear, buckskin pants and shirt, and an outer covering of bearskin tanned fur.

Abby watched, mostly in disbelieving silence, trying to think of any argument that would keep Jesse with her. "I don't like this," she eventually said. "Not one bit."

Jesse squeezed Abby's shoulders. "Don't worry. I'll be fine. There's not a cloud in the sky this morning."

"I don't care. I still don't like you going out there."

"I have to go. I just have to."

Abby followed her to the door, wanting nothing more than to grab her, hold her back, and fall to the floor with her arms wrapped around her legs if she had to. It was hard enough to breathe, let alone beg.

"I'll be back as soon as I can," she said, squeezing Abby tightly before kissing her. She put on the tan hide hat and mittens and grabbed her rifle.

"Please be careful. I need you to come back to me."

"I will. I promise."

Abby held onto Jesse in a long hug that neither wanted to end. The last time Jesse had promised her something would turn out all right she nearly died from a gunshot wound.

Abby stood in the doorway, the icy cold whipping around her as Jesse walked away from the cabin. An uneasy feeling grew in the pit of her stomach when Jesse vanished amongst the trees. She stood staring into the dense and desolate woods until Aponi took her by the arm, closed the door, and gently pulled her closer to the fire.

Jesse hiked along at a steady pace. As she made her way alongside the stream, she wondered if she might have worn too many layers. Already she could feel sweat trickling down her back. Heat seemed to be radiating from everywhere.

She paused at the lake, looking out over the vast expanse. On the last journey to the village, she had needed to travel around it. Now it was frozen. Though she'd never tried it, walking across would save valuable time. She weighed the risks against the benefits. This whole endeavor had been born of urgency; she would not slow down.

Mind made up, she planted her moccasin-booted feet on

the ice and started across. With nothing but her own frosty breath to accompany her, Jesse felt more alone than ever on the silent, frozen ice. Somehow it felt even more isolating than living alone on a mountain. Maybe it was because she had just left a place holding so much life, so much promise.

Jesse guessed it had been the better part of an hour before she set foot on land again. She continued up a steep incline, ignoring the burning ache in her legs as she powered herself to the top of a small peak.

The distant sky looked ominous, roiling with colors wholly unnatural. The clouds seemed to melt, their darkness contaminating the clear sky below. Bad weather was coming. Fast.

She searched for some kind of shelter. Anything would do. The only immediate option was a fallen tree, held at an angle by its root ball.

What is it with me and trees?

The wind increased, bringing tears to her eyes and stinging her cheeks. She managed to hunker down at the base of the tree just as the first flakes began to fly.

Hopefully it blows over fast.

She pulled her legs to her chest and rested her head on her knees. Hour after hour, the storm attacked the mountain. As the snow continued to fall, the drifts around her makeshift shelter engulfed her. She knew she was in for a long night.

Jesse woke in total darkness, buried in the deep snow. She panicked and feverishly punched her fists through the drifts that had entombed her. Relief rode on the daylight that came pouring through the hole.

After clawing her way out, scrambling on hands and knees like an animal, she leaned against the fallen tree to get her bearings. Overnight, the world around her had changed considerably. Everything was blanketed in several feet of snow. Nothing looked familiar.

She pulled off her fur-covered mittens, tucked them under her arm, and blew warm air into her cupped hands. She rubbed them together to generate some heat, but any respite was dulled by a gnawing pain in her stomach.

With prickly fingers, she took a piece of jerky from her pouch and ripped it with her teeth. She opened her canteen to wash down the dry, stringy meat, only to discover the water inside had frozen solid. She scooped up a handful of snow and let it melt in her mouth.

She needed to get to the village. Now.

Jesse put her mittens back on and picked up her rifle. As she trudged through the deep snow, she tried to find something, anything at all familiar in the landscape. The further she went, the more confused she became. Nothing was recognizable.

She stopped and turned around. Her tracks wove through the snowdrifts behind her, her short strides evident in the pits and ravines she left in the sparkling dust. She must have made a wrong turn along the way. She needed to retrace her steps.

Before she could move, she was struck from behind. The beast gave no warning before it attacked, driving her face into the snow. At once her mouth and nose were filled with the soft powder. Her struggle against the oppressive weight only pushed her deeper.

She flung her head side-to-side, gasping for breath. Snow stung her eyes and blurred her vision, but she could still see bits of fur being shredded from her coat. If not for the thick hides she wore, the hungry animal would already have sunk its fangs through to her flesh and beyond.

Her right hand was pinned beneath her, but the soft snow gave way when she jerked her arm. She reached down to pull out her knife. In one awkward move, she plunged her knife blindly at the side of the animal. When it recoiled, she seized the opportunity and rolled out from underneath her attacker. With quick, deep thrusts of the blade she stabbed repeatedly, the creature's light brown fur soaking a deep crimson as it collapsed.

Breathless, she lay on her back, staring up at the azure sky, feeling as if her lungs would explode. She lay still until her galloping heart slowed to a trot, then wiped the cooling blood from her face with the back of her mitten.

She pulled her knife from the lifeless mountain lion, stood, and wiped the blade on her pant leg, taking in the gory scene. She and the lion were in a patch of slushy red snow, trampled and splattered with blood. Her rifle, pouch of jerky, and canteen were strewn around the scene and dotted with blood.

In a race against daylight, it was imperative she get moving. Her only regret was leaving the meat behind, but the waste could not be helped.

When she moved to retrieve her provisions, the ground beneath her collapsed and she found herself falling, arms wind milling as she plunged into the dark abyss. Her body slammed into something hard and unforgiving before coming to rest at the bottom of the deep crevasse. Pain shot through her body and she cried out, clutching her side. Her breathing was hitched, each puff visible in the frosty air. She knew she had probably broken some ribs. Her right knee felt swollen and on fire.

She ran her tongue lightly across a salty laceration on her lip and spat out the blood. Trying to move only hurt more. She cried out again, her voice repeating off the walls of the large ravine—mocking her. She looked around. Panic built into an almost crippling terror when she realized she no longer had her rifle.

It must be laying up there, she thought, looking up at the opening in the rock above her.

She lay in an immense cavern. The gravity of her situation sank in.

No one will ever find me down here. Oh, Abby. I'm so sorry. Succumbing to the helplessness, her eyes fluttered shut, and the darkness swallowed her.

Hours later she woke. High above her, through the opening in the cavern ceiling, glimmering lights dotted the night sky. She tried to roll over again, but this only caused more pain. She cradled her ribs with an arm. It was hard to take in a breath. Her teeth chattered. She was cold, alone, and scared.

I'm going to die down here.

She stayed motionless for what must have been hours, in too much pain to move or sleep, trying to think her way out of the mess she had gotten herself into.

Nothing came to mind.

It was hopeless.

The night sky turned to day and back to night again. She was exhausted but too scared to sleep. If she closed her eyes, she may never open them again. She stared at the clouds floating across the stars until they faded, lost under the weight of lids too heavy to hold.

She woke with a start, teeth chattering and ran her tongue across dry, cracked lips. She pulled off a mitten, her hand shaking as she scooped some snow into her mouth. Her stomach growled.

How long has it been since I've eaten? She couldn't remember. Everything was jumbled in her mind.

Another day turned to night. She was weak, and growing weaker by the minute.

When she noticed the cold chill had left her body, she wondered what had happened. It didn't make sense as she knew she had to be freezing. Her mind was starting to play tricks on her, a sure sign she wasn't going to make it much longer.

Jesse had never been a quitter, but she didn't know if she could take anymore. She was beyond exhausted, the pain too overwhelming. She let sleep take her.

"Jesse, wake up." It was Abby's voice. "Jesse!"

Her eyes snapped open.

Relief flooded her veins. She found herself back at the cabin, in a warm bed, lying next to Abby.

"Abs, I'm so sorry," she said, holding onto her as if she hadn't seen her in a lifetime. "You were right. I never should've gone."

"I'm just glad you came back. I missed you," Abby said. She rolled on top of her and pressed her lips against Jesse's.

Jesse lost herself in the kiss. Somewhere, she heard someone speaking to her in the native language, the voice too muffled to make out. She ignored it.

"I missed you too," she said. "How long was I gone?"

No response came from Abby as the cries of babies drifted from the cradle beside the bed.

Jesse got up and felt as if her body almost floated towards them. Her heart lurched. The cradle was empty.

The world tilted around her and she found herself back at the church. A feminine hand rested in the crook of her arm. She followed the slender arm up and found it attached to a beautiful young woman. Jesse recognized her, but from where, she couldn't quite remember. She had looked deep into those blue eyes before.

"Gwen?" she asked, uncertain.

"Yes," Gwen said, then kissed her on the cheek. "Are you ready?"

It was as if Jesse had no control over her own feet. She floated again, this time leading Gwen down the aisle. A man stood next to the preacher at the front of the church. More familiar faces seated among the pews nodded up at her as they made their way past. Again, she heard the native language, chatter in the background.

Strange to hear that at a wedding, she thought.

Jesse turned back to Gwen, but she was gone like a wisp of smoke. The church began to spin, faster and faster, putting Jesse at the center of a tornado.

Abruptly, she came to a stop, hovering over two men. One of them, a black haired man, was attending to the other man's wounds.

Jesse drifted slowly to the floor, standing within arms reach of them.

"Excuse me. Sir?" she said.

The man acted as if he didn't hear her. She tried again.

"Sir," she said in a higher tone. Still, Jesse got no response and realized they could not hear her. She watched in silence as the man continued tending to his patient.

Treatment finished, the wounded man looked up at his healer. "Thank you, Doc McGinnis," he said.

Jesse's mind spun. She had no clue who the man was, but his name was familiar. She moved closer for a better look.

No. It can't be, she thought. *Jim?*

Everything went dark.

Next, Jesse found herself in an unfamiliar home. Whoever owned it had done well for themselves. Filling the space around her were the finest things anyone could imagine. On a settee nearby sat an older woman, crocheting. Although she looked familiar, Jesse again couldn't say for sure who she was. She became aware of the native voices once more. She wasn't sure how long they'd been back, but they were growing clearer and more urgent now. She could almost make out the words. As she concentrated on listening, something brushed past her arm. A man made his way over to the woman, kissing her before taking a seat next to her. Jesse moved closer in an effort to make out their conversation.

"The children are bringing their families over this evening for supper," the woman said, her voice instantly and uncannily familiar.

Jesse's legs went weak. She whispered in disbelief. "Abs?"

"Will be nice to see all of them," the man replied, striking a match. Smoke from his pipe hovered between the couple.

Abby moved closer to him and he put his arm around her. "We couldn't have raised better children," she said, her smile proud.

"I'm just thankful you came to your senses and left that daft mountain man."

THE DEVIL BEHIND US

"Me too, Sam. I don't know what I was thinking."

It was Jesse's worst nightmare come to life: that Abby would have chosen a life with Sam, that others would see her as obtuse because of her lifestyle. Her heart sank. This man was living the life she had wanted so desperately. It made her feel sick to her stomach.

A faint glow to the room quickly built to such a bright white she had to cover her eyes with her arm. She pressed her eyes shut tightly, but could not keep it out.

As the light faded, she slowly opened her eyes. The white glow had dissipated, and was replaced by the most beautiful hues of green she had ever seen. The lush tones morphed around her feet, transforming into blades of grass. It was no illusion. She could smell the sod and feel it against her toes. She looked up from the ground to find herself standing in front of the cabin. A lone figure sat on the old stump chair, whittling knife in hand.

Jesse rubbed her eyes, blinking as she tried to focus. *Who's that on the porch?* A gasp was all she could manage when the stranger's face took shape. Unafraid, she raced toward the cabin, calling out for Frieda as she went. She leapt the porch steps as Frieda dropped the knife, stood, and reached out for her.

"Frieda! I've missed you," she said, body quivering.

"Oh, I've missed you too. We don't have much time." Frieda's voice trembled as she broke the embrace.

"Am I dead?" Jesse asked.

"No, dear. But you must choose your path."

She cocked her head. "What do you mean?"

"You can choose to stay here with us—"

"Us?"

"Yes, everyone's inside waiting for you." Frieda tilted her head toward the cabin.

Jesse pointed at the door. "You mean my family's in there?"

Frieda nodded. "Along with Nathaniel and Patrick. We're all here for you."

When Jesse turned to run toward the door, Frieda grabbed her by the arm, grip firm. "Wait!"

"But I want to see them."

"I know you do," Frieda said, "but you must choose your path first."

"I don't understand."

"You can go through that door," Frieda said, pointing, "and stay here with us. Or you can go back."

"Why would I leave? I want to see them." When she tried to move again, Frieda's grip tightened almost painfully. The firmness was tender, not unkind.

"Jessica, we will always be here waiting for you, but think about the life you'd leave behind." This time, she pointed behind Jesse.

Jesse turned to see a vision form in the air so vividly she tried to reach out and grab it. She could see Abby pacing the cabin, worry written all over her face. The twins, the beautiful babies, slept in their cradle. The cradle she had made.

The scene flickered. Toby came into view. Something was happening to him. He was in pain. That was all Jesse could make out before the scene vanished, leaving her feeling like she'd been struck by lightning. She had been so caught up with the overwhelming desire to see her family, she had completely forgotten about them. She faced Frieda.

"I must go," Frieda said. "You have to choose now. You

can walk through the door with me, or you can turn, go down those steps, and go back to your life."

Jesse wrapped her arms around Frieda and squeezed her eyes shut. "I love you. Will you tell them I love them too and I miss them?"

"Jessica, I love you too and they already know," Frieda said, voice fading.

When Jesse opened her eyes, she was standing alone on the porch, her own arms hugging herself. Frieda was gone.

She kissed the palm of her hand, placed it on the weathered wood of the door, and then turned and walked toward the steps. As her foot touched the top tread, another flash of bright light overwhelmed her. She shielded her eyes.

CHAPTER TWELVE

J esse jolted awake, tears streaming down her flushed
cheeks. Dreams, vivid but elusive, evoked such strong
emotions she wondered if they were simply crazy imag-
inings or something more spiritual.

No longer an icy blue, the walls of her crevasse tomb had
changed considerably. The flickering shades of orange and red
she saw conjured up thoughts of hell.

Is this my penance for being with Abs? The thought stole the
air from her lungs.

She squeezed her eyes shut, blocking out the menacing
flames that threatened to engulf her. Inhaling, she swore she
could still smell Frieda, whose clothing always held the smoky
scent of her pipe. She shook her head to clear it.

Frieda is gone. It's just your mind playing tricks.

Fear unabated, she kept her eyes closed and inhaled again.
It wasn't the burning sulfur she had expected, but she recognized it immediately—the same herbal aroma that rose from
the pipe she'd shared with the tribal elders.

Slowly, cautiously, she peeked through eyelids which were

nothing more than slits. Shadows danced on the walls through a smoke-filled haze.

She gasped. Her whole body tensed at the touch of a hand on her shoulder. She looked up at a face both blurry and familiar, perhaps another trick of her eyes. "Toby?" So weak, the name left her lips like dry leaves crunched underfoot.

Her brother smiled wide. "I was beginning to wo-wonder if you were ever going to wake up," he said, voice thick with relief.

She closed her eyes again, mind whirling at how she had ended up in one of the caverns the natives called home during the winter months. The last thing she remembered was Abby standing at the doorway to the cabin, worry in her stance and sadness in her eyes.

Abby! Jesse called out. She sat up in a rush, sending pain shooting through her chest and leg. Moaning, she put a hand on her ribs and reached for the throbbing in her leg with the other. The touch only seemed to spread the inflammation around. It was too much. She collapsed back onto the pelt. "Did I break my leg?" she asked.

Toby shook his head. "I don't th-think so. But, the top of your knee was off to the side. You messed it up real good."

"How long have I been here?" She was still trying to put together the puzzle, but knew she had not yet found all the pieces.

Toby gently rubbed his thumb on her shoulder. "Going on three weeks now."

She noticed the stick he was leaning on for support. "Your feet. How are they?"

"I'm all r-right. Don't wo-worry about me."

"Where's Abby? The twins—" she said, trying to lean up

on an elbow. The simple action made her aching ribs sing out. She grimaced as she eased her head back down.

"They're all fine," he said. He shifted his focus. "Aren't they?"

Jesse turned her head and saw Aponi. "You left them there? Alone?" she asked, incredulously.

Aponi stepped closer. "No. Honovi and Onawa are with her."

Jesse breathed a sigh of relief. "How did I get here?" she asked.

"A few days after you left, Abby had a bad feeling. She felt something was wrong. She wanted me to come to village to see if you were here. When I found out you never made it, we started to look for you. We never would have found you if not for the red snow."

Jesse replayed the words over and over in her mind.

Red snow?

A thick fog hung over her memories. She struggled to process the information, reaching for the little bits and pieces visible through the haze.

Red Snow?

She closed her eyes, pushing back against the growing mist shrouding the memory she searched for.

Red snow?

Then it hit her. She recalled being back in the snow, flashes of fur and teeth as she fought off the mountain lion with nothing but her wits and an eight-inch blade. She remembered the bloody scene, the whole area looked as if it had been doused with red paint, unreal yet terrifyingly real. Her body shivered despite the heat of the nearby fire.

Aponi continued. "Not far from there, we saw a large hole in the ground. Saw you lying at the bottom—"

Jesse cut her off, suddenly recalling the fall. "How'd you get me out of there?"

"Kaga ran back to the village to get rope," Aponi said. "Then, he climbed down to get you. It took many of our men to lift you out. Now, you drink," she said, handing Jesse a wooden bowl.

Knowing the concoction was bound to be bitter, Jesse downed the warm drink as fast as she could. She grimaced and wiped her mouth with the back of her hand. "Does Abby know I'm all right?" she asked.

Aponi shook her head. "Weather turned. No way to get there. No way for them to get here." She took the bowl from her. "You rest now."

"She must be worried s-s-sick," Jesse said, her words already slurring. Fighting against the effects of the native medicine, she struggled for a few moments to keep sleep at bay. It was no use. Her eyelids flitted a couple of times and then closed, catapulting her into a bottomless sleep.

Jesse woke to hushed murmurings. Toby and Aponi stood close together, their muted tones too low for her to make out. She stayed silent, watching and trying to listen. Her eyes went wide when she noticed they were holding hands.

Sensing Jesse's watchful gaze upon them, Toby quickly let go of Aponi's hand. He limped over to her with the use of his cane.

"Are you in pain?" Jesse asked.

Toby looked down at his sister on her pallet. "Not really. Just trying to adjust to walking without tw-two of my toes."

Jesse gasped. "You lost toes?"

"Yes. Too far gone to save 'em." He shrugged. "Best to just cut th-them off."

Jesse wanted to be furious he'd put his life in jeopardy, but how could she be mad? If not for his heroics, she surely would have lost Abby and the twins. What her life would have been like after, she didn't want to imagine.

"I'm so sorry, Toby." She took hold of his hand. "I can't believe you risked your life like that." She squeezed. "You saved Abby and the twins. I'm forever grateful to you, brother."

"Aponi told me she had two. A boy and a girl." A smiled darted across his face. "I guess two toes for two babies is a fair tr-trade."

"Can you help me up?" she asked, reaching out, more than ready to get on her feet again. The sooner she was up and moving, the sooner she could get home.

Unfortunately, Mother Nature had plans of her own. The usual February snow fell relentlessly. For day after agonizing day, the blizzard kept Jesse separated from Abby and the babies.

A break came three weeks later, clouds giving way to cobalt skies and unseasonably warm temperatures. Soon, if the weather cooperated, it would allow travel across the mountain. It had seemed an eternity to Jesse—six insufferable weeks since she had last seen Abby and the babies. The extra time had been a blessing in a way. At least it had given her body more time to heal.

Jesse and Toby set out as the dawn kissed the horizon. They both struggled with their own injuries, almost hobbling at the more difficult points of the journey. When they reached the lake, they came upon Honovi and Onawa, who were also taking advantage of the weather to return to their village. Abby had sent them to see if they could find out what had happened. She feared Jesse had fallen victim to the blizzard.

Reaching the cabin and its vulnerable occupants became even more urgent. Honovi and Onawa continued toward the tribe, while Jesse and Toby pushed their bodies, racing to get home as quickly as possible. The gravity drove them, giving strength to their muscles and numbing the pain that screamed from their bones.

Jesse's heart thumped like a drum when she saw the chimney smoke hanging above the pine trees. They were close. She cursed the splint on her leg, the shackle prohibiting her from running the final yards.

After what seemed like an endless journey, they stepped onto the familiar old porch. It creaked under her foot, a happy song she knew so well and had almost forgotten. She opened the door.

The rockers on Abby's chair slowed, and her back and forth rock came to an abrupt stop. Frieda's old heirloom sat motionless for the first time in weeks.

Abby sat in stunned silence as she tried to comprehend what was right in front of her eyes. For a fleeting moment, it seemed surreal. Recognition hit her like a torrent. She leapt from her seat in front of the fire, abandoned chair teetering wildly as she ran into Jesse's waiting arms.

They wept, clinging to each other in an embrace neither wanted to break.

Abby's body went limp in Jesse's arms.

"Toby," Jesse said, using all her strength to keep Abby off the floor. "Help me."

They aided her to the bed.

Abby's eyes fluttered. "If this is a dream," she said, looking up at them, "I don't want to wake up. Are you real?"

"You're not dreaming. We're home." Jesse sat gently on the bed next to her. "Are you all right?"

"I thought you were dead," she said, breathlessly. "Honovi and Onawa told me you never made it to their village. I thought you froze to death out there."

Jesse leaned down and kissed her, letting her mouth linger on Abby's salty, wet cheek. "I'm sorry I put you through that," she said, looking her in the eyes. "How are the babies?" She craned her neck, trying to see inside the cradle.

"They're fine. It's just been a living nightmare. I still can't believe you're here," Abby said, pulling her close. Her pounding heart kept time with Jesse's. Abby shifted her focus to Toby. "It's good to see you too. Thank God both of you are safe."

He smiled. "Good to be home."

Jesse got up and went to the cradle. "They've grown since the last time I saw them," she said, taking off her coat. She blew warm air into her hands and rubbed them together before picking Jim up. "There's my big man. Did you hold down the fort while I was gone?" she asked, and then kissed him on the cheek. "I've missed you all so much." She cradled him in her arm and lightly ran her finger over his chin.

"We've missed you, too," Abby said, "More than you could ever imagine."

Jesse returned Jim to the cradle, placing him gently beside his sister. She reached for Gwen. "There's my beautiful girl," she said, kissing her on the forehead. Cradling her safely in her arms, she carried her to the rocking chair. She kicked her splinted leg out in front of her and took a seat, basking in the crackling heat.

Abby took a seat across from her. "What happened to your leg?"

Jesse filled Abby in on every detail, even telling her about the vivid dreams she still wasn't fully convinced were dreams at all. She knew her body was at the native village—at times she could hear them speaking to her in her subconscious—but her visions were too substantial to be dreams. They seemed more like premonitions. Frieda felt too real.

Abby was mortified to learn what Toby had sacrificed to get help. She would never be able to repay the debt to her brother-in-law, but loved him more than she ever had. He truly was her hero.

Toby slept soundly in the loft as night fell, his incessant snoring resonating throughout the cabin.

Jesse pulled the curtain closed and slipped into a pair of long underwear. She sidled onto the bed and leaned up on an elbow, watching in awe as Abby nursed Jim. "I'll burp him when he's done," she said. "I've missed doing that."

When Jim's suckling ceased, Abby handed him over and put Gwen to her other breast. Jesse stood next to the bed and patted Jim lightly on the back. Once he let out a soft belch, she kissed him and put him in the cradle. She sat next to Abby and waited for Gwen to finish. The thin lips pressed against her mother seemed so fragile she found herself overcome with emotion. She would do anything to protect these children— her children.

Abby handed Gwen to Jesse. "When she's done, don't put her in with him," she said. "They tend to wake each other. If you want any sleep tonight, it's best to keep one in the bed."

Jesse lay down next to Abby, Gwen resting on her chest. With an arm around Abby, she lightly rubbed Gwen's back, sending the infant straight to sleep. "I had a lot of time to think while we were apart," Jesse said. "I don't want to live up here anymore."

"But Jesse," Abby said, stunned, "this is your home. Our home."

"I know, but I don't think this is the best place for us anymore."

Abby sat up. "Where is this coming from?"

"I don't want them growing up in this old, drafty cabin surrounded by danger." She looked down at the tiny girl sleeping on her chest. "I don't want this life for them. I've seen what their lives can be and they won't have that if we stay up here."

"Where would we go?"

Jesse shrugged. "I don't know. We'll have to choose a path and see where it leads us. What do you think?"

Abby brushed Jesse's bangs aside and ran her fingers over her forehead, pausing on the small crescent-shaped scar. "I think you've just been through a lot. Things seem worse right now."

"Abs, I've lived here for twelve years. This wasn't the first time I've almost died up here." Jesse's tone was resolute. "I couldn't live with myself if something ever happened to any of you."

"This is what I didn't want." Abby shook her head. "I don't want us to be the reason you give up your way of life."

"It's not the life I want anymore. And another thing, we have no privacy." She flailed a hand at the small space around them. "We've been apart for weeks and I still can't be with you the way I want to."

Abby's lips stretched into a smile. She knew exactly how Jesse felt. "Having our own space would be nice. You know I have some money saved up. It won't get us too far, but it's a start."

Jesse put a hand behind her head, keeping the other resting lightly on Gwen's back. "If you could go anywhere, where would you go?"

Abby considered it. "Um…I think it would be wise to go to a big city. There'd be more opportunity for us, and everyone won't know everyone's business like they do in small towns."

"Like Big Oak?"

Abby shook her head. "Oh, no. More like San Francisco."

"Huh. I guess we have time to figure it out," Jesse said, eyes fixed on Gwen. "They're too little to make that trip now anyway."

"Actually, it might be easier on them to take them down while they're still babies. More than likely they'd sleep most of the way."

"So, you think we should leave this summer?"

"I don't see why we couldn't," she said. "Why put it off if it's what you really want to do?"

Jesse nodded. "I do, but I'm not sure how Toby's going to feel about it. I think he might want to stay here."

"What makes you say that?" Abby asked, cocking her head.

"I caught him and Aponi holding hands." The corners of Jesse's mouth twitched. "Something about the way they were looking at each other, well…might be something to it."

"Did you ask him about it?"

"Uh-uh. I don't think he wants me to know or he would've said something. I'll wait and see if he brings it up first. If not, I'll ask him about it and see what he wants to do." Jesse shifted the conversation. "Have you ever been to San Francisco?"

Abby curled up next to her. "Once. A few years ago, but it was only for a couple of days."

Jesse asked, "What's it like?"

Abby and Jesse lay awake for hours. The more Jesse heard, the more she wanted to see the sprawling city for herself. It sounded more like a place of fantasy than reality. Something in her gut told her it was exactly where they needed to be.

CHAPTER THIRTEEN

Notes of pine saturated the crisp, clean morning air. It smelled of freshness, of life returning to the mountain after another harsh winter. The songs of birds echoed through the trees, their melody in full agreement with the season as Jesse and Toby sat at the water's edge, their horsehair fishing lines slicing through the current of the stream. Jesse stared at the deadfall of leaves and twigs that had collected in an eddy. The detritus swirled like the words she contemplated, the ones she'd put off for far too long.

Her brother had feelings for Aponi, that much was certain. For whatever reason, though, he kept those feelings to himself. He couldn't hide his emotions from her, he never could. When he learned they were leaving Mount Perish, he said nothing. He didn't need to. Despite their years apart, Jesse still knew when something was eating at him, and she'd come to know all too well the grip of love. Their life on top of the mountain was coming to an end, as was the opportunity for this passion to bloom. The time was now to have the discussion.

She looked over at her brother. "I'm sure going to miss this fishing hole. Maybe we can find a better one when we get settled."

"Are you sure you wa-want to leave this place?" he asked, already pulling in a fish.

She could hear the apprehension in his voice. The world hadn't been kind to him and she didn't blame him for not wanting to go back to it. She'd felt the same thing. It wasn't easy for her to walk away from her home, either. Most days she walked around as if she'd swallowed rocks, a shaky smile forced into place and held aloft by invisible clothespins. But she knew it was for the best.

"I'm going to miss the mountain too, but it's no place to raise a family. Besides," she said, shrugging her shoulders, "what do we have to lose? If we don't like it down there, then we can always come back, right?"

"I suppose so. It's just..." he shook his head. "Never mind."

"No. Finish your sentence," she said, pulling in a fish of her own.

"It's nothin'."

She took her eyes off of the catch and looked at him. "I know," she said.

He met her gaze. "And just what do you th-think you know?"

She looked down and continued removing the hook. His words came out with the sting of accusation, but she knew him well. "I know you have feelings for Aponi," she said, pulling the leather thong through the gills. She set her pole down and continued. "I've seen you two together. It's pretty obvious you have feelings for her."

The relief that his sister knew the truth flitted by, a

butterfly too quick to catch. "Not th-that it matters. We're leaving soon."

"Does she know how you feel about her? You know she is welcome to come with us."

"She knows. She feels the same way 'bout me. I asked her to come, but she won't leave the mountain. She thinks her people won't approve of her being with a wh-white man. I told her to just sneak away and not tell th-them, but she won't. Says that would bring dishonor upon her."

Jesse tried to think of something, anything she could say or do to make things right for Toby and Aponi. "Um…I might be able to talk to the elders and see if I can get their blessing." She patted him on the back. "It's worth a try."

He combed his fingers through his beard. "Do you think th-they will come 'round and approve?"

"Not sure, but what do we have to lose by asking? Let's go and find out."

On their walk back to the cabin, Toby divulged some of Aponi's past only he had been privy to. Aponi was a few years older than he was and had once been married to the great-grandson of the tribe chieftain, Black Turtle. He went on to explain how chosen members of the Ponak tribe traveled to other villages each spring, a yearly ritual in which they observed the movement of the white men. One year after returning, the men of the tribe brought back not only vital information, but also a sickness that spread through their village. The plague seemed to hold no preference, indiscriminately striking down the young and fit as it did the older members of the tribe. Whether the victims were male or female mattered not. Not even children were spared. It showed no prejudice.

Nearly half the Ponak had been lost, including Aponi's parents. Then her husband fell ill and passed away not long after. Since his passing, no other man of the tribe would be with her. It wasn't that they had no desire. No man chanced insulting the chieftain by daring to ask for her hand. Aponi had been a widow for eight years now.

Jesse hoped it had been long enough for Black Turtle to free her from the shackles of her past.

Sitting at the table, Jesse swallowed the last bite of fried fish. "We'll be there by this evening. If all goes well, we should be back late tomorrow. Are you sure you're all right staying here by yourself?" she asked Abby. "I hate the thought of leaving you alone."

Abby shifted Jim in her lap, careful not to bump the table and spill the morning's cup of coffee. "Jes, we'll be fine. You two just be careful." She turned to face Toby. "I sure hope things turn out for you and Aponi. I like the idea of her being part of our family."

Jesse repositioned Gwen in her arms and scooted back in her chair. She picked up her plate.

Abby shook her head. "No. Leave it. I'll clean up. You two get going. The sooner you leave, the sooner you'll be back."

Jesse kissed Gwen before laying her in the cradle. She grabbed the supplies needed and met Abby, who waited at the door with Jim on her hip.

"You be a good boy for your mother," Jesse said as she adjusted the leather satchel around her neck. She bent down and kissed him on top of his head. Then she looked at Abby.

"You be safe and don't you step outside unless you have the gun."

"I know. Believe me, you don't have to worry about that. Be safe. Both of you."

Jesse picked up her rifle. "We'll see you tomorrow."

"I'm counting on it," Abby said, running her hand down Jesse's arm.

Abby watched from the doorway as they set out. When she lost their outlines to the dark of the forest, she closed and latched the door.

Conversational lulls throughout the trip gave Jesse time to plan, or at least try to. She racked her brain for anything that might convince these people to allow the joining of two races. While it seemed simple, she knew the wrong approach might offend them and sour the whole possibility.

They reached the village as the early evening sun stretched the shadows out across the mountain, much to Jesse's relief. She wasn't comfortable with Abby being alone. She wanted—needed to get back as soon as possible.

The people of the tribe were scattered about, clustered in groups, performing all types of tasks. Jesse spotted Aponi among the women tanning hides, and then saw Kaga seated with a group of men crafting arrows. She and Toby made their way toward Kaga.

"Good to see you, my friend," Jesse said.

Kaga stood and nodded. "And you."

"I have some news. May I speak with Black Turtle?"

Kaga held up his hand. "Wait here," he said, and then made his way toward a gap in the mountain.

Jesse took in the activity around her as she waited. She looked for more familiar faces among the teepees that now dotted the landscape. The native way of life fascinated her. The place had changed significantly since her last visit. In the winter months, they sheltered in the hollows of the mountain. When it got warm, they moved to the open grassy areas. Fires burned in front of many of the teepees, filling the air with a variety of aromas. Some made her stomach rumble, a reminder of the hours since she had eaten. Others were so unpleasant she could only imagine what the pots might contain.

She was thinking of her own experiences with the bitter native medicine, mouth going dry at the thought, when Kaga's voice rang out behind her. "Come."

Jesse grabbed Toby's arm before he took a step. "I think you should wait here. Let me test the water."

Toby nodded and watched as she followed Kaga into a cavern.

Inside, a group of men sat around a fire. Black Turtle, the chieftain who had performed her initiation into the tribe, waved her forward. He pointed to an opening in the circle of men. "Sit."

Jesse did as instructed, her legs crossed in front of her.

"What news you bring us?" he asked.

"I'm leaving the mountain on harvest moon and will be gone for many, many moons." She glanced at the men seated around her as she continued. "If I ever hear of white men crossing the river, I will return and together we will protect our mountain."

The circle of men nodded their approval.

"Here, I have something for you." Jesse reached into her leather satchel. She pulled out the envelopes of seeds she had purchased in Big Oak and offered them to Black Turtle. "You take these seeds. Grow many, many crops."

Black Turtle upended a packet into a weathered palm and examined the contents. She could tell by his expression he was pleased with the gift.

Holding up a hard black kernel as if it were the most precious of beads, he asked, "What you 'em want to make trade?"

Offering them the gift had been the easy part. She cleared her throat. "I want us to join together with a marriage."

The men looked at one another in confusion. She would have to be more specific.

"I make a treaty with tribe. To come with news if I ever hear white men are coming on our mountain. I give you seeds to plant all sorts of crops. I only ask one thing in return." At the last second she chose not to single out Aponi, in case they thought her idea one of lunacy. "I want to join my brother with one of your women."

Black Turtle nodded. "You leave us. We talk this trade."

She stood and left the group, leaving the men to discuss it among themselves.

Toby hurried to her side as soon as he saw her exit the cavern. "Well—what d-d-did they s-s-s-say?" he said, his words dragging more than usual in his rush to get them out.

"They're talking it over," she said, placing her hand on his shoulder. "But, I think it went well."

Jesse and Toby stood on the westward-facing ledge of Mount Perish, awash in the magnificent scenery. She tried to remain hopeful as the sky went from orange to pink to purple, the sun slowly dipping from sight.

The stars had all woken up by the time Kaga came and found them. Jesse and Toby trailed behind as they made their way back inside the cavern.

Jesse saw Tala first. The thirteen-year-old was dressed in a beautiful tunic, a woven garland of white and yellow spring flowers crowning her head.

"Tala make good wife for Toby," Black Turtle said, pointing to the offered bride.

Jesse looked at her. The whites of her eyes were large, standing out in stark contrast against her russet skin. The girl was terrified.

It had been a horrible mistake to leave Aponi out of her request. She scrambled for a way to decline without causing offense. She rubbed the scar on her forehead, racking her brain as she stalled to find the words. "Uh... Tala is good trade, but..." She pointed to her brother, "He wants Aponi for his wife."

The men remained silent and focused their attention on Black Turtle. Even members of the tribe who were interested in Aponi had never had the audacity to ask this of him. Everyone in the space seemed to be holding their breath, curious to see how the chief would react.

Jesse had the sense she would have to offer more—much more. She turned to Toby, hiding her mouth behind a closed fist. She whispered, doing her best not to move her lips. "Offer him the rifle."

Toby took the gun from her and extended it to Black Turtle. "Trade for Aponi?"

Black Turtle rose to his feet and took the weapon. He ran

his hand along the wood handle and traced it all the way to the end of the barrel.

Jesse held out the powder horn and a pouch of lead balls.

Black Turtle studied the items held out in front of him. "Aponi my family." He tapped his finger on his chest. "She daughter to me." The Chieftain looked down at his bare feet, trepidation visible. He lifted his head, wistfulness in keen eyes. "She mourn eight summers," he said. He reached for the powder horn and pouch of ammo. "Time she mourn no more. I make this trade. We join 'em this night."

Jesse and Toby stepped outside, both feeling giddy over the trade.

"I can't believe you gave th-them your rifle," Toby whispered.

She shrugged and whispered back. "I don't think we had a choice. We had nothing left to offer."

An hour later, Jesse stood in the mix with the tribe, wishing Abby could be there to witness the ceremony. Under a sky sprinkled with stars, she watched as Toby and Aponi took their places in front of Nateko.

The bride-to-be, looking more lovely than usual in the glowing firelight, was dressed beautifully in a white-leather tunic with fringe running down the sleeves. Blue and gold feathers hung from her ears, matching those adorning her outfit. Her hair, black as ink, was drawn into two long braids. They fell on each side of her face, framing her cheekbones.

Nateko draped a piece of beaded fabric over Toby and Aponi's outstretched hands, binding them together. He looked out at the gathering and spoke. "The Great Spirit here. Listen and you hear the voice on the wind." He turned his gaze to the couple in front of him. "Great Spirit say you see no more darkness, for you're each other's light. You will brave many storms, but will face it together. Remember in the blackest of clouds, the sun is still there." He paused and waited.

Black Turtle's wife, Lewonta, approached the couple and draped a blanket, woven with animal hide and fur, over the couple's backs.

Nateko continued. "You no feel the rain, for you're each other's shelter. You feel no more cold, for you're each other's warmth." He placed his palm on the fabric that bound their hands. "Two lives are now one. May the Great Spirit allow your days together in this world to be long, and may the Great Spirit bless you many sons and daughters."

Jesse waited for the traditional kiss, but it never came. It wasn't part of the native ceremony. Instead, Toby and Aponi were escorted to a raging bonfire. The entire village celebrated the couple by feasting and dancing around the red and orange pillar. Eager young men kept the fire stoked with logs, never giving it a chance to die down, for this was a night of celebration.

Tears welled in Jesse's eyes as she watched her brother and his beautiful wife dance. Aponi moved around Toby in a spirited fashion, her face aglow. The tempo of her steps, quick and agile, kept pace with the drumbeats. Measured at the start, they grew to a crescendo, the fringed sleeves of her tunic held high above her head. Her shadow, cast by the light of the bonfire, looked like a graceful bird ready to take flight. The smile on Toby's face was unmistakable in the light from the flames. Jesse wished so much that her parents could see him and what a wonderful man he had turned out to be. She wished Frieda could have had the chance to meet him, too.

Jesse pushed against the sadness, unwilling to let the past creep in and bite her when such happiness grew in front of her eyes.

Winded, Toby came over and dropped down beside her. "I can't believe it. I'm the luckiest m-m-man alive," he said, panting.

Jesse smiled. "Being in love is a great feeling, isn't it?" She nudged him with her shoulder. "Have you got to kiss your bride yet?"

Toby shook his head. "No. We n-n-never have."

Jesse couldn't help it. She laughed out loud at the thought of what was going to happen later. "Brother, I think tonight is going to be the best night of your life."

"I can't imagine being any happier than I am right now."

Jesse laughed even harder. "Just wait!" she said as she stood up and joined in the dance.

The celebration continued until the drumming and singing came to an abrupt halt. The women of the tribe giggled as they guided Aponi to a teepee, followed by the men of the tribe escorting Toby.

The drumming and singing resumed, even louder than before. Jesse wondered if it was to help drown out the sounds of lovemaking. Either way, she was grateful. There was no way she wanted to hear any of what went on in her brother's teepee that night.

CHAPTER FOURTEEN

"Jes," Toby said, kneeling down at his sister's side. Getting no response, he shook her by the shoulder and repeated her name, louder this time. "Jes!"

Jesse, lost deep in a dream, mumbled and pulled the blanket up to her chin.

"Jes! Wake up." He shook her more forcefully, which did the trick.

"What?" She bolted upright, sending the blanket to the dirt beside her. She squinted at him. "What's wrong?"

He sat down beside her. "Nothin's wrong. I just don't feel right 'bout wh-what you did."

"What'd I do?" she asked, rubbing sleep from her eyes.

"I know how much that rifle m-meant to you. Isn't there something else we can offer 'em instead?"

Jesse yawned and stretched, trying to cure the stiffness of sleeping on the hard ground next to the fire. "I don't have anything else. It's all right."

"But it wa-was Frieda's. And I know it means a lot to you."

"It does—did. But you mean more. Don't worry 'bout it."

She cracked a smile. "I think we came out better in the trade anyway. Don't you?"

"Yes. But—"

She raised a hand. "But nothin'. It's done and over with. So, did you get any sleep last night?" Her arched brow gave away that she already knew the answer.

"A little," he said, burning cheeks crowning his thick beard.

"Well, spare me the details. Are you two going to be ready soon? I want to get home." She stifled another yawn.

"I'll go get ready." He put his arm around her. "Thank you."

"Welcome. Now go," she said, eyes already closing as she reclined. A little more rest wouldn't hurt before the trip.

Toby returned to the teepee where he and Aponi had spent their wedding night. He found his new wife rolling up a hide, one of her few possessions. She didn't hear him come up behind her. He pulled aside one long braid, exposing her neck. "Good m-morning," he said, kissing the soft skin.

She put her hand on the back of his head, fixing his lips in place. "Mmm," she murmured.

He slid the leather tunic from her shoulders, not rushing the moment. She took his strong hands and guided him back onto the deer hide, pulling his body down on top of hers.

Outside, as the rising sun tinted the horizon, birds called out to each other by name. Jesse stared at orange embers, kept by her own thoughts from returning to her dreams. The dying fire popped, the first sound breaking the stillness as the mountain came to life. She lay silently, though three names echoed through her head. She pictured what waited for her at the cabin, the image clearer than any daguerreotype photo she'd seen. Being separated from them was pure agony.

Soon, a new song broke the early silence, this time coming from the newlyweds' teepee. Jesse buried her head under the blanket and hummed to herself. When that proved inadequate, she hummed louder.

It would be another hour before Aponi and Toby came out to join her.

The sun was sinking by the time the trio reached the cabin. Jesse's heart fluttered at the sight of Abby, who sat on the front porch waiting on them.

With Gwen in her arms, Abby rushed down the steps, closing the distance. "Oh, it's so good to see you. All of you. I take it things went well?"

Jesse took Gwen from her and lifted her playfully into the air. "Oh, look at those cheeks," she said. "I think you grew another inch while I was gone." She kissed her daughter's cheek and then cradled her in her arms. "How's Jim?" she asked, looking at Abby.

"He's fine. He's sleeping. So, how'd it go?"

Jesse grinned. "Let me introduce you to Mr. and Mrs—"

Abby grabbed hold of Aponi's arm. "You two are married?"

Aponi and Toby smiled, their heads bobbing in unison.

Jesse, anxious to see Jim, put her free arm around Abby. "Well, let's go inside and they can tell you all about it."

Toby and Aponi sat at the table with Abby, filling her in on every detail of their ceremony. Jesse lay on the bed, entertaining the three-month-old twins.

Abby could barely stay focused on the conversation around the table. As much as she wanted to hear everything, every little detail, the sight of Jesse playing with the twins was too much. Her heart felt like it would burst.

Toby and Aponi barely finished their story before Abby excused herself. She wished them good night as she pulled the curtain closed behind her.

Jesse glanced over her shoulder. "Look, he's trying to roll over," she said, her voice shaking with excitement.

Abby sat on the bed and slipped her hand beneath Jesse's shirt. "It won't be long before he's able to do it," she said, running her fingers over the soft-fine hair on Jesse's lower back. "I should probably feed them and get them to bed."

Jesse put on a pair of long underwear, stretched out on the bed, and waited on the twins to finish.

Once they were fed, Abby lay Gwen in the cradle and returned for Jim. "I'm going to put him in with her," she said, picking him up.

"You sure you want to put them together? Won't get much sleep."

Abby flashed a sheepish grin. "Who says I plan on sleeping tonight?"

Jesse got the hint. It had been months. Aching months, longer and more distant than most. Still, she whispered, "We can't."

Abby lay down beside her and put her mouth next to Jesse's ear. "I'm fine. Really. Don't be scared."

"I'm not scared. It's just...well, they're right there," Jesse whispered, tilting her head up toward the loft. "This is why I can't wait to get a place with some privacy."

"Mm-hmm," Abby murmured, nibbling on her earlobe.

Jesse let Abby explore her body, quivering silently each time Abby's lips touched her already heated skin. She leaned forward and drew Abby's face to her. "You drive me crazy," she whispered, grazing her lips over Abby's before guiding her onto her back. Jesse lay on top of her. "Let me show you how it—"

The wood above them squeaked rhythmically and Jesse and Abby traded knowing looks. Jesse rolled off of her and together they used a pillow to hide their muffled laughter. When the hilarity subsided enough for her to speak, Jesse pulled the pillow away. "See," she whispered, staring at the plank floor of the loft above her, "not an ounce of privacy in this stupid cabin."

Abby curled closer and placed her head on Jesse's chest, lightly running her fingers on the soft skin of her neck. "Soon. We won't have to worry about such things."

Jesse forked her fingers through Abby's hair, unfulfilled desire making her jumpy. "C'mon," she said, unexpectedly log rolling out of the bed to glance in the cradle.

Abby sat up. "Where are we going?"

Jesse pulled off the blanket and tucked it under her arm. She bent over to blow out the candle on the bedside table. "Outside," she said, in an evocative tone. Her eyes, the same deep shades of green as summer grass in the meadow near the cabin, sparkled with intention as she blew out the flame. Abby bit her lip as she slid from the bed and padded silently beside her.

On their last August morning on the mountain, Jesse woke early. Quietly, she dressed and went to the grave of her old companion. She sat on her heels next to a pile of moss-covered rocks. "Oh Frieda, I will always be grateful for all you did for me, and loving me like your own." She released a long, slow breath. "I think this is the right decision for us. I wish you were here to meet them. I know you'd love them as much as I do."

She used the back of her hand to wipe away the tears slipping from her eyes. She stared at the mound, ignoring the numbness in her legs, until Abby's hand on her shoulder roused her from thought.

Abby knelt down beside her. "I wish I had the chance to get to know you. Thank you, Frieda, for taking such good care of her. Thank you for everything."

Jesse laced her fingers through Abby's. "We should probably get going." She paused for one last look before leading the way back to the cabin.

Jesse hated to leave so many belongings behind. Frieda's carvings were some of the hardest to part with but there were far too many to take. She did pack a few of her favorites, along with Frieda's pipe. Caught up in collecting those most important to her, she failed to notice the lopsided deer missing from the center of the table.

When they went to leave, Jesse paused at the threshold, her eyes studying the cabin that had been her home for so many years.

Abby slipped her hand into Jesse's. "I'm going to miss this place," she said. "I know I wasn't here long, but it felt like my home."

"I know. It's not easy to leave," she said, still focused on the interior of the cabin.

A faraway look came into Jesse's eyes. For a moment, she

saw herself as a ten-year-old girl, lying in the bed as she caught her first glimpse of the woman who would have such an impact on her life. She could practically smell the stew as the scene unfolded in her minds eye, Frieda hunched before the fireplace stirring the contents of the large pot. The image shifted to the table where she sat with a book open in front of her, Frieda hovering close by to make sure she stayed focused on her schoolwork. Her eyes were drawn to the bed again. How hard it had been to sit there and hold Frieda's fragile hand, watching as the life drained out her.

Jesse was aware tears were streaming down her cheeks, but she made no move to wipe them. Her breathing came in hitches and her vision was blurred.

"Maybe you and I will come back someday," Abby said, resting her head on her shoulder.

"Maybe we will." She palmed her tears away and took a steadying breath. "You ready?"

"Mm-hmm."

Jesse closed the door on her past, at peace knowing it was the right decision for her family's future.

In the days leading up to their departure, Aponi had made cradleboards, native baby carriers, for the trip. With Abby toting Jim and Aponi carrying Gwen, Jesse and Toby led the way, each guiding a horse loaded with as many possessions as they could manage.

Jesse fought the temptation to turn back for one last look as the forest rose up around them. Instead, she decided to focus on the path underfoot: the path leading to the new life waiting for her and her family.

CHAPTER FIFTEEN

Jesse, Abby, Toby, and Aponi all traveled with heavy burdens as they descended the mountain. The weight of their physical possessions did not encumber them nearly as much as the mental burdens they carried, which only grew heavier with each step they took.

Jesse had made the trip numerous times, the route as familiar as her own hand, but now she saw the forest as if for the first time. The trees seemed to mock her, concealing danger in the thick underbrush flanking the trail. She kept alert, always listening and scanning the dense foliage for anything which could harm her family.

Every shadow morphed into a predatory animal, crouching, waiting to pounce on its prey. A black stump, rotten and crumbling, transformed into a bear, ready to attack. Even a timid brook, with a couple inches of water babbling over its rocky bottom, was enough to slam her heart against her ribs. How in the world did she think she could guide them all safely across the Devil's Fork?

At night, Jesse sat by the fire watching the twins, her

twins, consumed with worries for their future. Even though she had removed Frieda's gold from under the floorboards, and had all of it tucked safely in her saddlebags, she had no intentions of using it. Up until now she had been living by her own merits and she intended to keep going the same way. She needed to find a way to support everyone. When she cuddled under the blanket with Abby, too exhausted to keep her eyes open, the fear crawled around in her mind, keeping sleep at bay. She woke in the mornings fatigued, mentally and physically. Still, she forced a smile, not wanting to reveal all the uncertainties overwhelming her.

Toby had never been much of a talker, so his silence was not unexpected. Although he had come out of his shell since being reunited with his sister, no one could blame him for being unnerved. He was returning to a world that had been unkind to him and knew all to well what folks thought about him. He recalled the nights he had spent curled up alone in the back of the barn, a cut or bruise from some recent attack stinging on his cheek. His only comfort had been the sounds of the horses sharing the space with him. He had wished time and time again that he had died with his family on that horrific day.

As he grew, the physical beatings became less frequent. Instead, those who wanted to hurt him used words to attack. He learned to hide his pain, finding solace among the horses. With a hand on their withers, he'd rest his face against their necks, speaking softly, until he felt the stinging insults slip away. Even after all the years, some of the words never lost their power.

Toby glanced ahead on the trail at his wife. He never wanted her to experience the kind of torment he'd had to endure all those years and silently vowed to do whatever he had to do to protect her. He was a man now, not some wounded boy crying amongst the horses. If he had to, he would give his life for her.

Abby had heard women say you couldn't know love until you looked into the eyes of your child. She had always thought the words silly, the ramblings of women whose minds were as narrow as the confines of the homes their over-bearing husbands kept them in. Now, each time she heard Jim fuss, or turned to see Gwen's small head bobbing behind Aponi's, the words finally made sense. Even her love for Jesse, as powerful as it was, couldn't match the love she had for her children. With it came a burden she had never felt before: the need to protect and provide for them at all costs. The weight of it bore down on her so heavily she felt she couldn't breathe.

Not only did Abby have to worry about her babies, she knew Jesse, Toby, and Aponi were counting on her as well. She was the only one of them with any real-world experience. Abby worried especially for Aponi, about how she would be received. She knew there would be discrimination because of the color of her skin. With these extra burdens, it took all of her will to put one foot in front of the other and keep moving forward. Her driving force was her family. They needed her.

Aponi was terrified. She knew what white men were capable of. She had been hearing the stories for as long as she could remember. Her people had always been either fighting against those men or trying to avoid them. Now, she was giving up her way of life to be with one of them. Her husband was a good man. She loved him. Still, if a white man like Toby was reluctant to go back, how could she not be scared? The others said they understood how she felt, but could they really?

One person truly understood Aponi's fear: Black Turtle, the man who had been like a father for so many years. A single tear welled in the corner of his eye when they had said their goodbyes. Aponi pretended not to notice. She released his hands and turned to go, her own tears burning. She looked back one final time as she crested a hill, setting to memory an image of the chief waving to her, surrounded by a sea of teepees scattered across the grassy field. She wanted to run back to him and that life. Bravely, she turned and walked away without another look back.

They made most of the journey in silence, each one consumed by their own thoughts. Only their footsteps, the call of birds, and the occasional baby's cry broke the lingering hush.

"Whoa, Buck." Jesse pulled on the reins and brought the horse to a stop beside her. Jim's crying wouldn't stop and his cheeks were soaked with tears. He'd been cutting teeth, making him fussy. She took out her knife and cut a small piece of rawhide from the cradleboard. She pulled Jim from his carrier and returned to her place at the head of the line. Reins in hand and Jim cradled in her arm, somewhat pacified as he gnawed the leather thong, they continued down the mountain.

Four days later, Jesse stood staring at the Devil's Fork, moon-light glancing off the water as it rushed past. She could barely hear Abby humming softly to Jim as she nursed him beside her, the familiar melody broken by the thundering river. A fine bead of sweat broke out on Jesse's upper lip. She had been nervous when she brought Abby across the first time. What she felt now was terror. She had to take them all across. She forced herself to take a calming breath, took hold of Titan's reins and stepped into the water. The chill as it engulfed first her feet then her legs shocked less than she'd expected, owing either to her focus or her fear.

Slowly and cautiously, she led the horse across. The river pushed and pulled, a living thing with grasping tendrils that did not want her to pass, but it was no match for her resolve. Once safely on the other side, she wrapped Titan's reins around a tree branch before returning across the river. Buck went next. After unloading the supplies, she made the trip back.

The lives of her loved ones depended on her. This had to go right. The thought of a horse falling into the river was horrific, but what of the most precious cargo—her family? She pushed back against the fear before it could choke her. Her jaw clenched so tightly she thought it might shatter. The water roared in cacophony with her own heartbeat and the ringing in her ears.

On horseback, one meticulous step at a time, she ferried Abby and Jim across first. Then all together, she ferried Gwen, Aponi, and Toby. Not until everyone was across did her breathing return to normal, her legs feeling as bendable as willow branches.

When they bedded down for the night, Jesse fell asleep almost instantly. The stress of four long, tiring days, the stress she'd been walling in so she could take care of her family, finally caught up to her. She slept like a rock.

Jesse woke before dawn, listening to everyone's soft breathing punctuated by her brother's loud snores. Though calmer than she had been in days, she still felt on pins and needles. She analyzed everything that had taken place over the last few months, hoping she hadn't overlooked anything. Not wanting to hide she had a brother, she convinced Toby to go by the last name of McGinnis. And, in an effort to keep anyone from questioning the twins' paternity, she thought it wise to change their birthday.

Hidden in the trees on the outskirts of Ely, Jesse and Toby dismantled the cradleboards. They scattered the wood pieces in the dense underbrush, making sure not to leave any visible trace of native handiwork. The rest of the material they stowed in the saddlebags as Abby and Aponi slipped behind the trees and changed into dresses.

Finally, with horses in tow and babies on their hips, the foursome headed toward the Nicholas' house.

The door flung wide open, seemingly as soon as Jesse knocked on it.

"I'm so happy to see you," Edith said, beaming, looking from one person to the next. "All of you please come in." Once they entered, she asked excitedly, "Abby, which one is yours?"

"Both of them," Abby said, smiling.

Edith's hand went to her mouth. "You had twins?"

Abby nodded.

Edith turned and faced Jesse. "I wish I could've seen your face when you found out you had two," she said with a chuckle.

Abby lifted the brim of Jesse's hat, brushed her bangs aside, and put her finger on the pale scar on her forehead. "This was the reaction. Passed out cold," Abby said, grinning.

"Yeah. Ha, ha." Jesse pulled her hat back in place. "Edith, this is Jim," she said, indicating the baby in her arms. "And that's Gwen."

Edith ran her finger lightly over the infants' cheeks. "Aw. You two make beautiful babies."

Abby saw no signs of Edith's baby. She hoped nothing had gone wrong. "Where's your little one?"

"Oh, I put Burton down for a nap. He'll be raisin' Cain soon. He can be quite a handful." As Edith spoke, Abby noticed the dark blotches beneath her eyes. The woman's face told the truth. Abby wondered if similar things were in store for her. Only time would tell.

"Edith," Jesse said, "this is my brother, Toby. And his wife, Aponi."

"I remember you," Edith said, looking at him. "I didn't know you and Jesse were brothers."

"Yes, ma'am. Good t-t-to see you again."

Edith couldn't help but notice the drastic change in Toby. Although she had only met him once, briefly, he wasn't as simple as she remembered. He seemed to carry himself with more confidence now. She turned to face Aponi. "Well, you're lovely as a sunset," she said with a warm smile. "Please come in the kitchen and let's get caught up."

Rooted in place, Jesse asked, "Can I ask you for a favor?"

"Sure. What do ya need?"

"We're going to stay at the hotel, but I don't feel comfortable keeping all of our things there. Can we keep our stuff in your barn for a couple days?"

"You go right ahead. There's plenty of room for your horses, too."

"Thank you. Why don't you girls go on and Toby and I will be back shortly," Jesse said.

"Come on." Edith led Abby and Aponi by the arm. "Can't wait to hear everything about everything."

Jesse and Toby unloaded supplies and got the horses settled in stalls. Saddlebag draped over her shoulder, they headed for the hotel.

It appeared to be the finest building in town. The Ely Grand Hotel stood three stories high, with flag banners draped from each multi-level balcony. Jesse took hold of the iron handle and pulled open the heavy walnut door. A strong scent of fresh paint greeted them as soon as they stepped inside. Both of them craned their necks to stare at the ceiling high above, crowned by ornate molding. The walls had intricate molding as well, framing a floor so polished Jesse's own reflection stared back at her. In the center of the room hung a crystal chandelier. The facets of its many pieces cast blades of light across the room at all angles, slicing it into a million magnificent pieces. Off to one side of the lobby led a stairway, reptilian in the way it curled up the wall.

Jesse was a bit overwhelmed but swallowed her nerves as they approached the desk. She cleared her throat. "I need two rooms."

"How many nights?" the desk clerk asked.

"Two."

"That'll be eight dollars."

Her brow furrowed. "Eight dollars?"

"Yessir. Two dollars a room per night for two nights. That adds up to eight dollars."

Although surprised by the high price, she reached into her pocket and handed over the money.

"Rooms sixteen and seventeen." The clerk placed two keys on the counter and pointed toward the staircase. "They're on the second floor. And it's hotel policy, if you leave for any reason, you must bring me back the key."

She agreed, thanked him, and snatched the keys from the counter. As she and Toby climbed the stairs, she felt insecure. Would she really be able to fit into this life—the life Abby knew firsthand—the life she knew nothing about? She saw the same questions playing across Toby's face as she unlocked room sixteen. She turned the knob and they stepped inside.

"Well, there's nothing grand about this place at all," she said.

The room was small. A tall, narrow window at the foot of the bed allowed light into the room. The bed, much too big for the area, took up most of the space. Off to the side stood a three-drawer dresser. On top sat a porcelain basin and pitcher with a mirror hanging above it. A plain wooden chair had been pushed tightly into one corner, and a chamber pot stuck out from underneath the bed.

They found room seventeen identical. "It'll do," she said. "C'mon. Let's go see about getting tickets."

Downstairs, she set the keys on the counter. "What times does the stage run?"

The man behind the desk picked up the keys. "Depends on where you want to go and when." He turned and placed the keys on the allotted hooks on the wall behind him.

"The one that runs to San Francisco."

He turned back toward the counter. "Comes in at noon through the week. There isn't one on the weekends."

"I need to book two seats," she said. "Two days from now."

The clerk pulled a heavy book out from beneath the desk and tossed it down in front of him. He thumbed through the pages until he came to the one he was searching for. "Names?" he asked as he dotted his pen in the inkwell.

"Abigail and Aponi McGinnis. How long does it take to get down there?"

"That depends on the traveler. You can ride straight through and be there in a day and a half. Or, you can get off and stay at one of the stops along the way." He closed the book. "But if you decide to get off and stay, there is no guarantee that you'll get a seat on the next one going out. And that'll be twenty dollars."

Again, Jesse was stunned by the high cost. "For each ticket?" she asked.

"No, sir," he said. "That's for both."

Jesse paid for the tickets and she and Toby headed toward the trading post. She kept a tight grip on the saddlebag over her shoulder. It held all of Frieda's gold and she certainly wasn't going to let it out of her sight.

The bell above the door jingled, pulling Felix's attention away from the customer he was helping. He waved and then hurried to finish the transaction. While they waited, Jesse and Toby examined a steamer trunk.

A couple minutes later, Felix approached. "Well, how the hell are you?"

"We're good. Felix, this is my brother, Toby."

Felix offered his hand to him. "How long you boys staying in town? Is Abby with you?"

"She and the babies are with Edith."

His head jerked. "Babies?"

"Abby had twins—"

Felix ran his palm over his slicked back hair as he processed the news. "Well, I'll be!" One baby was exhausting enough. He had been totally unprepared and had no idea how fussy babies could be until Burton came along. He wasn't sure if he should congratulate Jesse or offer pity.

Jesse said, "We're leaving with the stagecoach on Thursday and heading down to San Francisco."

"Well, how about tomorrow evening you come to the house and have supper with Edith and me before you go?"

"We'd love to. Hey, you know those panniers I bought down in Big Oak?"

Felix nodded.

"Well, I don't need them anymore. Can I trade them in on that?" Jesse asked, pointing to a trunk.

"I think we could work something out." He twisted the ends of his curled mustache as he thought over a fair deal. "Tell you what. You give me the panniers and five dollars and I'll make the trade."

"Great. I'll unload 'em and get 'em to you tomorrow. If that's all right with you."

"That'll be fine. And go on and take the trunk now if you want."

Jesse and Toby each grabbed an end and carried it back to the Nicholas' barn. When they went in the house, they found the women at the kitchen table chatting away, each balancing an infant on their lap.

Jesse knelt on one knee beside Edith and took hold of the baby's tiny hand. "This must be Burton. That's a strong grip you've got there," she said when he latched onto her finger.

"Where did you two run off to?" Abby asked.

"Went to the hotel. Got our rooms and the tickets. And I swung by to see Felix." She let go of Burton's hand and stood. "We should get going."

"You don't have to head out already, do ya?" Edith asked.

Jesse said, "It's been a long trip and we need to put them down for a nap. I could use one myself. Felix invited us for supper tomorrow evening so we can catch up."

"Oh, that'll be wonderful. I'm already looking forward to it."

Jesse smiled at her. "Me too."

Jesse pulled out two of the dresser drawers and placed them on the floor beside the bed.

"What are you doing?" Abby asked, Gwen at her breast.

"Making a place for them to sleep." Jesse put a blanket in the bottom of each drawer.

After Abby finished nursing the twins, Jesse got them settled in their makeshift cribs. When she lay down next to Abby, sleep found all four of them quickly.

A few hours later, Jesse woke alone in the bed. She sat up and stretched. The twins, sleeping soundly, brought a smile to her lips before the yawn had fully escaped. The creak of the doorknob pulled her attention from the sleeping infants.

"Oh, good. You're up," Abby said, easing the door closed behind her.

"Why? What do you need?"

Abby sat beside her on the bed. "You, Jesse McGinnis. I need you. Now get dressed. We're going out."

"But they're still asleep."

"Aponi is coming to watch them as soon as they get back. They were hungry, so I went with them to the Tin Plate. I thought maybe you and I could have a nice night out. Just the two of us."

When Aponi arrived, Jesse draped her saddlebag over her shoulder. She escorted Abby down the hall. "I won't miss listening to that every night," Jesse said, laughing as they passed her brother's room. The door seemed to vibrate with his snoring, amplifying the noise.

"Something tells me you probably will," Abby said. "You're too sentimental not to."

After sharing a wonderful supper, an evening spent reminiscing about their first time at the Tin Plate and marveling over how much their lives had changed since, Jesse stood and retrieved her hat from the chair pushed in beside her.

"Would you mind if we swung by The Foxtail?" Abby asked as Jesse scooted out the chair for her. "I want to see if Mabel's there."

"All right." Jesse offered an elbow.

As they approached the saloon, noise spilled out into the street. Jesse felt uncomfortable already. Even Abby, once such a vital part of life at The Foxtail, found herself missing the serenity of their covered porch back at the cabin. How quickly she had changed. Abby had been unaware of the shift until Jesse pushed open the door to a packed saloon. Still, she was excited to see Mabel.

"C'mon, over here." Abby pulled Jesse toward the bar.

"Well, I'll be. If it ain't Miss Abby," said the man behind the counter.

Abby flashed him the smile of an old friend. "Hi Luke. How are you?"

"Good. Good. And you?"

"I couldn't be better. Luke, this is my husband, Jesse."

Jesse reached across the bar and shook his hand.

"Is Mab—"

Someone grabbed Abby from behind. She somehow knew it was Mabel before she even turned.

"I've missed you so much," Abby said, pulling Mabel into an embrace. The two women held onto each other, their friendship having diminished none by their time apart.

"It's so good to see you," Mabel said, finally breaking from the embrace to step back and get a better look at her. "I heard you came to town last year and got married. I'm so sorry I wasn't here."

"C'mon already." A man tugged on Mabel's arm, whiskey on his hot breath. "I'm not payin' ya to chit chat."

Mabel scowled. "Damn. Keep your shirt on. I'll be with you in a minute."

Abby continued. "I wish you could've been—"

A familiar face, one Abby thought she would never see again, came into view and stole the words from her mouth.

"Abigail Flanagan. It's good to see you," said a man with a husky voice.

Abby swallowed hard, felt the blood drain from her face. "S-Sam...Hi."

He gave her a quick peck on the cheek. "How have you been?"

"I'm good. Great actually." She put her hand on Jesse's arm. "Sam, this is my husband, Jesse McGinnis."

He extended his hand. "Sam Bowman. It's nice to meet you. Abby told me all about you. It's good to put a face to the name."

Jesse kept her grip firm as she shook his hand. "She told me all about you as well."

The Sam Bowman Jesse met wasn't the one she had conjured up in her mind. He was much more handsome, taller, and more distinguished than she had imagined. With soft hands and manicured nails, she could tell the man had never seen a hard day's labor in his life. Clean-shaven except for a fine-line mustache, and dressed in a tailor-made suit of the finest material, he was an imposing figure.

She groaned inwardly and wondered again how she had been fortunate enough to win Abby's heart.

Sam released her hand and reached for the elbow of the beautiful blonde woman on his right. "This is my wife, Helga," he said with a smile.

Standing a good three inches taller than him—long, curvaceous, blonde, and busty—no one could mistake the woman for an average housewife. She was gorgeous.

"Hej," Helga said in a thick Swedish accent.

Sam signaled for Luke to bring a round of shots. "These are on me," he said.

Luke placed four shot glasses side by side, poured whiskey into all four with one swipe of the bottle, and slid the glasses across the bar. Sam handed one to Abby.

"Uh…no thank you."

"Don't like our whiskey anymore?" Sam asked, teasing.

"It's not that. It's…well, I'm a mother now. I have to be up early and—"

"Abs, you had a baby?" Mabel said, interrupting her, excitement in her voice.

Abby held up two fingers. "Twins."

When Mabel and Abby hugged, Jesse glanced at Sam. He was looking quizzically at Abby.

Sam asked, "How old are they?"

Jesse spoke up. She and Abby had prepared for this moment, the words cocked and loaded days ago. "They were born April 15th."

He silently mouthed off the months of the year, counting off the time since he and Abby had been together. The fact the twins were premature only aided the deception, their small size easy proof they could be four months old instead of six.

"Ut of all der dayssen." Helga shook her head in disbelief. "Datten's a dayyen ve'll nevfar forget."

Neither Abby nor Jesse had any idea what she was saying and stared at her wordlessly. Before Abby could ask, Mabel chimed in.

"I still can't believe it. It shows you what a mad world we live in. If the President can be shot and killed, then how can any of us really be safe?"

Abby looked to Jesse. Both of them were shocked, but knew better than to ask about it. It wouldn't seem likely they'd both missed the news of Lincoln's assassination.

"C'mon, or forget it," the paying man said to Mabel. He tugged on her arm more forcefully than before.

Mabel allowed herself to be pulled away. "Abs, I'll meet you at the hotel in the morning. We have a lot of catching up to do," she said over her shoulder as she followed her customer toward the stairs.

Sam finished running his calculations. He picked up two of the shot glasses and handed them to Jesse and Helga. The remaining two he took for himself. After tapping his glasses to theirs, he tossed back both shots and slammed them back on the bar.

The piano began to play as Abby's replacement took the stage. Sam leaned in close to Abby. "She's not nearly as good as you. Can I have a word with you, in private?"

Abby looked at Jesse. She didn't feel she needed permission, but she wanted to make sure Jesse felt comfortable with it.

Jesse nodded.

"We'll be right back," Sam said.

He led her to the office he shared with Boone, where he took a seat in the leather chair behind the desk. Abby took one of the chairs in front of the desk.

"I just wanted to make sure you're all right. I know some women have to pretend when they're around their husbands. Are you happy? Does he treat you well?" Sam leaned back in his chair.

"I am happy and truly blessed to have such a caring husband." Abby knew she had probably hurt Sam when she broke off their relationship. She didn't want to add salt to any open wounds, so she reverted the question back to him. "Are you happy?"

"Yes. The first time I saw Helga, I knew she was the one for me," he said, leaning his elbows on the desk. "As a matter of fact, we're leaving first thing in the morning on our honeymoon. She wants to go to Paris. I just had to drop off some paperwork for Boone before I leave."

"Oh, that sounds like a lovely trip. How long will you be gone?"

"Three months," he said. He stood up, walked to the front of his desk and took a seat on the edge closer to her. "You know you'll always be special to me." A faraway look came to his eyes as he spoke. "As a matter of fact, there was a time I thought we would be the ones getting married."

"I did, too."

Sam shook his head, clearing the thoughts, bringing clarity to his eyes once again. "So, what are your plans? You raising your family in Ely?"

"No. We're going down to San Francisco."

"Well, it's a small world. I just bought some property down there a few weeks ago. Helga is having it renovated as we speak. She likes things kind of fancy, if you know what I mean."

Abby smiled. "I'm sure she just wants to make a nice home for you."

"The money she has me spending on it…" He paused and scratched the back of his neck. "Well, it's downright foolish. Hey, maybe we'll be neighbors."

"I doubt we can afford your neighborhood. We haven't found a place yet. We're going to look as soon as we get there."

Sam stood and went back behind the desk. He pulled a piece of paper from a drawer and jotted down an address. He handed it to her. "I'd offer you the main house but it's going to be a mess inside while they're doing the work. But you're more than welcome to the house next door until you find a place of your own. I'll send a wire in the morning before we leave and let Andrew know you're coming."

"Andrew?"

"Yes. He's my right hand. He's in charge while I'm away."

"Oh, Sam. Thank you. Thank you so much. You don't know what this means to us."

"You need anything, you just ask Andrew. Come on. They probably think we ran off together," he said, only half joking.

Abby hugged him. "Thank you again."

"You're welcome. Oh and hey, if you ever get the itch to sing, I have a new place down there. It's called The Bay Water. I'd be thrilled to have you."

"I appreciate that, but I think my singing days are over. For now, anyway."

They returned to find Jesse and Helga chatting up a storm. Abby was surprised. She had never seen Jesse so talkative.

The four spent the rest of the evening getting acquainted with each other. The conversation was fluid, as if they were long lost friends catching up.

Jesse could see why Abby was attracted to Sam. She wanted to dislike him. He had been with Abby, after all. But she couldn't. He was a kind man, and in the short amount of time she spent with him, she found herself enjoying his company. Again, she asked herself what Abby could possibly see in her.

Sam and Helga's stories of their life and travels enthralled Jesse. She knew she still had a lot to learn about the world and all the things in it, but the more she heard, the more she wanted to see these things with her own eyes. And it wasn't lost on her that Helga was living the lavish lifestyle that could have belonged to Abby. She could be traveling the world, living in the finest homes, and never worrying about money. Abby had given up all of that to have a life with her.

After a wonderful evening, the foursome made their way back to the hotel. The couples retrieved their room keys from the clerk and said their goodbyes. Sam and Helga went to their suite on the top floor, Abby and Jesse to room sixteen.

Jesse turned up the lantern, noticing right away the room was empty. "Aponi must be watching them in her room. I'll go get 'em," she said.

"Uh, no you won't. Aponi is keeping them for the night," Abby said, turning down the lantern. Only the soft glow of moonlight, spilling in through the window, lit the room. She unfastened the top button on her dress and went on to the next. "Tonight, you're all mine. No babies. No one sleeping in the loft above us."

Jesse took Abby by the waist and pulled her close. Their lips met, softly at first and then more frantic.

It had been a long time.

They hurried now, pulling at each other's clothes, rushing to see who could undress the other the fastest. Jesse's shirt and pants fell to the floor, followed by Abby's dress. Abby led Jesse to the bed, and pulled her down on top of her.

CHAPTER SIXTEEN

G unshots echoed through the dark woods, shattering the still of the night. Wildlife in the dense brush scurried away, their invisible paths marked only by the quick crunching of leaves and the rustle of dry grass. The birds in the treetops flapped their wings as one and disappeared. Clutching the wound on her side, Jesse, eyes large and white with fear, collapsed to her knees. Blood spat from the wound on Jake Roberts's neck. The ringing in her ears was so loud that she couldn't hear the deafening roar of the waterfall tumbling over the rocky bluffs behind her.

Jesse's pupils danced frantically beneath her closed lids and her legs fought to free themselves from beneath the tangle of sheets as the dream shifted. She found herself standing in an unfamiliar home, Abby seated at a nearby table. Fear took hold when she tried to move toward Abby and found her body unwilling to obey the simple command. It felt as if her feet were glued to the floor.

The snap of splintering wood broke the odd hush. Adrenaline tingled through Jesse's body when a man kicked open the door. Though she had never met him, she knew who he was—Silas. Her mind's eye had created its own rendering of Abby's deceased husband.

Jesse saw fear register on Abby's face. Desperately she willed her body to move, to step between the woman she loved and the man coming through the door. When it wouldn't budge, she watched helplessly, frozen, as Silas jerked Abby up by her arm. Horror accompanied her paralysis when Silas drew back his fist.

Jesse's arms flailed, a painful moan escaping her each time Silas landed a blow. The final punch connected with such force Abby crashed to the floor. Jesse shot up in bed, panting and sweat-soaked as her eyes snapped open. She glanced around the room, disoriented, her heart hammering. *It was just a horrible nightmare,* she thought as she fought to calm her racing pulse.

She slumped back against the pillow, contemplating the nightmare. For years after the brutal murder of her family, she had been plagued with terrifying dreams. It had been such a long time since she had had one; she hoped she'd outgrown them. The only conclusion she could think of was their return had been brought on by the uncertainty of living off the mountain.

It dawned on her then that she was alone in the room. No Abby. No twins. Her sleep-addled brain needed time to catch up. She glanced under the sheet and sucked in a breath when she realized she was naked. Slowly, she recalled Aponi had kept the babies last night. A smile tickled at the corners of her mouth as she thought about what had taken place in this bed a few hours ago, and how Abby had never been more beautiful than in the pale glow of the full moon. During the night their bodies had been bathed in soft light coming through the lone window, which now lit up the room like a flare.

Jesse threw off her thoughts like she did the sheet. She dressed, squinting against the bright morning sunlight. Sitting on the edge of the bed, she pulled on her boots, and noticed the chamber pot poking from underneath. It reminded her of Frieda and all the hours she spent sick, unable to care for herself. *No thank you,* she thought. With the heel of her boot, she pushed the container until it was out of sight. She would use the hotel's communal privy out back.

Finished with the morning necessity, Jesse went to Toby's room. "Anybody in there?" she asked, knocking on the door to room seventeen.

Aponi opened the door. "Just the twins and me."

Jesse entered the room, her eyes going straight to the babies. "They didn't give you any trouble, did they?"

"Oh, no," Aponi said, smiling. "They good for me."

"Good," Jesse said. "Where's Abby and Toby?"

"Don't know." Aponi shrugged. "When Abby finished nursing this morning, they left. Said they wouldn't be gone long."

Jim was fast asleep. Gwen, however, looked around with wide, alert eyes. Jesse picked her up. "Good morning, little girl. Did you sleep well?" She kissed her on the cheek and held her against her chest, breathing in the smell she had come to love.

The door opened. "Well, look who finally decided to get up," Abby said. She couldn't resist the opportunity to tease Jesse, who seldom slept in.

"Ha, ha. Where'd you go?" Jesse asked. When Abby stepped aside, it took her a moment to recognize the smiling stranger in the doorway. She ran her hand along her brother's newly clean-shaven jawline. "Well, I'll be. Soft as a baby's bottom."

"C'mon," Abby said to her as she picked up Jim. "I have something to show you."

Jesse noticed the envelope in Abby's hand as she followed her back to their room. "So, how'd you convince him to shave off his beard?" she asked.

"I didn't. Aponi did. She didn't like it. A man's beard can be very rough. So, he asked me to take him somewhere to get a shave this morning. Here," Abby said, handing her the envelope, "read it." Jesse lay Gwen back into the makeshift crib and took a seat next to her on the edge of the bed. Abby continued, "When I went downstairs, the man behind the counter said it was left for me early this morning."

Jesse pulled the letter from the envelope and read it.

Dearest Abby,

Helga and I had a fine time last night. We wish our visit wasn't so short lived. I've made arrangements for my driver to meet you when you arrive in San Francisco. He will take you to my estate. I hope this will lift some of the burden from you. Also, if you need anything, do not hesitate to ask Andrew.

I was impressed with your husband. I could use a man like him at The Bay Water. I've wired the head of my security, Mitchell Franks. He has orders to put Jesse on the payroll, if he's interested.

I hope to see you when we return. Wish us smooth sailing.
Bon Voyage,
Sam

Jesse folded the letter and slid it back into the envelope. "I can't believe he's doing all of this for us. Last night, when I first met him, I didn't want to like him. But the more I got to know him…then this." She held up the letter. "Well, I feel bad for not telling him the truth about the twins."

Abby put her hand on Jesse's leg. "Sam's a wonderful man, but I don't think he'd have any interest in raising children. He's always away on business. He'd be just fine placing his children in a boarding school and letting someone else raise them. That's not the life I would want for the kids."

"So, what do you think of me working for him?"

Abby's brow furrowed. "Absolutely not."

"But—"

"But nothing. You're not working in a saloon. You'd be out all night and it's too dangerous. I don't want them to be orphans," she said, glancing at the twins.

"All right. We'll figure things out as we go. I need to go pack up and get those panniers to Felix."

Abby picked up Jesse's hat and put it on her head. "Mabel will be here shortly. Then, I need to run by the post and get some more fabric to make extra diapers for the trip."

Jesse gave her a kiss. "Enjoy your visit and I'll meet you at Edith's later this afternoon.

Edith, Abby, and Aponi spent all afternoon preparing a feast. It had been a long time since Jesse had tasted Edith's cooking. She couldn't wait to put a taste to the smell. Everyone took places around the table. With hands joined and heads bowed, Felix gave the blessing. Afterward, they all dug in, the scraping of utensils against fine china plates filling the room. As the food disappeared, conversation flowed.

Jesse took a few more bites and then set her silverware down. She needed to discuss something serious with Edith and Felix. "I hate to keep asking, but I need another favor from you," she said.

"What can we do?" Edith asked. She set her own cutlery aside, giving Jesse her full attention.

"It's about Mount Perish."

Felix paused, focusing on Jesse, his knife and fork stationary above his plate.

"I need to know if men ever plan on stepping foot on it."

Felix went back to cutting his chicken. "You mean when they figure out how to cross the river," he said. He took another bite of food.

"Yes."

Felix swallowed. "Why do you care about that old mountain?" he asked, pointing with his knife over his shoulder in the direction of the mountain.

"I...I've just always been fascinated by it. That's all. I'd love to do some trapping on it. So, if you ever hear of them building a bridge or figuring out some other way to cross, will you please let me know?"

"You know Felix always hears all the gossip," Edith said, picking up her silverware. She smiled and continued, scooping up peas on her fork. "You think women like to talk? Please. You men have us beat."

Felix smiled. "You send us your address when you get settled and if I ever get wind of anything, we'll let you know."

The rest of the meal was ideal, except for Burton's screaming tantrums. Jesse couldn't believe the differences between the twins and him. No matter what Edith tried, nothing seemed to soothe him.

After a delightful evening, they left Sam Bowman's address with Edith and Felix, telling the Nicholas' they would forward the new address when they moved into a home of their own.

The big morning arrived and after a hot meal at the Tin Plate, the only thing left to do was to get the horses and meet the stagecoach at noon. Jesse and Toby headed over to Edith's barn to get Buck and Titan. Aponi and Abby stayed behind at the hotel, visiting with Mabel, who had come by to see Abby before she left.

Edith entered the barn to find Jesse and Toby mucking the stalls. "Well, you boys all ready to go?"

"Just about," Jesse said, dumping manure-caked straw into the wheelbarrow.

"Felix has to mind the store, but Burton and me are coming to see you off."

Jesse smiled. "I'd like that."

They led the horses through town while Edith walked alongside, trying to soothe Burton through another screaming fit. Jesse couldn't help but notice Toby's expression. She wondered if Burton's behavior would turn her brother against the idea of wanting children of his own, or if the twins' peaceful nature would convince him having children really wasn't that bad.

Everyone gathered on the street in front of the hotel, watching the approaching cloud of dust.

"I'm sure going to miss you—all of you," Edith said to the

small group huddled together. "Don't be strangers, and try to get back for a visit from time to time."

Jesse placed her hand on Edith's shoulder. "If you ever get down to San Francisco, you better look us up."

"We will. You be careful and have a safe trip."

The coach rolled to a stop, a swirl of dust settling in its wake. As the seven passengers got off, Abby and Edith hugged as best they could with babies in their arms.

The driver quickly unloaded the baggage and then gave a signal. Jesse and Toby hoisted the steamer trunk up to him.

Mabel kissed Gwen and handed her over to Aponi. She then wrapped her arms around Abby.

Jesse could see the sadness in Abby's red-rimmed eyes as she clung to her best friend. She knew the pain of leaving behind the ones you care about.

Mabel kissed Abby's cheek and took her place next to Edith. Both women's hearts weighed heavy as Abby mounted the stage steps.

"We'll be right behind you," Jesse said, helping Abby board.

Abby took her seat next to Aponi. "You two stay safe back there," Abby said, leaning through the small window.

"Yes, ma'am," Jesse said, winking.

After five other passengers loaded, the driver closed the door. Abby, still leaning out the window, waved goodbye as the stage rolled away.

Jesse turned to Edith. "Don't forget to send me that letter if you ever hear of anyone crossing the river."

"I know. I won't forget. Promise."

"You take care." Jesse swung up in the saddle.

Choked on tears, Mabel said, "You take good care of 'em."

Jesse smiled. "I will. And you know our home will always be open to you."

Mabel nodded and sniffled.

Riding out of town, Jesse stopped and turned Buck around for one final look. Edith stood with her hand waving high in the air. To Jesse, it felt like the sad ending to something safe and familiar, yet at the same time, the start of something new and exciting. She returned the wave, turned Buck, and with a quick click of her tongue she rode out of Ely.

CHAPTER SEVENTEEN

The few clouds drifting overhead did little to shield Jesse and Toby from the relentless heat of the sun bearing down on them. The only breeze they felt on their way to Big Oak, the first stop en route to San Francisco, was cast off from the stagecoach. It offered no relief, kicking up plumes of dust in its wake, the dirty powder feathering through tall tussock grass alongside the road as it rumbled past. Small groups of cattle huddled together under the trees, seeking shade from the scorching sun.

Jesse, coughing from the dust collecting in her throat, kept Buck at a smooth trot as she trailed behind. The mouthful of ever-present grit crunched between her teeth and sucked the moisture from her tongue. She tugged at her sweat-soaked collar and swatted away the horsefly buzzing in front of her face. Only an hour into the trip, she cursed it all: the sun, the insects, but most of all, the constant veil of dust that shrouded her.

An hour and a half later, the stagecoach driver sounded the

bugle. They'd arrived in Big Oak. Once the stage had rolled to a stop, she rode up alongside it. She bent down and rubbed Buck's sweaty shoulder before dismounting, kicking up her own small cloud as her boots hit the ground. The dirty particles had become an inescapable plague.

Abby stepped through the door of the coach. When she saw Jesse, she broke out in laughter before reaching the bottom step.

Jesse took off her hat and combed her fingers through her sweat-soaked hair. "What? What's so funny?" she asked, adjusting the hat back on her head.

Abby kept laughing. She couldn't help it. "You. That's what. You should see your face," she said, shifting Jim to her other hip.

Jesse swiped a hand down the side of her face. It only smeared the grime, her fingers leaving lighter streaks through the filth. It looked much worse, causing Abby to laugh harder. Jesse spat a murky glob into the street. "And you think riding inside is dusty. Ha! Try riding behind one." She offered a crooked smile revealing teeth, which stood out white as snow against her dirty complexion.

"Sorry. I know I shouldn't laugh. We'll be stopping in Lagro in a few hours. You'll have time to clean up then," Abby said.

It felt good to wash down the grit and stretch their legs, even if it was only for ten minutes. Jesse and Toby had barely finished tending to the horses when the driver signaled for everyone to board.

As the wheels of the stage started to roll, Jesse stood beside Buck, reins in hand. To the west, Mount Perish loomed in the

distance, its wild and towering pres
somehow comforting. It dawned on her ho
going to miss the mountain—home.

The realization took her breath away in
scorching sun and dust could not. Letting go of her
able, familiar life crushed her with a fear she did not u
stand. She had been parting with pieces of her true self o
the years, leaving them scattered on and around the mountain
she knew and loved, but it was terrifying to leave behind this
life. *Her* life. Still, something inside drove her to follow this
new road, if only to see where it would lead.

Buck's whiskery chin brushed against her cheek, offering a
welcome reprieve from her thoughts. She scratched away the
tickle and released a slow and steadying breath, trying to calm
her rising anxiety before swinging up in the saddle. There was
no quelling the inner fear as she rode out of Big Oak for the
last time.

It wasn't long before Jesse and Toby were riding on cracked
and bumpy terrain. Green meadows gave way to stunted
bushes and prickly, flowering plants. The countryside seemed
to consist of dirt as far as the eye could see, everything dry,
dying, or dead. Wilted scrub and withered trees, all in shades
of brown and ashen gray dominated the landscape. It was a far
cry from the lush vegetation growing in the foothills of Mount
Perish. A hawk screeched and circled overhead, searching for
anything skittering through the underbrush. *Poor bird is going
to starve to death looking for food here*, Jesse thought. She hoped
San Francisco didn't look so barren.

The brash call of the bugle sent a tingle down Jesse's spine.
They'd arrived in Lagro. Situated at the base of a canyon, the

a brown-thatched roof. The
towering in shades of gray
lated and sad ambiance. It
ernight stay, or they could
nce the stagecoach horses
es. Either way, the two
a bite of food and make

......ow plank bench at an oversized
......oard table. Dark patches spattered its top, tokens of previous travelers. Large tin platters, battered from years of abuse, sat spaced along the tabletop. Some were piled high with what appeared to be fried pork resting in hearty puddles of grease. Others had been heaped with biscuits, dry as the surrounding landscape.

Abby, motion sick from the last hour of the trip, couldn't bring herself to eat. Simply looking at the food made her stomach roil. She leaned over and whispered in Jesse's ear. "I don't want to stay here. Do you feel up to riding through the night?"

Jesse felt lighter. The odd building squatted in the middle of nowhere gave her a bad feeling. She swatted at a fly, keeping the bug from landing on her plate and said, "I don't want to stay here either." She shifted Jim on her lap and looked over the table at Toby and Aponi. "You two want to keep going? If not, we'll stay here tonight. It's up to you."

Aponi looked at Toby, her exceedingly anxious facial expression giving away her thoughts before she spoke. "I don't want to stay here, but I will if you want to."

Toby smiled. "Let's keep going."

Jesse nodded and swatted away another fly, or maybe the same one. "We best hurry up and eat before the flies beat us to it."

Abby shifted her body away from the food. "You go ahead," she said. "I don't want to eat. Besides, I need to feed them."

Jesse started to stand, but Abby stopped her with a hand on her shoulder. "You just stay here and eat. I'll be fine."

"You need to eat too," Aponi said.

Abby gave an involuntary shudder. "My stomach isn't doing well. If I eat that," she said, pointing at the greasy slab of meat, "I'll be sick for sure." She stood and repositioned Gwen on her hip.

"Stay close," Jesse said, reaching out to give Abby's hand a sympathetic squeeze.

"I'm just going to step out back. Besides, I could use the fresh air."

"You start feeding her and I'll bring him out when I finish," Jesse said.

Abby took Gwen outside and fed her in the privacy offered by the station's shadow, while Jesse gulped everything down as fast as she could. It wasn't the kind of meal for enjoying, anyway. Before heading out back she snatched one of the last remaining biscuits. It would be a long night, and Abby may want it later.

Jesse pulled on Buck's reigns, bringing him to a halt. The leather saddle squeaked beneath her when she turned to look behind. Mount Perish, an ever present and towering part of her life had been shrinking with each passing mile. Watching the transformation somehow made leaving more real. The mountain looked wonderfully bright and beautiful in the last throes of daylight and she stared at it, sad and fearful, watching as the sun dipped below the horizon.

Toby rode back to her. "What's wrong?"

"Nothing." She shifted her weight in the saddle. "C'mon, let's go." With a nudge to Buck's flanks, she and Toby were off to catch up with the stagecoach yet again.

She glanced over her shoulder one last time. The sky—a dark, purple-grey bruise—erased the mountain from her sight.

Everyone breathed a sigh of relief when the sun had set, taking with it the heat of the day. The sun-bleached landscape took on a milky-white glow in the light of the silvery moon as they continued onward.

After the second of two quick stops to switch out spent horses for fresh ones, the driver brought the stagecoach to a stop in the middle of the dirt road. Dark clouds had rolled in, heavy and pregnant with rain. He lit the lanterns hanging on hooks at the front of the stagecoach. They continued on at a much slower pace, the glow from the lanterns barely penetrating the blackness stretched out before them.

Jesse struggled against fatigue, willing her eyelids open that grew heavier by the hour. Silently, she sang the song Abby had written for their wedding. Over and over the melody played, a music box in her mind as she traveled in the wake of her family. Her mind raced throughout the night ride, its pace matched by Buck's steady hoof beats. She thought back on Sarah, one of many young girls forced to sell themselves to survive. She had wanted to do something, anything to help her and her situation, but Abby told her it was common for women and girls to sell their bodies to paying men. Abby forewarned her there would probably be more of that where they were headed and she needed to realize it was sadly the way the world was. Jesse pushed the disturbing thoughts from her mind and tried to focus on the positive things she had heard about San Francisco—the big city—their future home. In reality, she had no idea what it would be like. In her mind, she envisioned a place bustling with new and interesting things for her to experience.

As the first bands of sunlight crept across the sky, Jesse peeked over her shoulder. No sign of Mount Perish. Something sank in the pit of her stomach. The mountain had been the only constant in her life, a presence never more than a glance away. Now it had slipped below the horizon, taking with it the life she had known up until now.

Jesse jerked in her saddle at the sound of the bugle blast announcing their arrival in Cottonwood. She was thrilled to be there—anywhere. Exhausted, she desperately needed a break, as did Titan and Buck.

Pulled alongside a second stage, men had already begun shifting loads from one to the other. They rushed against the storm that threatened with dark clouds flying in their direction. Their current driver and stage would be returning to Ely. On the next leg of the trip, they would be on a different stagecoach with a new driver.

"How'd they do?" Jesse asked Abby as she stepped down from the stage, Jim in her arms.

"They got fussy last night, so I fed them some tiny pieces

of biscuit. It helped because it didn't take them long to fall back asleep. They just woke up when they heard the horn."

"You have to be starving." Jesse reached out to take Jim.

"I am," Abby said. She pointed to the dark clouds off in the distance. "Looks like rain is coming."

"Yeah, I noticed that, too. Come on. Let's go inside and get you something to eat."

The group went into the large farmhouse. A few people from the earlier stage were already eating at tables, ones much cleaner and more appealing than those at the last stop. The aroma of frying bacon filled the room, prompting Jesse's stomach to growl.

A woman approached. "Ma'am, you can use that room there to feed your youngins if you want," she said, pointing to a side room.

"Oh. Thank you."

Jesse turned to Toby and Aponi. "You two go on and get something to eat. We'll be right back."

Sitting in a well-used rocker, Abby fed Gwen, soothing the fussiest baby first. When she finished, Jesse took Gwen out to the well to change her. Holding her with one hand, she cranked up the bucket with the other.

Aponi came out to help. "I can do that for you," she said.

Jesse smiled. "You go on and get something to eat. I can manage. We'll be in soon."

Aponi walked back around the corner of the house. She stopped short when a man stepped in front of her, blocking her path. His dusty clothes had taken on the bleak color of the trail. He looked her up and down as the corner of his mouth turned up, half smirk, half sneer. "Well, look at that," he said to his companion, a gaunt man leaning up against the porch post. "A real live injun squaw."

Aponi's body trembled. She stayed silent.

The man leaning against the post stood up straight, grabbing the top of his head as if protecting it. "Best keep an eye open. She'll cut off your scalp when ya ain't lookin'," he said, squinting through the smoke of the cigarette dangling from the corner of his mouth.

Aponi's heartbeat hammered in her ears. She flinched, her feet coming off the ground, when a hand came to rest on her shoulder.

"Go inside," Toby said.

She made no effort to move.

"Well, lookit that. We got us an injun lover," the stranger said. He pulled the bent, hand-rolled cigarette from his lips with dirty fingers and spat on the ground.

Toby was used to this sort of harassment and had always thought it best to keep his mouth shut. In the past he would have cowered—let them give their licks. He wanted to be a different man now. Jesse told him his size alone was enough to deter most men. His sister's words rang through his head as he squared his shoulders, rolled up his sleeves, and walked toward the men. Inside, his heart tripped, but on the outside he presented himself as a fearless man who didn't take crap from anyone.

The man had to look up to meet Toby's eyes, as Toby stood half a head taller. "Now, keep your shirt on," the man said, flicking his cigarette onto the ground. "No need to get into fisticuffs 'bout it." He turned toward his friend. "C'mon," he said, walking off. "We got work to do."

Toby was stunned. For the first time in his life he had

stood his ground. *Jes was right.* Maybe things would work out all right after all. A sense of relief came over him as he took hold of Aponi's hand. He led her back inside, feeling ten feet tall.

Babies changed, Jesse and Abby finally sat at the table next to Toby and Aponi. Neither had any clue about the confrontation that had taken place.

They ate a breakfast of scrambled eggs, bacon, and a hunk of bread, all washed down with a cup of chicory coffee. It was the darkest, strongest coffee Jesse had ever had. It tasted glorious. They hadn't yet finished eating before the driver announced it was time to leave.

Jesse, saddlebag draped over her shoulder, reacted when she felt someone's hand on her. Without looking or thinking, she grabbed the offending wrist.

"I'm sorry. Didn't mean no harm," an older woman said. Jesse loosened her grip as the woman continued. "I just wanted to say I think it's lovely you help your wife the way you do. Charles here," she said, tilting her head toward the old man standing next to her, "wouldn't change a baby if his life depended on it." She chuckled.

"Come on, Harriet," the old man said. "Don't bother them." He led her away by the arm.

Jesse and the old woman exchanged smiles as her husband escorted her out the door and toward the stage bound for Ely.

Jesse shoved one last bite into her mouth, washed it down with a large swig of coffee, and headed to the stage. She looked up at the new driver. "How much longer until we get to San Francisco?"

"Depends on the weather. If that storm doesn't cause us

THE DEVIL BEHIND US

any trouble and nothing holds us up at the next few stops, we should be there in seven hours."

Jesse nodded. She swung up in the saddle as a bolt of lightning forked across the sky. She winced, not from the crack of thunder, but from the pain racking her already-sore muscles. She prayed nothing would delay them. She was dirty, tired, and more than ready to get there.

CHAPTER EIGHTEEN

They reached San Francisco in the afternoon, and Jesse followed the stagecoach as it rolled through the city. Despite being road weary and saddle sore, she was awestruck by her surroundings. Her head swiveled, like a weather vane in a storm, as she took in all the sights. The fatigue of the road evaporated when she thought back to her first trip to Ely. It had been merely a watering hole compared to this place. She remembered standing in the middle of the street, nearly run down like some lost child. That same feeling of naivety weighed on her again as she rode further into the sprawling city. She hoped she had made the right decision by leaving the mountain.

A bustling mix of faces and races in all manner of dress passed by, unseeing as they hurried along, scuttling through the maze of streets branching off of the main road. Unlike Ely, where everyone knew each other and often stopped to talk, the throng here moved along frenzied, anonymous, rarely speaking. They scattered like worker ants in all directions. Though Jesse noticed little interaction among them, the din all around her was surprisingly loud. It was as if the whole of the city was a busy night at The Foxtail.

Down an alleyway, several men stood at the back of a wagon. Jesse watched them wrestle a large barrel down a plank and through an opening into the side of a large, brick building. Their shouts, mingled with clomps from their booted feet on the wooden sidewalk, was an abrasive song with a drunken, chaotic rhythm. With her attention diverted, she barely managed to pull back the reins when a boy ran out in front of her. His small, filthy hand clutched a shiny red apple. She twisted in the saddle, watching as his dirt-smudged face mixed into the crowd behind her. Up ahead, angry shouts drowned out those of the barrel-hauling men. An older gentleman, white apron strings dangling, stood in front of a storefront waving his fist and yelling, his thick mustache twisting like some out of control caterpillar. She couldn't understand most of what he said in his heavily accented voice, but two words came across quite clearly: "Stop! Thief!"

The bellowed admonition fueled the boy's flight. Jesse watched as he frantically elbowed his way through the throng of people and disappeared. She wished she could vanish so easily. The clamor of the place was too much for her and she had to fight the urge to turn Buck around and let him carry her back to the relative calm of Mount Perish.

She caught sight of her brother up ahead. The look on his face told her he was feeling the same, probably worse. She could not imagine the memories triggered by being surrounded by people. For all she knew, he had been forced to steal much like the boy with the apple. *Never again,* she thought. She swallowed her fear and nudged Buck to close the distance with the stage.

No breeze stirred, yet she could still smell a hint of salt in the air, even above the stench of so many bodies pressed together. She focused her attention on the buildings crowding each side of the wide street rather than the swarm of people pushing in on all sides. A shimmer towered into view when she turned a corner. Before her stood the tallest, most ornate building she had ever seen. She had to crane her neck to see the entire façade, inlaid with high-arched windows of multi-colored glass fragments.

A clanging echoed through the streets, distant but loud. She twisted in the saddle again, using her hand to shield her eyes from the glare of the afternoon sun. She could make out the tops of sails on the clipper ships docked out in the bay. The crying of gulls circling overhead announced her proximity to the ocean.

The trip had been exhausting. In many ways the city felt more dangerous than the mountain. At least there she knew what to watch for. Here the unknowns seemed to be all around her, closing in, making her feel powerless. Still, she'd seen enough already to know this was what she wanted for her family. She knew if they'd stayed on the mountain her children would grow up to be fiercely independent and self-reliant. She wanted more for them than that: education, culture, and a better chance at finding love someday. She would make the trip a thousand times to ensure the twins had access to everything the world had to offer.

At last, the stage rolled to a stop and Jesse and Toby tied their reins to a hitching post outside the depot. Jesse hurried to meet Abby as she stepped off the stage. One look told her she was spent.

Although Abby tried, she couldn't quite force the thin line

of her mouth into a true smile. Jesse searched for any happiness in her eyes, but the puffiness rimming them was too dark to penetrate. Jesse hoped they didn't have much further to travel. They were all in desperate need of rest.

"'Cuse me, suh?"

Jesse turned to find herself face-to-face with the largest man she had ever seen, towering even over Toby. "Yes," she said, craning her neck to meet his gaze. Not only was he the tallest man she had ever seen, but also the first black person she had ever spoken to.

"You be Mr. McGinnis?" he asked, his voice a deep but gentle rumble.

She nodded. "Uh-huh."

"Suh. I'se Cuffy. I'se to bring you to the Bowman place."

"Nice to meet you, Cuffy. This is Mrs. McGinnis. And that is my brother, Toby, and his wife, Aponi," Jesse said, gesturing to her family.

Cuffy made no move to shake hands, but instead nodded greetings. "I'se needs your bags."

"The trunk is all we have," Jesse said, moving toward the stage. "We can get it."

"No suh," Cuffy said, reaching over her. "That's what I'se do." He lowered the heavy trunk onto the ground to get a better hold, the sunlight shimmering in beads of sweat on his bald head. "Come wid me."

Jesse watched in fascination as Cuffy wrapped the leather straps around his hands and hoisted the trunk with no assistance, nor even a slight grunt. She knew exactly how heavy it was. She could tell by Toby's face that he too was impressed by Cuffy's brute strength.

He led them to a carriage, polished red with matching

spokes. Two geldings stood waiting, black as ravens, their coats glistening in the bright sun. The clean, ornate vehicle stood in stark contrast to the dust coating everything in the street. Cuffy secured the trunk on a ledge at the back of the carriage. Stepping back around to the side, he opened the door and offered his gloved hand to the women. Abby, cradling a sleeping Gwen, took hold of his hand as she stepped inside. Her own fingers felt tiny in comparison to his. Aponi and Jim followed.

Jesse peeked her head inside. "We'll be right behind you." She couldn't help but notice the smell of the new leather seats. She gave Abby's hand a squeeze and then stepped back.

Jesse and Toby rode behind, staying as close to the carriage as possible, never letting it out of their sight. The plain houses and level streets soon gave way to larger homes along a gentle rise, which then gave way to a steep incline. She looked back over her shoulder. The homes they'd first passed looked like a child's blocks scattered at the bottom of the hill.

The finest homes Jesse had ever seen flanked the street at the top. The obvious wealth was stunning, almost in the realm of children's stories. She'd imagined many different versions of the city's opulence. The reality was like and yet so unlike all of them.

The carriage came to a stop midway between two houses. They were larger than any Jesse had ever known. She thought of the cabin on the mountain and the tepees stretched across the native village. That people lived in structures like these gave her a slight dizziness she shook from her head. It wouldn't do to let awe get the best of her now.

Jesse reined in her horse, bringing him to a stop. A raucous flurry of construction activity reverberated from the larger of the houses as men moved about, totally oblivious to the newcomers watching from the street. Behind the house being renovated, Jesse spied a smaller brick building. *That must be the guest house,* she thought.

Cuffy offered his gloved hand once more as Abby and Aponi exited the carriage. The physical strain of the trip was beginning to show in the weak but grateful smile Abby offered him. Beside her, Aponi stared wide eyed, her expression slightly anxious.

"Tie your hosses to the wheel, and I'se see to 'em after I gits this inside," Cuffy said, untying the rope from the trunk.

Jesse and Toby wrapped their reins around the carriage rim and followed as Cuffy led them toward the guesthouse. Jesse, not paying attention to where she was going, bumped into Abby, who had stopped abruptly in front of her. She had been expecting to go on to the brick house in the back. Instead, they were led to the large home facing the street.

"This is the guest house?" Jesse asked.

Cuffy said, "If'n you want to call it that."

"What do you mean?"

"Mr. Bowman gots both. Them workin' on that one now." Cuffy tilted his head to the house next door, then nodded to the house in front of him. "Then he be knockin' this one down."

Jesse was dumbfounded. They were set to demolish one of the finest houses she had ever seen. She wondered how many families could have used all that space. Curious, she asked, "What's that building?" She pointed to the brick structure in back.

"Carriage house," Cuffy said.

Carriage house? Jesse let the words echo in her mind. She

couldn't believe someone would spend all that money on a building made entirely for livestock and tack. A lot of people would feel blessed to have a home even a fraction as nice. She knew she would. The difference between her cabin and the carriage house alone was like night and day.

Cuffy set the trunk down on the stoop. He twisted the brass doorknob, pushed open the heavy, walnut door, and motioned for them to step inside. Jesse, hat in hand, had to remind herself not to let her mouth hang open. As nice as the house had looked from the outside, it had not prepared her for the extravagance within. The rugs looked far too expensive to be walked upon by dirty boots or the sweaty feet they contained. She suddenly felt self-conscious, fully aware of how dirty she was.

How do people live like this?

A well-dressed man with an olive complexion approached. "Well, you must be Mr. McGinnis," he said, extending his hand. "I'm Andrew. How was your trip?" He took Jesse's hat and hung it on the hall tree next to the door.

"Uh…good…real good," she said, stammering. She took Jim from Aponi.

Andrew nodded and directed his attention to the woman standing closest to Jesse. "You must be Mrs. McGinnis."

"I am. It's nice to meet you, Andrew," she replied. "This is my brother-in-law, Toby, and his wife, Aponi."

Andrew greeted them with a smile before turning his attention to Cuffy. "Take the trunk upstairs. Put it in the first room on the right." He turned back to his guests. "All right then. How about we get you folks settled. Come with me."

He began the tour of the twelve-room home by leading them up the stairs aside the front parlor. "The staff is happy you're here. They weren't supposed to start working until Mr. Bowman's return in November. Because of your arrival, he went ahead and had them start early."

"Staff?" Jesse asked.

"Yes, sir. Ulayla runs the kitchen. She's a fine cook. Mollie is the housemaid, and you already met Cuffy. We are all here to make sure you have everything you need during your stay." He pushed open a door. "Mr. and Mrs. McGinnis, this is the room you'll be staying in. I hope it's to your liking. Oh, and Mr. Bowman had two cribs delivered to accommodate your little ones. He told me to tell you they're yours to keep. Gifts from him and the Mrs."

Abby's hand went to her chest, touched by the thoughtful gift. "Thank you."

He smiled at her. "Don't thank me. It was the Bowmans' doing. You can thank them when they get back."

Jesse peeked into the bedroom. She thought for a moment her weary eyes deceived her. The entire cabin would fit into the space.

Toby and Aponi were given a similar room down the hall. Andrew stopped in front of another door at the end. "That's the privy," he said.

An outhouse inside, Jesse thought. She shifted Jim to her other hip and opened the door to have a look. While she'd heard of them, she had never expected to see one. She knew how she would sound even before she opened her mouth, but still, she had to ask. "I don't mean to be daft, but how does it work?"

"Water is stored in a large cistern up in the attic," Andrew said. He walked over to the sink and turned a handle. "Opening the faucet handle will allow water from the cistern to flow into the fixtures." He pointed to the toilet. "When you finish, just yank the—" He stopped speaking when he saw Mollie standing at the threshold. "Ah, perfect timing. Mollie is bringing heated water for the tub. Thought you would like to freshen up after your long trip."

Mollie smiled but said nothing as she carried in a steaming bucket. She poured it into the tub and then turned the handle on the faucet, mixing cool water with the hot.

"Still have to heat the water the old fashioned way." Andrew grinned.

Jesse held up her hand. "Hold on. Let me get this straight. Sam is tearing down this house?" she asked in bewilderment, pointing to the floor.

Andrew chuckled and nodded. "He is. There's a movement happening right now. People want large estates, not modest houses like this—at least in this area." He could tell by Jesse's expression she still didn't understand. "Mr. Bowman had to buy this one so he'd own the land. Right now, they're renovating the house next door. It's supposed to be finished by the time he returns in November. Then, they're tearing this one down to enlarge the home next door. Should be quite the mansion when it's all said and done."

The impossible babbling of water flowing inside came to an abrupt stop as Mollie shut off the faucet.

"Looks like the bathwater is ready," Andrew said.

Jesse looked at Abby and the twins. "I'll help you with them," she said. Without hesitation, Abby handed her Gwen and headed back to the bedroom for clean clothes.

As the others continued touring the rest of the home, Abby and Jesse gave the twins a bath. When they were cleaned and dressed, Jesse took them back to the bedroom.

Abby undressed and sank into the heated water. She was certain nothing had ever smelled better than the fresh lavender of the bar soap in her hand. Inhaling the fragrance, she rested her head against the cool copper at the back of the tub. She wanted nothing more than to wash away the dust of the road, curl up in the luxurious, oversized bed and sleep for days.

The hot water caressed her, begging her not to leave its embrace, but she knew Jesse was eager to take her turn. She stood and toweled off with one of the softest cloths she had ever felt before returning to the bedroom.

Jesse, feeling too filthy for the furniture, sat on the floor. Abby peered into the cribs to see silent, bundled lumps.

"They fell right to sleep," Jesse whispered.

"The water is still warm if you want to take a turn."

Jesse took a set of clean clothes and hurried down the hall, impelled by a slight excitement that defied her sleepiness. She couldn't wait to strip off her dirty garments and get clean again.

She dipped her foot in the water and found the temperature to be just right. *I could really get used to this,* she thought as she sank underneath the water.

A noticeable brown murk tinted the cool water by the time Jesse pulled the chain on the plug. The accumulated dirt and sand of their trip swirled down the drain, each grain on its own long journey.

Jesse had no problem sharing bathwater with Abby but knew it wasn't fair to ask the same of Toby and Aponi. She dressed and went downstairs in search of Mollie.

"Can you show me where the bucket is? I'd like to heat up some water for my brother and his wife."

"I does that," Mollie said.

"I can do it."

"No suh," Mollie reiterated. "I heat the water and brings it."

Being waited on made Jesse uncomfortable. She wasn't sure what to do, as she was still learning how things worked around here. With an awkward smile, she said, "Thank you. We appreciate it."

She went back up the stairs, noting the detail in the woodwork. The handrails and balusters had been fashioned from fine wood, polished to a sheen that looked almost wet. Each curve and groove was the painstaking work of master craftsmen who had devoted their whole lives to the art. Even the steps had been built with unexpected care. A thin but beautiful carpet was affixed tightly to the tread and riser of each step, running down the walkway in one smooth cascade that merged seamlessly with the carpentry.

Jesse still couldn't believe anyone could make plans to tear down such a fine place. It seemed like such a terrible waste.

Toby opened the door when she knocked. "Mollie is bringing more hot water for you two."

"Thanks. And Andrew told me to tell you th-that supper will be served in the dining room at s-seven."

"All right. We'll meet you then." Jesse tried to stifle a yawn. "I'm going to lay down and rest my eyes."

"I think w-w-we'll do the s-s-same," Toby said, his own fatigue slowing his words.

Jesse returned to their bedroom and locked the door behind her. She slowly pulled back the blanket and cuddled up next to Abby who was already asleep. Jesse, too, was asleep moments after her head met the pillow.

"Mr. McGinnis." Andrew rapped on the bedroom door. "Mr. McGinnis, it's going on seven. Ulayla has the table set."

"We'll—" Jesse cleared the frog from her throat. "We'll be down in a few minutes," she called out. She could tell Abby was awake but clearly as reluctant to move as she was.

"Yes, sir," Andrew said.

Abby and Jesse unenthusiastically rose and got dressed. Each one made ready to leave the room with a baby in their arms. Before walking out the door, Jesse, hesitant to let their valuables out of her sight, grabbed her saddlebag.

They entered the dining room to find Toby and Aponi already seated. Jesse sat down, placing the saddlebag at her feet.

The entire room, like everything else, had an air of newness about it. One large piece of off-white linen covered the table. Jesse ran her fingers over the intricate design stitched in light blue across the entirety. A place setting of fine china waited for each of them, along with goblets made of clear-cut crystal. She couldn't even begin to imagine the cost of the things she saw in this room alone.

A heavyset black woman pushed her way through a swinging door into the room, backside first. She turned, revealing the silver tray in her hands. "Welcome," she said. "I'm Ulayla. I made y'all a nice roast goose wid all the fixin's." Her smile came easy as she spoke. Her age was hard to guess based on her flawless complexion, free of lines. The only real hints of fading youth were the white hairs sprinkled throughout the tight braid she wore coiled around her head.

Jesse stood to help her but was quickly put in her place.

"Naw suh. You sit on down," Ulayla said, placing the tray in the center of the table. The wonderful smell filled the room even before she lifted the lid.

Humming softly as she worked, she skillfully carved the bird. Mouths watered as she placed a slice of meat on each plate, followed by a large dollop of mashed potatoes. After pouring on the gravy, she finished off the meal by adding generous portions of roasted vegetables to each plate using silver tongs. Ulayla wiped her hands on her apron, fetched a glass pitcher from the sideboard, and filled their goblets. Not one person seated at the table moved as they watched her work.

"Well, whatcha waitin' on?" Ulayla asked. "Dig on in 'fore it gits cold." She let out a small gasp. "Oh, I be right back," she said, hurrying out of the room.

They could hear the sounds of dishes clattering in the kitchen. Within seconds, she returned. "Made me granny's recipe. Best buttermilk biscuits they is," she said, placing the large platter on the table.

"Thank you," Abby said finally. "It all looks amazing."

"Welcome. You let me know if you be needin' anythin' else."

Jesse asked, "Aren't you going to join us?"

One plump hand quickly went to Ulayla's heart. To Jesse it looked as if she had just asked her to murder someone. "Lawd no, suh. I don't eat at this table. I takes my meals in there," she said, pointing towards the kitchen.

"Oh, sorry. I didn't mean—"

"No harm, suh. You jus' go on an enjoy. I be in there if you be needin' anythin'." She spoke with finality leaving no room for argument as she retreated to the kitchen.

Jesse shifted Jim in her lap and picked up her fork. The meat was so tender she didn't need a knife to cut it. In between bites of her own, she fed Jim small scoops of mashed potatoes and gravy. She looked at Aponi and asked, "You like it?"

"This is good food," Aponi said, smiling. "Never had anything like *this* before."

The group nodded their agreement.

The past week had been life changing for Aponi. Having never set foot off of the mountain, everything she encountered was foreign. She did her best not to let it overwhelm her. Most of the things she found amazing and felt, with time, she could adjust to. Her most pressing discomfort was the way some white people had looked at her. She had noticed it several times along the way, hateful stares here and there from beneath hats pulled low. She hadn't mentioned it because the others hadn't seemed to notice. She was afraid maybe it was only in her head, though the alternative was no better.

After they finished their meal, Jesse scooted her chair back and stood, plate in hand, Jim on her hip. Having heard the chair move, Ulayla was in the dining room before anyone could register her presence.

"Now, suh, you put that down." Ulayla shook her head at Jesse. Never had she seen a man wanting to be so helpful. It was a welcome sight even though she knew she had to decline the offer.

Feeling scolded, Jesse sat back down and looked up at Ulayla. "Jesse. Please, call me Jesse." She had never been comfortable being called sir.

"Lawd. I don't know where you is from but 'round here we

don't address men by their proper name. Especially ones we work fo'."

"Ulayla, you don't work for me. So, please call me Jesse," she said, standing up again. Before Ulayla knew what to say, Jesse placed her cutlery on her plate and picked it up. With Jim on her arm, she carried her plate and pushed through the door without another word.

Andrew was sitting at the table in the kitchen as Jesse placed her plate on the counter. "Tomorrow, I need to go to the bank first thing. Is there one close by?" she asked, shifting Jim to her other arm.

"There's one not too far actually."

"Can you tell me how to get there?"

He shook his head. "I'll do you one better. I'll have Cuffy take you."

"That's not necessary. I have a horse."

"Mr. Bowman already told me to have Cuffy take you around the city and show you and the Mrs. the sights."

Jesse felt relieved. The strangeness of being chauffeured was less uncomfortable than the thought of being lost in this metropolis. "Thank you."

"You're welcome." Andrew turned to see Ulayla, along with Abby, carrying in the dinner dishes. Toby and Aponi joined the entourage and helped clean up from the evening meal.

A *tsk* from Ulayla was heard more than once through the clatter of kitchenware. Once the last dish was dried and put away in the china hutch, she could no longer hold her tongue. Dishtowel clutched in hand, she placed her balled up fist on her hip. "Thank you fo' the help an all, but you's goin' to put me out of a job."

"What do you mean?" Abby asked.

"I can't be havin' yous in the kitchen. Mr. Bowman will string me up if him finds out his guest be doin' my work."

Jesse looked from Abby to Ulayla. "We just wanted to help—"

"I don't needs no help. Jus' lemme do what I hired to do. I don't want no troubles."

Abby knew Ulayla wasn't being rude. She understood how things worked. "We're sorry. If you haven't noticed already, we aren't the kind of people who feel comfortable with being waited on. I'm sure Sam wouldn't have an issue with us helping around here."

Ulayla shook her head. She tossed the dishtowel on the counter, speechless.

Jesse said, "We meant no harm."

"We'll try our best to not ruffle any more feathers around here," Abby said. "It's been a long day. Thank you for a lovely meal. I think we'll all turn in for the night. Goodnight, Ulayla."

Ulayla turned and faced them. "Night y'all."

CHAPTER NINETEEN

A bby's eyelids fluttered open. She rolled over and sighed, content as her gaze fell on Jesse. She lay sleeping on the feather pillow, her tanned face stark against the white fabric. Abby leaned up on an elbow, trailing the backs of her fingers along the curve of Jesse's jawline. She couldn't help herself. Her skin called out to be touched.

The soft caress roused Jesse from sleep, and she raised a hand to scratch away the tickle Abby's fingers left on her cheek. "It's morning already?" Jesse asked, voice raspy. She yawned into her cupped hand.

"I know. It feels like we just got to sleep," Abby said, laying her head on Jesse's chest. "This bed's like sleeping on a cloud, isn't it?"

Jesse ran her hand over the soft sheets. "I could get used to this. How 'bout you?" She slipped an arm around her. "Did you sleep well?"

"Mmm-hmm."

The comfort of the bed was almost too luxurious and

Abby found her eyelids growing heavy again. Before the nest of expensive linens and warm glow of intimacy could lull her back to sleep, the soft coos from Jim's crib escalated. Her silent request for another minute, maybe two, was met with an ear-piercing cry. "I'll get him," she said, slipping from beneath Jesse's arm. She plucked Jim from the crib and sat on the edge of the bed. She hummed quietly to soothe her hungry son as she hurried to undo the buttons on her nightgown. Chest bare, she guided him to her breast, her face twisting in pain the moment he latched on.

"They aren't getting any better?"

"No," Abby said, meeting her gaze. "Actually, they're getting worse."

"I can't imagine feeding one, let alone two."

Abby looked down at her nursing son. "I think we're going to have to wean them soon."

"Well, stop feeding him," Jesse said, throwing off the quilt. "Let's see if we can get him to fill up on solid food this morning. Same with her," she said, titling her head toward Gwen's crib.

Jim screamed when Jesse took him from his mother. His small fists beat the air as she fought to change his diaper. Gwen, upset by the noise, added her own cries to those of her brother's.

The siblings were red-faced but at least clean and dressed by the time they all went downstairs. Toby and Aponi were already seated at the table in the dining room. Jesse took a seat and used her finger to wipe away the tears streaming down her daughter's cheeks.

Ulayla jostled into the room. She set her tray on the sideboard and served plates piled high with scrambled eggs, slabs of fried ham, and thick pieces of toasted bread slathered in butter. After they thanked her, Ulayla nodded and returned to the kitchen without saying a word.

Jesse scooped some scrambled eggs onto her spoon and blew off the heat. She fed Gwen while Abby did the same for Jim.

Toby only managed a few bites before he stood and said, "I'm g-going to lay down. Not feeling—" He stopped speaking when Andrew entered the room.

"Good morning, everyone," Andrew said. "When you're finished, Cuffy is waiting for you outside. Much to see today."

Toby looked at the gathering around the table. "You guys go on without me."

Jesse held her spoon still, a tiny mouthful of fluffy eggs hovering over her plate. "You sure?" Gwen craned her neck, her mouth wide as she tried to reach the food just out of her reach.

Toby nodded.

Aponi said, "I'll be up in a minute."

Toby gave her a strained smile. "You do-don't have to rush." He turned and headed for the stairs.

"We're finished, but I need a few minutes," Abby told Andrew. "Jesse, can you help me in the bedroom?"

Jesse stood and reached for her plate. Then, she remembered the incident the night before with Ulayla. Even though she felt uneasy about leaving her dirty dishes lay on the table, she knew it was probably for the best.

Upstairs, Abby sat on the rocking chair and unbuttoned her dress. She wanted to make sure the twins had their fill.

Relief came quickly when each refused to nurse. As she refastened the buttons there was a knock at the door.

"Just a minute," Jesse called out, waiting for Abby to finish. Once she was decent, Jesse opened the door.

"I'm going to stay here with Toby," Aponi said as she entered their room. "I'll watch 'em for you."

Abby asked, "You don't want to come with us?"

"Maybe another time. I think something he ate didn't agree with him and I want to stay here in case he needs me," she said, reaching to take Gwen. "Besides, he'll probably sleep most of the day, so I'd rather have something to do."

Abby released Gwen to her. "All right. Thank you."

Abby lingered as she fretted over leaving her babies. Jesse, with the saddlebag draped across her shoulder, shifted her weight from one foot to the other as she waited. "C'mon. They'll be fine," she finally said, placing Abby's shawl around her shoulders. After kissing the twins goodbye, they made their way to the waiting carriage.

Cuffy hurried to open the door, offering his gloved hand to help Abby navigate the step. He waited until Jesse was seated before closing the door.

The scent of new leather was almost overpowering as Jesse admired the fine craftsmanship of the interior. "I've never been in one of these before. They're quite nice," she said, wriggling on the seat.

"I think you're going to like this. You just sit back and enjoy the scenery for once." Abby placed her hand on Jesse's leg.

The door to the carriage opened and Andrew stuck his head inside. "If you'd like, I can come with you and point things out."

Jesse and Abby nodded in unison.

Andrew took the seat across from them, tapping his fist on the glass behind him, signaling Cuffy to get the carriage moving.

Jesse looked out the window at the construction all around them as the carriage rolled through the streets. A few smaller houses were being demolished, and she assumed it was to make room for future mansions—like Sam Bowman was doing. The rivalry of the wealthy, this contest to build and own the biggest mansion no matter how impractical, seemed like such a senseless, wasteful competition.

The tree-lined streets soon gave way to multi-story buildings wedged next to even bigger ones. Everything was compacted tightly together, block after block of structures built practically on top of one another.

"That's Mr. Bowman's establishment," Andrew said, pointing out the window. "The Bay Water. Would you like to stop and go inside?"

Abby and Jesse exchanged looks. They had both spent more than enough time in saloons. "Maybe some other time," Abby said.

A little further down, on the same block, the carriage came to a stop in front of a large building with a stone facade. "Here is the bank you asked about," Andrew said.

"We'll be right back," Jesse said, grabbing her saddlebag. The door opened as soon she reached for the handle, courtesy of Cuffy. She stepped from the carriage and turned to help Abby, but once again, he beat her to it.

The noise of the street fell away as soon as they entered through the door of the bank. A man wearing wire-framed glasses, his gray suit neatly pressed, approached them. "I'm Mr.

Chapman," he said, offering his hand to Jesse. "How can I help you?"

Jesse shook his hand. "I read an article in the newspaper a while back," she said. "It mentioned you offer a place in your vault for safe keeping of valuables?"

"Ah, yes. You're interested in renting one of our safe-deposit boxes."

"Yes. How much are they?"

"Three dollars a month," he said, adjusting his spectacles, "and we require a two-month deposit up front."

Abby asked, "Can you show us one of those boxes before we decide?"

He looked at her over the rim of his glasses, but didn't answer. Instead, he turned his attention back to Jesse. "Sir, follow me." He led them down a carpeted hallway toward the rear of the bank. "I'll need you to wait here a moment."

Mr. Chapman disappeared around a corner. A heavy ratcheting sound could be heard as he turned a large wheel: once, twice, three times. This was followed by a loud clack and the creak of metal door hinges. He returned to his waiting customers. "Come along," he said as he escorted them inside the vault.

Several rows of metal boxes lined one of the walls and he walked over to it and pulled one from its slot. He placed the box numbered 32 on the metal table in the center of the room and opened the hinged lid.

Jesse knew as soon as she saw it that it was too small. "Can I rent two?" she asked.

"Yes, sir. That won't be a problem." He pulled box 33 from its slot and placed it next to the other. "You go ahead and put in what you want. Close them when you're finished," he said before stepping from the vault.

Jesse set her saddlebag on the table and opened the flap. She and Abby made quick work of divvying up the gold. They closed the lids and called out to Mr. Chapman. He returned, spun the small dials on the front of each box, and placed them back in their assigned slots.

"Come with me," he said. "I have some paperwork for you to fill out. And I'll need your payment."

Jesse left the bank feeling relieved the gold was in a safe place. She'd no longer have to worry about it constantly.

Abby, however, was irritated. Mr. Chapman had treated her like a second-class citizen. On the way to the carriage, it dawned on her. *That jackass still dealt with a woman and he didn't even know it.* She couldn't help but chuckle at the thought.

They continued on their sightseeing tour, Andrew pointing things out along the way. They soon came to an area where the homes were of a more modest size. Jesse felt her shoulders relax. She hadn't realized how tense she was until the dense city streets fell away behind them. Although she couldn't smell the scent coming off of the tall trees dotting the landscape, she knew the familiar fragrance in her mind. She liked this neighborhood and could see herself living there. It was neat and tidy, and it was obvious the homeowners took pride in their properties. This was exactly the kind of place where she could raise her family.

They next traveled through an area Jesse wasn't expecting to see in such a prosperous city. Lining the street, built with a hodgepodge of materials—anything available it seemed—were rows of homes which were nothing more than shanties. She looked at Abby with sadness in her eyes. *Buck's old shelter was better than this.* Thin and poorly clothed, the people loitering around the small shacks appeared to have little, if anything, to their names. The gaunt faces looking in their direction told Jesse that finding food must have been a daily struggle.

Abby pointed at a building, her voice somber when she asked, "What's that place?"

Andrew peered out the window. "Oh, that's the Orphan Asylum."

Jesse pulled her attention from the hovels and noticed the large, medieval building up ahead. Although it was warm inside the carriage, a chill passed over her as she stared at the structure.

Set back from the road, it loomed over the dreary area. No grass grew around the perimeter of the home as if worn away by the feet of all of the children confined in such a small area. Yet, not one child could be seen anywhere.

Jesse shuddered as she recalled being orphaned at a young age. She couldn't imagine what it would be like to grow up in such a place. Youth spent trapped between the cold stones, no streams to fish, no woods to hunt, and nothing but the walls closing in around her day after day. Reflexively, she reached out to take Abby's hand.

They rode in silence until the carriage came to a stop near the edge of a cliff. Out the window, they saw water as far as the eye could see. A million diamonds glittered on its surface. Abby smiled as she observed the awe on Jesse's face.

"This place is world-famous," Andrew said. "Come on. Let's stretch our legs."

Standing near the edge, Jesse looked down and saw something on the rocks far below. She had never seen animals like them. Their wet, glistening fur reminded her of beaver pelts, but their flat limbs were more like that of fish. They flopped about clumsily on the rocks but seemed to swim and dive as naturally as any creature born of the sea.

She was further taken aback when one cried out a series of sharp barks from its whiskered face. Its calls mixed with the sounds of breaking waves, crashing against the rock face beneath them. "What are those?" she asked Andrew.

"Sea lions. They like to come ashore and sunbathe. People come from all over to see them."

The view was spectacular. It was the first time Jesse had seen the Pacific Ocean or any ocean. She breathed deep of the salty air and was momentarily lost in the world around her as the crashing waves thundered in her ears. In the distance, huge ships seemed to glide across the open water. Overhead, seagulls cried to one another.

"More to see. We should get going," Andrew said.

The carriage continued until it came to a strip of risqué businesses flanking the road. "Welcome to Barbary Coast," Andrew said with either a grin or a grimace. Jesse wasn't sure which.

Dance halls, saloons, and brothels stretched endlessly. Packed streets held more people than Jesse's mind could take in: foreigners, drunks, prostitutes, miners, and sailors all mingled, hungry for lewd entertainment.

Jesse's mouth was agape as she took in the activity around her. Then, something—someone made her suck in a breath. She hit her forehead on the carriage glass as she tried to get a better look at what—who she was seeing.

Andrew leaned forward and looked out the window. "Oh, I heard about him," he said. "They've been advertising about him in the paper lately. He's the new addition to Mr. Myer's Marvels."

"Who?" Abby asked.

Jesse, face still close to the glass, steamed up the window as she spoke. "I've never seen anyone like him."

In a flash, the man disappeared into one of the buildings. Jesse turned toward Andrew. "How is that possible?"

"What are you two talking about?" Abby asked. She was leaning over Jesse now in an attempt to see out the window for herself.

"They call him Fred 'n Ed. He's a Siamese twin."

"A Siamese twin. What is that?" Abby asked.

"He was born with one body, two heads. For ten dollars you can reserve a table and eat a steak supper with him. Can you imagine?" he asked, shaking his head in disbelief.

Neither could.

"You'll want to stay clear of this area," he said as the carriage continued moving along. "It's nothing but lawlessness. People get killed here almost every night."

Jesse watched the faces staring back at them. She saw nothing but desperation. Several women, assuming a wealthy person must be on board, called out for them to stop. She couldn't help but think of Sarah at The Drake.

"I only brought you here to let you see what it's like," Andrew said. "To warn you both to stay far away from this place. Nothing here but thieving pickpockets, robbers, and murderers. And if you are ever foolish enough to come back, never, and I mean never, have a drink."

"And why's that?" Abby asked.

His normally mild expression took on a serious tone as he answered. "Have you ever heard the term, 'being shanghaied'?"

Abby nodded. "I have, but don't know the meaning behind it."

"I've never heard it before. What's it mean?" Jesse asked.

"Those sweet and innocent looking women back there… well, *pfft*, they aren't what they seem. When you're not looking, they'll slip a drug into your drink. It'll knock you out and you'll wake up only to realize it's too late. You'll be on a ship heading for God knows where. And when you finally make landfall, you'll be sold to the highest bidder."

It was an easy decision for Jesse. She had no desire to ever set foot in Barbary Coast again. The place terrified her.

The carriage soon rolled into a neighborhood known as Chinatown. Jesse's eyes, though still wide, couldn't take in everything going on outside the window. Of all the men gathered along the storefronts, one in particular caught her attention. She fixated on the piece of red silk tied in his long pigtail, braided and hanging almost to his heels, until Andrew spoke again.

"It's like another world here, isn't it? Oh, that's a joss house," he said, pointing.

"Joss house?" Jesse asked.

"Yes. It's where they worship. It's their church." He pointed to another building close by. "That's an opium den. Ever heard of one?"

Abby shook her head. "No. What is it?"

"I don't know much about it myself as I've never had the fancy to partake. It's something you smoke. I've heard it will put you in some sort of trance. A lot of people come here just to experience mind-altering drugs. Some say it takes them to paradise. I do recommend if you want to explore Chinatown further, you hire yourself a guide.

There are some less than savory establishments nestled in here."

Abby said, "I don't think we'd—"

"That place," Andrew said, pointing into the shadows of a dark alleyway, "is the worst—" He stopped speaking when he remembered he was in the company of a lady. He looked at Abby and shook his head. "My apologies."

"I've sung in saloons for years. I've heard many things that were unsettling. No need to sugarcoat things on my account. What is that place?"

Quiet filled the carriage as he searched for a way to describe it without being too offensive. A pained look flitted across his face even before the words were fully out. "You can buy girls there."

Abby, familiar with the ways of the world said, "Oh, I know all about men buying women for pleasure. It happens a lot, especially in the places where I've worked."

Andrew shook his head and looked down at the tips of his polished, black shoes. "I'm not referring to prostitution. I'm saying men can buy children. Own them. Any age is available, for the right price that is. I've even heard some purchase infant children to feed their perversions. Male and female."

Abby and Jesse both were overcome with a sudden and sickening feeling. They swallowed against the hot bile rising in their throats.

Andrew looked at them with a heavy sadness. "My apologies. I shouldn't have told you," he said, focusing his attention out the window, regretting he had even mentioned the place.

Abby used her hand to fan her face, suddenly in need of air as she tried to cope with a burst of anxiety that caused a breathlessness she had never experienced before. The thought of some vile man touching Gwen or Jim wracked her with fear and revulsion. Instinctively, she placed her hand on her belly, stomach roiling. She reached for Jesse's leg with the other and sidled closer, hoping the simple touch that had always made her feel safe would somehow calm her racing heart.

Jesse knew exactly how Abby was feeling. She too was desperate to go back and hold onto her children, but she also knew they were safe. She leaned over and whispered, "Don't worry. They're all right. They're with Aponi."

Then, without any warning, Abby felt a wet sensation. She peeked under her shawl and noticed her breast milk had soaked through her dress. Thinking about her babies somehow triggered her production.

Jesse caught a glimpse before Abby covered the evidence with her shawl. She slid an understanding hand over Abby's and asked Andrew, "Can we head back now?"

The words pulled Andrew's gaze from the window. "Sure thing, Mr. McGinnis. I'm sorry. I didn't mean to spoil the day."

"No need to apologize," she said. "It's been interesting. I've seen things I've never seen before. Things I never thought I'd see. But I think we've both had enough for one day."

Jesse kept a firm grip on Abby's hand as the carriage headed for the Bowman Estate. They both felt a sense of helplessness being so far away from the twins and an urgency to get back to them.

Abby stared out the window in silence, buildings passing by unseen. Her eyes, still the stunning blue Jesse had fallen for, held a distant look. Only hours ago, she'd complained about the pain of breastfeeding. Even the idea of having to do it had made her cringe. Now, she felt totally different. The only thing she desperately wanted, the only thing that mattered, was to get back and hold tight to her babies. She couldn't wait to feel them suckle again, regardless of the pain, knowing they were safe in her arms. She'd endure any pain—anything for her children.

CHAPTER TWENTY

J esse slid from beneath Abby's arm, unwound herself from the tangle of bed sheets, and tiptoed across the floor to peek into each crib. Both babies lay sound asleep, lost in dream. After grabbing her clothes, she slipped quietly from the bedroom and padded down the dark hall in the predawn hush still settled throughout the house.

She turned the knob on the gas-wall sconce in the water closet, enveloping the room in a warm glow. Having seen many modern amenities during her short time in the city, she thought the gas lighting was among the more ingenious. At the sink, she opened the faucet handle and cupped her hands underneath the running water. The splash to her face chased away whatever sleepiness still clouded her head.

As she patted her face dry with the hand towel, she studied her reflection in the gilded mirror. It struck her that she finally felt comfortable with the person staring back. She didn't feel like a man or a woman, she just felt like Jesse. When it had happened she wasn't sure. This was who she'd become—who she truly was. She smiled and hung the towel on the hook next to the sink. When she slipped into her trousers, she chuckled at the thought of having to put on a dress and high-heeled shoes like most women wore. She couldn't even imagine.

Dressed and ready, she headed straight for the kitchen in search of a cup of coffee. She could smell the rich, nutty aroma before she pushed open the door. She startled Ulayla, who was seated at the table, steaming mug in her hands.

"Good morning. You're up early," Jesse said, taking a seat across from her. "That coffee sure smells good."

Ulayla stood, her half-filled mug clutched in her hand as she walked toward the counter.

"Please, don't be like that," Jesse said. "I don't bite."

Ulayla turned to face her. "We don't share tables wid the bosses." A plump hand settled on her hip. "Or anythin' else for that matter. That's jus' the way it is."

"Ulayla, I told you, you don't work for me. I'm not your boss."

"Well, you sorta is." She turned her back and set her cup down, breathing out a sigh.

"That's nonsense. I'm no different than you. So what's the harm if both of us sit here at this table," Jesse asked, tapping her finger on the wood, "and have a cup of coffee together?"

Ulayla turned, hand on her hip again. "How's you like it? Black? Or cream and suga?"

Jesse shrugged her shoulders. "Never had it with cream and sugar."

Ulayla gave her a quick, sidelong glance. "Where's you from?" she asked, eyebrow arched quizzically.

"Up north. Hard to find cream and sugar where I'm from, that's all."

Ulayla said nothing as she reached into a cupboard for a

clean mug. She poured the coffee and added two heaping spoonfuls of sugar and a generous splash of cream. Cup in hand, she said, "Follow me," and pushed through the door to the dining room. She placed the cup on the table next to the day's newspaper and returned to the kitchen.

Jesse picked up the cup and paper and retraced her steps to the kitchen. "Did you read the paper already?" Jesse asked as she took a seat at the table again.

Jesse's tenacity confused Ulayla. Why would a man, a white man no less, want to be in the kitchen with her? It made no sense. "No suh, can't read. Now, I gots to start cookin' fo' they's all up." She took the heavy cast iron skillet down from its hook on the wall.

"How about this," Jesse said, holding up the newspaper. The pages crackled in her hand as she waved it. "You let me sit in here and I'll read it to you. Would that be all right?"

The older woman didn't know what to say. No one had ever offered to do something like that before.

Taking her silence as a yes, Jesse opened the newspaper and read. She took her time. She didn't want this to seem like an obligation she wanted to get out of the way. Besides, the longer she lingered, the less likely Ulayla would be to ask her to leave. She hoped.

After finishing the first article, a story about the seizure of a rum ship, she reached for the handle of her cup. She blew on the coffee and took a sip. Her eyes opened wide as the rich brew lit up her taste buds. The cream tempered the bitterness of the beans and added its own milky notes and silky texture, while the sugar elevated the drink to a luxurious dessert. She couldn't help smiling. It seemed almost wrong to have this before breakfast. "This is wonderful. I like it with cream and sugar. Thank you."

Ulayla, kneading the biscuit dough, glanced over her shoulder. "You's welcome."

Jesse could have sworn she saw the hint of a smile before she turned away again and went about preparing the morning meal. She had read several articles and was starting the fifth one when Ulayla unexpectedly took a seat directly across from her. Jesse glanced up momentarily but didn't pause. The pair sat together, sipping coffee, until she finished reading the last article.

"The rest is just advertisements," Jesse said.

Ulayla stood hastily. "I needs to set the table." She left her empty mug and went into the dining room.

Jesse had the notion to follow her and offer a hand. Not wanting to push her luck, she stayed seated, browsing the ads in search of property available for sale or let.

The very first one she came across had promise.

Cozy New Cottage, six rooms including bath, sunny side of Madison St. $30, water extra.

Jesse could picture her family in something like that. Six rooms sounded like plenty; the most difficult thing was imagining life without their own space outdoors. Skimming further, she found another one she thought she might want to check out.

New House, 902 Hickory Ave. Nine rooms, bath, basement, and yard. $50. Water included.

The price was higher, but it had more rooms and more importantly, a yard. She read on. The next one she came across sounded still more appealing.

For Sale or Let. Seven rooms. 317 Taylor St. Comes with

barn. *For sale on long term, payable monthly or annually, or to let $25 monthly, water included. Large lot: use of cow and chickens, if desired.*

Jesse nodded as she read the listing over a few more times. She went to take another sip of her coffee only to find the bottom of a dry mug. She folded the paper, laid it on the table, and picked up the two empty cups. She washed them and placed them on the rack to dry.

Outside the window, the pale light of sunrise painted the skyline. Jesse decided to go to the carriage house and check in on the horses. She followed a gravel path between the two houses to the rear of the property. She slid open the door of the carriage house, letting in the scant daylight and releasing the animal smell of the barn. The earthy bouquet wasn't nearly as offensive as she'd once thought. If anything, it was a comforting reminder of her past, something familiar in a strange city. She made her way down the aisle, looking into each stall until she came upon Buck.

"Hey, boy," she said, lightly rubbing her knuckles between his eyes. "What do you think? It's a lot different than the old place, isn't it?" She grabbed a currycomb from a nearby hook and brushed him down. When she finished with him, she moved on to Titan's stall and did the same, relishing her time with her old friends.

Loud banging from the renovation drowned out the crunch of gravel under her feet as she walked back between the houses. She paused to listen for a moment before curiosity got the better of her. The door of the larger home was already slightly ajar. She pushed it open and called out. "Hello?"

Getting no response from the cavernous manse besides her own echo, she went inside. The walls were nothing but lath and patches of plaster here and there. To her right rose a tall, unfinished staircase with no railing, only treads and risers. The pounding of a hammer reverberated from somewhere above.

Her footsteps on the stairs seemed amplified in the open space. She paused on the landing to look down at the vast area below. She was sure the entirety of the old cabin would fit neatly into the spacious foyer.

"Dammit! That's it!"

The shouted words echoed off the unfinished walls, coming from multiple sides and making her jump. She put a hand against the wall to steady herself, now acutely aware of the height and lack of railing. Her stomach did a quick somersault.

"You're fired!" a man yelled. "Get the hell out of my sight!"

A moment later, a young man carrying a toolbox brushed passed her, almost knocking her off the stairway in his haste. She turned and watched him run out the open front door.

"Well, today is your lucky day." It was the yelling man again, but his tone had shifted.

She turned toward the voice. Standing at the top of the stairs was a man, hammer gripped firmly in his oversized hand. The lines of his mouth were etched in a permanent scowl.

Jesse hesitated before responding. "…Are…are you talking to me?"

"You see anybody else?" His thick brow furrowed. "I usually don't hire people on the spot, so today is your lucky day."

She pointed at her own chest. "Hire me?"

"That's what I said. You aren't slow, are ya?"

She wagged her head side to side.

"That idjit has miscut more wood than you can imagine. I mean if I need a piece of wood 58 ¼, I can't use one at 58 ¾ or 58 ½. Am I right?"

Jesse nodded.

"You can cut wood. Can't you?"

"Uh-huh. I can."

"Good. I'll hire you for the day. If you don't screw up, you can have the job. Pay's twenty cents an hour. And so you know, right now we are putting in a minimum of sixty hours a week. You good with that?" He pointed his hammer. "If not, there's the damn door."

Jesse did a quick calculation in her head. At twelve dollars a week, she would bring home a monthly income of forty-eight dollars. That would be enough to let the house she read about in the paper.

"Yes, sir. I'm good with that." She hoped he couldn't hear the excitement creeping into her voice.

"Fine. Now, go cut me four boards at 58 ¼ and bring them up to me," he said. "The boards are in the room off the foyer."

She didn't move.

"Well, what the hell are you waiting on?"

She could see his nostrils flaring and the vein in his neck twitch. "Um…I don't have any tools."

"No tools?" The man's forehead wrinkled. "Who the hell shows up for a job and don't bring their tools?"

"Uh…I didn't know I'd get hired," she said, stammering. "So I didn't bring any."

He crossed his arms over his chest. "You do have tools, don't you?"

Her mind raced. Any that she once had were left behind in

the cabin on top of Mount Perish. She wanted this job desperately. Needed it.

Knowing she could purchase some later in the day, hopefully, she did the only thing she could think to do. She fibbed. "Uh…yeah. Just didn't bring them with me this morning. That's all."

The man raked a hand through his thick beard. He was pressed for time. "Tell you what," he said. "You can use mine today. Come here."

Jesse followed him to one of the rooms upstairs where he pointed to a wooden toolbox. "Use what you need. Just make sure I get 'em back by day's end."

Jesse sorted through them quickly, putting aside the ones she needed. Downstairs, she found several stacks of boards. She pulled one from the stack and set the corner of the board on the floor. She looked down the length of it, checking to make sure it wasn't warped.

After methodically picking out three more, she placed them all on sawhorses. She made sure all four boards were flush on the end and bound them with a clamp. With a pencil and square, she measured, scribed, and cut all four pieces at once.

With planks in hand, she ran them up the stairs. "Here you go."

The man cocked his head. He took the nails from between his lips. "You cut four of 'em already?"

"Yes, sir. Faster to cut all four at once instead of cutting one at a time."

"Yeah, but are they the correct length?" he asked, one thick brow rising in question. He took one of the boards from her and nailed it in place. He repeated the process three more times until all four boards were hanging. They were all exact.

"Name is Harry Tidwell. What's yours?"

"Jesse McGinnis."

"Get me six more. 72 ¾."

Jesse continued to run boards back and forth over the next hour, working alongside nine other men who had shown up to work on other areas of the house. She had just finished cutting a batch of boards when she heard someone yell, "Son of a bitch!" She looked across the room to see one of the workmen sucking on his thumb. Having done the same thing many times over the years, she knew what he was feeling. The banging sounds of men working with lumber quieted. Their apparent overwhelming concern for their colleague's mashed finger surprised her. She didn't see what the big deal was, but then she noticed the men's gazes weren't on the injured man. They were staring instead at Abby, who stood in the foyer.

"There you are," Abby said to Jesse. "What are you doing?"

"Working," she said quietly. "I got hired this morning. I can't talk now." She could sense the men's ogling gazes on Abby. "You should go."

"All right," she said. "I was just worried about you."

Jesse waved her off. "I'll talk to you later."

Only when Abby was out the door did any work resume.

Jesse spent the entire day cutting and running boards back and forth. At quitting time, she held back from leaving with the rest of the crew. She didn't want anyone to see her going to the house next door. If the people she worked with found out she knew the head boss, they might treat her differently. She didn't want that.

Finally, it was only Mr. Tidwell who remained. He stood at the front door, ready to walk out, when he noticed her. She could have sworn new lines of annoyance wrinkled around his mouth as they made eye contact.

"C'mon. I need to lock up," he said with a grumble.

Jesse handed him the tools she'd borrowed. He put them in his toolbox and stepped outside to lock the door. "You did good today. I expect you to be here at six o'clock tomorrow morning with tools."

"Yes, sir." Jesse lagged behind him as they walked toward the street. She wanted to see which direction he was going. He turned to walk past the house she was staying in, so she headed in the opposite direction. Walking slowly, she kept glancing over her shoulder until he was out of her sight. Then, she doubled back. She hurried to the carriage house and found Cuffy polishing tack.

"Do you know the city very well?" she asked.

He nodded. "Yes suh."

Her words came out in an excited rush. "How about Taylor street. 317 Taylor Street. You know where that is?"

"I knows the street. Not 317. But I's can find it."

"Can you show me?"

"Yes suh. I jus' needs to hitch up," he said, pointing to the carriage.

"No reason to go to all that trouble. You can ride Buck," she said, removing his bridle hanging on a nearby hook.

Jesse and Cuffy rode off in search of the property. They traveled through several neighborhood streets before coming to a two-story brick house with 317 painted on a shingle next to the front door.

Jesse jumped down and handed her reins to Cuffy. "I'll be right back." She brushed sawdust remnants off her shirtsleeves as she approached the door. She took a deep breath, knocked, and then fidgeted with her shirt collar while she waited.

The door opened only a crack, revealing an older man. "Can I help you?"

"Yes. Well, I think so. You had an advertisement in the paper this morning."

The man opened the door the rest of the way. "Ah, yes. Are you interested in buying or letting?"

"It said twenty-five dollars to let per month. How much to buy?"

"Eight hundred and it's yours." He looked Jesse up and down, as if assessing her worth. "Or you can purchase it on monthly installments of forty. Up to you."

Jesse could tell already she wanted to buy the property, but she didn't have enough to purchase the home. If things worked out with the new job, she would make forty-eight dollars a month. That would only leave eight dollars a month to live off of. It wouldn't be nearly enough to support her family.

She scratched the back of her neck. "I can only afford to let."

"Well, if down the road you'd want to buy, just contact Mr. Goldstein. He's my attorney and is handling the property for me. Come on in." He closed the door behind her. "So, do you have a family?"

"Yes. Married with twins."

"Twins?" A lady's voice came from another room off the hallway. She stepped into the foyer, peering around her husband for a better look at the visitor. "Did I hear you say twins?"

Jesse quickly removed her hat. "Yes, ma'am. A boy and a girl."

"Oh, how lovely," she said, clasping her hands. "I was hoping a nice family would move in."

The man put an arm around his wife, pulling her close. "This is my wife, Miriam." He extended his hand to Jesse. "I'm Richard Anderson."

She shook his hand. "Jesse McGinnis. Nice to meet you both."

"Come along and we'll give you a tour," he said.

They showed her around, pointing out features and what they saw as quirks. The latter seemed trivial to her since she had grown up in an old-mountain cabin. She wasn't about to turn down a home over a creaking floorboard or drafty window.

As she walked through the rooms, she could imagine her family living there. She looked out the kitchen window, taking in the yard. Some green space would certainly help her survive in this city. Staring out at the barn, she knew she had found the perfect place.

Back at the foyer, Mr. Anderson asked, "What do you think?"

"I really like it. Would it be all right if I bring my family over tomorrow evening? I'd like them to have a look before I decide."

"Sure. But to let you know, you can't move in until October 1st. And I'll need the first month's installment up front."

"I understand. What time should we come by tomorrow?"

"How's seven o'clock?"

"I'll see you both then," Jesse said with a wide smile.

"I's tend to 'em," Cuffy said when they returned to the carriage house. Jesse, for once, didn't put up a fight. It had been a long, exhausting day. She wanted to get inside and tell Abby the exciting news. As she was hanging her hat on the hall tree, she heard Abby call out, "We're in here."

Abby held Gwen. Aponi, seated next to Toby, had Jim in her arms. Jesse brushed her hand over the boy's head as she passed by. Her stomach growled and she realized she hadn't had a bite to eat all day. As if hearing her stomach's plea, Ulayla set a plate of food in front of her as she sat down. "Thank you, Ulayla," she said, reaching for a roasted ear of corn. It would have been too hot to handle had she been any less hungry.

Before she could take a bite, Abby asked, "Well, how was your first day?"

Jesse held the corncob over her plate. "It was good, but you won't believe what I did today," she said, smiling at everyone seated at the table. "I found us a place of our own." She took a bite of corn before the follow up questions could begin. It was as delicious as it smelled.

"Where? How?" Abby's brow furrowed. "When?"

Jesse stopped chewing, the sweet kernels in her mouth momentarily forgotten. "I saw an advertisement in the paper this morning." She swallowed. "I just got back from seeing it—"

Abby snapped. "Did you even think to discuss it with me,

us?" The heat of her ire had risen, evident in red splotches from her neck to her cheeks.

"It's not set in stone," Jesse said, setting the corn on the plate.

Abby stood. "I need to put the twins to bed." She pushed her chair in.

Jesse went to stand. "I'll help—"

Abby waved her off. "I'll do it. You just go on and eat." She left the room with the twins in her arms.

Jesse filled Aponi and Toby in about the new place in between bites of food. After she finished her meal, she carried her plate to the kitchen. Andrew was seated at the table. "Do you know where I can buy some tools?" she asked.

"Hello, Jesse," he said. "I heard you're working next door. Congratulations."

"Well, I won't be if I show up in the morning with no tools."

Andrew put his hands on the oak top and pushed away from the table. "I have an idea. Come with me."

Jesse followed him along the path to the far side of the carriage house as the sun was descending. He reached into his pocket and pulled out a ring of keys. They jangled in his hands as he selected the correct skeleton key and inserted it into the padlock. He flipped the latch, slid open the door, and motioned for her to enter. Even in the scant light, she could tell everything was covered in a thick layer of dust.

"When Mr. Bowman bought this place, all of this was included. Of course, he had no use for any of it so he had me lock it all up."

Jesse walked around the small workshop. She stopped in

front of a piece of equipment. "What's this?" she asked, her fingers trailing through the dust on the unfamiliar surface.

"That's a wood lathe. Put a slab of wood in it and you spin it by pressing the pedal there below." He then pointed to a group of hand tools, with sharp metal on the business ends. "Put any one of those chisels to it and it will put groves in the wood."

Jesse nodded in fascination. She continued to look around at what she realized was a wood-worker's paradise. She was pretty confident any tool she could ever want or need was there.

"Since you're friends of Mr. Bowman, I don't think he'd mind you putting them to good use." He pointed up to the rafters. "There's a bunch of scrap wood up there if you need any of it." He removed the skeleton key from the ring and handed it to her. "Just make sure you lock it up when you're done."

"I will."

Andrew left Jesse to explore the space on her own. Some things were familiar to her. Many she could guess at, puzzling their uses out of similarities to the instruments she knew. Still others, she hadn't a clue. She selected a chisel from the work-table, picked up a scrap piece of wood, and blew off the dust. Testing its sharpness, she dug the tool into the soft wood. It was like a knife through warm butter.

"I think we need to talk."

Jesse turned and was surprised to see Abby standing in the doorway. "Look at all this," she said, almost beaming.

Abby smiled at her excitement, but she had other things on her mind besides tools. She'd thought about what Jesse had done as she put the twins to sleep. She was upset with her at first for going to look at a house without her. They were supposed to be equal partners in this relationship and this was too big of a decision to make without discussing it together. Then her mood had softened. Jesse had given up her entire way of life for her and the twins. She couldn't have asked for a better partner and parent for the children. Letting her pick out their home seemed so trivial now. "So, tell me about this house. How much is it and can we afford it?" she asked.

Jesse put the hunk of wood and chisel back on the work-table. She walked over to Abby, placed her hand on her hips, and pulled her close. "I really think you're going to love it," she said, looking into Abby's eyes. "I can see us being happy there. I don't want to spoil anything, so I'm not going to tell you anything about it. You'll see it for yourself tomorrow evening." She took Abby by the hand. "If you don't like it, then we won't take it. Come on. Let's go inside. It's been a long day."

Jesse secured the padlock with a new sense of excitement, responsibility, and possibilities. She led Abby back inside, already looking forward to cleaning up and putting her head on the pillow.

After another long day of work, Jesse hesitated again. She tried not to let her nerves show as she waited for all the other workers to leave. Her excitement over showing her family the house on Taylor Street had grown during the day.

Gripping the dowel handle of her toolbox, she waited until the coast was clear before she hurried to the carriage house. Cuffy was putting the harnesses on Mr. Bowman's prize geld-ings when she stepped inside. "I'm almost ready. I just need to put these away," she said, holding up her toolbox, "and change my shirt." She locked the tools up in the workshop and tugged on the lock. Content they were safe, she hurried along the gravel path to the house, brushing sawdust from her clothes as she went.

After putting on a clean shirt, Jesse and Abby carried the twins to the waiting carriage, joining Aponi and Toby. Cuffy snapped the reins and they rolled down the street.

Jesse didn't realize she was bouncing her leg until Abby put a palm on her thigh. They shared a smile, each wondering if the other felt the same excitement or something more anxious.

When the carriage came to a stop, Abby looked out the window. "Is this it?" she asked, peering at the two-story brick house.

Jesse already had her hand on the carriage handle. She nodded. "It's nice. Isn't it?" she asked, opening the door.

Richard Anderson stepped outside as they approached the house. Jesse reached to shake hands. "Mr. Anderson. This is my family," she said before introducing each one by name.

Mr. Anderson greeted each of them warmly. "Come inside. My wife, Miriam, and I will give you a tour."

Abby looked around as she entered. *Jes was right. This place is lovely.*

The main entry hall had velour-patterned wallpaper accented by wainscoting. To the right was the parlor with a large fireplace, though Jesse had heard winters there were no more severe than spring on the mountain. A fancy-framed mirror hung above the brick hearth. With its patina, Jesse couldn't tell what it was made of, but knew for certain it was heavy. On each side of the fireplace, shelving had been built into the walls, filled to capacity with books and knick-knacks.

Several tasteful watercolors hung throughout the space, accenting the light green walls.

Sheer lace curtains covered a ten-pane window facing the street. Floor-length brocade draperies were pulled back at each end and tied with tasseled ropes. A sofa and matching loveseat, along with a lady's armless chair and an oversized man's armchair, filled the center of the room. A circular tea table sat beside the lady's chair. Flanking the sofa were end tables, each one holding an ornate, kerosene lamp. In one corner stood a curio cabinet, made of the same cherry wood as the tea table.

They went across the hall into the dining room next. Abby liked the large table, although the glass chandelier was not quite her taste. The walnut trim, stained a dark brown, stood out stark against the ivory walls.

The kitchen was at the end of the hall. A large, cast-iron, wood-burning stove took up one corner of the room. Overlooking the backyard were two windows. Beneath one sat a drop-leaf table. Abby could already picture starting her mornings with Jesse at that table, sipping their coffee. Next to the other window was a white, cast-iron sink. Two large hutches offered ample storage space. In the center of the room stood a large butcher block, its age marked by a forest of thin hatch lines.

Off of the kitchen was the water closet. While it wasn't as nice as the one they were currently enjoying, Abby was thrilled they would have modern amenities.

The group followed their guides up a narrow staircase. Upstairs were three bedrooms. The first was painted a light shade of grey with a darker tint for the trim. It contained a brass bed and an oak dresser. The second bedroom was painted a pale blue. Empty of furniture, the room was cluttered with boxes and crates.

"Please excuse the mess. We've been packing up some of our things for the move," Mrs. Anderson said.

The last bedroom was the largest of the three. The furniture filled the room with its oversized four-post bed and two matching dressers. The walls stood in stark contrast to the other two rooms. Abby knew right away that Jesse liked the wallpaper, lush and depicting nature scenes. Personally, she would paint it with a light mauve color if she had her druthers.

"Why don't you take the women into the parlor," Mr. Anderson said to his wife. "I'll show the fellas the barn. I'm sure the women don't care to look."

Mrs. Anderson joined the women in the parlor a short while later, silver tray in hand bearing a teapot, cups, sugar, and cookies. As she poured the tea into cups, Abby asked, "Can I ask why you are moving?"

Mrs. Anderson finished pouring and set down the teapot. "We have a family matter to deal with back in Connecticut," she said, using small tongs to drop sugar cubes into the teacups. Abby could hear the sadness in the older woman's voice. "It's going to be hard to leave this place." She sat on the sofa beside Abby and picked up her cup. "I'm just happy a nice family will be living here." Her spoon clinked against the porcelain as she stirred.

Abby placed her hand on Mrs. Anderson's arm. "I promise we will take fine care of your home."

Mrs. Anderson patted Abby's hand. "I hope you'll be happy here."

"I'm sure we will be. Will you be returning to San Francisco once you tend to your matters back east?"

Mrs. Anderson shook her head. "No. Mr. Anderson and I are getting too old to travel like we used to. We've decided to stay in Connecticut."

Voices drifted down the hall as Jesse, Toby, and Mr. Anderson made their way toward the parlor.

"Can I have a word with you?" Jesse said to Abby.

Abby excused herself and joined Jesse by the front door.

"Well, what do you think?" Jesse whispered.

Abby whispered back, "I really like it."

"Me too. So, I can sign the paperwork?"

Abby nodded in agreement. "I can't wait to move in."

CHAPTER TWENTY-ONE

Jesse sat on the edge of the bed, her bare feet planted on the plush rug. Yawning, she glanced over her shoulder at Abby who was still sleeping soundly. Her long-blonde hair was down and it spilled across the pillow in long waves. A fluttering sensation coursed through her body—a feeling now as familiar to her as her own flesh. It was still difficult for her to believe she had somehow managed to win the affection of such a beautiful creature. The knowledge that Abby still had such an effect on her caused a silly grin to tug at the corners of her mouth. She wanted more than anything to crawl in beside her and curl their warm bodies together but knew she couldn't. She had a job to get to and a family to support.

The house they were staying in was only a few years old. Despite its relative youth, the second stair tread creaked loudly when Jesse put her weight on it. With breath held, she stood frozen in place damning the workmanship of the builder as she listened for any stirring. After hearing nothing but silence, she continued to the kitchen and was surprised to see Ulayla. She glanced at the table and noticed a steaming cup of coffee, the light tan color revealing it had been made with cream and sugar, just the way she liked it now. Next to the cup was a folded newspaper.

"Good morning," Jesse said. "You're up early."

"Mm-hmm. Can't send ya off on an empty belly," Ulayla said over her shoulder, motioning with her head toward the cup on the table. "Gos on, fo' it gits cold." She turned back to the bowl and continued whisking eggs.

Jesse sat down and took a sip. "Boy, this sure is good."

"Mm-hmm," Ulayla said, pouring a generous splash of milk into the bowl. She continued whipping the eggy mixture.

Jesse picked up the newspaper and read aloud. As she read, the kitchen filled with tantalizing smells. She paused in between articles, trying to get a glimpse of what Ulayla was frying in the cast iron skillet but was unable to see past the woman's ample figure. It occurred to her that she could easily have stood up and investigated further, but she actually preferred to be surprised.

She continued reading until Ulayla set a plate down in front of her with a tiny pitcher of warm maple syrup beside it. The plate held a stack of three slabs of fried bread, melted butter pooling and spilling down the sides, along with four pieces of thick bacon. Heavenly notes of cinnamon and vanilla swirled up from the plate and into her nose.

Jesse asked, "You put syrup on toast 'round here?"

"Uh-huh. It be called French Toast." She watched Jesse pour the syrup over the toasted bread and waited intently as she took first one bite, then another. Unable to stand it any longer, she placed her plump hand on her hip and asked, "Well, whatchu think?"

"I think…" Jesse said, around another delicious mouthful, "this is one of the best things I've ever eaten."

She took her hand off her hip. "Secret's nutmeg an' pinch o' sugar," she said, wiping her hands on her apron.

Jesse devoured the food. After she finished she went to the sink to wash her plate, only to have Ulayla take it from her.

"Now ya ain't washin' that," she said. "That's what I does."

Jesse didn't argue, smiling slightly at the authority of the statement. "Thank you…I suppose I should get next door."

"They don't be poundin' over theres this early."

"I know, but I want to be there before anyone shows up."

Ulayla tossed a towel over her shoulder. "Why's that?"

"I don't want anyone to know I'm stayin' here or that I know Sam Bowman." Jesse could tell by Ulayla's expression she wasn't following her logic. "It's just…well, I don't want to be treated differently. That's all. Thank you again for the food. It really was good."

"You's welcome," Ulayla said. "Sees ya at supper."

On the afternoon of September 29th, Jesse heard Mr. Tidwell having a disagreement with the man who had been hired to complete the staircase. She paused cutting, leaving the teeth of her handsaw lodged in a board, as she listened to the argument escalate into an angry shouting match. Mr. Tidwell was now irate. His face turned an angry shade of red, reminding her of Ulayla's beet and sweet onion soup.

"We already agreed on a price when I hired you, dammit. I won't pay you one red cent more!" Mr. Tidwell shouted, spit flying. He jabbed his chubby finger twice into the man's chest to emphasize his point.

The man took a step back and pulled out his handkerchief. "Well, then," he said, wiping spittle from his face, "looks like my work here is done. Good luck meeting your deadline." He left Mr. Tidwell with a smirk before turning and walking out the front door, slamming it behind him on his way out.

Jesse released her grip on the handsaw and cautiously approached her boss. "Uh…Mr. Tidwell, is there anything I can do to help?"

"Yes, dammit! You can get back to cutting those boards like I hired you to do or you can leave too!"

She swallowed her nerves. "Uh…I can finish the staircase —if you'd like."

"For Christ's sake! I can't have some greenhorn do—" He stopped talking and both their heads turned when the front door opened. His jaw clenched at the unwelcome visitor.

Abby knew Jesse didn't want her coming to the work site, but she was too excited to wait. She had to share the news. "Mr. and Mrs. Anderson just dropped off the key to the house," Abby said to her. "Cuffy is going to help me take some of our things over while you're working."

Mr. Tidwell had reached his boiling point. However, he was still a gentleman in the company of a lady, so he did his best to remain calm. "Ma'am, you can't be here. We have work to do. I don't pay my employees to deal with personal matters while they're on the job."

Andrew stepped inside and asked, "Is there a problem?"

Mr. Tidwell answered, "No. Just a small hiccup, that's all."

Andrew turned to Jesse and Abby. "I got a wire from Mr.

Bowman. He hopes you two are enjoying the accommodations next door."

Mr. Tidwell's head turned in a snap. "You know Mr. Bowman?" he asked.

Jesse stayed silent. She had worked hard to keep her relationship with the Bowmans a secret for weeks, even being extra cautious to ensure no one saw her coming or going from the house next door.

Andrew answered for her. "Actually, Mr. and Mrs. McGinnis are good friends with Mr. Bowman."

Jesse was mortified. Her secret was out. She looked at Abby. "I need to get back to work. I'll see you this evening." She promptly returned to cutting the stack of boards waiting on her.

Once Abby and Andrew had gone and Mr. Tidwell's blood pressure returned to normal, he tentatively approached Jesse. "I'm sorry about what happened in there. I didn't mean to take my frustrations out on you." He chewed his bottom lip before continuing to speak. "So," he continued, "you really think you can finish that staircase?"

She noticed the prominent vein pulsing on his forehead earlier had receded. "Yes, sir," she said in a confident tone.

"Well, all right then. Why don't you get started on that? I can hire someone else to cut boards."

"Mr. Tidwell. I know someone who's lookin' for work. My brother, Toby."

The deadline for the first phase of the Bowman project was fast approaching. He was too pressed for time to be picky.

"Tell him to be here first thing in the morning," he said as he started to walk away. He paused mid stride and turned back around. "I hope he's not like you and knows to show up with his own tools."

"I'll make sure of it. Thank you."

Mr. Tidwell left her and went up the stairs. Jesse raced over to the carriage house, eager to begin work on the staircase. Already, she had something in mind, and couldn't wait to get her hands on some of those tools and start bringing it to fruition.

As soon as it was quitting time Jesse hurried inside the house. She found her family already seated in the dining room.

"Ain't gonna be same 'round here," Ulayla said, setting a tray of biscuits on the table.

Though she had been put off by Jesse's tenacity only a few weeks before, Ulayla now harbored an unexpected sadness. She had enjoyed the time she spent with all of them—none of it more than the mornings she spent with Jesse. Already she dreaded their departure. The kitchen would never sound the same as it did when it was filled with Jesse's voice, reading off the news of the day.

Ulayla prepared a feast for their last meal. Fried chicken, mashed potatoes, and a variety of roasted vegetables filled their plates. As if those things weren't enough, she baked a massive, three-layered chocolate cake for dessert.

As soon as Jesse finished eating, she took her plate to the kitchen. Ulayla took it from her, shaking her head in mock frustration. Jesse smiled knowingly. "I'm sure gonna miss seeing you in the mornings. Won't be the same," she said. "Oh, and your French toast."

"Now don't ya be gettin' all sappy on me," Ulayla said, setting the dish next to the sink.

"You know, I'll still be working next door. Maybe I can swing by and check on you from time to time."

"Yes suh. That be fine."

"All right then. Well…we'd best be on our way. Thank you again for everything."

Ulayla took two steps, closing the distance between them. "You's welcome, Jesse," she said, being careful to keep her voice low so no one else could hear.

It was the first time she had referred to her by her given name. Jesse smiled at her warmly knowing she had finally managed to earn the woman's trust. She wanted to hug her, but she knew that would be pushing the boundaries. Instead, she held up her hand and gave a quick wave before she left the kitchen.

Jesse and Toby led Buck and Titan out of the carriage house and joined everyone by the waiting carriage out on the street. Andrew said, "If you ever need anything, just let me know." He shook Jesse's hand.

"We will," she said. "And thank you for everything you've done for us."

Andrew helped Abby and Aponi board, along with the twins, and latched the door behind them. He tapped the carriage letting Cuffy know it was time to go.

"Hup!" Cuffy called out as he snapped the reins.

After getting Buck and Titan settled into stalls in the small barn behind the house on Taylor Street, Jesse and Toby went inside their new home. Jesse was stunned to see many of the Andersons' furnishings had been left behind. She looked at Abby for an explanation.

"Surprise," Abby said, eyes twinkling.

"I don't understand."

"They didn't want to haul all of this across the country. So, they made us a great deal. I spent most of our savings, but I couldn't refuse. They even sold us their old wagon for next to nothing."

Jesse had seen the dilapidated wagon out behind the barn the day Mr. Anderson gave her the tour. Even though it needed fixing, she was thrilled to have it. She glanced at the built-in shelving next to the fireplace. Filled with books the last time she had visited, it was nearly empty now, save for one book and a lopsided figurine of a deer propped up by Frieda's soapstone pipe. It was the first carving Jesse had made for Frieda—one of the few survivors of a vanishing collection she'd left behind on top of Mount Perish.

"It wouldn't have felt like home without that deer," Abby said.

Jesse shook her head. "I could have lived the rest of my life without seeing that ugly thing again." In all honesty, she couldn't help but feel touched Abby had thought to take the sentimental carving when they left the mountain.

"It may not mean much to you, but it sure does to me. One day, I'm sure the twins will cherish it as much as I do. It's a family heirloom."

Jesse reached for the lone book. The title *A CHRISTMAS CAROL BY CHARLES DICKENS* was scribed on the front. Surrounding the words were gold wreaths of holly. She opened the cover. A faint smell of vanilla and almonds greeted her as she read the words written on the light-green endpaper.

Mr. and Mrs. McGinnis
Welcome home,
The Andersons
September 29th, 1865

Jesse felt Jim tugging on the hem of her pant leg. She closed the book and placed it back on the shelf. After picking her son up off of the floor, she followed behind as everyone went up the stairs to their bedrooms. With the twins crawling around on the floor, Abby began putting her and Jesse's clothes away in the dresser.

Jesse stepped out into the hall. In the bedroom at the end of the corridor she caught Toby and Aponi in a warm embrace. They seemed happy with the new accommodations. She peeked into the room across the hall with its light blue walls. Abby, with help from Cuffy, had both cribs set up. Already the new place was starting to feel like home.

Jesse returned to her bedroom, shutting the door behind her. She stepped over the twins to get to Abby. After taking some clothing from her, she tossed it in the open drawer and took her by the hands. "Come here," she said, leading her toward the bed. They stretched out together. "Hey, this is comfortable. Sure beats the one at the cabin," Jesse said, wriggling on the soft mattress.

Abby rolled on her side and leaned up on an elbow to face her. "Can you believe we finally have a space all to ourselves?"

No sooner than the words left her mouth Gwen cried out.

"Well, almost," Jesse said, chuckling as she got up to get her daughter.

Abby got up and stood next to the bed. "Hey, why don't you go put them down for the night?"

Holding Gwen with one arm, Jesse bent down and scooped Jim up with the other.

Abby continued, "And don't take too long." Her eyes smoldered with intensity as she unfastened the top button on her dress. She glided closer, leaned up, and put her mouth next to Jesse's ear. "I have something planned for us tonight." She smiled when she heard Jesse's sharp intake of breath.

In less than ten minutes she had the twins down and was back in the bedroom, stumbling across the floor as she raced to get out of her clothes.

Abby pulled back the covers on the bed, giving Jesse a glimpse of her bare skin. "Get in here," she said, biting on her bottom lip as she locked eyes with her.

Jesse's pulse quickened as she gazed over Abby's ready and waiting form. She didn't have to be asked twice.

CHAPTER TWENTY-TWO

Jesse and Toby entered the smoke-filled kitchen to find Abby cursing over the wood-burning stove, gray smoke rising from the large cast-iron skillet as she lifted it away from the heat. Abby waved her hand in front of her face. "I thought I'd get up and fix you two breakfast," she said, coughing. "Found six eggs in the hen house this morning. It sure is nice to have chickens, isn't it?"

Jesse nodded and opened the window, trying to get the smoke to dissipate. It had been years since she had been around chickens. She thought back on her childhood and recalled the mean black rooster with the red comb and tail that hated people. Her sister, Jamie, had worn the proof. The mean cock left a scar on the back of her right calf where he came at her one day for no reason at all other than she had been in his vicinity. It felt like a lifetime since she'd thought about that, happening so long ago it was like it was someone else's memory.

"It's almost ready," Abby said, bringing Jesse back to the present. She set steaming cups of coffee on the table for them and went to the china hutch to fetch two plates. She piled each one with blackened slices of bread and three burnt pieces of bacon. "Ulayla showed me how to make her French toast," she said, setting the plates down in front of them. "She gave me her secret recipe, but it didn't turn out like hers. I think I had the skillet on too much heat."

Jesse looked up at her with a forced smile. "It looks delicious."

"Oh! I almost forgot," Abby said, hurrying to the cupboard.

While Abby's back was turned, Jesse darted a look from her plate to Toby. She grinned at his troubled expression. Ulayla's French toast had always been a nice shade of golden brown. Abby's was charred to a crisp—black as the liquid in their cups. The pungent smell of burnt bread had all but erased the usual mouthwatering aroma of nutmeg and vanilla that Jesse had come to expect.

"They left all sorts of food behind," Abby said, returning with a jar of maple syrup. She placed it on the table between them.

Toby and Jesse both poured on a generous amount, hoping to mask the unsavory flavor they both anticipated. Neither had the heart to say anything that would hurt Abby's feelings knowing she'd put a lot of effort into their breakfast. With smiles and *mmms* they graciously finished everything on their plates while maintaining their best poker faces.

Jesse tossed her napkin down, scooted back from the table, and asked Toby to fetch her hat from the hall tree. Once he left the kitchen, she approached Abby, who was hunched over the sink washing the morning dishes. "Thank you for getting up and cookin' this morning, but you don't have to do that. I can do it from now on. No reason for you to get up so early."

Abby straightened and reached for a towel. "I'm sorry. I know it wasn't very good. Ulayla's is much better," she said, drying her hands with a hint of dejection in her voice.

Jesse placed her hands on Abby's waist and pulled her close. She whispered in her ear, "That's not true. Yours was better. It tasted like love to me." Stepping back, she gave her a wink as Toby came walking in with her hat.

"You two have a great day," Abby said, still wearing the smile Jesse's words had left on her.

Jesse and Toby went to the barn, saddled the horses, and rode off to work.

Day after day, Jesse carved away at the wood, etching in intricate details and littering the floor below her with curled shavings of wood. Her evenings were always spent with the family, sitting in the parlor with one or both of the twins cuddled on her lap and reading aloud from *A Christmas Carol*. This precious time with her family was her favorite part of the day.

December 6th had approached quickly. It was the day before Sam and Helga Bowman were set to return and, coincidentally, the day before Thanksgiving was to be observed, courtesy of President Andrew Johnson's proclamation. It didn't feel like December to Jesse. Traditionally, she would have been shuttered alone in the cabin, up to her knees in snowdrifts by this time. Years of lonely isolation had been replaced by the warmth of her family. She was happy to break from that tradition.

It was fortunate for Mr. Tidwell and his crew that the Bowmans had been delayed overseas—this had given the workers two extra weeks to finish up some last minute details. Now, all that was left for Jesse to do was to finish installing the floral finial atop the carved-newel post.

It had taken her two months, sometimes even working late nights after everyone had gone to bed, to finish all the carved pieces of the staircase. Jesse had whittled meandering vines into the wood of the balusters and used a deep walnut stain that matched the banister, all finished with three coats of varnish to polish it off. After attaching the finial, she stepped back to have a look at her work and was startled to feel a hand rest upon her shoulder.

"That's some of the finest woodworking I've ever seen," Mr. Tidwell said, clapping her on the back. "You've exceeded my expectations by miles. How'd you like to be in charge of all the trim work when we start the construction on the next phase?"

"I'd be happy to," Jesse said with a smile that could not be contained. It felt nice to have her work recognized by someone as experienced as Mr. Tidwell.

"Listen, tomorrow is Thanksgiving. Why don't you go on home to your family and let them know about your raise?"

"Raise?" Jesse asked, her striking green eyes wide.

"How's five cents more on the hour sound?" he asked, offering his hand.

She gripped his hand, pumping it as if she was drawing water from a well. "Thank you, Mr. Tidwell."

"Call me, Harry," he said. "And get some rest this weekend

because we start demolishing that house next door on Monday. Now, get on outta here."

Jesse was still reeling from her unexpected good fortune when she went to the carriage house to saddle Buck. As she was tightening the cinch, Andrew came in through the open door. "I got a wire from Mr. Bowman. They'll be returning in the morning. He asked me to invite you and Abby over. Ulayla is going to prepare a Thanksgiving feast."

Jesse tossed the reins over Buck's neck and turned to face him. "I'm sorry, but we can't make it. Abby's been looking forward to our first holiday in the new place. She's been planning it for weeks."

"Hmm, I see. Well, how about you come tomorrow evening for dessert then? I can send a carriage for you."

Jesse thought for a moment. "We'd love to." She was sure Abby wouldn't have a problem with stopping by for dessert. Not only would it be nice to hear about their trip, she was eager to hear what they thought of her work.

The wonderful smells of Thanksgiving nudged Jesse awake. She inhaled deeply before opening her eyes, mouth watering at the thought of all the delicious food she was going to eat later that day. Abby and Aponi had been working hard at trying to perfect their cooking on the wood-burning stove, and judging by the aroma drifting through the house, it was obvious they had started to master it.

Jesse dressed and went into the twin's room. Jim was fast asleep, but Gwen was standing up in her crib, the rail gripped tightly in her pudgy hands as she swayed back and forth on unsteady legs.

"Pippa," Gwen babbled, reaching out with one hand.

Jesse leaned down and lifted her from the crib. "Pippa to you too," she said, kissing her daughter on the cheek.

Gwen's tiny hands cupped Jesse's face. "Pippa," she said again in her tiny voice.

Jesse carried Gwen downstairs making her feel like she was riding horseback. She bounced her up and down in her arms all the way into the kitchen, making an abrupt stop next to Abby that caused Gwen to burst into laughter.

Jesse said, "Abs, she said her first word."

Abby wiped her hands on her apron. "What did she say?" she asked expectantly.

"Sounded like Pippa. I don't know what it means, but she said it twice."

Abby smiled and placed a loving hand on her arm. "I think she is trying to say Papa."

An awkward yet familiar feeling enveloped Jesse. A few times now, she had heard Abby trying to teach the twins to call her Papa and had never felt comfortable with the epithet. "I actually like Pippa better than Papa anyway," she said, cheerfully.

"Well then, Pippa it is. Can you put her in her chair so I can feed her?" Abby said. "And will you go get Jim?"

She put Gwen in one of the highchairs next to their drop-leaf table. "Do you think when they're older they'll understand why I chose to live this way?"

"I do," Abby said, picking up the dishtowel from the table. "We have plenty of time before they'll be old enough to understand those things."

"I know. I just don't ever want to hurt them."

Abby stood on her tiptoes and kissed her on the cheek. "We'll figure it out later. I promise. Now, run up and get your son," she said, playfully snapping the towel on Jesse's behind in an effort to lighten her mood.

As the mantle clock in the parlor struck twelve, Jesse and Toby put the twins in their highchairs next to the dining room table and took their seats. Jesse gazed across the table at the wonderful array of food Abby and Aponi had prepared. She stood and picked up the large carving knife and fork, more than ready to slice into the golden-brown turkey.

"Wait," Aponi said, raising her hand. "I—we have something to say."

Jesse placed the utensils back on the table and took her seat.

Aponi looked at Toby seated next to her. "You want to tell?" she said, placing her hand over his.

Toby shook his head. "No," he said, his thumb grazing her fingers. "You tell 'em."

Aponi's face, normally introspective, lit up when she blurted out proudly, "I'm with child."

Jesse glanced over at Abby. She got the sense she had already heard the news since the two women had grown as close as sisters. "Congratulations, you two. I'm so happy. Just think, our kids will grow up playing together. When are you due?" Jesse asked.

"Should be-be here sometime in June," Toby said.

"I can't wait to meet my nephew—or niece. This year we

have something extra to be thankful for," Jesse said, standing. She carved the bird, placing several slices of meat on each plate. She put extra meat on Aponi's.

Although Jesse could hear the conversation flowing around her, her mind was focused on her blessings. They had made it to San Francisco without troubles. They'd found a wonderful home and were blessed to be all together. She and Toby both had jobs. The twins were healthy. Toby and Aponi were going to be parents. There were so many things she felt thankful for this year. So many, in fact, it was almost frightening. If anyone knew how a happy life could be torn away in an instant, it was her.

That evening, with the twins under the care of their aunt and uncle, Cuffy escorted Jesse and Abby in the carriage to the Bowman home. After thanking him, Jesse offered her elbow to Abby, and they made their way toward the stately home. They stopped at the oversized double doors that were each adorned with black-forged horse head knockers. When Jesse reached out and tapped the wrought-iron ring against the strike plate, Abby quickly ran her hands down the front of her periwinkle blue dress in a last minute effort to look more presentable. Both doors opened simultaneously and Andrew appeared on the other side, dapper in his black suit and white gloves. He greeted them warmly and invited them inside.

Jesse shook his hand and stepped into the enormous entry-way. Abby stared in amazement as she took in the interior of the home. Though she had never known indigence in her life, it still took her breath away to be in a place like this. It had changed considerably since the last time she had been inside, and it was the most extravagant home she had ever seen: high ceilings, marble flooring, high-end décor, and crystal chandeliers.

Abby's eyes landed on the stairway built up against the wall. She approached it slowly, taking in all the elaborate details of Jesse's handiwork. She had caught glimpses of it now and then when Jesse was working out in the barn late at night, but she had no idea it would turn into such a breathtaking finished product. She ran her hand over the finial atop the newel post. "It's beautiful," she said, looking at Jesse.

Andrew said, "My sentiments exactly. Now, please follow me." He led them toward the parlor and slid open the pocket doors. "Mr. and Mrs. McGinnis to see you, sir."

Sam stood in front of the fireplace, brandy snifter in hand. Helga, her dress billowed in layers beside her, sat on a large embroidered couch.

For the next hour, Jesse and Abby listened intently as they regaled them with stories of the wonderful excursions they'd had on their honeymoon. Neither Jesse nor Abby were able to get a word in edgewise. When they had finished sharing all the details of their lavish trip, Sam asked Jesse to accompany him to his office. She glanced at Abby before leaving the room, noticing Abby was still fidgeting with her dress. For some reason, she had been doing that all evening.

Sam closed the door to his office. "Have a seat," he said, pointing to one of the leather armchairs facing his desk. He walked over to a cabinet and retrieved a crystal decanter and two glasses. After placing them on the desk, he took a seat in a large leather chair, and opened an ornate box on the desktop. He removed two cigars and handed one to her. He held his cigar in his mouth and poured them each a glass of scotch.

Sam placed the glass stopper back in the decanter, and then struck a match under his desk and lit his cigar. He waved the match a few times before flipping it into the ashtray. The odor of sulfur swiftly gave way to the rich aroma of tobacco. Glancing at the end of his cigar, he seemed to contemplate his words before he spoke. He leaned forward, placing his elbows on the desk. "Mr. Tidwell tells me you were the one who did all the work on the staircase," he said, tossing her the matches.

Jesse fumbled as she caught the small box. "I just finished off what was already started."

Sam took another puff. She watched the glowing tip of the cigar, waiting on him to continue.

He stood up and reached for a rolled up document on a shelf behind him. Pushing everything on the desktop aside, he unrolled a set of blueprints. He used his scotch glass to hold down one edge of the paper and the palm of his hand to hold the other.

She stood to get a closer look.

"These are the plans for the addition. Once the house next door is torn down, this will be going up in its place. It will attach to this house flawlessly. No one will ever know it started out as two buildings."

Sam paused to puff once more before he continued. Using the tip of his cigar, he pointed at a spot on the blueprint. "You see this? It's where the main staircase will be," he said. He raised his eyes from the paper to her with intensity. "Notice how it sits in the middle of the grand foyer? It will be the first thing people see when they enter. I don't want just a plain staircase. I want a piece of art—I want a masterpiece."

Jesse focused her attention on the blueprint and saw the area indicated for the staircase. Her eyes wandered further down the plans. She saw it, spelled out in black ink: Bowman Estate. Phase number two: Estimated cost of one hundred and fifty thousand.

Sam lifted his glass and released the blueprint, causing the whole thing to neatly roll up on itself. He reached into the inside pocket of his suit coat and pulled out an envelope, handing it to her emphatically.

"What is it?" she asked.

He took his seat again. "Open it and find out."

She sat back down and opened the envelope. It was full of money. More money than she had ever seen.

Sam smiled warmly at her. "I've seen what you can do and I want to hire you to build the new staircase. You interested?"

Still taken aback by the contents of the envelope, she paused for a second to regain her words. "Of course I'm interested. But I work for Mr. Tidwell."

"You work for Mr. Tidwell," he said with a cheeky smile, "but Mr. Tidwell works for me. I already had a discussion with him this morning." He pointed toward the blueprints, jabbing toward it with his cigar for emphasis. "I want the entire project completed by July first. Mr. Tidwell is hiring as many men as he needs to meet my deadline so he can get by without your help. I want you to focus your attention on the staircase." He tapped his cigar, knocking ash into the ashtray. "Helga and I think you did exquisite work on the one out there. It far exceeded what we were expecting. We decided to pay you a small bonus of sorts—three hundred dollars. And the other thousand is for a down payment should you take on my proposal. It should be plenty to support your family while you're working on it. I'll pay another thousand upon completion." He leaned back in his chair. "So, two thousand to do the job. You interested?"

Jesse dropped her cigar when she heard him say two thousand dollars. She was glad she hadn't lit it yet. She reached down, picked it off the floor and settled back in the chair. Reluctantly, she put the envelope on the desk and slid it toward him.

Sam's brow furrowed in confusion. He leaned up on his desk. "What's wrong? Isn't it enough? To be clear, the money is just for your labor. Every business around here knows who I am. I have accounts all over. You take Cuffy and he'll assist you in getting any supplies you need. Just put it on my account."

She was speechless.

He took her silence as disinterest, which only enticed him further. In an effort to sweeten the deal, he said, "Tomorrow, all the furnishings in the house next door are going to be auctioned off. I was going to include all those tools out in the carriage house since I have no need for them. I know you've been using them. Tell you what. You can have them." He set the cigar in the ashtray and placed his finger on the envelope. "So, all those tools and two thousand dollars. Do we have a deal?" he asked, pushing the envelope back across the desk.

Sam was a dealmaker, and Jesse was beginning to feel the power of his persuasive skills. Still, she made no move to take the envelope. "I'd love to do this for you, but I can't. I know how to carve wood, but I don't know how to build a staircase like you want. Figuring out the bones of it...well I've never built anything like that. You need someone who knows how to construct it properly. It wouldn't be right to take your money."

Sam picked up his glass and leaned back in his chair again.

He swirled the scotch as he contemplated the dilemma. Then he downed the liquor before placing his glass back on the desk. "How about I have Mr. Tidwell and his crew frame it out? Then, you finish it off with your carving work. After all, that's what everyone is going to see. I'll still pay what I offered. So, what do you say?" He drummed his fingers on the desk as he waited on her reply.

She picked up her glass and tossed back the scotch. "Now that I can do," she said, cringing as the alcohol burned her throat.

He leaned back in his chair and propped his feet up on the edge of the desk. He took another drag of the cigar and blew the smoke toward the ceiling. "Not that I have any doubts about your skills," he said, "but I suggest you do your best work. I'm having a gala on July Fourth to celebrate the completion of my estate. People from all over are going to be here. They'll see your work up close." He drew on the cigar again.

Jesse was grateful he was blowing the smoke upward— between that and the scotch, she was starting to feel woozy.

"I want you and Abby to come. My gut says once people see what you can do they will be lining up to hire you. What you do...well, it's art. And people pay big money for that, especially around here." He swung his feet off the desk and stood. "All right, I've kept you long enough. Let's go join the women. Ulayla made her famous peach pie."

Jesse folded the envelope, and put it in the pocket of her trousers. Though it was only filled with paper, she felt heaviness in the envelope—a representation of power that she had never been acquainted with.

She knew exactly what she was going to do with some of

the money. First thing in the morning, she was going to meet with the Andersons' attorney and purchase the house on Taylor Street, giving the deed to Abby as a Christmas present. She followed Sam to the door. "Can you not mention any of this to Abby? I have something special I want to do for her. It's a surprise."

He smiled perceptively. "I suggest the place on Sacramento Street. It's Helga's favorite."

She hadn't a clue what he was talking about. Her confusion must have shown on her face because he went on to clarify.

"The one thing all women have in common is shopping. Especially when it involves getting a new dress. Am I right?"

Jesse nodded. He was right. It hadn't dawned on her until then how worn Abby's periwinkle dress had become. The blue had faded so much it could hardly be called blue any longer. The formerly white cuffs were now more of a cream color. In that moment, Jesse knew the reason for Abby's fidgeting—she must have felt like a worn out rag doll sitting next to Helga, who was dressed like royalty. Jesse still found Abby to be the most glamorous woman in any room no matter what she was wearing, but she realized what a boost of confidence an enhanced wardrobe would bring to her.

"Tell you what," he said, putting his hand on the doorknob. "I'll send Cuffy over to your place tomorrow with the carriage. Say, around one? He knows the places Helga likes to shop and can take her around the city." He opened the door. "And don't worry. Your secret is safe with me."

CHAPTER TWENTY-THREE

The room was bright when Abby woke. Realizing she had overslept and her babies must be hungry, she threw back the covers and fought to get her arms into the sleeves of her housecoat as she hurried across the hall. Finding both cribs empty, she went downstairs and found Jesse on her hands and knees chasing after the twins on the parlor floor.

"Morning," Jesse said. "They were up early so I scrambled 'em up some eggs."

Abby tied the belt of her housecoat as she went to sit on the sofa. "You should've woken me up," she said, yawning.

Jim turned his head and looked at his mother through his long bangs. A crooked smile came across his face. He crawled over to her as fast as he could and started to fuss.

Abby picked him up and brushed the dark black hair away from his eyes. "Want to help me cut his hair this weekend?"

"Sure," Jesse said, picking a piece of dried egg out of Gwen's blonde locks. "I have a couple errands to run this morning. I shouldn't be gone too long."

"Aponi will be up soon," Abby said, rocking Jim in her arms. "If you wait, I can go with you."

"I'm just going to look at some lumber for Sam. You'd be bored to tears." She kissed Gwen and got up off the floor. "I should be back before you and Aponi leave this afternoon, but if I'm not, Toby can watch 'em."

Abby tilted her head and kissed her goodbye. "Be careful."

"I will."

Jesse swung astride Buck and rode down the tree-lined street, eager to get to the attorney's office. To pull off the surprise she had planned, she had fibbed to Abby about what had transpired in Sam's office the night before, keeping secret how much he had actually given her. Even though she had to deceive her, it was going to be worth it when she got to see the look on Abby's face when she handed her the deed to the house. She too was beyond thrilled at the prospect of actually owning property.

Distracted in her euphoria, she didn't notice the familiar carriage parked in front of The Bay Water or Sam as he stepped down. It took a moment for her brain to register that someone was calling out her name as she passed by. She pulled on the reins and turned Buck around.

"Morning! Have you come up with any ideas yet?" Sam asked as he brushed a speck of dust from the lapel of his tailored three-piece suit.

"No. Not yet. I like to see the wood I'll be using first. It kind of speaks to me in a way."

He nodded approvingly. "Monday, I have two cargo ships coming in from Europe. While Helga and I were there, we purchased a lot of materials we want used on the home. I have all kinds of exotic lumber on board. We can go down to the wharf and you can have a look for yourself." He pointed over his shoulder to the building behind him. "Have you been inside The Bay Water?"

"No. I noticed it before but haven't had a chance to go inside."

Sam turned toward the carriage. "Cuffy, see to Mr. McGinnis's horse." He turned back to face her. "Come inside and I'll show you what it looks like now." He took a drag from his thin cigar.

"Now?" she asked with curiosity.

He nodded and exhaled the smoke. "I'm going to have it renovated. I'm turning it into a gentleman's club. Only members will be allowed." He pointed up and down the street. "My place happens to be in the center of the business district. I'll have lawyers, bankers, and all sorts of businessmen joining. No more rowdy drunks to deal with." He took another drag and flicked his cigar into the street.

She had no desire to go in, but she wanted to keep him happy. She swung a leg over the saddle, slid down, and handed the reins to Cuffy. "Thank you. Won't be long."

Anticipating another ordinary saloon, she was surprised to find the establishment clean and tastefully decorated with expensive furnishings. She was also surprised to see several men already seated inside—according to the pendulum clock hanging on the wall it wasn't even ten o'clock in the morning.

A man approached them. "Mr. Bowman, Mr. Randolph is waiting in your office," he said.

Sam nodded. "Jesse, I need to take this meeting. Why don't you have a seat and have a drink on the house," he said, motioning to the man behind the counter before disappearing to his office.

Jesse took a seat at the well-polished mahogany bar.

"What'll it be?" the bartender asked as he wiped the area in front of her with a white rag and placed a small napkin and a bowl of peanuts onto the bar.

"Just a glass of water."

He tossed the rag over his shoulder, poured water from a pitcher into a glass, and set it on the napkin. She picked it up but before it reached her lips, a young man a few seats down from her spoke.

"Non drinker, hein?" he asked in his thick French brogue.

She had never heard anyone with an accent like his. It was obvious he wasn't from the area. "Just a little too early for anything stronger," she said. She took a drink and set her glass on the napkin again. "Your accent…where are you from?"

He sat up tall. "Je viens de France!" he said proudly.

She assumed Je veins de must be his hometown in France. She swiveled her seat to face him. He was a slender young man with a thin mustache and well defined features. Thick, black curls flowed from underneath the brim of his hat. She guessed his age to be about the same as her own. "I've heard of France. It's far from here, isn't it?"

"Oh oui, very far."

"How'd you end up in California?"

"Work brought me to this great country."

With her curiosity piqued, she ventured another question. "What kind of work do you do?"

"Vineyards." He dropped his head as he continued. "I have known nothing else."

She detected the anguish in his voice. "The way you said that, it must be awful work."

His head perked up again. In a flash, he moved to the

barstool next to her. "Non," he said. "It is not awful work and I am in fact good at it. It is in my blood—my family's blood for generations."

"I don't know anything about vineyards. What is it exactly?"

He motioned for the bartender and asked for two glasses of something Jesse had never heard of. She watched as the man behind the bar retrieved a bottle, popped the cork, and poured a red liquid into two long stemmed glasses. Then, he placed the glasses in front of them.

The Frenchman picked the glass up by the stem and held it up to the light. He moved it in a circular motion, swirling the fluid, his other hand fanning the aroma toward his nose before he took a sip. She watched as he sat there with it held in his mouth, sucking air through his teeth. Finally, he tilted his head back and swallowed. He turned to her. "Inhale the bouquet," he said, "then you taste."

Jesse picked up her glass and did her best to mimic the process. She inhaled the sweet scent before taking a sip. "What is this?" she asked, enjoying the fruity aftertaste.

"It is a red port. Sorry to say, not one of the best I have had," he said. "They picked the grapes too soon. A little longer on the vine and it would have been much better."

Jesse asked, "So, do you own a vineyard?"

"My family owns one of the finest vineyards in all of France." With his palm facing down, he held out his hand three feet off the floor. "I worked that land from the time I was tout petit. Several years ago, I read about California. I have always wanted to make my own way in this life. I know every-thing there is to know about grapes. California is the lieu parfait for me to make a name for myself. I sailed across the ocean and well…voilà, here I am," he said. He took the last sip, and set his glass down with a heavy sigh.

She motioned for the bartender and held up two fingers. "I've never seen a vineyard. Is there one close by?"

"Oui. Not far, but I no work there anymore. I am going back to France."

Jesse cocked her head. "Why?"

"I got a letter from my maman. My papa is gravely ill. I must return home." He reached into his pocket and pulled out a folded document. "I bought one hundred acres in Neva." He set the property deed on top of the bar. "I have to sell it. I need the money to book passage to France."

His despair rolled off him like the thick fog that sometimes moved inland from the bay. Jesse remembered what it was like when Frieda got sick; the heavy sense of helplessness she carried around like a lead anchor. "The name is Jesse McGinnis," she said, reaching out her hand.

"Bonjour," he said, shaking it. "Armand Baptiste."

One simple handshake told her a lot about the man. His firm grip wasn't what told his story, but the numerous callouses covering his palm, revealing he didn't shy away from hard work. It was a way of life she respected and admired, so it was a welcome encounter to meet another person with a similar work ethic.

"My dream was to come to America and work on a vineyard until I have money to buy my own land. Then, I start my own vineyard." He tapped his finger on the deed. "I own my land for two months. Now, I must sell and return to my country."

Jesse took another sip of the sweet wine before she spoke. "Life doesn't always go the way we want. Sometimes things happen out of order from what we plan. Maybe you can return someday and start that vineyard."

"Oui. Peut-être." Perhaps, maybe one day he would, he hoped.

"So, what's an acre go for in Neva?"

"Six to ten dollars—sometimes more—sometimes less. I bought my parcel at four dollars because of the sand in the soil."

Her brow knitted in confusion. She used her finger to lift the brim of her hat. "I know a little about soil, but isn't—"

Armand waved his hand in the air. "I know what you are thinking—nothing grows good in sandy loam, but it is parfait for growing grapes. It is the same kind of soil we grow our grapes in on my family's vineyard."

"Never heard of Neva. Where is it?"

"On a fast horse, it is about an hour from here."

Jesse stood up and grabbed the bar, momentarily off balance, courtesy of the sweet red liquor. "You have a fast horse?"

"Oui."

"I might be interested in your land, but I'd like to see it first."

Armand agreed and Jesse settled the tab, telling the bartender to let Sam know something had come up, and she would see him on Monday. They exited The Bay Water, mounted their horses, and rode off.

After riding for close to an hour, they came upon the outskirts of a quaint little town. A wooden sign stood next to the road that read, *Neva: Established 1858*. They slowed the horses to a walk and made their way down Main Street. Jesse studied the storefronts. Every business was fairly new and well maintained. It was obvious the owners in this town took pride in their establishments. One man, washing the large plate glass window in front of a feed store, paused and waved at them as they passed. A few doors down, another man was arranging merchandise on a table in front of a store. He also stopped what he was doing and turned to smile and wave. Two women nodded their greetings as they crossed the street in front of them. No matter who they passed, they were met with a friendly gesture. It wasn't until they had come to the end of the street Jesse realized not a single man loitered anywhere.

"Where's the saloon?" she asked, glancing back down the street.

"There are no saloons in Neva. This is a farming town. Farmers get up with the sun and work until it goes down. They are too tired for anything else."

Now, this is my kind of place, she thought.

"Come on. We are almost there." With a click of his tongue, Armand got his horse to pick up his pace.

Ten minutes later, Armand pulled back on his reigns. "Here it is," he said. He let his arm swing wide as he did his best to indicate the starting and ending points of his property.

Jesse scanned the landscape, taking in the rolling hills, lush meadows, and sprawling forest off in the distance that stretched out before her.

Armand saw the gleam in her eye when he pointed and said, "There is a river in the woods." He kissed his fingertips. "Délicieux trout. Follow me."

He led her further onto the property and came to a stop in

a field. He jumped down, knelt, and picked up a handful of the loose soil. "This is where I was going to plant my grapes," he said, letting the sandy grains fall between his fingers. "When I had saved enough money, I was returning to France. I would get the best vine cuttings from the vineyard of my family and bring them back with me. I would grow the best grapes in all of California."

Jesse swung a leg over the saddle and dropped down to the ground. Kneeling beside him, she scooped up a handful of the soil. "I know nothing about grapes and vineyards, so would you be interested in being partners?" she asked, running her thumb over the gritty dirt.

"Excusez-moi?"

"Partners," she said. "Do you want to be partners?"

"What are you proposing?" He stood and rubbed his hands together, brushing off the grit.

Jesse dropped the handful of soil and wiped her hand on her pant leg. "What if I buy your land so you can get home," she said, standing up to meet him face to face. "Someday, if you decide to return to California, you bring your vines, and I'll deed you back fifty acres. We'll be equal partners. What do you think?"

"You'd do that for me? Pourquoi? You don't even know me."

She looked out over the meadow. Her thoughts shifted to Frieda and how the woman had been there for her when she had needed someone the most. She thought of Edith and her willingness to help her when she first went to Ely. She didn't know why those women took a chance on her, but they did. She turned to face Armand.

"In my past, I've had strangers take a chance on me. My

gut is telling me to do the same for you." She reached into her pocket and withdrew her money. She counted out four hundred dollars and glanced momentarily at the bills in her hand, knowing if she handed it over, she would no longer be able to afford the house on Taylor Street. Instincts told her that this was the place she wanted to call home one day. She didn't need to give it another thought. "So, do we have a deal?" she asked, extending the money to him.

Before he reached for it, he asked, "Pardon. But what if I do not come back?"

She shrugged her shoulders. "Then you don't. That will be up to you." She smiled at him. "I think you will, though."

Armand extended his hand to shake. "Merci. Merci beaucoup," he said as his other hand quickly went into his breast pocket.

For a split second, she feared he was reaching for a gun. Automatically her hand went to her pistol. Before she had time to draw, he had already pulled out a piece of paper.

He handed her the deed. "Let me show you the river, and then we ride to Neva. I know someone who can witness the transfer of the land."

It was dusk by the time they returned to San Francisco. Small points of light came into view and they slowed their horses to a trot. The hypnotic thrum of chirping crickets was drowned out by the noises of the city.

When they reached The Bay Water, Jesse leaned in the saddle. "Safe travels, my friend," she said, reaching out to shake his hand one final time. "Hopefully, I will see you again. You remember my address?"

"D'accord. I will come to 317 Taylor Street, should I return. Au revoir, Jesse McGinnis."

Jesse rode home even more elated than she had been when she rode into town that morning. It had been one of the best days of her life. She was now the proud owner of her own piece of land. She was bursting with pride and couldn't wait to share the news with Abby. There was no way she was going to be able to keep it a secret until Christmas.

After she got Buck settled in the barn, she whistled on her way to the house. Entering the kitchen through the back door, she kicked off her boots.

"Jesse!" Abby called out as she rushed into the room. "Where have you been? I thought something happened to you."

"I'm fine. Sorry. I didn't mean to make you worry."

Abby collapsed into a chair at the kitchen table.

Jesse sat across from her, noticing her bloodshot eyes. "What's wrong?" she asked, reaching for her hand.

"When Aponi and I went shopping we were confronted by a couple of men outside one of the shops." Abby paused to wipe away her tears. "They said terrible—hurtful things."

"What'd they say?"

Abby sniffled. "One of them ran his hand through Aponi's hair and said he could get good money for a scalp like that. Then he called her a savage and spat in her face. Called me an injun lover. It was awful. She wants to leave and go back to Mount Perish."

Jesse's chair screeched across the wood floor when she stood.

"Where are you going?" Abby asked, grabbing her by the arm.

"To talk to her."

"No. Don't. It's late. Hopefully she's sleeping now." Abby sniffed again. "You know if she goes, Toby would go with her."

Jesse sat back down as Abby continued. "She told us it wasn't the first time she's noticed things. We just haven't been paying attention and we should've."

"What the hell is wrong with people? I will never be able to understand how a person can be treated so badly just because of the color of their skin. It makes me furious," Jesse said through clenched teeth. "Maybe we shouldn't have brought her here."

"What are we going to do?"

Jesse took off her hat and tossed it on the empty chair next to her. She realized she had an opening to deliver the news to Abby. "Maybe Toby and her would be more comfortable living in the country." She reached across and took hold of Abby's hands. "I did something today. I hope you won't be upset with me. I purchased some land in a little town called Neva. It's beautiful there. Hills, pastures, woods, and—"

A frown creased Abby's forehead. "You did what?"

"I bought a hundred acres. There's no house on the land, but we could help Toby and Aponi build one. I was hoping maybe someday you'd like to move out there, too. I think you'll love—"

Abby jerked her hands free. "I can't believe you sometimes! You just go off and do things without discussing it with me. Like I have no say in the matter." Her eyebrows furrowed over her incensed blue eyes. "And how did you come up with money to buy land anyway?"

Jesse sat up straight. Even though she knew Abby was furious, she still couldn't squelch the thrilling feeling of being a landowner. It was a huge accomplishment for her. "Look. It's been a long day," she said. "Why don't we go upstairs and I'll explain everything."

The following morning, after an unusually silent breakfast, Jesse and Toby hitched Titan to the Andersons' old wagon Cuffy had helped them repair. Abby and Aponi climbed into the back and Jesse handed up the twins. Once they were settled, Toby took his seat up front next to Jesse and she drove them out to see their property.

Aside from the twins' gibberish, no one spoke as the wagon rolled through the countryside. The trip was taking much longer this time in the slow moving vehicle, only making the awkward silence that much more noticeable.

Abby was still fuming over the fact Jesse would do something as important as buying property without even speaking with her about it first. Toby and Aponi were contemplating their own woes. Jesse was the only person who seemed to be even remotely happy, but she was careful not to let it show. Left to her own thoughts, she stared straight ahead, dreaming of a life out in the country.

She eased the wagon through the town of Neva at a crawl. Several people along the way waved at them as they rolled past, and she returned their greetings with a nod. She glanced over her shoulder and saw Abby returning their waves, and she hoped her mood was starting to soften. A smile lifted the corners of her mouth when she saw the twins waving to strangers as if they were the grand marshals of the Neva Fourth of July parade. She hoped that Abby's first impression of the town had been similar to hers.

Twenty minutes later, Jesse pulled the wagon out in a field and pulled back on the reins. "Well, this is it. We own all of this," she said, using her hand to indicate the property boundaries as Armand had done when he had showed it to her. "Isn't it perfect?"

As much as Abby hated to admit it, it was a beautiful piece of land.

Jesse set the break on the wagon. "C'mon. Let's go for a walk," she said, jumping down. She tossed her hat in the back of the wagon, picked Jim up, and set him on her shoulders. Once everyone got down, she continued. "This is the field where I hope someday to have row after row of French grapes. Just needs a little clearing." She turned and pointed. "That's where I'd build our house. Over there, in those woods is my favorite. There's a river. Well, Armand called it a river but it's more of a stream—nothing like the Devil's Fork. We can fish and hunt…"

Abby shifted Gwen to her other hip and listened as Jesse went on and on. Her excitement was contagious. The longer she spoke the more excited Abby became. She too was starting to picture the country life Jesse was describing, and she was beginning to see for herself how Jesse fell in love with the land. It was picturesque.

Jesse felt Abby's hand on her back. It was the first time she had touched her since she had pulled away from her the night before, and the electricity she felt flowing into her body from the simple touch told her the answer to her next question before she asked it. "So, what do you all think? Do you like it?" she asked.

Abby looked up at her. Jim was running his tiny fingers through Jesse's hair giving her a windblown look. "This place really is pretty," Abby said. She took a deep breath, not knowing until that moment just how much she missed the country air.

Jesse, hair stuck up in all directions, turned to face Toby and Aponi. "I know we don't have the money to build anything fancy. But look at those trees. We could harvest the wood and use it to build you two a cabin. Would you like to live here?"

"It's like home," Aponi said, tears pooling in her eyes.

Jesse turned back toward Abby. "Someday I'm going to build you the home of your dreams. Don't you like the idea of raising our children in a place like this? I can teach them to hunt, fish—"

Abby held up her hand. "Breathe," she said. "You already have me sold. You did good buying this place."

Aponi reached out and took hold of Toby's hand. "I wish we didn't have to go back to San Francisco. I want to stay here." Tears spilled, and she hurried to wipe them away.

Jesse got the sense there was more behind Aponi's emotions. She too loved the property but it didn't bring tears to her eyes. She chalked it up to pregnancy mood swings, as she knew all about those first hand. "You and Toby can start building now if you want," she said. "I won't be able to help much because I have a job to finish for Sam. But, I can come out on the weekends and do what I can."

Abby took hold of Aponi's hand. "I'll come too," she said eagerly.

Jesse was moved by Abby's willingness to help. It was one of the many reasons she loved her so much. "See? We'll have you a home built in no time. So, what do you think?"

"But I have a job w-working for Mr. Tid—"

"You don't need to work for him," Jesse said, interrupting. "You just get your home built. That's more important right now."

"But wh-what about money? I have a family to support."

"We'll worry 'bout that later. Right now, I think it's important to focus on getting a home built. You have a baby on the way."

Unable to contain her emotions, Aponi began to sob in an unusual outpouring that alarmed everyone.

Toby took her face in his hands and used his thumbs to brush away her tears. "Are you all right?"

"I'm sorry," Aponi said, voice breaking. She stared into his eyes trying to muster the courage. "I'm so sorry. I lost the baby early this morning."

Toby pulled her close and held tight to his trembling wife. "You have nothing to be sorry for. We can try again if you wa-want."

The news was devastating to him, but he didn't want to add to her heartbreak. She had enough of her own. He shifted the conversation. "Let's build a new life here. We can live off th-the land just like we used to. The woods will provide everything we need," he said pointing to the trees behind them. "We just have to hunt for it. So, wh-what do you think?"

Aponi sniffled. She palmed away her tears and nodded her agreement.

Abby handed Gwen to Jesse and wrapped her arms around Aponi. Jesse, managing both kids, watched as Toby quickly wiped away his own tears before Aponi could see them. Her heart broke for her brother. She couldn't imagine what she would have done if Abby would have lost the twins. It was too unbearable to fathom.

Jesse had learned from Frieda the best way to help someone cope with loss was to keep them busy so they wouldn't have time to dwell on their sorrow. She hoped focusing all their attention on building a new home would do just that for the grieving couple.

CHAPTER TWENTY-FOUR

CHRISTMAS, 1865

"Yes, wake up," Abby said, sitting down on the edge of the bed. "I want to show you something."

Jesse rolled over, yawned, and rubbed the sleep from her eyes. She yawned again and leaned up on an elbow.

Abby handed her a piece of folded newspaper. "I want us to start our own family traditions. This was printed in the paper a few weeks ago. I love it, and thought maybe you could read it to the children."

Jesse rested her head in Abby's lap and took the piece of paper. Unfolding it, she read the poem titled, *A Visit from St. Nicholas.*

Abby brushed Jesse's bangs aside and lightly ran her fingertips across her forehead. "I know it's make believe and all, but the kids don't. I know they're too young to understand now, but I like the idea of them growing up believing in something magical. So, what do you think?"

"What kid wouldn't like believing in a man who brings them presents for no reason?" Jesse said, tilting her head back to look at Abby. "I know I would've. I love the idea of starting traditions with you and them."

"C'mon," Abby said, her blue eyes dancing. "Get dressed."

Jesse tossed back the bedcovers and rolled out of bed. As she dressed, she watched Abby pulling wrapped packages from underneath the bed.

"It's fun playing Santa," Abby said, her face flushed with delight. "Hurry up so we can take 'em downstairs before everyone gets up."

Abby's enjoyment was contagious. Jesse was now excited and hurried to finish dressing, fumbling the last button on her shirt as she rushed.

They carried the gifts downstairs and placed them on the floor in front of the sofa. Abby said, "Now, let's go get everyone up."

Soon, the entire McGinnis clan was gathered in the parlor. Abby said, "Look, Santa came last night." She handed Toby and Aponi each a gift. "You two go first," she said. She picked Gwen up and took a seat next to Jesse and Jim on the sofa.

Jesse couldn't help but notice Abby's joy as she intently watched Toby and Aponi pull the ribbons and tear away the fancy wrapping paper.

Jesse chuckled at Toby's expression when he opened his gift. It wasn't surprising. He reacted the same way she imagined most men would to a plaid flannel shirt.

Even though Abby had been excited for Toby to open his present, it was clear it was Aponi's reaction she seemed to be waiting for more anxiously. She bit her lip as Aponi pulled out her gift. "Well, do you like it?" Abby asked, the words gushing out.

"It's beautiful," she said, holding up the new dress under her chin. "Thank you."

Abby's blonde lashes blinked over sapphire eyes. "Don't thank me. It was Santa Claus." Shifting on the sofa, she turned to face Jesse and Jim. "We're going to have to help them. You two go first."

Balancing Jim in her lap, Jesse helped him rip open the paper on his present. Inside was a colorful red, yellow, and blue wooden toy top. She put him down and gave the top a good spin, sending it skipping across the wood floorboards, skittering out of his reach. He quickly crawled off after it, laughing and cooing in his pursuit.

On the sofa, Gwen, sitting on Abby's lap, tore at the paper on her present without much need of assistance. She giggled as she yanked her new doll up by its arm.

"Jes, come here," Abby said, patting the cushion next to her.

Nearby, Jim had scooped up the top and was biting on the handle to ease his teething pain. Jesse took it from him and gave it another good spin, grimacing when she grabbed the drool covered handle, before heading over to the sofa.

"No peeking," Abby said, placing her hand over Jesse's eyes.

When they were confident she couldn't see, Toby slipped out of the room.

Moments later, Jesse felt something being placed in her lap.

"All right," Abby said, lowering her hand. "You can open your eyes now."

The gift wasn't wrapped. It was a rifle, the exact model and year as the one she had traded to Black Turtle. The second she saw it, something inside of her broke loose. With her heart in her throat, she made no effort to hold back her tears. She couldn't have even if she wanted to.

"I kn-know it's not Frieda's," Toby said, "but I hope you like it."

Jesse used the palms of her hands to wipe away her tears. "How," she asked, her voice shaking. "Where did you get it?" She ran her fingers along the wooden butt of the gun.

"Abby helped. I think she went to every gun st-st-store in San Francisco to help me find one."

"I don't know what to—there aren't words to say how much this means to me. Thank you." She glanced at the smiling faces staring back at her, realizing she had become the center of attention. In an effort to get the focus off of her, she looked at Abby with a gasp. "I'm sorry, Abs. I didn't get you anything."

"Of course you did! Look around you. All of us are here together sharing this day. What more could I possibly want?" Abby said, happy tears pooling.

"Now do you think I would really forget about you?" Jesse asked, rolling her eyes. "I'll be right back," she said, springing up from the sofa.

Jesse hurried through the kitchen, slipped on a pair of boots, and headed outside to the barn. Inside her workshop, she reached under the far end of her workbench and pulled out the present she had hidden behind some scraps of wood. Back inside, she kicked off her boots and headed to the parlor, anxious to see if she could replicate the same kind of response with her gift.

Abby sat with her hands clasped together, drumming her foot against the floor. Although the appearance of the package looked more like something the twins had wrapped, she chose to ignore it, focusing instead on what was inside. All types of things ran through her mind: a sterling-silver brush with matching mirror, a jeweled hairpin, perfume, or maybe a pearl necklace. Based on the weight of the box, she knew it couldn't be any of those items. She was stumped.

"Open it already," Jesse said, anxious to see her reaction.

Abby ripped open the paper, peered inside the box, and sat with her mouth falling open.

Jesse asked, "Well. Do you like it?"

"Uh...well...is it what I think it is?"

Jesse reached over and pulled it from the box. "This is going to make your life so much easier." She pointed to the small fuel tank attached to the back of the iron. "See, you put kerosene in there. No more waiting for one to heat on the stove," she said with a satisfied smile as she placed it back on Abby's lap.

Toby chuckled under his breath. He didn't know a lot about women, but even he knew an iron wasn't the gift most wives fancied.

Abby stared at the modern apparatus, which was supposed to simplify her life. "Thank you," she said. "How thoughtful."

"You're welcome." Although Abby was smiling, Jesse could tell by her tone the gift was a disappointment.

Abby placed the iron on the floor at her feet and patted Jesse's leg. "Well," she said, standing. "I need to get started on dinner. It isn't going to cook itself."

Jesse reached up and took hold of Abby's hand, gently guiding her back to the sofa. "You've done enough." She leaned in to kiss Abby's cheek. "I'll take care of dinner." It was the least she could do.

The Christmas of 1865 started a McGinnis family tradition which continued from that day on with Jesse taking charge of the holiday meal. A day of relaxation surrounded by her family, rather than one spent standing over a hot stove, was the best gift Abby received each year.

What began as a seed of hope had already taken root now that construction was well underway on Toby and Aponi's log home. After speaking to the owner of the local sawmill in Neva, Jesse had managed to hire three capable men to work alongside her brother. She too wanted more than anything to be out in the country, working beside them as trees were harvested from the property and transformed into a home. She knew the feeling of creating something with your own hands. There was nothing more gratifying. Unfortunately, financial obligations kept her tethered to the city.

Taking advantage of the hired help and having plenty of natural resources on the property, Jesse and Abby opted to start construction on a small log home for themselves as well. It wasn't going to be anything lavish, just a modest one-bedroom cabin not much different than the one back atop Mount Perish. It would be their weekend retreat, a place to get away from the hustle of city life and spend quality time together.

Ever since the construction had begun, mornings inside the home on Taylor Street had turned chaotic. Gone were the days when everyone had time to sit around the table enjoying a relaxing cup of coffee together. Now, they were spent in a mad rush as everyone scrambled with preparations to get on with the day's agenda. Having one-year-old twins only fueled the morning mayhem. After scarfing down a quick bite together, they scattered, rushing to get on with the day's routine. Jesse and Toby would go over the inventory in the wagon, loading any tools or other materials that were needed out in Neva. Inside, Abby hurried to tend to the twins while Aponi hastily tossed together a basket of food for them and their workers.

Once the women and children were settled in the back of the wagon, Jesse said her last-minute goodbyes. Toby took the opportunity to check over his supplies one final time. The hour and a half wagon ride was too long of a commute to turn around and come back for something he had forgotten.

Throughout the week, Jesse followed them out into the street as they pulled away. She stood and waved, her hand as heavy as lead as she watched her family head off to the countryside without her. Once they were out of sight, it was off to work for her as well.

Over time, she had transferred all the tools from the Bowmans' carriage house into an area of her own barn, which had been converted into a workshop. When she wasn't working on one of the more intricate pieces of wood in her shop, she was over at Sam's learning the process of erecting the framework of the staircase, courtesy of Mr. Tidwell.

Even though she enjoyed working for herself, she hated the solitude. Throughout the day she caught herself talking aloud to Buck as she worked, reminding her of those isolating winter days on the mountain. By days end, her feet were buried in shavings, her heart smothered in loneliness.

As the hours turned into days and then to weeks, the wood Jesse fashioned with her blades took shape. Her vision was coming to life. Although she was pleased with the way it was turning out, nothing filled the void of being separated from her family. Being apart from her children was a pain like no other. All day long she looked forward to seeing them return safely. As soon as they got home she loved all over her babies, listening to Abby, Toby, and Aponi fill her in on the day's events.

Leaving Jesse in the mornings wasn't easy on Abby either. Still, she found herself looking forward to working on their land. With the wagon parked under the shade of a large oak, the boxed-in bed was perfect for keeping the twins corralled and out of harms way. Once she had them down for a nap, she spent the time being useful: sawing, sanding, or cooking over an open fire. She did whatever she could to contribute.

No matter how busy Jesse was she always made sure to stop whatever she was doing to get supper on, knowing everyone would be exhausted by the time they got home, especially Toby. She knew it would have been easier on all of them to camp out on the property, but he was adamant about making the long commute back and forth every weekday. If it was only him, he would have stayed, but he felt the women deserved to sleep in a warm bed. And moreover, he knew it wouldn't be fair to his sister. He was fully aware of how hard it was on her to be separated from her children and the sacrifices she made. Watching her dote over the twins when they got home made it all worth it.

Weekends became Jesse's favorite. Every Saturday morning she would make the trip with her family and was able to see first hand the progress being made. Every week she was amazed by the changes being wrought. She spent the entire day working alongside the others until they lost the light, then they would settle by a fire and sleep out under the stars or shelter together under a canvas-tarp tent on rainy nights. At dawn, Jesse and Toby would sneak off while the others were still sound asleep hoping to pull a few trout from the river before the trip back to San Francisco later that day. Then, in a flash of an eye it was Monday again, and it was back to the same long weekly routine.

As the walls of the cabins were going up, the ones surrounding Aponi were crumbling down. Being in the country seemed to open something in her the others feared had closed off for good after the loss of her baby. It was obvious to all the woman found her solace in nature. When she wasn't working on the log structures, she was foraging in the woods. Much to her surprise, she discovered many plants with medicinal properties like the ones on the mountain. She soon came to realize the ground beneath her feet wasn't much different than where she had grown up—it was home.

CHAPTER TWENTY-FIVE

J esse stood in front of the dresser and lifted her chin, allowing Abby to straighten her tie.

Abby tugged the black fabric a little side to side. "There," she said. "Perfect."

Jesse fastened the three buttons on her embroidered, silk, maroon vest. "I can't believe how much you spent on this. You know what we could have bought with that much money?" she asked, looking down at the cuffs of her pressed white shirt as Jim used the pant leg of her black cotton-twill trousers to pull himself up.

"I know it was expensive," Abby said, "but try to think of it as an investment. You want to look the part, don't you?"

"I know, I know." She looked at the cuffs on her shirt. "There aren't any buttons," she said, quirking an eyebrow.

Abby smiled at her. She went to the dresser and pulled a box from the top drawer. "Just a little something I picked up for you. I hope you like it."

Jesse removed the lid from the box. "What are they?" she asked, staring at the gold jewelry inside.

"They're cufflinks. Here, let me show you." She stuck the pins through the fabric and clipped the studs with the fasteners. "So, what do you think?"

Jesse pulled her sleeves down and looked at her cuffs again. "I like 'em. Thank you," she said, giving her a kiss on the cheek. She felt Jim clinging to her pant leg. "Abs, go sit on the bed. Let's see if he'll walk to you."

Abby smoothed out her ball gown and sat, reaching out with both hands. "Jim. Come here," she said, raising the pitch of her voice to entice him to come.

Jim looked at her but didn't move. Jesse gently pried his fingers loose and turned him in his mother's direction. "Go to your ma," she said, letting go of his hands.

He stood, tottering in place as Abby continued to encourage him. Finally, he moved one hesitant foot forward. Jesse bent over and followed behind him, hand at his back, ready to catch him should he fall. They watched attentively with breath held as he swayed back and forth with each step. Each time he leaned too far to one side, both women leaned as well, as if their movements somehow had the power to keep him on his feet. Five monumental steps later, he reached his mother's outstretched hands.

Jesse scooped him off the floor and held him high in the air. "You did it! That's my big boy."

Jim cupped her face in his tiny hands and giggled.

A knock on the bedroom door interrupted the momentous occasion.

"Cuffy's here," Toby said.

Three weeks ago, he and Aponi had finally moved into their new home in Neva. They had come back into town earlier in the day to sit with the twins.

"We'll be right down," Jesse said. She put Jim on the floor next to Gwen and reached for her black-silk tailcoat. Glancing into the mirror, she took one last look at her short hair, which had been slicked back with a hint of Madagascar oil before donning the top hat.

"You look very nice," Abby said.

Jesse turned to face her. Abby was wearing a flowing, maroon, ball gown, which matched the embroidery work on Jesse's vest. Her hair was pulled up into a loose bun and pinned into place with a jeweled hairpin. She was wearing little makeup, just enough to enhance her beauty.

"And you're still the prettiest woman I have ever seen," she said, running her finger lightly down the soft skin between Abby's breasts.

"Now don't go starting something," she said teasingly as she pulled Jesse's hand from her cleavage. "So, you think you'll remember the steps I taught you? Because tonight, when we dance, I want to get lost in your arms," Abby said as she slipped on her lacy-black gloves.

"I guess we're both going to find out soon enough."

At precisely eight o'clock, Cuffy pulled the polished carriage to a stop in front of the Bowman mansion. He opened the door and stepped aside, allowing Jesse to step out first. Then, he offered his white-gloved hand to Abby, assisting her down the carriage steps. She curtseyed a small thank you to him. He returned the salutation with a warm smile and a bowed head.

Jesse offered her elbow and the couple strode together through an opened gate along a brick-paved path. They paused next to a five-tiered fountain to take in the sprawling estate. The grandiose forty-three-room granite mansion sat on a well-manicured lawn, surrounded by meticulously shaped hedges. Its three stories were topped off with a wrought iron widow's walk on the mansard roof.

Just beyond the splashing sound of the fountain, they could hear the muffled chatter coming from the large gathering of people visible through the open double doors.

Jesse turned to Abby. "I'm not sure this was a good idea." The lines of worry in her forehead only deepened. "Look at all those people."

"I know you hate crowds, but you'll be fine. I promise. Besides, I can't wait to see it. You worked so hard." She tightened her grip in the crook of Jesse's elbow and pulled her along before she could talk herself out of going inside.

They entered into a grand foyer with eighteen-foot-tall ceilings, held up by massive Corinthian marble columns. They were cordially greeted by one of the uniformed staff who offered to take Abby's shawl. Distracted, she mumbled an unintelligible thank you as she tried to see through the throng of people gathered around the staircase.

The stairway had a towering presence, unlike anything she had ever seen. The attention to detail was extraordinary. The handrail had recessed patterns of acanthus leaves, which seemed to grow right from the wood. The spindles had been carved to look like vines of climbing ivy. While these details were beautiful, they were nothing compared to the heart of the structure. The real masterpieces were the two, five feet tall newel posts.

Jesse had gotten her inspiration from the Bowmans' door-knockers. She had fashioned the newel posts to look like rearing black stallions with red eyes, their manes flowing in the wind. A few of the guests were reaching out for a touch as if they almost expected to feel hot air snorting from their flared nostrils.

Abby's mouth was wide open in shock, and she quickly covered it with her hand. "Jes," she said finally, "I've never seen anything like it. It's beautiful. How'd you get the eyes to look like that?"

"I went to a glass shop and had them—"

"There's the man of the hour," Sam announced, his voice carrying over the crowd.

Jesse watched as he made his way toward them, mingling and quickly greeting people along the way as he fought through the sea of guests.

He reached out to shake her hand and leaned in close. "I'll bait. All you have to do is set the hook," he whispered.

The line of people that had fallen in behind him as he made his way over now congregated around them, each one eager for a chance to meet the new artisan in San Francisco.

Sam raised a quieting hand. "Ladies and Gentlemen, it is my privilege to introduce to you, Mr. McGinnis. As most of you know, I've been all around this world. He is by far the finest craftsman..." He paused, trying to find a better word, and continued, "...artist I've ever seen. I am honored to have his presence here with us this evening."

As soon as he finished speaking, the guests swarmed in closer around her and Abby.

Abby released her grip on her arm. "Don't be too long," she said, smiling at her sweetly. "You promised me a dance."

Jesse watched her walk over and stand next to Helga. "So?" she heard a man say. She turned toward the voice. "So, when could you start? The Mrs. and I would like—"

A man stepped in front of him. "Do you have a waiting list? If so, I'd like to be placed on it."

An older woman holding a small poodle in the back of the group raised her hand, her voice loud in spite of the crowd. "I'd like to hire you."

Sam raised his hand in the air again. "Honored guests, please. Don't crowd. If you'd like to speak with him, then follow me."

He led Jesse and a small group of people toward his office. "Mr. McGinnis," he said, pulling his big leather chair out from behind the desk.

Jesse took the offered chair while Sam pulled one of the smaller chairs around the desk and took a seat next to her. He dotted his pen in the inkwell and held it poised over a blank sheet of paper. "If you're interested in hiring Mr. McGinnis, I will take your name and address and he'll be in touch. He is very particular about his work. Not every home can have an original McGinnis statement piece, so please don't take offense if he declines."

For the next forty-five minutes, Jesse spoke with potential clients to get an idea of their visions and then Sam took down their names and addresses if she felt the work was in her wheelhouse. Most of them were willing to hire a contractor to install her handiwork if need be. All she had to do was carve.

After Sam had penned the last name, he escorted the couple out of his office and closed the door. He went to the liquor hutch and retrieved a bottle of scotch and two glasses.

"That went better than I ever imagined," he said, pouring the liquor. "You're going to make a fortune, my friend," he said, handing her a glass.

Jesse held it up, toasting him. "I'm forever grateful to you. If I can ever do anything for you…just name it."

Sam nodded and tapped his glass against hers. He sat on the edge of his desk. "You know most rich people are fools with their money. Look at the folks who just left. They'll claw at each other to get you to build them a staircase—or whatever. Don't get me wrong, you do exquisite work, but the more costly something is the more rich people want it. If it's expensive, they have to have it."

He drank down his scotch and refilled his glass. "My advice to you is to be absurd when you shoot them your price. Mark my words. They'll pay anything you ask." He tapped his glass against hers again, clearly happy to be passing along his wisdom to someone potentially heading up the social ladder. "Oh, and make sure you ask for half up front."

Jesse's head was whirling even before she took a drink. She tossed back the scotch and sat her empty glass on the desk. "Can I ask why you're doing this for me?"

Sam opened the box on his desk and pulled out a cigar. He offered one to her, but she declined with a shake of the head. He struck a match and lit his cigar. After a couple of puffs, he asked, "Can I be honest with you?"

"Of course."

A smile lifted the corners of his mouth. "There was a time when I thought Abigail and I would marry. Even though things turned out differently for us, I'm still fond of her. She holds a special place in my heart. Always will." He held up a hand. "Now, don't think I have any intentions of chasing after your wife. I've moved on and am quite happy with Helga. It's obvious that Abigail is in love with you—always has been. You're a good man. You do right by her. I like that. I just want her to have a comfortable life and don't want to see a good family have to struggle."

"I want her to have everything she could wish for. Same for the twins. After tonight, because of you, I think I'll be able to make that happen."

He puffed on the cigar, shaking his head in bewilderment. "Twins. I can't even imagine."

An instant wave of guilt ate at her insides. Had Abby been wrong about him wanting children? The thought flitted through her, and she considered maybe he had the right to know the truth. "Do you and Helga plan on having children someday?" she asked, wanting to know what was in his heart.

He laughed and snuffed out his cigar in the crystal ashtray. "I can't imagine Helga ever wanting to have children. I'm sure she'd think it would ruin her figure," he said with a chuckle.

His reply didn't answer whether or not *he* wanted children, and Jesse sensed a bit of deflection in the way he had answered with a joke. She pressed on. "How about you, though. Do you want to be a father?"

"Never really considered it."

In an effort to pin him down further, she dug deeper. "But what if Helga came to you and said she was having your child. Would you be happy with the news?"

Sam shrugged. "Hardly. I'm always away on business. And, to be honest, I don't have a fondness for children. Never have."

Hearing his answer erased any guilt she was harboring. *Abs was right.* Her conscience was cleared in that moment, and all she felt now was gratitude. "Thank you again for everything you did for me this evening."

"I was glad to do it. If you ever need anything, just ask and I'll do what I can." He stood. "I suppose we've kept the wives waiting long enough." He folded the piece of paper with the list of names on it and handed it to her. "Why don't you take my carriage and let Cuffy take you around the city? He knows how to find the addresses."

She stuck the paper in the pocket of her tailcoat and smiled at him. "Thank you! And I'll take you up on your offer."

Jesse found Abby in the ballroom, watching as other couples moved in rhythm with the music. She approached her from behind and placed a hand on the small of her back. "This has been one of the best nights of my life," she whispered. "I have so much to tell—" She wasn't even able to get her words out before guests began coming up and introducing themselves.

Over the next hour, she met more people and received even more compliments on her work. So many, in fact, Abby was starting to get a little annoyed. Not because she didn't enjoy meeting people or because she disagreed with their assessment, she just wanted Jesse all to herself for a change. Each time a song drew to a close, her frustration grew.

With Jesse consumed in yet another conversation, Abby slipped away undetected. She worked her way through the crowd, searching among the dozens of faces until she spotted Helga. After getting her attention, she waited off to one side until Helga had detached herself from the circle of women gathered around her. She felt bad for pulling her away from her guests, but knew the only way to get time alone with Jesse was to ask for her help.

After speaking with her, Abby made her way back to Jesse and did her best to stay pleasant. She was polite when Jesse introduced her. She played her part of the smiling, devoted wife. Still, she couldn't help but glance anxiously at the large wall clock, watching as the minutes rapidly faded. *Funny how I was the one who was looking forward to this and had to convince her it wouldn't be so bad.*

When the clock struck ten, Abby tugged on Jesse's arm, pulling her from her conversation. "They're getting ready to play the last song of the night," Abby whispered.

Jesse couldn't believe the evening had passed in a blur. Turning back to the railroad tycoon who was still speaking to her, she said, "My apologies. I need to excuse myself for a moment." With Abby's hand gripped firmly in hers, she led the way onto a floor already filled with other couples.

Jesse and Abby stood facing each other, waiting for the music to start. When the first trilling notes of the piano rang out, Jesse exhaled slowly. This was the dance she felt most confident with, which was why Abby had asked Helga to make it the last song of the evening.

After bowing to one another, Jesse put her right hand on Abby's waist. With her other hand, she took hold of Abby's right. Though her hand was shaking slightly, Abby's was steady. She tried to draw confidence from the wink Abby gave her as they set off across the floor with the other dancers.

Jesse did her best to keep up with the fast-paced tempo of the Galop. There were many spins and turns and double reverse spins, and more than once she knew she had missed a step and landed on Abby's toes.

Abby's smile never once faltered, though. Instead, she kept her chin held high as if nothing were amiss.

When the song had ended and the room erupted in cheers, Abby and Jesse couldn't help but mix in claps of their own. As they stood catching their breath, Jesse noticed Abby's wide smile and she wondered if she had even noticed her missteps. As she was about to ask, Sam called out, requesting everyone's attention.

His announcement asked for all the assembled guests to follow him to the rear of the estate. Jesse and Abby filed in line with the others as they headed toward the back of the manor where hired staff in white coats moved among them carrying silver trays loaded with flutes of champagne. Jesse took two and handed one to Abby. Just as their glasses clinked together in a toast, a loud boom shook the night. Jesse instinctively dropped her glass on the lawn and moved to shield Abby with her body.

"It's all right, Jes," Abby said reassuringly. "It's only fireworks. Look."

All around them explosions were going off; raining down sparks of multi-colored lights. They stood shoulder to shoulder, watching in fascination as one explosion after another went off. The spectacle lighting up the night sky was unlike anything Jesse had ever seen before, and she hadn't the slightest understanding of how it was being done. She only knew it was beautiful.

Abby stood on the tips of her toes and whispered into Jesse's ear. "Happy birthday, My Love."

~

Following the Bowman Gala, Jesse found herself with more requests for her services than she ever thought possible. Wealthy socialites wanted to hire her for all sorts of custom woodwork: crown moldings, wainscoting, doors, chair rails, and intricate window casings. Whatever they could imagine, they were willing to pay for. For the majority of them, cost was of no concern. One potential client, a white-haired widow with so much of her late husband's money she had run out of ways to spend it, asked for a life-sized statue of her pet poodle, Priscilla.

Jesse was still shaking her head in disbelief when Cuffy dropped her in front of the house on Taylor Street. It had taken four days to meet with all the names on the list, and nearly everyone had paid her a handsome deposit for the future work. After thanking Cuffy for his services and wishing him goodnight, she started for the door, whistling as she went. Short of robbing a bank, she had collected more than she ever dreamed of.

"How much does that make now?" Abby asked, staring at the roll of money Jesse placed on the side table next to the sofa.

Jesse tossed her hat on one of the empty chairs and dropped down next to her. "I can't believe it," she said, shaking her head in disbelief. "Thirty-six hundred. And that's only half of it. Sam was right. Rich people don't bat an eye when it comes to spending money. I probably could've made more if I asked for it."

She reached down to pick up Gwen, who had crawled over and was swatting at her foot. "Oh, I swung by and talked to

Sam," she said, raising Gwen in the air, eliciting a happy coo. "He's arranging for us to meet with an architect this Friday."

"Did he say how long it would take before the plans would be ready?"

Jesse lowered Gwen and blew raspberries onto her daughter's stomach. Gwen's laughter increased and Jesse couldn't help but chuckle herself now. "Says it depends on what we design."

"I guess that makes sense. I have so many ideas for the new house—"

There was a knock on the front door. Jesse stood and handed Gwen off to her. It had already become a common occurrence for people to show up unannounced, seeking out Jesse's services. She heard Jesse explain to a man at the door she was tied up on other projects and the best she could do was take down his information and put him on a waiting list.

The man had obviously come ready to do business. In an effort to entice her, he offered her a substantial monetary bribe. He wasn't the first to do this, nor would he be the last.

Jesse never knew exactly whose voice it was she heard in moments like those: her mother, her father, or Frieda. Maybe it was a combination of all three. It didn't really matter. Whoever it was speaking to her conscience, their moral guidance reinforced to her the only ethical thing to do was to decline. Staying true to her principles, his name was added to the bottom of the list.

Like the changing of seasons, so came changes for the McGinnis family over the next two years. Abby had taken the twins and moved permanently to the one-room cabin in Neva in order to oversee construction of the new home and barn. While the separation was hard, Jesse and Abby knew it was a necessary sacrifice if they were going to make their dreams come true. If not for Toby and Aponi living on the property, Jesse never would have agreed to go along with it.

The only time Jesse got to spend with them was on the weekends, holidays, or when she needed Toby's help on a job. She spent most of her time working alone in the barn behind the home on Taylor Street. Her skilled hands guided the tools, shaping the wood day after day. The shavings flew until her tired eyes could no longer focus.

After finishing a good day's work, she would often stand outside under a star-studded sky brushing the traces of her work from her clothes. That was when her family's absence struck her hardest. Instead of going in to share a meal and then tuck her children in bed, she faced an empty house alone. When she stared into the night sky and took in the majesty of the moon, the seemingly endless arrangements of constellations, and the occasional shooting star, she often wondered if Abby was doing the same. She hoped so. She liked to think they were at least sharing something. Sadness always cloaked her like a shadow as she headed to the house for the night.

Jesse couldn't wait for the construction to be completed because she was quickly outgrowing the barn space on Taylor Street. The new, larger barn had become a necessity. She already had visions of what it would be like to work from her own woodshop in the country. Even though she'd be the one who had to commute back and forth for work, to be able to make the move to Neva and join her family permanently was going to be worth it.

Toby had made a life for himself in Neva like he had never been able to do anywhere else. One day while at the mercantile, he overheard some of the men talking about the unexpected death of a local man. The deceased had been the only farrier in the area. Given his experience with horses, and not wanting to rely on his sister for financial support, he spoke with the blacksmith in town and became the new farrier. After years of degradation, he finally felt worthy as a man.

Much to everyone's chagrin, Aponi suffered another miscarriage. With the loss of the second child, fear took root in her. Whereas before she had envisioned herself as the mother of several children, now she wondered if she would ever be able to bear any at all. Plagued with doubt, uncertainty ate away at her constantly. It grew like a weed, destroying the landscape of her mind, one tendril at a time. She did the only thing she could and kept as busy as possible as she tried to come to terms with yet another unbearable loss.

Aponi focused her attention on the things around her she could control. She spent hours in the woods harvesting plants. When she wasn't foraging, she was in the large garden she had planted. Eventually, all of her hard work paid off and she was able to reach into the ground and pull out vegetables—ones she had grown from seeds with her own bare hands. It was at least something tangible she helped create.

After the loss of his second child, Toby gave up on the idea of ever having children. He had never seen so much blood. Knowing he had almost lost his wife, he tucked the idea of ever being a father in the back of his mind where it could do no harm. Burying his stillborn son was soul shattering, and subsequently watching his wife struggle to heal and move forward with her life was hard to bear. The toll it took on her physically and mentally was something he never wanted to put her through again. Her well-being, above all else, was the most important thing to him now. Besides, he reasoned, being extremely close with the twins, he knew what it was like to be a father—he loved them as if they were his own flesh and blood.

CHAPTER TWENTY-SIX

SPRING 1868

J esse had begun to doubt this day would ever come. Construction on the new home and the large barn with a gable roof seemed to lag and drag on indefinitely. After returning the key to the house on Taylor Street to the Andersons' attorney, she left his office and climbed onto the wagon seat next to Abby and the children. With a click of her tongue she got the wagon, loaded with the last of their belongings, rolling out of the city.

Her anticipation was at an all-time high since she hadn't seen the new home in nearly a month and a half since construction had been completed. She had decided to leave the interior decorating to Abby—she had never cared much about such things, and given how swamped she was with work, she was happy to relinquish control of the finishing details.

Abby was thrilled to take on the task of decorating their home. She had given Jesse strict instructions there would be no peeking allowed inside on her weekend visits until it was finished. She wanted the reveal to be a complete surprise to her.

The wagon wheels traced over the well-worn tracks as it made its way along their lane. Jesse steered Titan to the front of the three-story home and set the brake. She helped the three-year-old twins down first. As usual, they were off and running as soon as their feet touched the ground. They raced toward the open arms of their aunt and uncle, scaring off the chickens that were unfortunate enough to get caught in their path.

Hand in hand, Abby and Jesse stood facing the white home with the full-length covered porch held up by four grand columns. Jesse had been here many times since the house had been completed, but something about standing there in front of it with Abby really hit her. It was done, and it was theirs. This was the place where their children would grow up and memories would be made.

"I hope you like what I've done," Abby said.

"Well, come on and show me already! I can't wait to see what it looks like."

Once at the door, Abby placed her hand over Jesse's eyes as she guided her across the threshold. "All right," she said, lowering her hand and placing it on Jesse's lower back. "Open your eyes."

Jesse stood in place, head scanning side to side as she tried to take it all in. "It's...it's beautiful," she said. "Abs, you outdid yourself. I don't even know what more to say."

"I can't wait to show you the rest." Abby took hold of her hand and led her across the tiled foyer to a set of closed pocket doors. "I hope you like what I've done in this room." She slid them open, studying Jesse's expression as she looked over the parlor.

Jesse scanned the beautifully decorated room with fine furniture and décor before her eyes settled on the rock fireplace and its thick wood mantle. She walked across the large navy-blue, tapestry rug atop the polished oak flooring and reached out to touch the stone face. The large rocks, taken from their property, were cool against her palm as she ran her hands over their curved fronts.

"I know the mantle looks plain right now," Abby said, "but I'm pretty sure you can do something about that."

Jesse listened as words continued to rush from Abby. She spoke of the troubles she had encountered with the workers—how they had found her to be too demanding, even threatening to quit at one point. Abby's words soon morphed into nothing more than background noise as her attention was drawn to the objects sitting atop the mantle. There, lopsided as ever, stood her first deer carving propped up by Frieda's soapstone pipe.

Abby slid her hand up Jesse's back. "It wouldn't have been our home without them."

Her heart rose into her throat at the thought of Frieda. She felt tears welling up in her eyes.

"All right, let's go," Abby said, understanding Jesse's emotions. "Much more to see."

She took hold of Jesse's hand and led her down the hall and into the next room. "This is probably my favorite room of all."

Again, she studied Jesse's expression as they entered the room, watching as she took in the bookcase-lined walls of the den. "You need someplace to keep your growing collection."

Abby walked into the center of the room. "This is where the piano will go," she said, splaying her arms wide. "It should be here next week. I can't wait until Jim and Gwen are old enough for me to teach them to play." She was practically dancing with excitement.

In each room on the ground floor, Abby explained the process of how she had gone about picking out each and every object, down to the paint color and wallpaper. Finally, at the end of the hall just outside the kitchen, Abby paused, her hand on the glass knob of the door.

"I hope you like this room," she said, turning the handle and pushing open the door. "Surprise! I know this wasn't what we planned. Someone with a business like yours needs an office, don't you think? So, I made an executive decision and made the changes. Besides, we don't need a large pantry anyway."

Jesse stood in the doorway.

"Well, go have a seat at your desk," Abby said, giving her a nudge.

Jesse pulled the tall-backed chair from behind the desk and sat down on the leather seat. She ran her hands along the wood top of the desk, admiring its fine craftsmanship. After peering in the drawers she turned to Abby. "It's perfect. I love it. Thank you."

Abby walked over and sat in her lap. "Welcome home, Jes—"

They both cringed in unison.

"What is that?" Abby asked, leaning to one side.

Jesse shifted in her seat and reached into her pocket. "Stick out your hand." Whatever it was she removed from her pocket, she kept hidden in her cupped hand. "Someone told me once about this tradition of setting down roots." She placed an acorn in Abby's upturned palm. "I thought we could get the kids to help us plant it this time."

"I love it," Abby said, her lashes wet with tears as she wrapped her arms around Jesse.

As they embraced, Jesse felt a wave of panic roll over her. There weren't many things in life that frightened her. For the things that did, she usually had the fortitude to face them. But she learned years ago the people you love could be gone in the blink of an eye, and that thought was always lingering in her mind. It terrified her to know the happiness she felt could be stripped away in a split second and there wasn't a thing she could do about it.

Abby leaned back. "Are you all right?"

"Yes," she said, trying to clear her mind of her worst phobia. "Why?"

"You just had the strangest look on your face."

She patted Abby's hip. "I'm just so happy. You really have done a remarkable job."

"Well, let's go upstairs. I can't wait to show you our bedroom." She unfastened the top button on Jesse's shirt.

"What are you doing?" She took hold of Abby's hands and sat up straight. "The kids could come in here any second."

Abby's expression revealed she wasn't concerned about them being caught in a precarious situation. "Don't worry about them. Your wonderful brother offered to take them exploring in the woods." She pressed her mouth on Jesse's, using her tongue to tease open her lips.

Jesse stood holding Abby firmly in her arms. She carried her up the stairs, and pushed open their bedroom door with her boot. Gently, she laid Abby on the bed and all talk of paint and wallpaper was quickly forgotten as she fell on top of her.

Three and a half weeks later, Abby and Jesse were in the kitchen preparing supper when there was an unexpected knock on the door. It couldn't be Toby and Aponi because they never knocked, and it was unusual for anyone else to stop by unannounced. Abby shot Jesse a questioning look and Jesse shrugged her shoulders, indicating she hadn't a clue who was calling at their door.

Jesse dried her hands on the dishtowel and went down the hall. When she opened the door, it took several seconds for recognition to set in as she looked at the man standing in front of her. She had completely given up on the idea that Armand Baptiste would ever return, but there he was, on her porch with a wagon full of French vine cuttings parked out behind him.

"I went to 317 Taylor Street. When I found out you no longer lived there, my only other thought was to come here. Are you still interested in being partners?" He extended his hand.

Jesse hadn't exactly forgotten the deal they made three years ago, but it was something she hadn't thought of in quite some time. As she scrambled to make sense of his return, she realized she was being rude. She tossed the dishtowel over her shoulder and shook his hand. "Please," she said, "come in."

She led him to the kitchen.

"Abby, this is Armand Baptiste. Armand, this is my wife, Abby."

He hurried to remove his hat. "So nice to meet you, Madame," he said, bowing slightly at the waist.

"Likewise," Abby said warmly. "We were just about ready to have supper, Mr. Baptiste. Would you care to join us?"

"Oui. I would like that very much. Thank you, Madame."

"It's not quite ready. Jesse, why don't you two get caught up in the parlor while I finish?"

Jesse escorted him down the hall. They were discussing all the changes to the property since the last time he had been there when Abby walked into the room carrying a silver tray bearing three glasses. He jumped to his feet.

"Thought I'd make us some sweet tea while we're waiting," Abby said.

"Thank you, Madame," he said, taking the offered glass.

"Abby," she said, her smile welcoming. "Please, call me Abby."

"Oui, Abby." He nodded.

They took their seats. As he apologized for not returning sooner, his look turned to sorrow as he went on to explain the delay had been caused by the death of his father, and his need to remain at home until his younger brother was competent to run the family business alone. Jesse and Abby both assured him there was no need for an apology. Knowing he needed a place to stay, they happily offered him lodgings in their vacant cabin. Once all the arrangements had been made, he jumped to his feet again when Abby stood and excused herself. While Abby finished in the kitchen, Armand and Jesse went outside to tend to his horse and wagon.

Over the course of the meal, they all sat transfixed as Armand explained the process of planting grape vines. Before they could even think of planting, he told them, the fields would have to be worked over. He assured them that as long as they kept the roots of the vines damp, they had plenty of time to prep the land. But first, they would need to get a plow and a couple of capable horses to pull it. Titan and Buck were too small and getting too old for the job. Luckily, Toby knew exactly where to find the perfect draft horses for the task.

After purchasing the necessary equipment, Jesse, Toby, and Armand each took turns behind the plow, struggling to guide the heavy piece of steel in a straight line as it bit into the ground. The one not steering the plow walked alongside the newly purchased draft horses, urging them along as the other hauled upturned rocks off the field.

The Belgian horses strained against their harnesses in the heat of the midday sun, white foam dripping from their mouths. Jesse, Toby, and Armand were soon as lathered as the mares. Dust stirred up by their hooves clung over everyone, coating them like a second skin until exhaustion finally pulled them all from the field.

After spending two weeks breaking their backs over a plow, they finally had the twenty-five acre field ready for planting. Jesse ignored the large pile of wood in the barn for the new-client project she was supposed to be working on. Even she couldn't help but be involved in something so groundbreaking.

Over the next two years, Jesse made more than enough money to purchase another two hundred and fifty acres from her neighbor. In addition, she added two large barns, one to house the growing number of livestock, the other for everything pertaining to the vineyard. When she looked out her bedroom window in the mornings, instead of seeing a meadow filled with wildflowers, she saw a field lined with row after row of thriving grapevines. Off in the distance, well beyond the vineyard, she could see the roof of Armand's home. It was the one they had helped him build on his fifty-acre spread; the one he now shared with his wife, Celia, who was expecting their first child. Jesse often wondered how different all their lives would be if she hadn't chanced upon Armand that day at The Bay Water.

Jesse's creations were still some of the most highly sought after status symbols in San Francisco. Business hadn't slowed since the event at Sam's, and she had little free time left over at the end of each workday. What precious little she did have, she cherished, spending it with her family. Although she was completely exhausted most nights, she couldn't have been more grateful for the life she had been given—until her deepest fear came out to bite.

"Jesse! Wake up!" Abby shouted.

"What?" Jesse said, sitting bolt upright in bed. "What's wrong?" She threw back the bedcovers and jumped up, fear constricting her chest.

"It's Jim! He's burning up!"

They ran down the hall and into his room. Their five-year-old son's cheeks were flushed an angry shade of red. In an instant, Jesse was by his side, her hand on his fevered forehead. His skin felt as if it were on fire.

Jim looked at her with glossy eyes. "Pippa, I don't feel good."

"I know you—"

"I don't want to die," he said. His small, clammy hand clutched hers. His voice was strained and he struggled to swallow as if his airway was constricted.

Jesse forced a smile. "Now, do you think your ma or me would let anything happen to you? You're going to be just fine. I promise. I'll be right back," she said standing, gently pulling her hand away. She motioned for Abby to follow her out into the hall. "I'll be back," she whispered.

"Where are you going?"

"To get Aponi."

"She's gone. Remember her and Toby left yesterday?"

Jesse had momentarily forgotten she had gone with him. He had been hired for a farrier job for a yearly horse round up, and they wouldn't be home for at least two more weeks.

"I'm going into town to get the doctor, then," Jesse said. "I'll be back as soon as I can."

She hurried back to her room and threw clothes on over her long underwear. Her feet barely made contact with the stairs as she ran down them and rushed out the front door. Once inside the barn, she didn't bother with a saddle for Buck. She simply slipped on a bridle and tore down the lane, galloping into town bareback.

Abby sat on the bed next to Jim, fighting back tears as she waited for Jesse to return. The cool rag she placed against his fevered head did nothing to quiet his weak cries. Stroking his black bangs back from his forehead, she did her best to soothe him, promising him he would feel much better soon. Inside, she was a writhing ball of agony. Every minute Jesse was gone felt more like an hour, and it was all she could do to sit there, whispering reassuring words to her son.

After what seemed like an eternity, Abby heard the bang of the screen door, and the sound of several pairs of boots walking over the foyer tile. She released the pent up breath she hadn't even realized she was holding as she stood and moved to make room for the doctor. Consumed with worry, she hadn't noticed the doctor wasn't the only person Jesse brought home with her until the preacher placed his hand on her shoulder. She reached out and took hold of the bedpost for support. Her own pulse was the only sound she could hear, and for a moment, she thought she might faint.

"Mrs. McGinnis," Reverend Tucker said, "while Doc Montgomery tends to your son, why don't you and your husband come pray with me?" He motioned for Jesse to follow him out into the hall.

It wasn't Jesse who had sought him out and brought him back to the house with her; it was more a case of divine intervention. He happened to be with the doctor when she rode into town. He had offered to come along, and she wasn't about to waste a single second trying to persuade him that his services weren't needed. All she wanted was to get back to Jim.

Despite his kindness, the last thing she wanted to do was pray with him. All she wanted was to be with her son. He needed her. She felt Abby nudge her and saw her bow her head. Jesse followed suit and stared at the floor.

"Heavenly Father..." were the only words Jesse heard before she completely tuned out his prayer. She tilted her head and peeked through the open doorway. The doctor had removed Jim's bed shirt and was examining him. Her eyes widened when she saw the bright red rash covering her son's chest. Fearing her knees would buckle, she put her hand on the wall for support.

During his examination, the doctor instructed Jim to open his mouth. Jesse didn't know what the physician was seeing, but she could tell by his expression he was concerned. Terrified now, Jesse squeezed her eyelids shut and prayed. She didn't know who she was praying to—God or Frieda's Great Spirit, or whether she was even being heard, but she felt helpless and didn't know what else to do. *Please don't take him from us. I'll do anything. Take me instead.*

"How long has he been sick?" Doc Montgomery asked.

Jesse and Abby both hurried to the bedside. Abby's answer came out in a rush. "He complained of a sore throat yesterday. When he woke up this morning, he said his ear hurt."

The doctor nodded in understanding. He stood and opened the window by the bed. "Best to keep it cool in here. Let him rest. Try to get him to drink as much as you can."

He looked down at Jim. "We'll be right back," he said, snapping his black bag closed. "Let's step out into the hall."

The doctor waited until they were all out of Jim's earshot before he continued. "He's got the fever. Not much I can do for him. Best medicine is to keep praying. He's in the Lord's hands now."

"There has to be—" Jesse lowered her voice. "There has to be something you can do. You must have something to help him in that bag of yours."

"There is no remedy for what ails him. How's your daughter? She showing any signs?" he asked.

"No," Abby said. "She's fine."

"I suggest you keep her away from him. Don't want her catching it too."

"Abby, take Gwen over to Armand's. Tell him what's going on—and tell them to stay way."

As soon as Abby disappeared into Gwen's room, Jesse turned back to the doctor. "Be honest with me, Doc. Will he die?" It took all of the strength she had to utter those words.

"I honestly don't know. Some children pull through. Some don't. No way to know."

"When will we know if he'll make it?"

"Should know in about a week."

Reverend Tucker placed a hand on Jesse's shoulder. "Tomorrow, during Sunday service, we'll all pray for him."

For the next week and a half, Jesse and Abby sat vigil at Jim's bedside as his sickness worsened and he struggled to breathe. While he spent most of that time sleeping, unmoving for hours on end, they went without rest, caught in a waking nightmare. He was a thin boy to begin with, but he became thinner still as the sickness sunk its teeth into him. Other than the ugly quilt of red dots covering him, he was still their same little boy, albeit a paler version.

Jesse and Abby both suffered from their own weight loss and fatigue seeped from their bodies. Food and sleep had become an afterthought to both of them. They were terrified to leave their son's side, afraid they would come back to find he would never wake up again.

Finally, on the eleventh day, Jim showed small signs of improvement. Another two long days would pass before the doctor would declare him well enough to be considered one of the lucky ones.

Although Jim had beaten the fever raging through him, it left devastating effects on his heart. The permanent organ damage would leave him prone to fatigue, fainting spells, as well as bouts of shortness of breath. Even so, he proved to be exactly like Jesse. He too was a survivor.

CHAPTER TWENTY-SEVEN

ELY, CALIFORNIA - SPRING OF 1873

Eight-year-old Burton sat at the kitchen table pushing food around on his plate. Edith was cooking over the stove, and like most mothers, she knew her son's behavior without having to look.

"Eat your breakfast, son, and stop fiddling," she said, flipping the ham steak in the cast-iron skillet.

"Listen to your ma," Felix said, entering the kitchen. He patted Burton on the head, tossed the day's newspaper on the table, and took a seat across from him. "When you get done with your chores this morning, I need you to come to the store." Edith set a steaming cup of coffee down in front of him. "I got a shipment coming in and those shelves won't stock themselves." He unfolded the paper and reached for his mug. He stared at the headline, his coffee cup suspended and forgotten as he turned toward his wife. "Edith, come look at this."

She wiped her hands on her apron and made her way over to the table. Over his shoulder she read the headline: *Corp of Engineers To Conquer Mighty River.*

"Says they'll have the bridge in Granite Falls finished in four months," he said. "You should send that letter we promised."

"Oh, I will. Hopefully when Jesse comes through, he'll bring the family with him. We have a lot of catching up to do."

Edith had no understanding of the seriousness of the article, or the true impact it would have on Jesse. So, it wasn't until she had her family fed and the kitchen cleaned before she gave it any attention.

Later that morning, Edith took a seat at her desk. Pulling open the top drawer, she took out a sheet of ivory colored stationary and found her pen. After dotting it in the inkwell, she wrote. By the time she had finished, the page was so crowded with words there was barely enough room for the elegant flourish she added at the bottom. She had just finished sealing the envelope when there was an unexpected knock on the door.

Burton ran right past his mother who was still seated at her desk. He opened the door to find Hank Johansen standing there, his hand poised, ready to strike again.

"Where's your Ma?" he asked, with a tone of urgency.

Before Burton had time to reply, she was already standing behind him.

"What's wrong?" Edith asked, her voice cracking with worry.

"It's Felix. He was patching the roof and a shingle slid out from under him. He took a nasty spill."

Burton instinctively made as if he was going to run out the door, but Edith, unsure of Felix's condition, reached out and held him by his shirt collar.

Hank continued. "Didn't mean to give you both a fright. He's fine but needs you to come run the store. Says his ankle's bothering him."

Edith nodded to Hank. She took hold of Burton's chin and tilted his head. "I need you to run over and mail those letters for me," she said, gesturing toward the desk. "When you're done doing that, head right to the store so you can start stocking the shelves like your father asked you to." She gave her son a quick peck on the forehead, and left with Hank.

Burton went to his mother's desk to retrieve the letters with every intention of doing as he was told. He was, however, an eight-year-old boy with an overactive imagination.

Two months ago, he had been forced to ride along with his mother when she went to Granite Falls to shop for fabric. Bored, he had wandered the aisles, messing with the many items lining the shelves. Worried he'd break something, Edith had sent him to the front of the store to stand while she finished her shopping. He had waited for her with his nose pressed against the glass, watching as the people outside moved along the busy street. Out of the corner of his eye, he noticed a throng of people running toward the courthouse.

Burton cast a swift glance over his shoulder to see what his mother was up to. He could tell she was preoccupied with the salesclerk, and knew from past experience she took forever to pick out her materials. His curiosity quickly got the better of him. He took one last glance over his shoulder and slipped out the door, joining in with the crush of people making their way down the street.

As he neared the steps of the courthouse, he overheard someone nearby say, "They reached a verdict!" Burton had no idea at all what the words meant, but he was determined more than ever to find out. He followed the people filing into a room. Inside, the courtroom was packed, and foot traffic came to a standstill. Standing on the tips of his toes, he tried to get a peek toward the front. When that didn't work, he hunched down, using his elbows to push his way through the crowd, ignoring the irritated looks he got as he shoved his way through the sea of legs.

He made it to a row of chairs and craned his neck, straining to see over the heads of the people in front of him. He saw a man seated at a desk on an elevated platform. The man's black robe was stretched taut over his large paunch and gave him a foreboding look. In front of the robe wearing man stood a lanky fella, his manacled hands before him. He had an ugly bruise over one eye, its color the same grayish black as the thick stone of the building.

Burton heard men whispering behind him.

"What's he accused of?"

"Murder. They had so much evidence against him, there's no way the judge will find him not guilty."

Now, murder was a word Burton was familiar with. He had overheard it once in a conversation his parents were having. When they had explained to him what it meant, it had elicited even more questions from his young mind.

Burton could see the man in shackles trembling as the judge rendered his verdict. When the gavel slammed down onto the mahogany wood block, the sound echoed through the room like a gunshot blast. Startled, Burton jumped, his feet coming off the floor. The convicted man exploded in a rage, and he had to be dragged from the room by two constables. An icy shiver ran down Burton's spine. The entire scene had been both frightening and exhilarating.

With nerves already on edge, Burton leapt again when a hand landed on his shoulder. Without having to look, he knew whose hand it was—he had felt that exact grip many times in his young life already. Humiliation stained his cheeks as his mother pulled him by the ear and led him through the crowd of onlookers, yelling at him for scaring her half to death all the way down the courthouse steps. The escapade earned him one of the worst whippings he had ever gotten from his father when he got home. Still, what he had witnessed at the courthouse was a thrilling experience he would never forget.

Burton eyed the stack of letters sitting on his mother's desk. He pulled the chair out and took a seat, his back straight in an effort to seem taller, as he tried to emulate the judge. The toes of his shoes barely skimmed the floor as he looked out over the empty room, visualizing it packed with spectators. Jumping back up, he searched for the one thing he needed to complete his illusion. He snatched his father's coat from the peg by the back door.

Draping it around his shoulders, he returned to his seat and cleared his throat. In the most commanding voice he could manage, he said, "Order! Order, I say!"

In the absence of a proper gavel, he finished the edict by pounding his small fist on the desk. He pulled open a drawer and selected a blank piece of stationery. A scowl creased his forehead as he pretended to read the imaginary words. He turned to the empty chair next to the desk. Frowning, he glared at the accused as he repeated the words he had heard in Granite Falls. "Clyde Holmes, I find you guilty and sentence you to hang."

Burton's courtroom erupted as soon as he read the verdict. Such behavior would not be tolerated. "Quiet!" he yelled. His hand swung through the air, and he slammed his fist down in another call for order. "Order in my court—"

He sat in stunned silence when he realized what he had done. His mother's inkwell was resting on its side. He immediately set it upright, but the damage had already been done. His relief over the fact none of it had spilled onto the desk was short lived when he noticed the sinister puddle of black liquid on the top envelope. Wasting no time, he jumped off the chair and sprinted to the kitchen in search of a rag. Running fast, he skidded to a halt and did his best to dab away any evidence, but his efforts only seemed to make matters worse. Instead of getting rid of the spot, somehow he had managed to make it larger. It was of no use. His mother's letter was ruined.

Burton knew he would be in trouble—big trouble. His parents had warned him countless times not to horse around in the house. As with most kids his age, scared of being caught, he panicked. He pulled the bottom drawer from its slot and tossed the envelope to the back. After putting the drawer back in place, he slammed it shut, snatched up the remaining mail, and hurried out the door. At the bottom of the steps, it suddenly dawned on him. He hurried back inside and fetched the ink-stained towel. On his way down the street, he quickly tossed it behind a bush. Then, he sprinted the rest of the way, laughing to himself on the inside. "They can't find me guilty if there's no evidence."

CHAPTER TWENTY-EIGHT

NEVA, CALIFORNIA

The following summer, with the early sun starting to show along the eastern horizon, Jesse and Gwen hunkered on the ground using a fallen tree for cover. Birds chirped in the branches high above their heads. Their songs, along with Gwen's measured breathing, were the only sounds cutting through the stillness of the morning.

Jesse watched as her eight-year-old daughter lifted the rifle, her heart overflowing with pride. The scene sparked memories from her own childhood: reminiscences of climbing tall trees with gnarled branches, fishing in the inlet, and pestering her siblings. Of all the memories she had from when she was Gwen's age, not one of them included hunting. Her parents had their beliefs and stayed true to them, believing their daughters should follow the same standards society deemed appropriate. Some things were acceptable and some weren't. Her parents deemed hunting unladylike. As much as she loved them, she had a much different perspective on what girls should and shouldn't do. Gwen would never be denied any opportunities because of her gender as far as Jesse was concerned.

"Hold steady," she whispered to Gwen. "Aim just behind his shoulder."

As Gwen took careful aim, flapping wings overhead beat the air and nearby wildlife scattered. She fired. A white tail disappeared through the break in the thick undergrowth as the large buck fled for his life.

"Sorry, Pippa," Gwen said, lowering the rifle.

Jesse went from a crouching to sitting position, resting her back against the tree. "No need to be sorry. I don't always get one either. Besides, he knew we were here."

Gwen cocked her head. "How'd he know?"

"Those birds gave us away. They've been sending out warnings for some time. They flew away just before you fired. When they did, it was a signal for all the other animals to flee. The woods will speak to you if you're smart enough to listen."

Gwen sat on the ground beside her and placed the rifle in her lap.

"I'm sure you'll get the next one," Jesse said. "It's getting late. We should probably head back, don't you think? I'm sure your brother is chomping at the bit waiting on us."

"Are you disappointed he doesn't like to hunt and you have to take me instead?"

Jesse put her arm around her and pulled her close. "Never. Hunting isn't his thing and that's all right. I love spending time with you."

Gwen wrinkled her nose. "He's crazy. He'd rather have his nose in a book reading about things instead of actually doing 'em."

Jesse smiled down at her daughter. "Don't you like to read anymore?"

"No. Not really. But, Ma makes me when she has me doing my schoolwork. I'd rather be outside."

Jesse's smile widened. Gwen's words took her back to the mountain—to a time when she stared longingly out the cabin window. She remembered how much she had hated being made to sit there and read. As a child, she never could understand why it was so important for her to learn math and all the other subjects Frieda forced upon her. Thankfully, her old mentor had been a patient woman.

Naturally, as an adult, Jesse knew the importance of an education. "I used to feel the same when I was your age. But trust me, even though you don't believe it, the things your ma teaches you will come in awful handy one day." Jesse stood up and reached out her hand. "C'mon, let's get going."

In an effort to give Abby one day a week to sleep in and relax, Jesse had started a Saturday morning ritual with the twins. For the past few years, they had been getting up early and going into town to get pastries.

As Jesse, Jim, and Gwen went to board the buggy, Jim asked, "Pippa. Can I drive?"

Jesse tapped her finger on her lips. "Hmm." She looked to Gwen. "What do you think? You trust your brother?"

Gwen scowled. "Heck no! He'll crash us for sure."

Jesse laughed out loud. "Oh now. I think you're being a little dramatic, don't you? You do know if he's old enough to drive, then so are you."

Gwen squared her shoulders. "You mean I can drive the buggy into town?"

"Well, now that wouldn't be fair would it, since he asked first. Jim, how about you drive to town and Gwen can drive us home. Sound fair?"

"Fair," the twins said in unison.

Jesse's heart was bubbling over as her son kept a tight grip on the reins, steering the buggy into Neva. She thought back to the conversation she'd had with Gwen earlier about how Jim didn't like to hunt. She knew he preferred to be inside, usually in the den with his nose in a book. He was a quiet child. In many ways, she found it difficult to relate to him. On the other hand, Gwen was a miniature version of herself. The similarities were uncanny.

It wasn't just small things that set the twins apart. They were as different as corn and peas. Abby had also noticed their differences and couldn't help but think something got switched in the womb. While it caused Abby some concern, Jesse respected their individual personalities. Never would she force them to be something or act a certain way because society considered it proper. As long as she drew breath, they were free to live a life of their choosing.

Jim steered the buggy down Main Street. He guided the horses into an opening in front of the bakery and brought them to a halt.

"Set the brake," Jesse said.

"I know. I know what to do," he said in a confident tone.

Gwen was halfway to the door by the time her brother jumped down. He raced to catch up to her. Although they were eager to get inside, they were well behaved enough to wait on Jesse before entering the store.

The three of them were greeted kindly by the middle-aged woman standing behind the long-glass counter. "Well, if it isn't my favorite twins in town."

Jim and Gwen had been hearing the same greeting since the first time Jesse had brought them to the bakery. They weren't actually her favorite twins. They were the only twins in town.

"Good morning, Miss. Dottie," Jesse said.

"Morning." She began putting their usual order together—two-dozen plain doughnuts.

The twins stood at the counter, their foreheads pressed against the glass. For two kids who had talked nonstop on the ride to town, they were now unusually quiet. Jesse placed a hand on each of their heads.

"Pippa, I want that one," Jim said, pointing at one of the chocolate-covered doughnuts nearest him. "Please!"

"Me too," Gwen pleaded, her head bobbing in agreement.

"Miss. Dottie, can you add in two of the chocolate ones?" Jesse asked, rubbing her hands through their hair.

"Will do," Dottie said, smiling. "I'll add a couple more for you and the Mrs."

The twins' mouths watered as they watched her wrap the doughnuts in wax paper and place them in a brown paper sack.

Jesse placed her money on the countertop.

"Thank you. See you tomorrow at church," Dottie said, handing her the paper sack. "Oh, I just love hearing your wife sing. She's got the voice of an angel."

Jesse nodded. "Yes, she does." She held up the sack. "Thank you and we'll see you tomorrow."

For the past three years, Dottie had seen the McGinnis

clan at church every Sunday. What she didn't know was the real reason behind their attendance. When Jim had been battling Scarlet fever, Jesse had made a promise to God. In return for sparing her son, she had promised Him she would do anything. Part of that bargain had included attending church. He had kept His end of the deal. Since then, she had seen to it she kept hers as well. To this day, she still wasn't sure who she was actually praying to—God or the Great Spirit. For all she knew they could be one and the same.

Jim and Gwen raced each other back to the buggy and climbed up onto the seat. Gwen never hesitated as she moved onto the driver's side, eager for her turn at the reins.

Jesse handed the sack of doughnuts up to Jim. "Now, no eating them until we get home." Then, she tried giving Gwen her most stern look. "And don't you leave without me. I'll be right back," she said half teasingly before turning away. A smile twitched at the corners of her mouth as she walked across the street and disappeared through the door of the mercantile. Once inside, she picked up a week's worth of mail and a newspaper. As she paid for the paper, she glanced at the twins who were clearly visible through the large window on the front of the store. Seeing they were fidgety, she tucked the paper beneath her arm and left, thumbing through the letters on the way back to the buggy.

"Hurry up, Pippa!" Gwen shouted.

Jesse looked up from the mail in her hand. She thought it was Gwen who had yelled but wasn't for sure. At their age it was hard to tell their voices apart. She quickened her step, knowing her daughter was anxious for her turn to drive.

Heading down the lane leading up to their house, Jesse asked Gwen to stop when she saw Armand, his head visible over the rows of grapevines. She turned to Gwen. "Go tell him to come up to the house and have doughnuts with us."

Gwen leaned over Jesse and shouted at the top of her lungs. "We. Got. Doughnuts. Come to the house."

Armand turned and waved. "I will be there shortly," he shouted in reply.

Although it wasn't exactly what Jesse had meant, she couldn't help but chuckle. It was just the sort of thing she would have done. With her ear still ringing, she stuck her finger in ear and rubbed. "That's not what I had in mind. C'mon driver, take me to the house."

Abby was seated in a rocker on the front porch, coffee cup in hand, when they pulled up. Gwen let go of the reins with one hand and waved to her mother, smiling as if she were the star of her own parade.

"Both hands on the reins, young lady," Jesse said. "Pull it up to the barn. Since you two are old enough to drive now, you're old enough to tend to the horses."

As soon as the buggy came to a stop, Jesse jumped down, making sure to grab the sack of doughnuts off the seat. "When you're done with the chores," she said, holding up the brown sack, "these will be waiting on you." She turned to walk away but then stopped abruptly. "Oh, and when you've finished, run over and get your aunt and uncle."

Jesse climbed the porch steps and set the sack on the table next to Abby's chair. She sat down in a matching rocker, the folded newspaper and bundle of mail piled in her lap.

"You let her drive?" Abby asked with raised eyebrows.

"Actually, they both did. Jim drove on the way into town. They're growing up so fast. I've been thinking—"

"You make me nervous when you say you've been thinking," she said, half teasing.

Jesse stopped rocking and leaned over to put her hand on Abby's leg. "Aren't you witty this morning?" She sat back and resumed rocking. "I know you thought the twins were too young last Christmas, but I think this year would be perfect. Don't you?"

Abby knew what Jesse was referring to. It was a discussion they had had many times. It was something Jesse had wanted to do for more than two years, but Abby was always adamant that the twins were too young.

Abby glanced toward the barn. Jim and Gwen had already unharnessed the horses. Something about the prospect of a bag of fresh doughnuts had put their work ethic into overdrive. Each one had a horse in tow as they led them into the barn. There was no denying how fast they were growing.

"All right," Abby said her words coming out in a sigh. "Let's do it this year." Although she was reluctant, she could already see the joy it would bring them. "Can you picture their faces when they see them?"

"I know. I think it will be their best Christmas yet. I'll have Toby be on the lookout for the perfect ones."

"Uh…Maybe we should start them out with ponies."

"Nah, ponies are for babies." Jesse glanced at the bundle of mail on her lap. "Oh, I almost forgot. You got a letter from Mabel." She picked it from the stack and handed it to her.

Once a month, like clockwork, Abby had been getting a letter from her dearest friend. Mabel's life was much different than when they had last seen her. The changes had been slow to come. Initially, when Abby first left Ely, Mabel had spent a lot of months lonely and alone. She had done her best to hide her despair in her letters, but she and Abby had been friends since they were children, and she was able to pick up on it even if it wasn't written in ink.

Abby worried about her friend for a very long time. Until one day, she wasn't. Something in the tone of one of her letters changed. Happiness seemed to leap from the page. And then, two paragraphs down, she read the reason why. Mabel had met a man. Not just a man—*the* man.

Abby was thrilled for her, but it quickly turned to apprehension when she learned Mabel's fella was thirty-two years her senior. She had let the letter fall in her lap as she tried to process what she had read, coming to the conclusion that who was she, of all people, to judge? Besides, age was just a number, she reasoned. The gentleman was a widower, and one very well off from the sound of things. More importantly, he was good to Mabel. That, she told herself, was what mattered most.

After that letter, everything happened very quickly—so quickly there wasn't even time to send word of their upcoming nuptials. Before Abby knew it, Mabel was married and living on his homestead in Omaha, Nebraska. Despite her reservations, Abby could tell by the tone of Mabel's letters she truly had found the happiness she had been searching for her entire life.

Now, Abby tore into the envelope, excited to read about the newest installment in her dearest friend's life.

"Oh, how wonderful, "she said when she had finished. She clutched the letter to her chest, tears pricking the corners of her eyes.

"What?" Jesse asked.

"Mabel. She's expecting their first child this winter. Do

you think someday we could go visit her? She wrote here in her letter we could be in Omaha in a week if we took the train."

"I don't see why not," Jesse said, her rocking chair coming to a rest. "You know I've always wanted to ride one. I wonder how much tickets would cost?"

Abby handed her the letter and pointed to a certain paragraph. "She said it's around seventy dollars for each of us to ride in a sleeping car. And, she said children under twelve are half price. I'm dying to meet her husband. I just hope he'll be a good father."

Jesse knew the question she was about to ask was a tenuous subject. She decided to ask it anyway. "Speaking of fathers, do you ever think about writing to yours?"

Abby's brow furrowed. Her rocking faltered before resuming its normal pace. "No. Why would I do that?"

It wasn't the first time they'd had this discussion. Jesse thought often of her own father. She would give anything to be able to see him again, even if he had been a drunk.

"I was just wondering if you were curious about him. I know he had problems with alcohol. But I can't help but think about what would've become of me if I'd have lost you and the twins during childbirth." Jesse glanced uncertainly out of the corner of her eye. "Maybe he's changed over the years. I'm sure he'd want to know he's a grandfather now."

As if by divine intervention, the twins came racing toward the house. "The kids are coming," Abby said, her tone clipped and somewhat distant.

Jesse knew from her tone the conversation was over. She also knew better than to say anything more on the subject in front of the children. They knew nothing about their grandfather in Missouri.

Jim took a seat on one of the steps. Winded, he struggled to catch his breath. Jesse's thoughts shifted to her son, and all talk of fathers was forgotten for the moment. Both women hurried to his side.

"Slow, deep breaths, Son," Jesse said, placing a calming hand on his back.

It had been this way for him ever since his bout with the fever that nearly took his life. He forced one wheezing breath after another from his taxed lungs until his breathing returned to normal. It was always a scary thing to witness.

Abby could tell Jim was starting to get his breath. "Better?" she asked.

"Better, Ma," he said. "Can I have a doughnut now?"

Abby was about to answer when she looked out across the yard and saw Toby and Aponi. Toby walked at her side, his hand resting lightly on the small of her back. Aponi's hands were laced beneath her oversized belly as if she were carrying it across the lawn. Her gait was more of a sway, and it was comical, though no one dared laugh.

Abby turned to Jesse. "If she doesn't have that baby soon, I think she might pop. I thought for sure she would have it last night."

"I did too," Jesse said. "I'll be right back."

She went inside to the kitchen and dropped the folded paper and the rest of the mail on the table. After making herself a cup of coffee, she returned to the porch and sat on the steps in between Jim and Gwen, enjoying the precious time spent together with her family.

CHAPTER TWENTY-NINE

It was midmorning by the time Jesse, Jim, and Gwen headed to the barn to work on their special project. The twins were her co-conspirators on a surprise for Abby. When she managed to have their attention, she helped them guide the chisel to carve a floral pattern into the wooden door of the master bedroom.

It didn't take long before they lost interest, choosing instead to swing from a rope hanging from one of the barn's exposed beams. Jesse continued to work on the intricate details, the sound of her children's laughter lightening the atmosphere of her normally hushed workspace. To her, their playful noises were like music playing in the background. Unfortunately, even the rope swing wasn't enough to keep them entertained.

"Pippa, you almost done?" Gwen asked impatiently.

Jesse looked up from her work. "Almost."

"How much longer are you going to be?" Jim asked.

Jesse straightened up, hands on the small of her back. "All right. Since I'm not likely to get any work done with you two pestering me, go get your poles—and run over and get your uncle," she said, waving them on with a smile. She watched them race out of the barn, nearly knocking Abby over in the process. She remembered being their age and how excited she got at the prospect of pulling in a big one. The memory made her chuckle as she hurried to drape a heavy piece of canvas over the large slab of wood resting on sawhorses.

"You didn't read the paper this morning, did you?" Abby asked, newspaper held in hand. Abby considered burning the paper after she read it, ensuring Jesse would never see it. Her heart told her to destroy it, but her head told her she had to tell her, regardless of the consequences.

Jesse laid the chisel on top of the canvas. "No, not yet." She bent over and brushed the wood shavings off her denim pants. Knowing how much Abby liked to shop, she asked, "Why, is there an ad for another sale at The Dress Boutique?"

Abby unfolded the paper and placed it on the canvas. On the verge of tears, her voice broke. "I'm so sorry."

Jesse looked at the paper, her eyes wide with shock, as she took in the headline. There it was, in large-black font: *Massacre on Mount Perish*. She felt weak, her knees began to buckle and she had to grab hold of the wood slab for support as she read the article. The written words blurred as her tears pooled in her eyes. Then they spilled over, causing some of the letters to bleed into black-ink starbursts.

Jim and Gwen came racing into the barn, a fishing pole gripped in each of their hands.

Jesse turned and hurried to wipe away the evidence before they saw, but she was too late.

"What's wrong, Pippa?" Gwen asked. It was the first time she had ever seen her father cry. Fear made her voice small.

Jesse didn't answer.

Abby leaned down to her level. "Friends of your fathers were hurt."

"Are they going to be all right?" Jim asked.

Abby placed her arm around him. "No, Son. They were hurt very badly. Can you take your sister and go to the house, please?"

Jim and Gwen left their fishing poles resting against the canvas tarp. They cast a glance at Jesse over their shoulders as they left the barn, fear and confusion twisting their young features.

Abby ran her hand up Jesse's back. "Are you all right?"

Jesse used the back of her hand to wipe the tears from her eyes again as a spark of anger ignited inside her. "Lies," she said. She threw the newspaper into the wood chips at her feet. "They're saying the troops were attacked. You know damn well that's not the way it was. I have to go."

Abby grabbed her by the arm. The color drained from her face. "No. No you don't have to go," she said, pleading. "There's nothing you can do now."

Jesse scowled. "You don't know that. Maybe some of them are hiding. I have to find out."

"Please, please don't go," Abby said, falling into her arms. She knew she sounded pathetic begging, but she didn't care. She didn't want Jesse to leave or be killed in a fight they both knew she couldn't win.

"I'll be fine. Don't worry." She pried Abby's arms from around her and turned to walk away.

"Then take Toby with you."

Jesse shook her head. "No. Aponi's due to have their baby any day now. He needs to be here with her. Besides, I'll make better time if I go alone." She bent down and picked the paper out of the pile of shavings. "Burn this rubbish," she said, handing it to her. "I don't want Aponi to see it."

"Let me help you pack your things at least. And don't you dare leave until I get back," she said.

Abby rushed to the house. Her mind was jumbled. It had been so many years since they had done this sort of thing. Upstairs, she threw whatever provisions she could think of into one side of Jesse's saddlebag: clothing, toiletries, and some cash they kept hidden in a sock. She paused when she went to hurry out of their bedroom and added a personal token before going downstairs. She snatched one of her scarfs and gave it a squirt of her favorite perfume. Then, she ran to the small smokehouse out back and retrieved a smoked ham. In the kitchen, she loaded the other saddlebag with a large hunk of the smoked meat, hard-boiled eggs, a wedge of cheddar cheese, three apples, and a loaf of bread.

As she hurried down the front steps, Jesse was leading Buck out of the barn. Toby was crossing the lawn, his fishing pole propped over his shoulder.

"Aren't we goin' fishin'?" he asked when he reached his sister.

Jesse shook her head. She handed the reins to him. "Where's Aponi?"

"She's sleeping, or tying to when sh-she can get comfortable. Why?"

"Abby will fill you in. I'll be right back." She rushed inside the house, oblivious to the twins sitting in the parlor, as she hurried down the hall to her office. She opened one of the drawers and pulled out her long blade. She attached the sheathed knife to her belt and then strapped on her holster.

When she reached for her rifle hanging on the wall, she heard Gwen ask, "Where are you going?"

Jesse turned to face her. "I have to ride into San Francisco to see about a job. It can't wait."

Jim, standing next to his sister, said, "But you never take your rifle with you."

Already tears were in their eyes and Jesse knew they had to be scared. Her breakdown in the barn was the last thing she wanted them to see. She placed the rifle on her desk, got down on her knees, and motioned them over. Both of them ran into her arms, nearly knocking her down with the impact. She held onto them as tightly as she could.

Wanting to look at them, she forced herself to break the embrace. "You know about my friends who live up on the mountain?" she asked. They nodded. "Well, they were hurt. I'm going to see if I can help them."

"Can I go with you?" Jim asked.

"No, Son. But I need you both to do me a favor. You mustn't tell your auntie where I'm going. If she gets wind of this, she would be very upset. So upset it could cause her to lose the baby. And we don't want that to happen, do we?"

"But we aren't supposed to lie," Gwen said.

Jesse felt like the biggest hypocrite when it came to lying. "I know. But sometimes we have to lie to the ones we love in order to protect them. I hope one day you'll understand that." She hugged them as if it would be the last time. "I'm going to miss you both so much." She leaned back on her heels and looked at Jim. "You take care of them while I'm gone. Will you do that for me?"

Jim swallowed hard, trying to dislodge the lump in his throat. "I…I…I will," he said, stammering.

Jesse placed her hand under Gwen's chin and tilted her head. Her daughter had always been the ornerier of the two. "And, Little Miss, you behave yourself while I'm gone," she said.

"I will," Gwen said, sniffling. She wiped her nose on her sleeve.

Jesse stood and grabbed her rifle from the desk. "I love you both and I'll see you soon."

Jim and Gwen both said, "I love you, too," before following her outside.

Toby, securing the saddlebags on top of Buck, asked, "You sure you don't wa-want me to come with—"

Jesse, with the twins clinging to her waist, slid her rifle into the leather sheath. "No. You stay here. Aponi needs you. And please don't tell her anything. No reason to upset her right now."

"How are you going to cr-cross the river? Moon isn't g-going to be full for days?"

"I should get there by tomorrow afternoon," she said. "No reason to wait and cross at night anymore." She glanced down at the twins who were clinging on to her. "You two remember what I told you," she said, gently prying their hands free.

Tears rolled down their cheeks as their heads nodded in response.

Jesse stepped closer to Abby and she drew her into a hug. "I'll be back as soon as I can."

Abby, barely maintaining her composure, reluctantly let go, and watched Jesse quickly swing astride the saddle. "I love you," she said, placing a hand on Jesse's leg. "Please be safe. I —we need you to come home to us."

"I love you too, and I will."

Toby handed her the reins. "Take care of yourself out there, and d-don't do anything foolish."

"I won't." She took one last, long look at her family. "I'll see you all soon." She turned Buck. With the click of her tongue, she got him galloping down the grapevine-flanked lane, leaving behind plumes of dust kicked up by his hooves in their wake.

Jesse kept to the main roads, setting a punishing pace. She pushed Buck to his limit and beyond—never stopping—never pausing.

She wasn't even halfway to Ely before the sun sank below the horizon, and with no moonlight to help guide her, she was forced to bed down for the night. After finding what seemed the safest, most secluded place she could, she practically fell from Buck's back, fatigue pulling her from the saddle.

After tending to Buck, she spread out her bedroll and dropped down on the ground. No breeze stirred. Howls of coyotes, chirps of tree frogs, and songs of crickets broke the lonesome silence as she leaned her back against the saddle.

Not wanting to go through the effort of starting a fire, she opted to put on a pair of socks over the ones she was wearing in an attempt to stay warm throughout the night. She opened the flap of her saddlebag and noticed Abby's silk scarf lying on top. She held it under her nose, breathing deeply of the familiar honeysuckle fragrance. An image of Abby came to mind, warming her insides, and she had to squeeze her eyes against the welling tears.

She sank down, resting her head on the saddle. Even though she was exhausted, adrenaline still coursed through her veins and sleep eluded her. Blanketed in darkness, she lay there struggling to slow her racing thoughts. Not only was the unknown outcome of events on Mount Perish weighing on her, but also her conversation with Gwen from earlier in the day.

The twins, her twins, were growing up way too fast. With each passing day their perception and understanding of things around them was growing as well. She couldn't help but wonder if it was time to reveal to them the truth about her, a truth that had been gnawing at her for eight years.

She had faced many dangers in her life. None of them scared her half as much as telling her children her shocking secret. Knowing she could potentially devastate two people who meant more to her than her own life overwhelmed her. Even if she managed to get the words out, it was the outcome that terrified her most of all. What if they rejected her? It was a possibility she knew for certain she wasn't strong enough to withstand.

She'd had the people she loved most taken from her before. She could still feel not only the lingering pain of their absence, but the cold, icy shock of their loss, even decades later. Now, she imagined a new terror—not one of lives stolen from her but of love rejected outright. She wondered which was worse and hated herself for it.

All around her in the darkness, insects whirred, mocking her, binding her already jumbled thoughts. A tear rolled from the corner of her eye, but she made no effort to wipe it away. "I need your help, Frieda. I sure got myself in a mess this time. I desperately need your guidance," she said, staring at one twinkling star up in the night sky.

Another coyote yip was the only answer she got. She shook her head side to side, and let out a sigh.

What did you expect? She's been gone for twelve years. Maybe

I made the wrong choice that day. Maybe I should have chosen to go through the door. Maybe there was something else, some other option I missed.

She closed her eyes and put her palm to her forehead.

What the hell do I even know?

She took a deep breath. When she exhaled, she tried to blow the manic thoughts out of her head. Like ash from a spent fire, they blew right back in her face.

Feels like they would've been better off if I died that day.

The leaves rustled all around her from the gust of wind shuttering through the branches, and a cold breeze blew across her face. An icy shiver raced down her spine.

I'd rather die than—

She bolted up from her bedroll, eyes wide, new energy filling her body. Her fingers worried at the wool blanket, unsure what to do with the sudden inertia.

It's so simple, she thought. She couldn't believe she hadn't thought of it sooner. The whole thing was so obvious now. Her burden had been lifted, her dilemma resolved. Things were, in fact, going to be all right.

I'll just disappear.

Financially, she knew her family would be taken care of for the rest of their lives. The vineyard was beginning to flourish. Everything they owned was paid for. They had thousands of dollars in the bank account—not to mention all the gold still in the safe deposit box.

They'll be fine without me. The twins will never have to know the awful truth.

Whether it was from fatigue, stress, or a sign from up above, whatever the reason, Jesse's decision was made right then. She knew in her gut that not returning home would be the best thing for Jim and Gwen. Recovering from her assumed death would be much easier for them to cope with than finding out she was never their father to begin with and they had been deceived their whole lives—that she was really a fake, a fraud, a phony.

For the first time in years she let herself cry. She cried from the depths of her soul, her heart breaking as the reality of a life without Abby, her children, and her brother sank in.

Walking away from everyone she loved would be the hardest thing she had ever done, but she knew she could start her life all over again. She had done it before.

Jesse clutched Abby's scarf in her balled fist and wrapped her own lonely arms around herself. Tears burst from her eyes, spilled down her cheeks and drenched her shirt until there was nothing left to shed. She was spent, physically, mentally and emotionally. As the last tethers of wakefulness snapped, before the restless sleep, she had one final thought.

Why does walking away from your life and starting over seem easier when you're ten?

A NOTE FROM THE AUTHOR

Dear Reader,

Thank you for reading *The Devil Behind Us*. I truly hope you enjoyed the story as much as I enjoyed writing it. If you're inclined, please leave a review on Amazon, Goodreads, or your favorite book website. Even if it's only a few words, I'd greatly appreciate your feedback. Thank you again for your continued interest in the incredible life story of Jessica Pratt.

I would also like to let you know that the third book in the Devil Series, *The Devil That Broke Us*, is in the works. Please follow me on Facebook at The Devil Between Us or Twitter @SCWilson_Author to find out the to be released date.

S.C. Wilson

ACKNOWLEDGMENTS

I would like to give a heartfelt thank you to some wonderful people who had a hand in making this novel with me: Erica Alexander, Andrew Donaldson, Sue Hurst, Amy Mullen, Jodi Myers, Paul Saylor, Judith Silberfeld, and Linda Wilson. Without any of you, this novel would not have been possible. I am forever grateful to each and every one of you.